Rush to Nowhere

Rush (to) Nowhere

by
Howard Lewis Russell

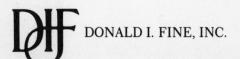 DONALD I. FINE, INC. ◦ *New York*

Copyright © 1988 by Howard Lewis Russell

Library of Congress Catalogue Card Number: 87-46253

ISBN: 1-55611-075-8

Manufactured in the United States of America

10 9 8 7 6 5 4 3 2 1

Library of Congress Cataloging-in-Publication Data

Russell, Howard Lewis.
    Rush to nowhere.

    I. Title.
PS3568.U7666R87   1988   813'.54   87-46253
ISBN 1-55611-075-8

THIS NOVEL IS DEDICATED TO THE
AMERICAN POET, ROBERT PHILLIPS.
HE OPENED THE DOOR WHEN OTHERS
REFUSED.

If you live long enough, you win in a hurry.
UNKNOWN

Part

I

LIFE'S COMEDY

A BLUE SUMMER SKY

or

Chapter

I

IT IS ONE of those horrible experiences on the subway that makes Dancer wish he had never left the South. First of all, they're working on the B & D lines, which he usually takes, so he now has to take the 4-5-6 from Grand Central to Union Square and then transfer to the N, the Q or the RR to get to Dekalb Station in Brooklyn. (He never dreamed when he was growing up that there could be a place so aesthetically deprived as Brooklyn, much less that he'd ever have to live there.) Anyway, from Dekalb he has a fifteen minute walk to the corner of Washington Avenue, and since he has to pass right beside Fort Green Park, he runs the inevitable risk of being mugged, raped or shot at, not to mention that it is uphill all the way. And this is just a normal day.

But normal days never happen because no matter what, things always get worse. Today is no exception. He is down in the grimy bowels of Grand Central (The Antechamber of Hell), and he is about to pass through the turnstile so he can proceed onward to The Train of Tears, when he realizes that he doesn't have either a subway token or the dollar it takes to buy one. So he is trying to decide what to do. And while he's deciding, he just stands around looking stupid, but nobody notices because they're all in too much of a hurry, and stupidity is not at a premium here anyway, so he's hardly going to stick out like a sore thumb. At least he isn't singing a song.

But somebody else is—a fifty year old hippie. The hippie's playing a ukelele, and his ukelele case is open by his feet and there is money in it—money that says, "Dancer I'm yours." While Dancer is figuring out how he's going to steal a dollar without being seen, something mangy walks toward him and asks him if he can spare some change. Dancer says he doesn't have any. It says, "God bless you anyway," and continues on. Dancer also sees a blind man begging. He's holding a pewter cup over a diseased dog which is sleeping in his lap, and there is a fat woman—a grotesquely fat woman—by his side holding a sign that reads, "I am hungry. I have no home and four kids to feed. If you do not help us we will starve to death. Please help us. God bless you." Dancer is thinking about introducing her to the ukelele-playing hippie, but he is accosted by a skinny black man with a beard in a white robe, wearing a hat which he stole off an organ grinder's monkey. "Would you give to the children of Islam?" the black man asks. Dancer says no and hears another "God bless you" in return. He thinks that Heaven certainly awaits someone who has been blessed as many times in one day as he has. Still, his hallowed state isn't helping him to get home.

Something catches his eye. Three little boys are wrapping their lips over the hole of a turnstile and sucking out tokens. "Get away from there," shouts a policeman. "Don't you know that's illegal?"

"So's child abuse," one of them yells back. "We could have *you* arrested." Dancer can't believe he's hearing such insolence from a kid who is eye level with his knees.

"You little brats," says the policeman. "Scram before I get mad. You hear me, get."

"You don't skeh me," says one of them defiantly. "My deddy would keel you if ah aksed 'em."

"Yeah," says another through a mouthful of tokens, and he spits them into his hands and screams, "up yours pork face!" and throws the tokens at the policeman. The other two do the same and yell, "Run!"

"Little brats," shouts the policeman, and he chases after them while a mob of people descend like vultures on the slimy, rolling tokens. Luckily, one of them rolls right over to Dancer. He stomps on it and now he has a ticket home.

But all's not well that doesn't end. Naturally the Train of Tears is naturally not at the platform, neither an express nor a local, and Dancer is certain that when one does finally pull in, it *will be* a local... and it will be one of the old rickety, graffiti-covered ones with no air conditioning, packed like a sardine tin with a grim cross-section of humanity, and he will have to stand next to someone who stinks.

He waits and he waits. The concrete island is getting more crowded by the second. Everyone looks utterly exhausted. The air reeks of urine and sweat, and babies are screaming and people are carrying on conversations with themselves—but none of this is unusual. Neither is it unusual that the uptown island across the tracks is all but deserted. This is because Dancer needs to go downtown, and because Murphy's Law is true.

"Would you give to the children of Islam?"

"You asked me that once already," Dancer says. And he wonders who these ubiquitous "children of Islam" think they are. He hates people who make him feel guilty. This time though, instead of God blessing him, he merely tips the monkey's hat.

Suddenly, whether it's from the heat, the congestion, the chaos around him, or just the normal New York ambiance that forces normalcy to break down—whatever the cause—a sense of anxiety descends on Dancer. He whips around quickly, but the only thing behind him is a steel column painted turquoise. Still, something has most definitely gone awry.

The man of Islam has turned his back on him to beg from someone else for his children. Dancer can see the lights of an express train approaching as he looks down the black tunnel. He is thankful it's an express, since it will save him maybe a minute or two. The person that the Islamic is begging from is deceived, and she gives him a few coins. He blesses her, and not having a good memory or else believing that persistence is holy, he turns back around and asks Dancer again if he would like to help.

Dancer is fed up. "Listen, I've told you no twice already, and if I had ten million dollars in my pocket, I wouldn't give you a thin dime!" After this, he tells him just where he can go. Several people actually applaud. The Islamic's eyes widen, but then he smiles serenely and turns back around. A woman in a white dress standing next to Dancer says, "Honey, I love you." She is unfastening a gold chain that hangs around her neck, thinking she will put it in her purse so that no one will snatch it. The Train of Tears is entering the station, and the noise is like a mountain moving. Dancer turns quickly around again, but the turquoise column is still the only thing behind him. The woman's gold chain misses her purse and clinks to the ground. Being chivalrous, he bends down to pick it up. Above the tumult he hears or maybe just feels a whooshing noise as the Islamic, with lightning speed, spins around and shoves the air where Dancer is supposed to be. But the woman in the white dress is there instead, and when Dancer stands back up again things have changed.

The train is blurring past him. Its brakes are screeching like a giant claw raking down a blackboard, and people are screaming in horror. They can't believe what they are witnessing. One man is yelling, "Stop him! Stop that man!" because the Islamic is shoving people out of his way and stepping on children and cursing at everyone as he races toward the exit stairs. His monkey's hat flies off, and he looks over his shoulder back at Dancer. His face registers surprise and shock. He hesitates a moment, sweating, and someone shrieks, "Don't let him get away!" But he bounds up the steps three at a time and disappears. Dancer turns to where the woman was who dropped the chain... but she isn't there anymore. The Islamic has pushed her in front of the train, and blood is splattered everywhere.

Welcome to New York.

Dancer is still in shock and surprised he's even alive, especially that he is alive and sitting on the edge of the fountain in front of the Plaza hotel. He has no idea how he got here, but by now it is almost dark, and the stars are out, and a cool breeze is blowing. At least he's through throwing up, so he feels a little better, but still he can't believe it…that poor, poor woman. Surely he, Dancer, didn't actually witness a death! No, not only a death, but cold, calculated murder! He can't help thinking that he was the one the Islamic meant to kill.

He folds his arms across his chest and shudders. Slowly though, after he breathes in deeply a few times, he starts to feel a little better. And after a few more minutes, a general numbness toward the whole incident begins to set in. Is this what a year in New York has done to him—made him immune to any outrage, no matter how brutal? He hopes not, and now wishes he'd stayed to help. But what could he have done? He sighs and looks around, thinking vaguely about God and life and death and other abstractions. He just wishes they would turn this fountain on every once in a while, but they never do. It might even eclipse the Bethesda fountain as his favorite in New York if only they would give it a chance.

Dancer, where's your heart, he asks himself. A person was just killed, a person who had hopes and dreams and a family, just as you do, and here you are comparing fountains. He stands up, thinking he'll never forgive himself if he doesn't go back, but then he loses his determination. Nothing could be done at this point. Besides, he still doesn't have any money, so even if he did go back, he wouldn't be able to get down to the platform. And certainly none of the eyewitnesses would still be there. It would be a whole new crowd, few if any knowing that just a short time before a woman had been killed in that very spot. Yes, everything would be back to normal now. All the blood would be gone. The body would be gone. The tracks would be open again. It would be just like nothing had ever happened.

So Dancer doesn't do anything. He settles back onto the fountain and just stares into it. Something about fountains is so soothing. He still has the woman's gold chain, which he dangles in front of him to make it sparkle. He figures that at the very least he should perform some noble epitaph with it, yet he realizes he scarcely knew the woman, except that she said she loved him, so any commemorative gesture would probably be in poor taste. Besides, it hardly seems appropriate to throw a gold chain into a fountain of dry concrete. Somebody would only steal it. So he fastens it around his neck and doesn't take it off again as long as he lives.

But despite his newly acquired gold, Dancer is back to square one again. How is he going to get home? Ordinarily this isn't a problem, and it wouldn't have been today were it not for the divine intervention he experienced on his way to work this morning. He had accidentally given the fake nun in Grand Central a $10 bill instead of a $1 bill. The only reason he even gives her money is that she doesn't beg like all the others. She just sits in her chair holding a dish in her hands. So Dancer usually gives her any spare change he has rattling around in his pockets. Today though, he had felt generous and decided to give her a dollar. In fact, he could have sworn it was a dollar because he only had the ten and the one in his wallet.

The faux pas wasn't even discovered until he was already inside McDonald's. He'd ordered coffee and an egg McMuffin because he just couldn't take another morning of bagels. The insolent, pimple-faced girl behind the counter just sneered when he opened his wallet and found only the dollar. Feebly, he said, "I guess I'll just have coffee."

So now he has no money except for maybe the eight or nine dollars left in his savings account. He can't even get at that because the magical money machine won't give him anything less than a ten, so it looks like he's out of luck until he gets paid tomorrow. He sighs and chews on his fingers. Why does life have to be so hard? He doesn't ask for much, he really doesn't, but lately he's found himself obsessed with mere nickels and dimes. To think that he'd scrimped and saved to make his measly pittance last two full weeks only to be swindled by a thankless nun. And not even a real nun at that!

Don't be self-pitying, Dancer, he tells himself, and he breathes in deeply again, cracking his knuckles and trying to take his mind off his impecunious state. He suspects it must be around eight o'clock, because the sky is just turning that hard-to-describe color it gets right before nighttime devours it. Hey, he thinks, suddenly inspired, maybe I can sell the chain. But immediately he rejects the idea, realizing it would be a kind of sacrilege. Besides, it's really too pretty to sell, and he has just noticed an oval cartouche attached to the end of it. The cartouche is monogrammed with Egyptian hieroglyphics which Dancer thinks might spell the woman's name. Or maybe they're a symbol of love. He doesn't know, and he's sure he'll never attempt to find out. This is because he believes some things in life should retain a sense of mystery.

"Do you think I'm beautiful?"

"What?" Dancer suddenly realizes he is staring a hole through a woman seated next to him. She begins to laugh, but it's not the laugh of lunacy so commonly displayed here on the streets of New York. No, she is laughing because she thinks she has gotten one up on him, or perhaps it's the laughter of self-mockery. Obviously, she's quite used to people opening conversations by commenting on her beauty, and maybe she no longer falls for the line. Or maybe she no longer believes it herself. Whatever the reason, its effect is successful. Dancer looks wounded.

"I'm sorry," she says, now flashing a smile. "I don't know why I said that," and she glances over one shoulder to the hotel entrance, craning her neck as though looking for someone. Distractedly she adds, "Really, I didn't mean to sound so resentful."

"Oh no, that's OK," he says and quickly shoves the chain under his collar. "I was just daydreaming...I didn't mean to stare at you...but yes, I do think you're beautiful." A goddamn goddess, he wants to add.

"Well, I'm not going to give you my autograph, if that's what you want. I don't do those things anymore. I don't have to."

Autograph? thinks Dancer, and he's wondering, Who *is* this woman? After a moment he says, "Don't worry. I never impose on famous people. They have just as much a right to their privacy as anyone else, even more so in my opinion."

"Really?" says the woman, diverting her eyes from the hotel for a second to see if he is sincere. "You mean you don't want my autograph?"

He thinks quickly. "Well naturally I'd be delighted of course, but I'd never presume to expect it of you." And still he's wondering, Is she really famous? Her face does look familiar; he has a vague recollection of seeing it somewhere before. Television maybe? A movie?

"Maybe I'll make an exception for you," she says, still craning her neck. "But just this once." Yet before she can open her bag for a pen, someone comes out of the hotel and she quickly turns toward him and says, "Kiss me first though, hurry!"

"What?" But before he can even register her command, she's on him, smothering her lips into his—the most passionate, sensual kiss he's ever experienced in his whole life. And wow, does it taste good.

Slowly, she pulls back, leaving him staring doe-eyed into her lovely face. "I suppose you deserve an explanation," she says, wiping an imaginary smudge of lipstick from the corners of her mouth. She fumbles through her bag and comes up with a pen and a Kleenex. She presses the tissue against the top of his thigh and scrawls a totally illegible name. The first part of the name looks like it starts with an "A," and the last part with an "M," but he can't make out any of the rest of it and he's too embarrassed to admit he still has no idea who she is.

"A collector's item," she says, handing him the tissue. She adds, "I hope you don't read anything into what I just did—with the kiss, I mean." She looks to the hotel once more, then around the fountain area and relaxes a little. "You see, there's this weirdo who has some strange obsession for me, and I saw him getting in the elevator as I was coming back into the hotel. I'm sure he was looking for me. That's why I came out here, to wait him out. When I saw him coming out of the hotel just now, I panicked. I hope I didn't offend you."

"Oh no, no," he says, his head still giddy. He's not sure he understands the explanation but smiles anyway. "Stars kiss me all the time. I mean...I like getting kissed." He nods his head. "I mean it was nice." The woman laughs. Dancer can't tell if she's making fun of him or just being sympathetic. He fidgets about on the fountain and says, "Uh, is he dangerous, this guy?"

"Only to himself," she says. "Too much of everything, you know the type."

He does not, asking, "He didn't see you, did he?"

"I don't think so, but who cares," and she dismisses him with a wave of her hand. "He's really not worth the bother, believe me." Now she sort of pats Dancer on the head and smiles sweetly, as though actually acknowledging him for the first time. She stands up and dropping her facade of stateliness, gives him a sort of thank-you-for-saving-my-life-but-I've-got-to-run look. Before turning to leave though, she pauses and the ends of her lips go up; not quite a smile, more a look of pity. He guesses that he must look as if the weight of the world is resting on his shoulders. As a parting act of charity she says, "That's a pretty chain you have. A gift?"

"Well sort of... but she died."

"Oh no, I'm sorry."

"Don't apologize. I barely knew her. I don't even know her name in fact, and the only thing she ever said to me was, 'Honey, I love you.'"

The woman laughs again, this time a merry sound, and Dancer thinks she is definitely the most beautiful woman he has ever seen, her hair especially. It's a deep brown color, all loose and combed away from her face in a way that makes it seem to flow when the wind catches it. And her teeth. He has never seen such a perfect smile, yet it's not so much her features that make her beautiful, but more that certain something that urban women especially seem to have. He can't quite put his finger on it, but it falls into that same category as style, worldliness and survival of the fittest. He guesses she doesn't have to worry about money either, since she seems to radiate a sort of bored-with-life casualness, as though she's only in New York temporarily and might have spent the entire day shopping on Fifth Avenue, but hasn't bought anything simply because she can afford to buy it all.

Teasingly, she says, "Well, if all she ever said to you was that she loves you, then I'd say you're a lucky guy. Personally, I can't think of another combination of words I'd rather hear."

"It's not quite as romantic as you think," he says, and glancing down at her ruby-studded wristwatch asks if she has the time. "A pretty watch," he adds.

"A gift," she says, "from a former blood-sucker. Yes, it's 8:14."

He wonders what a blood-sucker is, but she didn't say it too pleasantly, so he doesn't ask. Instead he says, "Don't you think the sky's beautiful this time of night? What color would you call that?"

She sits down again, crosses her legs, smirks and taps a platinum colored cigarette case against her wrist. She opens it and the cigarettes are all different colors, like hard candies. Pulling a manicured nail across the ridges, she selects a water-blue one and says, "Teal maybe... or cobalt."

"Indigo?" he speculates.

And she says, "Only far over there to the East." She points with her cigarette, "There... where the Atlantic meets the horizon. But over there, to the West, it's azure or maybe..."

"Cornflower."

"And just five minutes too late for aqua."

"Royal."

"And soon to be midnight," she says.

"Or how about plain sky?"

"Yes," she agrees, "plain sky blue," and they both laugh together. This is followed by a silence, but a silence that is soon broken. "I'm sorry," she says, "my name is Anne. Anne Monet."

"Oh, of course," he says, extending his hand. *Now* he knows who she is. He's talking to a real life movie star. "My name's Dancer."

She smiles, repeats it and says, "What an exotic name. It makes me think of India for some reason... and ivory, and bolts of silk and pools with reflections of palaces rippling across their surface."

He ponders this. "Well, I don't know about India, but my grandfather on my mother's side is an American Indian... My dad's people are originally Irish. You're French, I guess? Any relation to the painter?"

"None. I'm not French at all. My mother is Venezuelan and my father's Dutch."

"No wonder you're so attractive. A blend of dark and light."

"Shadows and light," she corrects. "But thank you. Monet... well I made that up." Now she looks at her watch again and asks, "Do you have to be somewhere?"

"Not now. Earlier I was trying to get home, but the Gods are preventing it."

"Where's home?"

"Brooklyn."

"Oh," she says, a bit sympathetically. "Like it?"

He considers a moment, then asks her a question. "Have you seen a public Christmas tree with jagged tin-can lids for ornaments and toilet paper for tinsel? Well I saw one this past Christmas in Brooklyn. Let me tell you, it put Rockefeller Center's to shame." She begins laughing and blows a plume of smoke into the air. "It's the truth."

"I know it is. You don't have to tell me; I'm from Brooklyn originally." And she smashes out the cigarette with her toe.

"You?"

She nods and combs her fingers through her hair. "Yes, oh yes, I've come a long way," and she stares pensively toward Central Park across the street. She doesn't speak for a few seconds, then turns back to him. "Did you grow up there too?"

"No, I come from Alabama."

"Oh," she says, "a Southern boy. My goodness, no wonder you're so polite. But what happened to your accent?"

"What happened to yours?"

"I got wise."

He nods. "So did I. I hate Southern accents. They sound so affected and... well, illiterate."

"Oh no, they're wonderful... so charming and, and sexy. Now a Brooklyn nasal..." She throws up her arms and rolls her eyes. "Oh my God! I didn't think I'd ever get rid of it. See, I'm an actress, and there just aren't too many scripts that call for Lady Macbeth of Flatbush. It was either lose it or die, professionally speaking." Now she pauses. "What do you do?"

"That's a good question. Unfortunately, I don't have a good answer this year."

"Well, what brought you to New York? I'm always fascinated by people's reasons for coming here."

He sighs and parrots the same story he's told a hundred times. "I came to get a book published, a children's novel, but so far, no takers. It's been rejected about fifty times, but I've told myself I won't leave until it's accepted."

"So what are you doing for money in the meantime? I'm sorry, it's really none of my business."

"No, no, I work for an advertising agency. I'm an assistant in the creative department . . . sort of. Whatever I am, the title doesn't mean too much. I spend most of the day sending out unpublishable stories and working on a new novel."

"Well, that doesn't sound bad. It seems like the ideal job for a writer, I mean, you're getting paid to do just what you want to."

"If you want to call it pay. I shouldn't complain though. I've got access to the Xerox machine, the mailroom, free use of a typewriter, self-correcting, too, and all the supplies I could ever need —envelopes, paper, pens, ribbons.

"The company doesn't mind?"

"It's not something they'd notice. There's so much fat at the place. One girl on my floor doesn't even show up except to pick up her check. That's how much they care."

She laughs again and lights up another cigarette. This one is poppy red. "Do you smoke?" she asks as she offers the case to him.

"Only dope," he says, but he isn't serious.

"Honey, what do you think *these* are?" and she is.

What-the-hell, he thinks. "Thank you," and he selects a grass-green one.

She hands him hers to light it with. He takes a long draw, coughs like an emphysema victim and says, "You won't believe why I'm sitting here."

"Oh, let me guess," she says, smiling. "You're gathering material to write a compare/contrast essay on the desperate plight of jaded uptowners versus the plight of downtown homeless. You're trying to discover which group is at lesser risk of being busted by a narcotics agent when buying the things they need to live at the corner of Fifth and Central Park South. Am I right?"

"Close. Actually, I'm sitting here because the subway nearly killed me, literally. Some crazed black man tried to push me in front of a train." She gasps appropriately. "But he missed, because I bent down to pick up a chain that the woman next to me dropped. And now, now she's dead. It is just so unbelievable." And he stares out into space.

"Damn," she says. "It sure makes you believe in an unfulfilled purpose, doesn't it?" She taps her cigarette so the butt will drop.

"And a God."

She nods silently. "Or at least a Hell."

He thinks about this one but leaves it alone. She is pretty high by now.

"Listen," she says, suddenly jumping up and turning to face him, "have you eaten dinner yet?"

"No." He politely stands too.

"Then I'd love for you to join me. It'll take my mind off that creep." He agrees and they begin walking up Fifth, under the canopy of colossal sycamore trees. "What are you in the mood for?" she asks.

"Whatever you like; I'm not particular. I didn't eat any lunch ... or breakfast either for that matter." He draws on his cigarette. "Well that's not entirely true. I did have some coffee this morning, but the counter girl forgot to give me a stir stick and I burned my finger trying to mix up the sugar with the non-dairy creamer." He wonders why on earth he's going into detail about this.

She stops to take a sip from a water fountain. "Are you on some sort of weird starvation diet or something?"

"No, it's just that I gave all my money away by mistake."

"A philanthropist," she says in a Jewish mother imitation. "And you coulduv been uh doktah." They stroll into the park, past the Henry Moore sculpture glazed in pigeon excrement, past the pond and the ice skating rink, over to the Sheep Meadow, which looks eerie and enormous undappled by sunbathers and kite flyers.

"Where are we going?" he asks.

"This perfectly hideous place I know of on Columbus across from the Museum of Natural History."

"You mean the one with the paper palm trees, the checkerboard floor and the copper torsos in the windows?"

"Uh huh," she says, "decadence never looked so cheap."

"You realize I only have about thirty-seven cents."

"Don't worry about it. My life is plasticized. Do you like fireworks?"

"Doesn't everybody?"

She opens her purse and takes out a box of sparklers, the kind sold at Woolworth's. "I never know when I'll see my nieces, so I always try to have something for them. Here." She lights one and hands it to him, then lights another and begins running across the meadow as though the Statue of Liberty had jumped off her pedestal. He watches until she blends into the shadows and becomes a firefly in the distance. "Come on!" she yells. "Put some spark in your life; it's fun!" So he runs after her.

"Can you juggle?" she asks when Dancer catches up.

"Can a rug lie?" She tosses him three lit sparklers, and he drops all three.

"Yes, and so can you," she says. "God, I'm having a good time. Come on, let's go over to Strawberry Fields and stand on Yoko's IMAGINE mosaic. I want to wish I were a movie star."

"Aren't you?"

"Yes, but I want to be the kind I dreamed of as a girl, not a real one. She always had such fun being famous."

"Have you ever been in love?"

Dancer sips his cuba-libre with extra lime and finally says, "Twice."

"And... come on."

"Well, the first was with a girl in high school my senior year... Sharon Renko."

"Just a minute. Oh waiter..." Anne nods at a bored person standing beside a Warhol fake and points at their glasses. "Okay, her name was Sharon Renko."

"I think she was a genius, a bona fide one. She made A's effortlessly, but if she didn't respect a certain teacher, she wouldn't even turn in her test paper. We used to sit on the bus together and rub knees and go on champagne picnics and take rides in the rain in my dad's convertible. She'd stand up in the front seat with her hair flying and wave her arms like she was at Woodstock or something."

"What happened between you?"

"Nothing... just nothing. After graduation night, I never saw her again. We didn't have a fight, and we didn't break up. We didn't even say good-bye. But we both knew it was over...I just drove away. It was that simple."

Anne smiles and crosses her arms on the table. "What a rapport you two must have had. I've never, I mean *never* been that in tune with my lovers. So where is she now?"

"I don't know. I have no idea. She was planning to go to Harvard that fall and eventually become the first female Supreme Court justice. Sandra D. beat her to it though. I think about calling her sometimes, but you know how it is—people change. And I'd rather remember how it was."

"How perfectly lovely. And your other love?"

"Well, it was more recent...and more confusing, looking back on it."

"What do you mean?"

"Well, she was very sophisticated and well-mannered, and tall. She was over six feet, so she wore flats all the time. She was also older than me, by about ten years. I don't know why, but I've always liked older women."

"Ummm, that's because they're so much more worldly and wise."

"I think that was part of the problem. She never lost her temper. She was always polite and thoughtful, but I really think she was more in love with her lifestyle than anything else...in love with her cappuccino machine, her three VCR's, her condo, even her dog. She liked her damned dog more than me."

"I've known a few of those myself."

"Yeah, but we did have some great times together. There's one night I'll never forget. It was my birthday, and it was snowing. She flew in that afternoon—she lived in Washington—and stepped off the plane loaded down with gifts. She said, 'Pick a hotel, a restaurant and a show.' So I chose the Plaza—a room with a view—and Tavern on the Green because it's so garish, and for my show I picked 'Vampire Lesbians of Sodom' because I've always liked to suspend reality. We rode in a carriage to the restaurant and ate by a window and drank wine and laughed at those ridiculous gold and silver balls strung through the trees, and at the chandeliers that look like therapy work from a mad Venetian glass blower. And after the show we went back to our room where we lit candles and made love and ate chocolate truffles with the window open and the snow blowing in."

"Oh, God, it's like a mail-ordered romance."

"Yeah," he says, sipping his drink. "That's what it was, and that's all it was. There was never one bit of reality in our relationship. I think I was too young for her."

Anne plucks an orange wedge from her sangria and chewing on it admits, "I've never been in love. Lust of course. Why, that's as common as dirt." Now she throws the mangled wedge back into her drink and fishes out a lime. "And infatuation a couple of times, but I think love is something you can't really look for. You see, I have this theory that you can't attract real love until you've botched it up a few times first. Or hell, maybe I'm just too damn driven to ever fall in love. I demand too much. It comes from growing up poor and having a television. I learned two things— that I was every bit as pretty as any girl on the tube, and that a more beautiful world did exist outside of Brooklyn. From there, it was just a matter of course. I decided I was going to be a star and live in a beautiful house by the sea. I set a goal; I pursued it, and what I had time for I did, but what I didn't have time for I did without. Somehow, the love slot is still vacant."

"I'm sure you'll find the right person someday," he says, then thinks a moment and adds, "but you're right; you can't go looking for it. It just happens."

Dinner is over and they are walking around the reservoir in the middle of the park. Both are smoking again. "Who do you think she was?" Anne asks.

Dancer picks up a stick and drags it along the fence as they walk. It makes a pleasant clackity sound. "Who?"

"The woman in the subway?"

"I've no idea; I guess I ran out of there as fast as I could. There wasn't anything I could do anyway. It's sad when you think that someone was probably waiting for her to come home, a husband or even kids, or at least a pet or a houseplant that needed watering."

"I'm sure it'll be in the paper tomorrow."

"Probably." He throws his stick over the fence into the lake. "I should really find out who she was and return this chain to her family. I mean, hell, it's not even mine. Yeah, I guess that's what I ought to do, don't you think?"

"It would be best," she says, lighting up another colored cigarette. "The classy thing." Now they walk in silence a few minutes gazing at huge buildings beyond the line of dark trees that ring the park. A squirrel scampers across the path in front of them. The moon begins to rise up from the tops of skyscrapers in the distance. Everything is washed in purple. "You know, when I was little I used to think of this park as Paradise. I still think it's the only thing that keeps half of Manhattan sane."

"And what about the other half?"

"No hope for them, Honey."

He points to the middle of the lake. "Look at the ducks."

She stops, thinks a moment. "What idyllic lives they must lead just floating around all day not worrying about a thing. No one is going to kill them; they've got plenty of food and lots of water. What more could a duck want?"

He can't think of a thing.

A woman jogs by and Anne flashes her one of her dazzling smiles. The woman smiles back but jogs on. "Did you see her? Know who it was?" He says he doesn't. "Diane Keaton. I don't think she even recognized me...it used to be magic, Dancer— being a celebrity. It was like everything you ever dreamed of. But it's so fucking hard to stay on top and so fucking easy to fall, and the funny thing is that the same ones who prop you up are the first to knock you down." She picks up a stone and throws it at the ducks. They scatter into another spot. "My next movie starts shooting in two weeks, my first film in four years. Do you know why I haven't worked in four years?"

"You've been waiting for the right script?"

"Not the right script...*a* script, any script at all. And do you know how I got this part...how 'the most promising new actress of 1969' got this part?" He does not. "Because," and she flings down her cigarette angrily, "because that maniac who won't leave me alone is suddenly a very popular rock star. He's British and he's crazy. He used to send me these fawning fan letters saying his life wouldn't be worth living unless I was part of it. Sometimes I'd get three a day! Well, of course I ignored them, but that just made him send more, and he'd enclose pictures of himself naked and playing his guitar with his penis; I mean strange stuff, telling me he was going to become famous just so I'd marry him."

"And he did?"

She kicks the graveled path with her heel. "Oh, he did all right. In the past year he's had four number one singles and produced a movie that's still breaking all box office records."

Dancer is rifling through the files of his brain trying to figure out who she's talking about. "So now he wants you to co-star with him in his next movie?"

"You got it. I play an heiress in distress."

He finally asks. "What's this guy's name?"

"Turk."

"Oh yeah. I don't listen to the radio that much, but I've heard of him. He's been in all the magazines. Are you going to marry him?"

She stops walking and turns to Dancer. "The man is crazy. He's an ethyl addict, an alcoholic and he can't even read. Dancer, the man has made more money in the last six months than most countries have in their treasuries, and he can't even read!"

He thinks about this a moment. "But how does he send you letters if he can't read?"

"What?"

"Who writes his letters?"

"Well, I don't know. Secretaries, I guess."

He says nothing.

"Please," she says, "let's not talk about him any more. It makes me sick." She composes her face again. "What do you want from life, Dancer? Fame? Fortune? A wife, two kids and a Toyota?"

"I want something of mine left behind. That's all really, just something that a person three hundred years from now can look at and say, 'He made a contribution. As trite as it is, and as small as it is, he did give something of himself that's preservable. Maybe the world is a little better for it, and maybe it isn't, but hell, he gave it a shot just the same.'"

"Well, I think that's quite admirable. I do." And she starts quacking at the ducks, but the ducks aren't fooled. "I'll bet you're a romantic, aren't you? Yes, I can tell you are. I'm a romantic too."

"Are you suggesting we be romantic together?"

She gives a playful smile. "I'm asking if you'd like to come back to my hotel. I'm staying at the Plaza. It's a room with a view, the most spectacular view. Of course, I can't do much about the weather. I mean I can't order any snow, at least not *outside* the room. And chocolate truffles, well, you can get those anywhere."

Diseases too, he thinks. And he wonders why the 80's have transformed love-making into something to be feared. But he doesn't wonder too hard because he just might come up with an answer. "I'd love to," he tells her. So she smiles, and he takes her hand and the moon follows them back to the Plaza.

GREASY SLEAZE BUCKET

or

Chapter

2

PAYDAY!

Dancer thinks it is not a second too soon. He still has his thirty-seven cents, and if he were a nervous sort (which he is) he would worry about being so flat broke in a city like New York. But he's used to it. Besides, he has always thought of poverty and a lack of funds as two distinct ways of living. He has never been poor. He has only been without access to money. He fools nobody but himself.

He has some extra time before he has to be at work, and since it is only a short walk from the Plaza to Madison and 47th, he decides he'll go out of his way to Grand Central and give the last of his money to the fake nun. He just hopes that the truck that delivers the checks did not get crushed under a toppled concrete gargoyle or that the driver hasn't been smoking crack for breakfast and run the vehicle off the Manhattan Bridge.

As he strolls, he savors thoughts of the night before. Most of it is just a blur by now but a deliciously pleasant blur, like a wet dream remembered. There was the bath they took, a steaming bubble-bath with the air conditioning turned down as low as it would go. And then the room-service of blueberry pancakes leading somehow to his dribbling syrup all over Anne's stomach and slowly licking it off. He smiles, thinking of it. He must have been really high—or excited—to have done that. After they had achieved mutual satisfaction, they had fallen asleep exhausted in a nest of blankets by the window. He is a little hung over now though. And his clothes are crinkled and wrinkly—he is sure someone will say something about it at work.

He stops to gaze in Bergdorf's at the things that pass for fashion, and then he crosses Fifth to gape at the $800 glass apples at Steuben's and at the pearls and diamonds in Tiffany's, thinking to himself that the pearls in the window aren't naturally pink, because he once read an article in "National Geographic" that said all colored pearls are secretly dyed by the Japanese using techniques that are ancient and highly coveted. He imagines that some rich matron is really going to be bamboozled, and he chuckles to himself.

He glides by Godiva and thinks that he would sell his soul right about now for a chocolate-covered apricot jelly, even though a half hour before, he and Anne had stuffed themselves in the Edwardian room on marmalade-covered croissants and coffee. Anne had been a little distant or maybe just hung over like himself. She gave him her number in L.A. though and said, "If you're ever in California..." He thinks she knew damn well that he wouldn't make it out there before the next ice age. But he was polite and followed suit by giving her his home number and his number at work. He asked her to call him there today if she liked. She said she would. She said they should get together again later in the week, take in a show or something. He said that would be nice. "Wonderful," she said, "I'll call you this afternoon."

The fake nun does not even say "Thank you," much less "God bless you."

Tuesday morning. 9:15 A.M.
Dancer is the only person on the whole creative floor. The other floors—Media, TV Production, IRC, Personnel, etc., etc., the floors where you have to wear suits and ties—are already buzzing. The creative floor, though, is an exception to every rule. After

all, the creatives are the ones who *make* advertising. They deserve and expect preferential treatment. They wear what they want; they come in when they want; they leave when they want, and the rest of the agency be damned.

This is no less true of Dancer who, most of the time, does nothing. But his desk that he does nothing at is a nice laminated white one, resplendent with an elaborate phone (that he can dial long distance on and nobody cares), a desk calendar, a stapler, a typewriter, and a two-tiered tray that says "Out Box" and "In Box."

His desk is in a sort of wide, blindingly lit hallway that he shares with the potted palms, the water cooler, the beiged-out walls and carpet and two other "creative assistants." One is a black girl who simply doesn't bother coming in half the time. No one ever questions her excuse, it being some vague concoction about her mother's dying of tuberculosis. And the other, the one whose desk is closer to his, is a perennially late, gum chomping, unnatural blonde named Suzanne Bernstein.

He looks up and sees the first "creative" to arrive after himself, Judith Meyers. She is Irving Koenig's private secretary. Irving Koenig is *the* senior creative director of the whole creative floor and the entire package goods division. He has a corner office and has to wear a suit. Judith's resplendent white, laminated desk is next to Irving's corner door. She has a sort of make-shift office—a cubicle. It is made of sectional aluminum walls about six feet high on three sides of her desk. Dancer thinks that Judith is probably one of the sweetest girls on the floor, but he has suspicions that she may suffer from anorexia. So far, he has yet to see her eat so much as a cracker. Also, she is frighteningly skinny, though obviously from a well-to-do background, and he has read that this sort of girl is most likely to be afflicted with the disease. "How are you today, Dancer," she asks over her *Times*. "It's payday, you know." Her voice is softer than silver wind chimes.

"Oh, that's right," he says. "I forgot all about it."

"Do you have another story for me to read today? I was telling my friends all about how I work with a guy who's one day going to be a famous author." Tingles run down Dancer's spine. To someone as afflicted with self-doubt as he, Judith's words are like a rallying cry.

"I think you've read everything," he says, concealing the disappointment he feels over not being able to spark more praise. "Everything worth reading. I may have a few random chapters from some unfinished novels in my desk, but they don't make any sense to anyone but me."

"Are they violent, too?"

"Do you think my writing is violent?"

She looks down at her paper. "Well, a little macabre maybe, and sometimes unnecessarily cruel, but that's what sells I guess... They're written well, though. Really, well."

He thinks about this, wondering if she wants a date.

"Will you promise to write something beautiful...for me. Something with a happy ending, something ethereal and full of music and light?"

He wonders if Judith hovers in a delicate balance between fantasy and reality, and if she does, is it a result of malnutrition? "Would you like to go to dinner some night, Judith?"

"I'd love to, but I'm... well, I'm sort of on a diet."

"Oh."

"A movie then?"

"Well, I'm sort of dating someone too."

"Oh. Well, if your boyfriend sort of dies and you get sort of hungry let me know." He doesn't know whether Judith realizes it is a joke or not. She laughs though and her eyes blink quickly, and this time the tingles go all over him. "Judith, could I borrow your *Times* when you're through reading it. I want to check the obituaries."

"A friend of yours die?"

"Not really a friend, just someone I barely met."

"Well here, I'll give you that section right now," and she does, but he doesn't see any mention of the lady in the white dress. Of course, how would he find it since he doesn't know her name? But he doesn't recognize any of the pictures either. He'll have to check the *Post*. It likes to run articles on gory deaths.

He thinks that maybe Suzanne Bernstein will have a *Post* but she isn't in yet, so he sits at his desk and debates whether he should resume his novel to pass the time or just say fuck it all and stare at the water cooler until lunch hour.

Soon though, his lethargy is broken by the arrival of two account executives who work with his boss on a detergent account.
One is about 6'3", the other about 3'6". "Hey Dancer baby,
where's all the other reindeer?"

Dancer looks up from what he is not doing and with a pencil
punches the button that says TIME on his elaborate, technologically advanced desk telephone. "It's only 9:45."

Both of them stare, but they do it well. This is why Dancer and
his boss, Nova Grey Lovejoy, secretly call them Tweedle Dumb
and Tweedle Dumber. "When is Nova getting in?" asks one of
them, probably Tweedle Dumber, since the names are reversible,
so whoever speaks up first automatically gets to be dumber.

"Maybe her train was late," Dancer offers.

"What time does she usually get in?" Tweedle Dumb asks.

"Same time as everybody else."

"I guess everybody's train is late," says Dumber.

"It's only 9:45."

"Prima donna," says Dumb.

And Dumber says, "Well, tell her we came by. Neither one of us
thinks the insert here at the bottom of this print should have the
powder version of the product in it. I mean it *is* an ad for *Liquid*
GLORY. We don't want to confuse the consumer. I do agree
though that showing both the powder version and the liquid version together creates an association in the consumer's mind, like
hey, I have a choice now, two different forms of my favorite brand.
But we think it clutters the ad just a little. Clean, sharp and simple—that's what we want."

"I'll be sure to tell her."

"Super, Dancer. Super."

Dumb and Dumber trot away leaving Dancer to wonder how
grown adults can possibly take so seriously something as irrelevant as dishwasher detergent. Do people really care whether they
use a liquid or a powder? Maybe he just doesn't make enough
money to care, or maybe he takes technology for granted. He has
always taken technology for granted. Advances have never impressed him. Not computer chips. Not laser discs. Not satellite
videos. And certainly not dishwasher detergents. He doesn't care

how or why a liquid is an improvement over a powder. And he doesn't worry how a liquid will stay in the little dish built into the door without oozing down the sides once the door is shut.

He starts doodling on a canary legal pad. Why then does a sensible woman like Nova Grey Lovejoy care? He supposes it's because she's paid to care. After all, she *is* the art director—the one single person solely responsible for the rise or fall of the Liquid GLORY automatic dishwasher detergent campaign. Amazingly or not so amazingly, thinking of Nova summons her in the flesh.

"Good morning, Dancer," she says as she skips in clad in a houndstooth jumpsuit and crystal prism earrings. She looks at his clothes. "Never made it home last night?" He shrugs a you-know-how-it-goes-sometimes shrug. "When you've got a minute I need you to run an errand for me."

"Tweedle Dumb and Tweedle Dumber just came by."

"What do they want?"

"They think the GLORY print ad is too cluttered."

"Well fuck 'em. Where do these A.E.'s get off thinking they know my job?"

"They don't think the powder version should be in the insert, since the ad is really for the liquid version."

She flashes a "Why me, Lord?" look and says, "I never asked to be on this account anyway, and now these . . . these morons . . . you know, this is really the shit of the business. It's accounts like these that make us whores. We have to create a need for something no one wants, no one cares about." She strides into her office.

"Is the product even any good?" he asks, following her in.

Nova has a lovely, if a little run-of-the-mill office. Its principal furnishings, besides the obligatory desk and chair, are a pink gabardine sofa, a black lacquered Chinese screen for models to undress behind, a floor lamp in the shape of a human skeleton (the light shines through its eye sockets) and something that looks like a rosewood chest-of-drawers done in relief, which Dancer imagines Nova stole from a monastery. In one corner stands a green fluorescent life-size Crayola crayon and adorning her walls are the usual sort of things—a lithograph of Josephine Baker stripping, a poster of fishing lures that reads THE LURES OF AD-

VERTISING and a black-and-white glossy of a hyper-chic woman in a man's underwear with her legs spread and her back to the camera as she pisses like a man into a urinal. Dancer can't decide if it is Nova or not. On her door is a flap of black construction paper that says 25¢ 50¢ A PEEK. He has not lifted it to see what there is to peek at. Sometimes he thinks about it, but as with the cartouche, he feels it's more important that the mystery be preserved.

"Are you kidding? GLORY is trash," Nova says, sitting down at her desk and rummaging through a box of markers. "The liquid's even worse than the powder."

"How are you going to sell it then?"

"By claiming that because it's a liquid it dissolves easier than a powder, which it doesn't, and that being a liquid it doesn't streak or leave water spots, which it does."

"So you lie?"

"Of course you don't lie," she says as she starts drawing on a small board. "You create truths." Now she bobs her head from left to right while she sketches a bottle of GLORY. "That's why they call us creatives... on the creative floor... of a creative business."

Nova is a woman in her late 30's. She has hair the same color red as the middle Gucci stripe, combed forward like Elizabeth Taylor's in *Cat on a Hot Tin Roof* but much shorter. And she is model thin, hyperactive; she dresses exactly like you would expect a New York advertising creative type of independent woman of the 80's to dress.

Dancer likes her. She is sleek, slick and she doesn't patronize him... except when she is lazy. "Dancer, I know it's reverse sexism, you don't have to tell me again, but could you, would you please please please get me a tea and an orange?"

"Nova..."

"I'm sorry. I shouldn't have asked. I would never take this kind of crap from a person like me if I were you. It's just that I am so busy. You can get something for yourself too."

He sighs. "Lemon?"

"Please, and if they've got a little honey... you're so sweet. I'll pay you when you get back from the cafeteria." But he knows she won't. She never does. It's just one of those things.

You're young.
You're talented.
You're ambitious.
You're crazy about advertising.

Dancer is back from the cafeteria after remembering he still doesn't have any money since the checks haven't come up from Payroll yet. He decides not to tell Nova that he's too broke to buy tea. Let her get her own damned tea. She won't remember she asked for it anyway. She's scatterbrained like that. So he sits back down at his desk, and within a few minutes most everyone begins shuffling and slouching in.

Chomp, chomp, chomp. It is Suzanne Bernstein. "Oh Dancer, I am *so* late. But I had to cut my fruit. Miles isn't in yet, is he?" A shake of the head. "Good. Now Dancer," she says as she opens Miles Caesar's door, "I know you'll be honest with me." Laugh. "That's the one thing I can count on from you. But do I look thinner to you?" Nod. "Yeah? It's that new diet I'm on. It's really fantastic. My sister told me about it. You've met my sister, haven't you?" Nod. "Yeah, I thought you had." Smile. "Anyway, you only eat fruit in the morning, nothing but fresh fruit, and in the afternoon when you reach that, you know, low sugar slump, well, you're allowed say, an orange or a banana or whatever you like— but nothing heavy. You know, before I would eat a bagel, say, with just a little cream cheese, never too much though, and I'd have a soda maybe with it, usually a diet soda, but I'm finding that I can actually be satisfied with just a mango..."

"Did you buy the *Post* this morning, Suzanne?"

"Yes, I did. You can borrow it just as soon as I do the crossword."

"Morning earlybird." It is Miles Caesar, Nova Grey Lovejoy's copywriter and Suzanne Bernstein's boss.

"Hi, Miles," says Dancer.

"Morning Miles," beams Suzanne.

Miles is a shuffler and a middle-aged poet from Delaware (a state that Dancer can't quite seem to place on the map). He is congenial and likes to tell filthy jokes, but he has never really been an advertising sort of man. He is really a poet, but of course nobody can make a living writing poetry, not until they're dead, so he has to slum in advertising. Miles has a son in college, a mortgaged house in the burbs and an "unusual" wife named Azalea that he has to keep locked up most of the time in a place that doesn't look like a prison. It's the cost of keeping her there that's kept him here.

"Here" happens to be GS & B, the seventh largest advertising agency in the world, and just about the last one still on Madison Avenue. Dancer has asked several people what the initials stand for. "The original founders' names," Nova has told him, but she can't remember who they are. A less plausible but perhaps more apt explanation is that GS & B stand for Greasy Sleaze Bucket.

> You're young.
> You're talented.
> You're ambitious.
> You're crazy about advertising.

Uh oh, in walks Irving Koenig. "Good morning, Irving; good morning, Irving; good morning, Irving..." until he stalks into his corner office, where he can close the door and wolf down some more superiority pills. Rumors fly rampant that he is a reformed alcoholic and that he "straddles both sides of the fence." Like all rumors, this one has an element of truth, though Dancer suspects that Irving prefers one side of the fence to the other.

"Good morning, Dancer...Judith."

"Good morning, Irving," they say in unison.

"I think Irving likes you," Miles whispers to Dancer.

"Please," Dancer says.

Miles takes a closer look at him. "God, you look ravaged. What'dya do last night anyway, dodge traffic?"

"I made love to a famous actress."

"What a coincidence, so did I...Azalea didn't even know it."

"I guess that makes us both starfuckers then, doesn't it?"

The checks have come up from Payroll and Dancer has distributed them beneath every door of every person in his group. Luckily, they did not forget to print one for him, so if the crack-addicted truck driver did run off a bridge, he at least saved the right bag from getting wet. Dancer endorses the back of his check, debating whether he wants to contend with the line at Chase Manhattan. Of course, he can't eat until he cashes it, but the croissants this morning were filling. So he'll wait. He stares at Suzanne Bernstein's broad backside as she reads her *Post*. Apparently, she isn't taking her diet too seriously, because instead of her fruit she is wolfing down a knish with mustard and a diet Pepsi ...She swivels around. "You can have my paper now, Dancer. Doing anything special for lunch?"

"I don't know yet."

"You know, I'm in a sushi sort of mood. I know of this little place I heard about through this restaurant hotline." She licks mustard off her thumb. "But I need to go to Georgette Klinger too or maybe to Lord & Taylor and do a little shopping. I couldn't find my shoes this morning, my blue ones; you've seen them before, and I needed them to match my belt. You know, you always match your leather, but my sister, you've met my sister haven't you?" Nod. "Well, she had worn them on her date last night, and it's so weird because he was my old boyfriend, and he knew that he'd seen the shoes on me when *we* used to date, and now that I'm dieting again"—she bites once again into her knish—"he's like, you know, interested again." Smile.

Dancer stares at his phone wishing Anne would call him. He has already replayed the movie of their night together about a hundred times. The *Post* makes no mention of the woman in the white dress. Instead, the murder-of-the-day story is about a discontented Haitian from Queens who took a machete to the SRO crowd inside the Roosevelt Island sky tram. Apparently, New York has such an overstock of grisly daily deaths that the *Post* gets to pick and choose—the most titillating being those involving the largest number of butchered victims. He guesses the woman in white will be in tomorrow's paper for sure.

Meanwhile it's lunchtime, and his usual routine is to go to a salad bar and then maybe buy a coconut DoveBar, and then it's off to Barnes & Noble where he checks out the weekly magazines and snoops through the biography section, because he likes to read about celebrated people. But he finally decides he just might as well not go out. It's too hot, and he's still too hung over, and if he eats he'll only feel sick. Besides, now would be a good time to get some work done on his novel... or at least a short story.

So he goes down three floors to the stock room and orders a stack of canary legal pads, a box of #2 pencils, bond typing paper and several bottles of liquid paper. But of course as soon as he sharpens the pencils and sits down to let the fluids flow, he is summoned. "Dancer?" Nova Grey Lovejoy calls out from her office. "Can you come in here a minute? I've got to come up with a name for a pitch product, and I've been thinking about calling it 'Extra.' How does that grab you?"

"What's the pitch for?"

"A brilliant new fabric softener. It not only adds a fresher than Springtime scent while reducing the horrors of static cling but as an extra bonus, it prevents odors from building up on your clothes. Personally, it excites me so much I could piss a river."

"But don't you think 'Extra' might be just a little overused?"

"That's what I need you to find out." She begins to blush which is very unusual for her. Meanwhile, he is busy trying not to block the beams from the skeleton's eye sockets. "I think there's a prophylactic called 'Extra.'"

"Probably several, what with the condom market exploding like it is."

"Yes, well, what I need you to do is fill out a petty cash voucher and run over to the drugstore and buy every brand with 'Extra' on the box."

"No?"

"Yes."

"Nova."

"So," she says, shrugging, "everyone will think you have a healthy libido. Is there anything wrong with that? And be sure to ask the pharmacist if he has any behind the counter as well. Sometimes they keep them out of sight."

"You don't say," he says, cocking his eyebrows archly.

Nova makes a half smile trying not to look uncomfortable. This is her sign that the game shouldn't go any further than it already has. Dancer is intrigued by the sexual tension that their relation-ship is founded on. Of course, neither of them would ever dare pursue their interest beyond this stage of innuendos and double entendres, because they're both too conscious of job propriety and office dictums. Besides, Nova just isn't the philandering type.

Sexual overtones aside, however, she has this strange tendency to treat Dancer like her only trusted friend, always calling him into her office to purge her frustrations, both personal and profes-sional, as though he alone knew all the answers; like the time she'd asked him how she would ever be able to live with the idea of an early death. This was on a day she had to leave work early for a sonogram, because her doctor had discovered a polyp the size of an orange in her uterus during a routine gynecological exam the week before. "Today an orange, tomorrow a grapefruit," she'd said. "I'll die if it's malignant." Luckily though, it turned out to be benign. Still, a polyp in one's uterus is not a subject most people discuss around the office.

He can't figure her out. Although once, way back when he first started working for her, she did mention how he looked a lot like her younger brother whom she respected and admired and felt very close to. He was flattered but remembers the embarrassment that followed when he asked how old her brother was. Nova said, "He was about your age when he was killed in a car accident about five years ago."

"Oh," he said, fumbling for words, "I'm sorry," and she never mentioned the subject again.

As long as he has to go to the drugstore anyway, he might as well stop by the bank and cash his check. He imagines he's prob-ably paid more than someone like Suzanne Bernstein or the seldom-seen black girl, even though they've both been with the agency much longer than he has. He thinks this because he is a male and GS & B is very sexist. On the other hand, Judith proba-bly makes at least what he does, because not only is she pretty, friendly and intelligent but she also works for Irving Koenig. And Dancer knows that where Irving Koenig is concerned, attractive-ness is next to worthiness.

While he's waiting for the elevator, Dancer tries to think of something to say to the receptionist, but he can't even remember the sex of the person let alone its name.

"Hi, Dancer," he/she says.

Dancer says, "Good book?"

"Fairly, if you like Stephen King. I don't particularly."

Please hurry elevator, Dancer thinks. He/she winks at him. The elevator opens and Dancer quickly jumps inside and stabs the "G" button with his pen, but it doesn't turn orange like it's supposed to.

"Hold the doors!" two assistant copywriters shout. He decides to pretend that he doesn't hear them and stabs the button harder, but still it doesn't light up. Finally, he remembers that it is touch sensitive and only his fingers will make it work, but it's too late. He's going to have to share the ride with the two copywriters, and he can't remember *their* names either.

"I didn't get screwed all weekend," says one, who presses the "one" button by mistake but fails to notice.

"But you're single, you're supposed to get screwed," says the other.

"I know, but I didn't."

"Did you get back those chromes yet?"

"Not yet. I can't do anything lately. I haven't been screwed."

"What about the color stats?"

"I haven't been screwed."

The doors open on floor one and both copywriters glare accusingly at Dancer. The doors close again and open a few seconds later on the ground floor. Dancer says, "Hope you get screwed," and smiles. They smile back. All is forgiven.

Lunch hour is over. Everyone reluctantly drags back in, everyone except Suzanne Bernstein, who decided she was feeling ill after seeing how cloudless and absolutely gorgeous it was outside ...perfect tanning weather. Dancer wonders why she even bothered coming in at all, because he read in the *Post* that today is some sort of minor Jewish holiday. He thinks to himself that Suzanne will really be mad when she finds out she wasted a sick day. But he also wishes that there were either more Jewish holidays or that Suzanne Bernstein was a sicklier sort, because he's always glad when she's out.

Miles Caesar seems to be just as pleased. Her absence gives him a legitimate excuse to give Dancer all the work she ordinarily doesn't do. Dancer likes Miles anyway. Miles has lots of connections in publishing, and on more than one occasion has shrewdly advised him on where to send his short stories. Alas, to no avail. They are rejected without fail.

Miles sets a storyboard on Dancer's desk and asks Dancer if he would mind typing it up for him, seeing as how Suzanne is sick. Dancer says he doesn't mind. "By the way," Miles says, "how's your S.V.A. course going? You had a class last night didn't you?"

Uh oh, he thinks, trying to remember what S.V.A. stands for. Oh yes, the School of Visual Arts. Then he tries to remember the last time he actually went. He can't. "Yeah," he says, "that's right. Fine. It's going fine."

"Have you decided what you want to be yet—a copywriter or an art director?"

"A copywriter," he says, inwardly grimacing at the thought of being a copywriter.

"Well, I don't want to see you doing either. You're too good a writer to waste yourself on disposable fiction. You can make it, kid, just hang in. Perseverance—that's the key. That and luck... but you know what they say about luck, that it's just the residue of hard work." He now throws up his arms, "And everything that goes around..."

Dancer thinks that for a poet, Miles uses too many clichés.

Later. Much.

Dancer is again replaying his movie of last night while pressing sharpened pencils into assorted colored condoms to see just how strong they are. He's thinking about writing a story about an employee on the assembly line of a rubber factory, and he is trying to decide if it will be a comedy.

"Dancer?"

"Yes." He goes into Nova's office.

"Can you believe this memo from Ice Man Irving?" She passes it to him and he reads:

> Please make sure that when you fill out your weekly time sheets you properly allocate the time you spent working on GLORY liquid.
>
> This particular product is on a fee basis which means the Agency gets paid based on the hours we submit. The implications are obvious.

"I don't understand why you're so upset," Dancer says. "Isn't this just standard procedure?"

"Of course it is, but you don't go around reminding people with memos. For God's sake, this is on *paper*. A spy could see it."

"Well don't scream at me. I didn't send it."

"I hate that Irving. You know he killed some of my best boards. I came up with this great new idea—an animated commercial for GLORY; I mean real quality animation using parables like Aesop's fables, not this Saturday morning shit. And he killed it. Nothing like it has ever been attempted with a dishwashing detergent, and that bastard killed it... not the client, Irving Koenig." Nova throws up her arms. "It's amazing anything ever gets the go-ahead around here. I'll bet you that for every *one* of my ideas that slips through, there are twenty that don't. Dancer, will you be honest with me?"

"Sure."

"Do you think I'm being discriminated against? No wait, let me rephrase that. Every woman here gets discriminated against, but do you think I get discriminated against more than other women?"

"I believe so. You're too assertive and sharp, which I think is intimidating to someone like Irving, who apparently has an inferiority complex. That's why he's so impersonal, but then who said he has to be friendly? After all, he is the one in the corner."

"Did you know he has a priority list of people to axe if we lose too many accounts? That's why Gwen Perry was fired last week. We lost the Topaz Cola account, and because her head was at the top, it rolled first. I just wonder whether I'm far behind."

"They won't fire you, Nova. They've got too good a thing. You work twice as hard as anyone else here."

"And I guarantee you I get paid half as much. It's a crime what they pay me to kill myself. You know I've only been able to go to my tap class twice in the last three months, and it doesn't start until 8:oo!"

"So go above him and ask for a raise."

"Are you kidding? He'd fire me in a second."

"Then what are you going to do about it?"

"Don't tell anybody; I mean this is only between you and me, but I'm seeing a headhunter during lunch tomorrow."

Back at his desk, Dancer is incredibly bored. But staring at his telephone isn't making it ring and staring at his pad isn't making him write. Having cashed his check, he counts his money, wondering why he didn't deposit it, but it's too late now. The bank is closed. So, for the time being he just sticks it into an envelope, all but the few dollars he'll need to get home and eat tonight. Then he shoves the envelope into a drawer. He'll deposit it tomorrow. Now he stares back at his blank writing pad and wonders why a story can't write itself. He taps a pencil against the bridge of his nose. He wonders if his nose is bone, or if it's only cartilage.

He stares at Suzanne Bernstein's empty chair. He wonders if he really hates her or if her personality just bugs him. He has already thought of the infinite number of ways she could accidentally be killed between her apartment and work—she could see a new diet book in a window, go into the store to purchase it not realizing that her sister is in the store about to purchase the same book and is wearing Suzanne's blue leather pumps on top of it all. Suddenly, in walks the boyfriend who knows that Suzanne's sister is wearing the shoes that are really Suzanne's. Panic stricken, Suzanne tries to hide behind the mango stand, but she accidentally knocks off one of the mangos which starts an avalanche, and a thousand mangos are crashing around her feet drawing attention to the fact that she and her sister cannot afford separate wardrobes. Thus she dies of shock and embarrassment and even a few bruises. . . .

"Dancer, have you got a minute?"

It is Ned Helix, and his lovely window office is just behind Dancer's desk. It looks exactly like Nova Grey Lovejoy's, except that Ned is a stuffed shirt, so his office is bare but for a desk and some files. Ned is sort of tall, sort of grey, sort of bland-looking and innocuous. His sense of humor is known as arid. Nova calls him Mr. Personality, mainly because he has none. He is poker-faced and dead-panned. He tells a joke and no one laughs simply because they never realize it is a joke to begin with. He's just that dry. "Dancer, I want you to look at something."

Oh, God.

"Do you know what a push-pin is?" He's holding out two closed fists like kids do when they want you to guess which one the spider is in.

Dancer nods that he does.

"Good, now look at this." Ned opens the left fist to reveal a shiny, silver thumbtack. "This is an authentic push-pin. And this," and he opens the other fist, "is what the supply room delivered to me yesterday."

Dancer sees that it looks exactly like the other, and he is desperately trying to decide if Ned is playing a joke on him or if he really does think they're different. He takes a gamble. "Yeah," he says, "the one on the right looks inferior."

"That's right."

My God, Dancer thinks, emotion.

"Tap the head on this one." Dancer obeys. "Metallic, right? Now tap the other."

"Plastic," gasps Dancer.

"Can you believe it? Shit! That's what they're ordering down there. I wonder how much money they're saving?"

"I'd imagine millions," Dancer says.

"Do you know I pushed this into the wall and nearly punctured my thumb."

Dancer begins to wonder where this conversation is going. "Do you want me to see if I can order the metallic kind?"

"Hell, son, if they made them anymore, don't you think we would have them in stock. But they don't make them anymore.

They're all just trying to save their own money while stealing others'. And the end result is shit."

Dancer thinks that shit seems to be a popular word in advertising. "Then what do you want me to do?"

"I only wanted to tell you that it's good to be a little cynical at times. Don't grow old accepting what comes along. Fight! You only get what you fight for."—and Ned punches the air.

Dancer thinks this is probably good advice but with limited results and questionable applicability for the case at hand.

Dancer tries to pick up his pencil again, but Otis Molansky and his prize-winning writer are arguing by his desk. Otis Molansky has the pompous title of Creative Director. In the chain of command, his authority is second only to Ice Man Irving's. Otis is a spineless fifty-year-old with a salt and pepper beard. He's also the new father of an ugly baby girl. Dancer knows she's ugly because Otis carries around scrapbooks of her photographs, and he makes everyone look at them. Miles says he only does it to prove that he can still get an erection.

Otis is yelling at his prize-winning writer, and the prize-winning writer says, "But I hate mimes, and I am not going to use one in this commercial."

Otis yells, "My daughter likes mimes. My daughter likes toys. This is a toy account, and you will use a mime."

The prize-winning writer begins to contort his body in jerky motions and pretends to build a brick wall. He says, "Did you know that people in San Francisco have to go all the way to France to buy their mimes. That's where they sell them, in France—little miniature mimes. So the Californians play with them a while, but when they get sick of their mimes, they just flush them down the toilet. Down in the sewers they grow and get bigger, until they turn into people who build glass boxes and do shit like this. That's why I'm not using a mime." The prize-winning writer walks away, and Otis Molansky doesn't know whether to fire him or fire Dancer, who is laughing.

Dancer realizes that since he has not won any awards, he will probably be the one to get fired. The fact that he has never been in a position to win an award is totally irrelevant. *Relevance* is not laughing at Otis Molansky. Otis turns to Dancer, his face a persimmon. Fast, fast, Dancer tells himself. Think of something fast.

"Otis, I didn't get to see that picture of your daughter that you were passing around this morning. How old is she now anyway?"

"What? What? My daughter? You mean my new baby girl? You didn't see that picture?"

"No Otis, I didn't, but I'd love to."

"Well she's 6 ½ months old now. How old was she the last time I showed you her picture?"

"6 months."

"Well she's grown like a tree since then. Here, I've got it in my wallet. You know she can say Da Da now too."

"You're kidding!"

"Better believe it. And I started her on swimming lessons just yesterday. It's never too early to make an Olympic champion. That's what I say."

"That's what I say too," Dancer agrees.

Tick tick tick... thank God it's finally five o'clock. Anne never called. Dancer should never have expected that she would. Hell, she's a world famous actress. What is he? Just a nobody from nowhere. "Damn," he says. Another day wasted and not a word written on his book.

SUNGLASSES IN THE SHOWER

or

Chapter
3

MONEY.

Money!

MONEY!!

Dancer trudges up the steps of his building and as usual, this is the only thing on his mind. Not even sex occupies a greater percentage... and he thinks about sex all the time. He asks himself, what is the point? Why does he put up with this filthy city? Is the dream of becoming a published author really worth the sacrifice?... worth the third-world living conditions, the garbage blowing through the streets, the noise, the lack of any stability whatsoever? How does a young person survive?

Think about it, he tells himself. Already his check is spent. Well not literally, but it might as well be. And worst of all, he will have nothing to show for it... *absolutely* nothing. Take his car payment, for instance. This is a car that he drives maybe once, or at most twice, a year. This is a car that sits in his mother's driveway in Alabama where it is slowly decomposing before nobody's eyes. This is a car that he refuses to sell because it is the only thing on this earth that he owns other than the clothes on his back... he refuses to sell it because he tricks himself into believing that New

York doesn't really have an iron-clad grip on him after only a year here...that, of course, he can leave anytime he wants to. New York is strictly a city to come to in order to get your career primed, then get out of...and that's all it is.

So, this is why he makes payments on something that he never uses, that he can't afford, and that he wouldn't use if he could afford, because living in New York turns most necessities into impracticalities, and because he would never in a zillion million years leave, because you just can't go back to the farm once you've seen the bright lights of Paree.

Somehow though, his astronomical Macy's and Visa bills aren't as easily justified as his car. This doesn't mean that they *aren't* justified. Of course they are...it's just that they are a little harder to accept. But look, he has to have clothes, especially in the winter. Lots of them. God, the winters in New York! He caught three different strains of flu last winter, probably because, until he moved here, snow was something he saw only on television. But he has never smoked, not cigarettes anyway. And he doesn't really drink, not regularly, and only when necessary does he use foul language. So he figures that in exchange for his sainthood, he deserves a few new threads once in a while.

But aside from these minor craters through which his paltry pittance plummets, the real black hole is rent. Dancer shares a two room shanty with a ditsy punker on the fourth floor of this sleazy tenement, and guess how much his half of the highway robbery is?...$500! He can't believe that two college-educated people would in their right minds pay $1,000 per month to live in putrid squalor. Really, it isn't even living. It's more like staying. Living, by definition, is "the condition or action of maintaining life." Staying, by definition, is "the ability to endure a given place or condition." Need he say more?

But he can't complain (he can, but he won't). No one dragged him forcibly to New York. (Conversely, neither did anyone tell him that a one-thousand-dollar-a-month shanty in Brooklyn, though outrageous, would cost *at least* double if it were picked up and set down in Manhattan.) But Dancer *had* to come to New York, to be successful, to pursue his "art." And through the history of the world, people have suffered and persevered more for art's sake than for any other cause. Dancer is a martyr.

He turns the key, pushes the door . . . the door is chained from the inside. "Zinc," he calls. "Zinc, the door is locked." No answer. "Zinc, open the door." Still no answer. Apparently, Zinc is not home. Then how did he get out of the apartment? Dancer wonders. Through the cracks in the ceilings? He hits the door with his fist and screams Zinc's name a final time but realizes it's futile. He thinks that maybe Zinc left by the fire escape through the bedroom window. If so, then the window should be open. So he walks up three more flights of stairs to the roof where, on opening the door, he immediately gets gummy hot tar all over the soles of his shoes. Cursing, he clambers onto the rickety fire escape; and as he ginger-foots down the side of the building, trying to keep his eyes on the wall, he's thinking that with his luck the window will be open but the burglar bars will be locked. And sure enough, they are.

So the question remains; if the front door is chain-locked from the inside, and the burglar bars covering the only other exit are locked as well, then how did someone with an I.Q. equivalent to the number on a tube of sun-screen possibly get out? He ponders this Houdinian feat as he leans against the window-box full of magenta petunias and red geraniums that Zinc had planted. He stares into the bedroom. His roommate is probably at his girl-friend's, whose number Dancer can't ever remember, and God only knows when he'll be back.

Suddenly, Dancer hears a faint noise from underneath one of the petunias. He sees that the pigeon eggs have hatched, and there are now two matted, eyeless creatures squeaking for food. He hopes the mother comes back to feed them soon, but he guesses she won't. From his observations, pigeons are neglectful parents. They don't even build nests. They just drop their eggs anywhere. And this is the second time this summer that one has laid her eggs in this flower box. Last time, the mother pigeon had sat patiently on top of them for three weeks, but once they hatched she just abandoned them. The poor things starved to death in less than a day. He thinks that the wonder isn't that there are so many pigeons in New York. The wonder is that the species isn't extinct.

So he wishes them luck and back-tracks, figuring he'll just have to bust the front door in like they do in the movies. But walking across the roof again he gets even more sticky tar stuck on his shoes, and soon he can't even pick up his feet at all. About ten yards stand between him and the door. He looks down. His shoes, a pair of foam-green docksiders which he bought over a year ago, are literally starting to sink. His mind flashes tortured pictures of saber-tooth tigers being sucked helplessly down into the La Brea tar pits. Quickly, he pulls up one foot, which lifts right out of the shoe, and since it's summer, he isn't wearing any socks. So he stands there like a stork with one bare foot dangling next to the knee of his other leg, in the middle of a lake of tar on the roof of a broiling building in downtown Brooklyn. How has his life descended into such a farce?

He wonders what T.V.'s Lucy would have done in this situation. She probably wouldn't have reacted quite as vigorously as he is doing now. He imagines that the lava-like tar will begin pouring in over the top of his other shoe at any second, melting his flesh. Frantically, he looks around for an escape, holding his arms out for balance. Surrounding the roof is a brick wall about three feet high. He wonders if he could jump toward it and sort of swing one leg over the ledge so that he could shimmy along the top of it to the door.

But the molding on top of the ledge is made out of that chalky-colored bluish-green copper like the Statue of Liberty, and it's triangularly sloped and certainly hotter than a furnace fire. He looks down at his shoe again, which has sunk another half inch. Realizing he has no other choice, he strips off his shirt (a brand new one), folds it up like a towel and throws it down on the tar about five feet in front of him. He leaps onto it, leaving his shoes behind. Swiftly, before the shirt has time to absorb the tar, he wriggles out of his pants, grabs his keys and his wallet, and throws his pants in front of him. So in this stepping stone fashion, he somehow manages to reach the door, although he's left with nothing on but a pair of underwear, remnants of what was once a perfectly acceptable summer outfit...

Muttering vile oaths, he hobbles the three flights back down the stairwell. He throws his weight against the door with such force that not only is the chain bolt wrenched off but the board it's screwed into. As the board dangles from the latch against the inside of the door, he sees behind it a lovely view of the mice inside the woodwork in the kitchen. He slams the door and makes a mental note to buy a different kind of mouse trap, then notices that the refrigerator door is open. He pours the spoiled milk down the drain, closes the fridge, hangs the phone back on the hook and turns off the iron. He has long ago stopped asking Zinc why he can't do these simple chores himself. His roommate only shrugs and says he's got too many important things on his mind. So Dancer doesn't say anything more. After all, the lease is in Zinc's name.

For some reason this apartment is always dark and airless. Dancer turns on the fan and opens the window to let the brick wall shine through. He peels off his underwear and drops it in a garbage bag in the corner. Neither of them has any furniture other than the bed (a mattress on the floor), a sofa which Dancer sleeps on, and a table that they eat on occasionally. Hefty garbage bags serve as their dresser and shelves. One bag is for clean socks and underwear, one bag is for towels and miscellaneous items, one bag is for dirty clothes and one bag is actually for garbage. Zinc naturally gets them all confused though, and more often than not Dancer finds rotten banana peels stuck to his clean underwear and chicken chow mein juice on the towels. The floor serves as their closet... the original closet being the bathroom.

Dancer thinks a nice long bath would relax him and do him good. In spite of his careful efforts, he still got tar on his feet. But at least they're not permanently ruined like his shoes are. Somehow, either directly or indirectly, one year of living with Zinc has completely obliterated a wardrobe that had taken him a lifetime to build.

As he pauses to reflect on this, he becomes aware of something amiss in the fish bowl in front of him. He peers over into the glass sphere on the table and notices that the only fish swimming around is Lily. "Lily," he asks, "where's your sister?" He thinks Ambrosia might have tried to escape, but she isn't flopping about on the floor. Maybe a mouse got her. "Lily, did you let the mice eat your sister?" Lily doesn't say anything. "I guess we'll just have to get you another sister," he says. "Are you hungry?" And he drops a pinch of this stuff that looks like colored sawdust into her bowl. Lily likes it a lot.

Now he shuts his eyes and turns on the light in the bathroom. This is to give the roaches time enough to crawl back into the cracks before he sees them. He opens his eyes, but one of them is still scrambling around in the bathtub. He turns on the hot water in order to boil it alive, but only cold comes out, and it doesn't get any hotter. Still, the roach is swept down the drain where Dancer hopes it will drown. Zinc has painted the whole bathroom black, even the porcelain toilet and sink. He did leave the bathtub white though, and the effect is such that the tub seems so bright that Dancer is forced to wear sunglasses in the shower. So he puts the plug in the drain and fills the tub with ice cold hot water. He slides into it slowly, wearing his Vuarnets and thinking of the eerie sound teeth make when they chatter.

Eventually it becomes comfortable, and he settles back to dream of Anne. Maybe she was busy today and didn't have a chance to call him. Maybe she'll call him tonight instead. That's what she'll do, he thinks, and after a while he is absolutely convinced of this. So he hums a song that he makes up as he goes along, hums it contentedly until the front door opens.

"Hi there," Zinc shouts. "Dancer?"

"I'm in here." He gets out of the tub and wraps a towel around his waist.

"What happened to the front door?" Zinc asks, poking his head into the bathroom.

Dancer glares at him. "Some idiot locked it from the inside."

"Oh. Yeah, I couldn't find my keys last night and you never showed, so I had to come down the fire escape and in through the bedroom. I guess I forgot to unlatch the door when I left again this morning."

"But the window was locked too."

"No, no, it wasn't. That lock doesn't even work. I just put it on there to fool the burglars. Look, I'll show you." Zinc goes to the bedroom window and pulls the lock. "See, it opens right up."

"I guess it would have been too easy to leave through the front door?"

"Well, like I said, I couldn't find my keys. They were at Cheryl's." He looks at Dancer's feet and smiles. "I see you tried the roof too."

"My shoes and clothes are still up there, permanently mired."

"Sorry."

Dancer brushes his fingers through his wet hair. "And what happened to Ambrosia? She seems to have vanished."

"Oh, Ambrosia. You mean your goldfish?" Zinc sort of shifts his weight from one leg to another while he massages his tan. Zinc is perpetually tan, not just bronzed a little, but totally tan...black! It's what he does. He's supposed to be an artist of some sort, having won a scholarship to Pratt, but Dancer has never seen him paint or draw so much as his name, much less attend any courses, and he doesn't dare ask Zinc where his money comes from. He prefers to think his roommate is an independently wealthy California surfer who got blown off course and accidentally spilled bleach in his hair. Zinc's head is whiter than cocaine. "Yeah, about Ambrosia...well man, you know those pigeon eggs hatched last night and the mother never came back to feed them."

"No," Dancer says, "tell me you didn't."

"Man, I tried to pour some milk down their mouths but they wouldn't drink it, and then I put some bread crumbs in the flower box, but they wouldn't eat those either."

"You fed Ambrosia to the pigeons!"

"Well, hey, I figured we could get another goldfish at Woolworth's for a buck or two, and I meant to replace her today before you noticed, especially since the little birds wouldn't even eat her, but they were starving. I had to try something."

"Did it not even occur to you that Ambrosia was twice the size of those chicks? Didn't even occur to you."

"No, you don't understand. I cut her into little pieces."

"You cut Ambrosia into pieces."

"I tried feeding her to them whole, but she kept flipping around."

"So you cut Ambrosia up alive." Dancer falls against the sofa.

"No, I cooked her first. I thought the little birds might be able to digest her easier that way."

"I don't believe this. Did you bake her in a pat of butter and squirt lemon on her, too?"

"Just boiled her, that's all."

Dancer shakes his head back and forth and stares at the fish bowl. He crosses his arms. "I guess I should just be thankful you didn't do the same thing to Lily."

"I'm sorry, man, I didn't know you were so attached to those fish. I'll get you another, I promise. But you know, I just thought they were more exp . . . expede . . ."

"Expendable?"

"Yeah, I just thought they were more expendable than the birds were."

"Yeah, New York has a real shortage of pigeons. Next time, Zinc, just let Mother Nature handle things in her own way. Okay?"

"Okay . . . hey, where'd you go last night anyway? I was goin' to ask you over to Cheryl's to barbecue with us. And where'd you get this chain?" Zinc pushes his face against Dancer's chest. "Hey Dancer, this is real gold, man."

Dancer pulls the cartouche back and finishes toweling off. "It's personal, thank you."

"Got lucky huh?" Zinc is grinning from ear to ear.

"You could say that."

"She rich? Hell, she must be loaded."

Dancer scrounges through one of the garbage bags until he comes across a pair of short pants. He pulls them on. "Rich and famous. She's an actress."

"Oh yeah, who?" Zinc drops some colored sawdust into the fish bowl.

"Don't do that! I just fed her. My God, you're going to kill Lily too."

"Sorry."

Dancer snatches the fish food out of Zinc's hand. "Her name's Anne Monet. She's going to call me tonight."

Zinc laughs. "I may look stupid to you, Dancer, but I'm no moron. There's no way you made it with Anne Monet. She doesn't even live here."

Dancer goes into the kitchen and takes a pitcher of iced tea— warm iced tea—out of the refrigerator. "Believe what you want," he says, "but she's in town to film a movie with that British rock star, Turk." Dancer pours the tea into a glass, wishing he could add ice but knowing that, even if Zinc hadn't left the refrigerator door open, there wouldn't be any ice, because Zinc never refills the ice trays. All six of them are sitting empty in the bottom of the sink.

Zinc squeezes past Dancer and takes this long frozen raspberry thing out of the freezer. "And I guess you just ran into her on the street, huh?" He squeezes the bottom of the plastic tube and the raspberry thing pops up. He takes a bite.

"In front of the Plaza," Dancer says. "That's where she's staying." Now he closes the fridge and they both sit down at the table and look at each other through Lily's bowl.

"What were you doing at the Plaza?" Squeeze...bite. Squeeze ...bite.

"I don't know. I nearly got killed in the subway by some lunatic, and then I didn't have any money, because I gave it all to the fake nun." Zinc nods, squeezes his treat, bites it and nods again. "It's a long story," Dancer says.

"And she's gonna call you tonight?"

"She was supposed to call me today."

"She wanna three-way?"

"Dream on, Zinc."

"Just a thought." Zinc finishes squeezing his frozen raspberry thing and tosses the plastic wrapper under the table. "Damn, it's hot. Wanna order Mexican?"

"I don't know."

"Is she tan?"

"Who?"

"This Anne Monet chick."

"I don't know . . . a little I guess."

"You know this summer has really been the pits. We haven't had a decent weekend yet. All of New York is so fuckin' paaaale. I'm really one of the lucky ones." Zinc examines his legs to see just how lucky he is. "So what's she really like? Is she a whore dog?"

"A what?"

"You know, a bitch. Is she a Hollywood snit bitch? Does she flaunt lots of jewels and priss around like she's better than all the rest of us?"

"No, she's just like you and me . . . a little more jaded maybe."

"How old is she?"

"I didn't ask. Late 30's maybe, but she looks great."

"Late 30's my ear. I remember seeing one of her movies back when I was just a kid; and hell, she had to have been at least as old back then as we are now. I'll bet her face has been lifted from here to the moon. Does she have one of those Betty Ford smiles? You know, does she look like she just came out of a wind tunnel?"

"She's not that old, I told you. She just got started back when she was real young, that's all. Why are you so interested anyway? You didn't even look twice when we passed Raquel Welch on the street the other day."

"Well for one, you didn't go to bed with Raquel Welch. I'm just trying to figure out why a big Hollywood movie star would be interested in someone like you."

"You talk like I'm a creature from outer space. Maybe she found me attractive. Not all celebrities go for just other celebrities you know."

"She was probably just horny and you were the easiest fish to catch."

"Thanks Zinc, that really makes me feel good." Dancer lays his head on top of the table with a sigh. "Let's just drop it."

"Hey, I didn't mean it like a reflection against you. I only meant these movie people aren't like the rest of us. They don't have the same values we do."

"Please Zinc, don't go casting the first stone."

"The first stone? What are you talking about?"

"Nothing. I said let's drop it, okay?"

"Cool with me. I was just trying to help." He starts playing the drums on the table. "By the way, your mother called last night. She has the sweetest telephone voice, like Snow White or something."

"You mean like the sea sirens. Anything important?"

"She wants to know if you're going home to the plantation over the 4th of July. I told her I didn't know, that I hadn't seen you, that you could have been mugged and had your throat slit and dumped in a ditch so far as I knew."

"Thanks, Zinc. Any mail?"

"Somewhere." He looks around. "I know I put it around here somewhere. You got a letter from some friend of yours in Atlanta."

"Tommy?"

"I don't know. The envelope didn't have a name. All it said in the top corner was, 'The Confederate of Dunces.' And I think you got a rejection on that weird children's novel you wrote too. Oh, and we got a note from the landlord...uh, the rent check bounced."

"What do you mean...bounced. The fifth of July isn't until next week. It's not even due yet."

"Not July's...June's."

"You bounced June's rent!"

"Hey man, don't blame me..."

"Oh, I guess Ambrosia did it and then committed suicide."

"I told you that you're the one who should be takin' care of these things."

"Zinc, can't you even manage a little responsibility? I gave you my half over a month ago."

"Hey man, I put my half in the account too, but I guess the check must have hit the bank faster than I thought it would."

"Great, Zinc. Just great."

"So what do I do now?"

"You tell the landlord to redeposit the check, that's what."

"Well," says Zinc, "there's only one problem," and he gets up and paces around the room. "The landlord wants it in cash now ...from now on in fact."

"Wonderful."

"That's not all...I sort of, well I may have spent a little of it already."

"You spent last month's rent!"

"Not all of it man...just a little. But hey, don't blow a fuse. I'll make up the difference. Don't even worry about it."

Dancer leans back in his chair until it balances against the wall. He rubs his eyes. "Oh sure, and this is coming from someone who doesn't even have the sense to put the phone back on the hook."

"Hey, chill out. You know, it's just that I've got a lot of pressures on me now, things I can't talk about, you know."

"No, I don't know."

"Look, I'm sorry. You know I—" He leans against the window sill and stares into the flower box. "They're dead."

"What?"

"The baby pigeons...they're dead. Should we bury them?"

"Why don't you just feed them to Lily?"

"You think she'd like them?"

"It's a joke, Zinc."

"Oh. Oh yeah, I guess they're a little big for her, aren't they?"

"Just a little." Dancer taps the table. "Zinc?"

"Yeah?" Zinc is digging a pit between two geraniums. He pushes the little chicks into it and covers the pit back up. "There," he says, "fertilizer."

"You're not in any kind of trouble or anything are you?"

"Hey, I said don't worry about it."

"Are you going to have enough money to cover July once you pay off June?"

"Sure, no problem. I'll have plenty of money." Zinc pats the freshly covered grave. "Should we say a prayer?"

"Yeah, let's pray we have a roof over our heads next week."

"Hey, just don't worry about it, okay! Jeez, you worry too damn much. Relax a little, huh." Zinc's face lights up. "What do you say we go out for a drink? It'll do you good."

"You go ahead. I think I'm going to try and write a little."

"Man, don't you do enough of that at your job?"

"Enough of it? I barely do any."

Zinc rinses his hands off and smirks in the mirror. "I get it. You're hopin' to make it again with this Anne Monet tonight. Hang it up, Dancer. You were nothin' but a one trick stud for her. She's got a thousand just like you in every port."

"Oh, you know I guess?"

"Hell, she's an *actress*...a fuckin' famous Hollywood actress." Dancer stares into Lily's bowl. "Think about it, man. She can have any *body* she wants...anybody." Zinc changes shirts, stuffs a small celophane package into his pocket, shakes his head and hits the door. "See ya, dude. Uh, I'll be at Cheryl's." And the door swings open behind him.

APOSTLE AND LACTOSE

or

Chapter

4

TWEEDLE DUMB AND Tweedle Dumber have already performed their morning trick. "Just touching base, Dancer baby. Tell Nova we came by." Dancer is now chewing on a gummy raisin bagel with cinnamon/walnut cream cheese. He imagines it has about 10,000 calories and he doesn't care. He eats this with coffee every single morning of the week (except for the mornings that he has egg McMuffins), and he hates bagels. But like beer, it is one of those tastes that is so loathsome you just have to have more.

He stares into his coffee, which with the added non-dairy creamer is the color of a melted paper bag. He is thinking about Anne, wondering what she is doing and who she's with, telling himself that she was really only a one-night stand...that he should never have expected a call in the first place. She doesn't even remember your name at this point, he tells himself. Just forget her. Still, he can't help think that maybe Zinc was right: She *might* have called if only he were a more successful person. What would a woman like her want with a would-be like him anyway?

* * *

Nova Grey Lovejoy—black leather micro mini, metallic gold fuck-me pumps, blue satin blouse and a Donna Karan $550 jacket that she got at Loehmann's for $120—comes skipping in. "Pssst, Dancer, come in and close the door behind you."

"What's wrong?"

"Don't tell anybody because the memo won't be out until this afternoon..." She cracks a grin. "...but I've been made a vice president...me."

"Nova, I can't believe it. That's wonderful, congratulations, and to think you were going to see a headhunter today."

"Yeah, all my overtime finally paid off."

"So are you and Sal going to go out and celebrate tonight?"

"No, I have to work."

> You're young.
> You're talented.
> You're ambitious.
> You're crazy about advertising.

"Oh and Dancer, while I'm thinking about it, I need you to type up some boards for me and run off some quick Xeroxes, ten on each board, and then I need you to call Elite, Ford, Wilhelmina and Zoli for the books on these girls." She throws down some pictures that she's ripped out of magazines. "But first I guess you have to find out their names, and I don't know how you're going to do that, unless you call the magazines that ran them."

"What's the poop?"

"It's for GLORY. The client has decided that the YUPPIE market is the one who buys the shit, not apathetic housewives, and they want a new girl—one that's young, fresh and intelligent. You know, the kind who has blue water in her toilet bowl and white tulips in her all-white living room on Central Park West. Miles wrote the copy in the third person so hopefully she won't have to talk. That way I can get a more beautiful girl. All she has to do is stand around looking gorgeous by her dishwasher..."

Dancer turns to leave her office. "And if anybody calls, you pick up the phone. Tell them I died, even Sal. We had a fight this

morning because he was poking along, and I told him we were
going to miss the train from Connecticut. Sure enough, we're
driving to the station, and the train is just about to pull out.
Anyway, I dashed through the doors just in time, but Sal said
he refuses to run because machines are taking over his life,
and it isn't right. But I had all the money on me, so when the
train pulled out Sal was just standing there like a lost puppy as
I waved bye. God knows whether he ever got to his office or
not."

Suzanne Bernstein slouches in with a tan to kill for.
"Feeling better, Suzanne?"
"Yeah, you know I think it was just one of those twenty-four
hour things. All I did yesterday afternoon was just kind of lie
around."
"How was Jones Beach?"
Suzanne laughs nervously. "Oh you mean my tan?...I guess
it's from all those harsh lights in the doctor's office."
"Your doctor works on a holiday?"
"What? Oh yeah, yeah well you know how Jews are, work work
work." She is fidgeting with her hands, "I was feeling better by
dinner and went to Temple with my sister. Then we played a little
Scrabble. She's not nearly as good as you, but what's so weird is
that I drew an "A" so I got to go first. Well, I made a seven letter
word right off, and you know how rare that is, but sometimes you
just know the letters you have are like seven-letter material. Well,
I drew a blank and an "A," an "L," an "S," an "E," a "T," and an
"O," so I spelled "APOSTLE." Imagine, and I've never even studied the Bible or anything. But then, and get this, my sister drew
exactly the same letters, the other blank and everything! So guess
what she spelled?"
"Um, 'APOSTLE'?"
"You'd think so wouldn't you, but no, she spelled "LACTOSE,"
so she got to put her "S" at the end of my "APOSTLE," making
"APOSTLES" going across and getting those points plus the ones
for "LACTOSE" *and* the fifty bonus points for spelling a seven-
letter word. I couldn't believe it! Can you even imagine what the
odds must be for picking out the same letters, blank and every-

thing, in two consecutive turns? It's just boggling, and she's never even studied biology or chemistry either, so how do you even think she knew it was a word?"

"Maybe she picked it up out of one of her diet books, probably the section that deals with everyone's afternoon low-sugar slump period."

"Yeah, you know that's what I was thinking. To me it doesn't matter what you read, you're still going to learn something. That's what I say. Well, my mother actually used to say. . ."

Dancer is getting a sudden headache.

"Oh," Nova shouts from her office, "Dancer, before I forget, will you call the in-house travel agency, Mr. . . . Mr. . . . What's his name?"

"Mr. Forester."

"That's right. Please call him and book me on a 6:00 o'clock flight to LAX for tonight—first class and I want a dietetic tray of tuna packed in water and a small salad, no dressing. Book me for a night at the Beverly Hills and a return flight tomorrow afternoon."

"What's up?"

"It's that fuckin' SILKEN body bar account. I've got to meet with Nina Blanchard and select a winner from the five finalists in that college girl contest that ran in all the fashion magazines."

"What? I don't remember this."

"Sure you do. SILKEN ran the ad about four months ago, and the winner gets a wardrobe and makeover and her picture on a billboard peddling the shit."

"What if none of them are very pretty?"

"It scares me to death, but at least it won't run in anything like *Vogue* or *Harper's Bazaar,* and if she's a real wolf then we'll just run it once and send her back to Idaho. So can you do that for me?"

"Same meal on the way back?"

"Hell, I guess so. Don't let Linda Evans fool you. It's a bitch turning forty."

You're still young.
You're talented.

You're ambitious.
You're crazy about advertising.

Miles rushes over to Dancer's desk and whispers, "Did you know it's Nova's birthday—the big four/OH!"

"So that's what she was hinting at," Dancer says. "I wish someone would have told me earlier. But I guess I can still get her a bottle of wine or something. Did you get her anything?"

"This card." Miles hands Dancer a photo of a young, tan, athletic young man in a grocery cart, naked except for a red bow and ribbon wrapped around his crotch. The young man is smiling lasciviously. The card reads, "Your birthday..." Dancer opens the card, "...is a hard thing to miss." Needless to say, the lascivious young man has now not only removed his ribbon but he is obviously not thinking about his grocery list either.

"Isn't it a hoot," Miles says, laughing. "He looks kind of like you."

Dancer takes a closer look at the card, and the young man does look a little like him. He wonders if this is why Miles bought the card.

Suzanne then puts in her two cents worth. "Of course," she says, "you'd have to unzip your pants for us to see if you're really twins..."

"Right," Dancer says uncomfortably. He is reminded of what Suzanne said last week when Dancer came in wearing some slacks with lots of snaps and buckles on them. Referring to Otis Molansky's prize-winning writer, Suzanne said, "What do you think about Keith Halley?"

"I think he's a nice guy, strange but nice. Then again, who isn't a little eccentric around here?"

"Have you seen the box on him?" Suzanne put one hand against her face like it was *too* scandalous. "My God! He was in my office the other day wearing those tight Murjani jeans that he must have to jump off the Pan Am Building to get into, and I swear he turned sideways, and I like thought there was going to be an eclipse of the sun!"

Dancer thinks it's interesting, the things Suzanne observes.

* * *

The mail boy comes by pushing his mail cart and, as always, Dancer thinks that this might be *the* day he gets that acceptance from *The New Yorker,* or maybe a letter from some publisher offering to buy his children's novel. Hope springs eternal. "How ya doin', Dancuh?"

Why is it, thinks Dancer, that everybody can remember his name, but he can't seem to remember anybody's? "Fine," he says after an awkward moment.

"Let's see here," the mailboy says. "Nova... Ned... Keith... Otis, nope, nothin' for you."

Dancer isn't too surprised. The publishing industry has been ignoring him for years. Why should today be any different? "Wait, before you go, do you have any stamps?"

"What?"

"Stamps."

"Uhhh. You mean like for letters?"

No, thinks Dancer, like for hydraulic turbines. "That's right."

"Let me check." The mail boy digs through his pockets, but all he comes up with is a condom that says 'Extra' on it. "Oops," he says, and Dancer wonders if the mail boy sifts through everybody's garbage cans, or if he has an exclusive contract on Dancer's alone. "Nope, no stamps."

Dancer is now curious. He is sure that he threw all of those condoms out yesterday after Nova was through examining them. So either the mail boy just happened to notice them and decided to take advantage of the opportunity, or else somebody has solicited him to pore over everybody's garbage. But the only reason anybody would do that is to find out something they have no business knowing. And there's no way the mail boy could be an outside spy. So it must be an inside job. *But who's putting him up to it?*

"See ya' latuh, Dancuh."

"Oh, there you are son," Irving Koenig says, smiling at the mail boy... Ice Man Irving is smiling. "Come into my office, son. I've got something big that needs weighing."

Dancer silently sorts the mail and pretends he isn't a witness to this. Judith has gone to the bathroom (probably to stick a finger down her throat), and he debates whether he should risk eavesdropping outside Irving's door. Even from his desk he can hear hushed whispers, and he knows that if he could only get a little closer he might be able to hear the discussion... if it is a discussion. He has always wondered why Irving's two office sofas fold out into beds. But just as he's standing up, two secretaries from the other side of the building walk by gossiping. They are both enormously fat. "Well, where's Miss Judith?" one of them asks.

"The skinny one?" the other says. "She's probably in the bathroom flossing her teeth with her arm."

"Hi, Dancer," they both say in unison.

"Hi." *Dear God, please let me think of their names.*

They stop at his desk. "Oh," says the first woman who's sorting through everyone's mail, "look at this, Nova's got a pass to the Palladium for tomorrow."

The second woman sighs. "I hate these art directors, they're always getting passes to everything—the Palladium, Tunnel, Limelight, the Milk Bar, even Nell's."

And the first woman says, "Dancer, do you think she'd notice if we borrowed it? I mean, my boss never even looks at her mail. I take her passes all the time and she doesn't even notice."

The two women laugh conspiratorially and Dancer says, "Well, of course I wouldn't mind, but Nova has a friend at the door, so sometimes she likes to go."

"Wouldn't you know it," they both say at the same time, and they wander on, apparently having nothing of importance to do. Dancer is thankful he doesn't have to remember their names after all.

By now, Judith is returning and the mail boy quickly slips out of Irving's corner door and closes it stealthily behind him. He feels around his waist (to make sure his shirt is tucked in, Dancer presumes), and then he pushes his mailcart on around the corner... Dancer wonders.

He passes out the mail and thinks, "Why not?" So he conveniently forgets to give Nova her Palladium pass, and somehow it ends up in his desk drawer.

* * *

Suddenly, his elaborate and technologically advanced telephone begins bleeping and flashing bright red lights announcing that several calls are incoming at once. Nova Grey Lovejoy shouts, "Dancer, I'm dead."

Dancer picks up the receiver and punches Nova's button. It's Sal. "She's dead, Sal. Hold please." Punch. "Nova Lovejoy's line."

"Hello, this is Mr. Forester. Nova's tickets to Los Angeles are ready."

"Could you send them up please?"

"Could you come down and get them?"

"No, could you send them up please?"

"No, could you come down and get them?"

"Fine," Dancer says.

"Okay, we'll send them up."

"But I just said I would come down."

"Well, all right, but are you sure you wouldn't rather we send them up?"

"Fine," Dancer punches another button. "Hold on, Sal." Punch. "Hello, this is Dancer."

"Hey there, man."

"Zinc, I've got someone else on the line. What is it?"

"Chill out, guy. I just called to say that it's cool with June's rent."

"You paid it?"

"Every penny, man. And hey, I'll probably be stayin' the rest of the week over at Cheryl's place."

"Well, don't forget about July. It's due by the 5th."

"No problem. Just put your half of the cash under the carpet in our usual spot. I'll give it to the super myself."

"Fine, but Zinc, I've got to go now, there's . . ."

"No sweat, but hey, how'd your date go last night?"

"She . . . she never called."

"Oh hey, I'm sorry man. I warned you though. These actresses are nothin' but—"

"Yeah, yeah Zinc. Talk to you later."

"Catch ya, Dude. Bye."

Punch. "Hold on, Sal." Punch. "Ned Helix's line."

"Hello, my name is Dale Mandarino. May I speak to Ned please?"

"He's in a client meeting." Standard lie. "Can I take a message?"

"Yes, this is Dale Mandarino returning his call." Dancer thinks since it is a return call, chances are that Ned may actually want to talk to this guy.

"Hold please." Punch. "Hold on, Sal." Punch. "Ned," Dancer shouts, "it's Dale Mandarino returning your call."

There is no response from the office behind him. Dancer thinks he is probably so busy examining a new box of push pins that he didn't hear him. He holds the phone and watches the red lights blink until finally they stop altogether meaning that both Sal and Dale Mandarino have hung up in disgust.

"DANCER?" Ned's voice registers restrained fury.

"Yes."

"Dancer, could I see you a moment?"

"Certainly." Ned Helix is seated at his barren desk staring out the window with his back to Dancer.

"Dancer, do you know who Dale Mandarino is?"

Oh God, here we go again, Dancer thinks. He says, "The name sounds familiar."

Ned leans back into his chair apparently mesmerized by the window pane. "Is Irving's door open?"

Dancer sticks his head into the hall. Judith smiles at him sweetly. He smiles sweetly back. "Yes."

"Dancer, do you know who Dale Mandarino is?"

Dancer wonders if Ned has a bad memory, or if repetition is his way of covering one up. In any case, he plays along and jumps from the skillet to the fire. "The name sounds familiar."

"Dale Mandarino is a headhunter. Do you know what a headhunter is, Dancer?"

Dancer loves the way Ned condescends to him all the time. It makes him feel all of three-years-old. He says, "Isn't it like a Mr. Potato Head?"

Ned doesn't get it. He whips around in his chair. His sunglasses are on and he looks like a Herman cartoon. "Dancer, I would appreciate it if from now on you wouldn't shout through my door any messages I receive. It just isn't good practice, if you know what I mean."

He certainly does. Ned Helix is job shopping.

"In the first place," says Ned, "I never called Dale Mandarino. These bastards are nothing but snakes, always trying to make a commission, so they'll stop at nothing just to get you on the phone. And in the second place, Irving probably heard you, and everybody knows who Dale Mandarino is... everybody but you it seems. Dancer, I just don't think you displayed real professionalism here."

"Professionalism?" Dancer says, looking indignant. For a moment, he considers challenging *Ned's* professionalism. Instead, he bows his head in an act of contrition and says, "Say no more, Ned. You can be sure that any future calls for you from headhunters will get no further than me." Ned wears a stricken look as Dancer leaves the office.

Noon.

Nova rushes out of her office. "Dancer, I've got to go to that client meeting now. Did you get the names of those models?" Dancer hands her a list. "Good. Did Sal call back? I'm still dead."

"I told him."

Miles appears, grinning mischievously, and hands Nova the card.

"Oh, Miles, how did you know?" She looks at the front of the card and laughs. "I don't know whether I should open this or not." But she does. "Wait, is this Dancer? Oh, I love it! How did you get Dancer on this card?" Now she covers her mouth in mock horror. "Oh my god, Dancer, I had no idea..."

Dancer believes Nova should have her eyes examined. He gives her his wine; they cut the cake, have a few bites, and then Nova is off to see her client. Miles asks Suzanne what's thick and about twelve inches long.

Suzanne says, "Certainly nothing Caucasian."

And Miles says, laughing, "You're right, not much of anything."

It looks like it's about to rain, and naturally Dancer hasn't brought an umbrella, so he decides he'll just eat in today. He goes down to the cafeteria and gets a tuna on pumpernickel with tomato, even though the tomato is one of those artificially red kind that's been blasted with ethane gas, and he brings it back up. Suzanne must have forgotten her umbrella as well. She's eating a sausage dog and peeling an avocado as she reads her *Post,* which reminds him that he hasn't checked today to see if the woman in the white dress is mentioned.

"Suzanne, could I please borrow your *Post* again when you're through."

"Jesus, Dancer, they're only thirty-five cents."

"Well, excuse me for asking. I'll buy it from you then."

"Here—" she flings it at him—"there's nothing in it worth reading anyway."

He looks through it and decides she's right. There's no mention of the woman. He wonders if maybe he just imagined the whole incident, but the chain certainly didn't materialize from thin air. Oh well, he thinks, maybe it's best he doesn't know after all. He chews on his sandwich and contemplates the day's agenda, thinking he should try and write something, maybe a letter or two. He hasn't written his parents in months, but then again, they haven't written him either. He decides he'll wait for them to make the first move. Besides, he's in no mood to write. If he writes a story, it'll only be rejected. If he writes his parents, it'll only be ignored. All he's really in the mood for right now is sex. He thinks of Anne again and stares at her autographed Kleenex but then makes himself stop. He turns his attention back to Suzanne. Now, not only is she eating her sausage dog and peeling her avocado, but she's also typing something, polishing her nails and talking on the phone at the same time. He wishes he'd brought a camera. Miles is talking on the phone too, but he's in his office so Dancer can't hear what he's saying. Suzanne can, however. Suzanne is good at hearing one side of a conversation, filling in the rest with what she thinks the other party is saying, then offering unexpurgated versions of the whole.

Dancer watches as Suzanne throws her avocado rind into the wastebasket, wedges the phone between her ear and shoulder, reaches into a bag and pulls out a purple fig. She chews on it while she jabbers away, then pulls her right foot up to her desk top and begins painting her toes. Suddenly, she spits out part of her fig and says, "Oh you won't believe this. Miles..." She places one hand over the receiver. "...you are not going to believe this, Miles. I mean it is *so* weird. You know how you just said 'testosterone.' Well, I was typing that very same word just when you said it. Isn't it weird? I mean it's not exactly the most common word in the world, and for you and me to both use it at the same instant, well..."

Dancer begins humming the theme song from *The Twilight Zone*.

Suzanne hesitates a second then bursts out laughing. "Miles, did you hear that? Wait Didi, I'll be back with you in just a minute. Dancer, you crack me up sometimes. Okay, Didi, I'm back. Didi? Damn, she hung up."

Keith Halley walks by in his Murjani jeans, drawing numerous sets of eyes to an area above his knees but below his waist. "Oh, Suzanne," Keith says with mock surprise, "you've had an operation."

Suzanne, chewing on her fig, says to his crotch, "Whatdayamean?"

"Why, you've had the phone removed from your ear."

She smiles and bites off the top half of her fig. Now she squeezes the bottom half so it puckers out juicily. "Remind you of anything, Keith?"

Keith puts a finger to his mouth, thinking very hard about it. He examines the fig from all angles, pushing his nose practically into it. Finally, he leans down and whispers something in Suzanne's ear. She throws the fig at him.

Hunched over his desk, Dancer squeezes and squeezes his brain for a drop of inspiration. His latest attempt at a novel is some apocalyptic science fiction mumbo jumbo in which all the earth's women have suddenly and mysteriously become infertile. For a moment he wonders if this concept is inspired by his daily association with the likes of Suzanne Bernstein, but then he chides himself for his condescending attitude. Just what makes you so great? he asks himself. Do you really believe you're unique, that you are somehow better than everyone else?

He'd like to think so but he has a nagging feeling that if he were destined for greatness, he would have received some sign by now. He also suspects that Darwin was right, that it *is* the fittest who survive, and that writers—even the successful ones—were never intended to be masters of all they survey.

It will probably be the Suzanne Bernsteins who inherit the earth.

Later, much.
The memo has arrived.

> To the organization:
>
> I am happy to inform you of six new Vice Presidents:
>
> > Blah, Manager of Special Markets
> > Blah, Print Traffic Manager
> > Blah, Account Supervisor
> > Blah, Executive Art Director
> > Blah, Executive Art Director
> > Nova Grey Lovejoy, Creative Supervisor
>
> Please join me in congratulating all these deserving officers of the company and in wishing them continuing success.
>
> > Chester A. Lark, President

Dancer passes the memo out to his group wondering if he is the only one who realizes that print is cheap. GS & B already has several *hundred* vice presidents. Can it be just a coincidence that the newly appointed ones are all overqualified, underpaid, overworked and threatening to leave?

Within minutes, the sycophants and would-be vice presidents start congratulating the new inductees. Flowers arrive and the phone doesn't stop. A big cut glass vase of lilies appears from somewhere and Miles, who is brainstorming with Nova in her office says, "Those flowers look like something just picked from the median on Park Avenue."

"Don't you like them?" Nova asks.

"Well, they're a little wilted. You know, I planted a hundred lily bulbs last weekend in my backyard."

Nova doesn't look up from her storyboard. "So you can wave your lily at your neighbors?"

"I felt like waving my lily yesterday when he revved up that chainsaw at six in the morning."

"Well, I wouldn't wave my lily in front of a chainsaw."

"You're right. Talk about mixing metaphors."

Nova's phone rings again. Dancer would rather not answer it, but since Nova is in her office he guesses he has to. "Nova Lovejoy's line." It is Tweedle Dumb.

"Dancer, who loves you baby? Is Nova there? I just got the memo."

"Hold on. Nova, it's Dumb. Are you still dead?"

"Fatally."

"He wants to congratulate you."

"Screw him. I don't have time for these cretin A.E.'s. Tell him I'm still at the client."

"Dum...Shane, she's still at the client."

"Rad, Dancer. Just tell her I called and that no one deserves it more."

"Will do."

"Dancer," Nova calls out, "did you get those tickets to L.A. yet?"

"They just came up."

"Good." She comes out of her office to get them. "But now we've got another problem. The client has decided that they don't want to use a new girl on GLORY after all. They just got the latest results from the focus groups, and it contradicts the information from our mall survey. It seems that housewives really are the ones buying the shit, so now we've got to change all these boards back to first person, and we've got to do it this afternoon before I leave for L.A."

Suddenly, a group of soon-to-be-graduating college kids appears, led by the seldom-seen black girl, who is playing tour guide. "And this is the water cooler where we all refresh ourselves. Eight glasses a day, that's what the human body needs. And here is where I sit, although due to an illness in my immediate family, I haven't been able to attend work on a regular basis, but..."

Nova looks at Dancer and Dancer looks at Nova. Miles comes out of her office and asks both of them what the difference is between a two inch penis and an anaconda. "You don't want to fuck with either one of them."

Suddenly, Suzanne Bernstein starts crying. She does this most every afternoon. She hates her non-job, but the idea of looking for a real one terrifies her. Right now, she happens to be scanning the help wanted ads, having already consumed a bag of figs, called her friends in California and finished the daily diagramless cross-word.

Down the hall, Otis Molansky, future Olympic swimming champion's father, is shouting for no reason, "The price of freedom is eternal vigilance! The price of freedom is eternal vigilance! The price of..."

"...and this is a ti plant, a native of tropical climates. It was just moved to this spot, so we haven't had time to see if the lack of direct sunlight or adequate nightfall will have any long-term harmful effects..."

Ding-a-ling. "Dancer, who loves you baby? Is Nova back yet?"

"Nova, it's Dumb again...or maybe this is Dumber."

"Tell him to shove a chair up his ass."

"How do you fit four gay men on a bar stool?" Miles asks.

"...and if you'll look to your right, you'll see that even in the unlikely event of a fire, we are equipped..."

"The price of freedom is eternal vigilance!"

Ding-a-ling. "Just don't answer it, Dancer."

"Turn it over!"

"...and this is our novelist in residence, Dancer..."

Ding-a-ling. "Don't Dancer. Dancer! Dancer!!! DANCER!!!!"

Every day, Dancer. Every damned day.

A BLOODIER WAY TO DIE

or

Chapter

5

DANCER DOESN'T WANT to contend with the congestion at the Antechamber of Hell, and there's no point in going back to Brooklyn so early. All that waits for him there are assorted pests and rodents. (Well, at his apartment at least.) So why doesn't he write?

The answer is that he can't write at night. He doesn't know what it is about darkness that shuts off his creative flow, but he just can't do it. If he had brought his gym bag he could go work out, but as usual he forgot it. He thinks about calling Zinc and Cheryl to see if they want to see a movie, but he doesn't know Cheryl's number, and he doesn't want to see a movie alone. He wishes he knew some other people in New York, but it's so hard to make friends here. Everyone's so busy.

Finally, he decides to bum around the West Village for a while. He removes the envelope of money from his desk drawer and puts it in his wallet, asking himself whether it's safe to carry around. He figures that, even in New York, the chances of his being mugged on this particular night are very slight, but just in case, he folds up a hundred and tucks it down behind his Visa card.

The sky hasn't changed. It remains overcast, but the inevitable downpour has yet to occur. He is walking downtown along Sixth

Avenue, less commonly known as the Avenue of the Americas, trying to absorb the energy while ignoring the frenzied rush to nowhere. Until now, the Avenue's pseudonym had seemed rather dubious, but he notices now that on each side of the road are strung aluminum plates with an American country printed on them. He sees Uruguay, which conjures up no imáge whatsoever, and Panama, which only brings to mind hazy news stories about contras. Next comes Venezuela, which of course makes him think of Anne Monet. And now he sees Bolivia, Canada and Guyana, making him remember Jim Jones and his cult who committed mass genocide back when Dancer was a freshman in high school ... but then he thinks of Anne Monet again.

He's hornier than ever. What is it about warm muggy weather that makes him this way? Food is a poor substitute for sex anytime, but the latter isn't available, so by the time he makes his way through the Chelsea blocks into the Village, he is salivating for Moo Shoo Pork. He knows of this little Chinese place on Hudson that has the very best. They serve a heaping portion on steaming white porcelain platters, along with the prerequisite plum sauce. He loves the pork but has never quite mastered the technique of folding it into the rice pancakes. It always falls apart on him.

Later, as he's eating, he thinks that the Chinese actually are an advanced race of people, even though they've never carved the sort of niche into the American culture that the Blacks and Hispanics have. They've always been a little bit on the fringe, and he suspects that this is because they prefer to keep to themselves and secretly believe other races are subservient. This is why they smile all the time, and why they are about the hardest working and most polite people he has ever encountered. The reason he suspects this is because he is now a jaded, debauched New Yorker, and anyone friendly deserves the utmost suspicion and doubt.

His appetite sated, Dancer takes to the streets again, pleased that he's well fed and in no hurry to get anywhere too quickly. It's a nice feeling, and he just meanders along until...until he's nearly killed. He walks through a DON'T WALK light, head leaning back like the village idiot. Horns honk, brakes screech, and a messenger boy on a bicycle just misses a collision with his groin, grazing the side of a limousine instead. The messenger boy yells to the limousine driver, "Hey, mothafucker, you coulduv killed me!"

The limousine driver, a burly black man, rolls down his window and hollers, "Big shit roadrunner, you're no fuckin' loss to this city." And he turns around to grin his large white teeth at his passenger—a silhouetted female figure behind the tinted glass. She cracks her window and taps her pink cigarette impatiently. Dancer steps back into the curb. He brushes off his pants and shrugs apologetically to first the driver and then the passenger. He sees the cigarette just as it's pulled back in and the window closes.

"You okay, kid?" the driver asks... "hey kid, you okay?"

"Anne?" Dancer asks softly, "is that you?" and then louder, "Anne?" but the cars in the street are blasting their horns and people everywhere are yelling at the driver to let them by.

The messenger boy is shaking his fist and his face is purple. "You fuckinsonofabitch! My bike! My bike! You fuckinsonofabitch!" The silhouette looks at her watch, leans forward and whispers something into the driver's ear.

"Anne?" Dancer says, but the silhouette doesn't hear him.

"My bike!"

"Hey buster, get your battleship moving, will ya."

"My bike!"

"Watch it, asshole," the driver says to the messenger as his window rolls closed. He steps on the gas, leaving the messenger boy and his broken bicycle in a cloud of carbon monoxide.

"Anne?" Dancer asks one more time, but the silhouette in the back seat gets smaller and smaller, and then it disappears.

It happened so quickly. It all happened so quickly. Was it her? Dancer asks himself. Was it really? He doesn't know. At first he was sure, but now he isn't—it's like trying to recall a dream once you've awakened... what seemed real at the time is only an illusion in retrospect and fading by the second. He leans against an iron fence that surrounds a small park at the intersection of Hudson and Bleecker. Some children are playing in the water gushing from a fire hydrant. *If it was her, was she ignoring me on purpose?...Don't be silly, she didn't even see you...did she?* He kicks at the sidewalk and shoves his hands in his pockets. *Of course she didn't, otherwise she'd have spoken.* Now he looks at the children and wonders if he'll ever have a kid. He'd like a little girl, because you can spoil little girls, especially if they're beautiful. And beautiful children are really the only kind he'd want anyway—that is if given a choice.

Dancer sits down on a bench to watch the people go by. The Village is so different from where he was raised—a true melting pot, all manner of abnormalities converging to become the norm. Nothing is unexpected and everything is accepted, even the colors. Colors have always fascinated him. Here, black seems to be the definitive, except for hair, which tends toward shades favored by Rousseau and Monet...*Don't think about her Dancer, don't.* And most of the couples are the same sex, and sex is mostly what keeps them couples. He thinks it is a Disneyland scraped raw and turned inside out. He loves it.

The dusk seems earlier tonight because of the heavy cloud cover. He gets up and wonders where the umbrella vendors are when you need them. He walks east on Hudson, or is it west? Whatever it is, it runs parallel to the Hudson River—inspiring him to guess which was named first. From somewhere appears a shabby dog. *Why isn't it on a leash?* It trots toward him wagging its tail; but suddenly it bares its teeth and growls. Dancer feels the same nervousness he felt down in the subway when he was accosted by the Islamic. He whips around quickly and a fat bum, probably the only fat bum in New York, is behind him. Dancer nods, but the dog starts growling more fiercely. The bum attempts to pet it, but the dog runs yelping into the street where a cab hits it and it dies. Dancer is stunned. Of course the cab doesn't stop, but luckily the dog looks as though it died instantly. The bum shakes his head and walks away, muttering, "I guess there's a bloodier way to die."

Dancer picks up his pace as he turns left onto Christopher. He pauses in front of a junk shop to gaze at the bric-a-brac. Tin carousels and frowning paper clowns seem to be moving in the play of shadows, and he watches them while eavesdropping on a man and woman to his right arguing about the fate of Mr. Reagan.

"He will too," the man insists. "All the presidents elected on a year ending in zero have died in office. And furthermore, they are the *only* presidents who've died in office."

"That's ridiculous," the woman says.

"Name one who hasn't then." Dancer tries to think of one.

She says, "Mmmmm, Roosevelt... Franklin."

"He was elected in 1940," the man says, obviously pleased with himself.

"Harding, then..."

"1920. Kennedy, Roosevelt, Harding, McKinley, Garfield, Lincoln, and I forget who 1840 was, but it goes on back. It's an Indian curse." Dancer never realized this before.

He walks on. It has finally begun to sprinkle, and the steamy rain muffles the street noise. He is getting wet, but he knew it was inevitable, so he just ignores it as much as he can. Umbrellas sprout like toadstools; soon he is dodging murky black pools that could be an inch or a fathom deep. He can't imagine why he doesn't just go on home. Up ahead an old man wearing gloves with holes in the fingers is holding out a plate with a few nickels on it. The man says, "Make a wish and change the world." Dancer tosses in whatever change he has and hears the fossil say, "God bless you, son." He swishes the money about on his plate and grins at the noise it makes. Dancer ponders the differences between himself and this old man. Aside from their ages there must be many, but he can't think of a single one.

A few seconds later he comes to a cross street, and on one corner sits a woman under a tatty, candy-striped canopy that drips like a coffee machine onto the parasol she is holding. Under the parasol, she squats on a big vinyl cushion, the kind that water races off of, and her mustached customer sits on the stool. A flimsy, fold-out tray separates them. "So be careful in July," she warns.

The customer rises, twitches his mustache and whispers to Dancer, "She's the real thing, worth every cent," and he rushes on into the wetness. The woman scoops the dirty cards into her hands and shuffles them slowly.

She says, "Take a picture and ya can luk at me longer."

Dancer has always wanted to have his cards read. "I'm sorry. Will you take on one more?"

She pulls the sweater about her and stands up from the cushion. Her parasol pokes a hole into the tatty canopy. "Well, it's gettin' a little late," then she looks him over, "but ya, I'll try to do ya. Sit. My name is Tequila Mockinbyrd. Ya been swimmin'?"

"I . . . I forgot my umbrella."

She smiles. "Bust mah bubble, an I thought ya was bleedin' nectar."

Dancer feels a little uncomfortable. "Excuse me, but what do you charge?"

"Only what ya tink I deserve."

"Fair enough." And they both sit down.

Tequila is a short woman wearing gray hair and cropped bangs over a pasty face. Somehow, she looks like she ought to be selling apples in Wisconsin rather than charging for wishes on a sleazy street corner. Her accent is the strangest. It sounds a little southern and a little Eastern European. "Now tell me nothin'. I tell ya instead. First, I tell ya what I see about de wurld," and she doesn't lay a single card on the table. He is suspicious. "Next week . . . three countries . . . France, Italy and Germany, I see acts of terrorism, very violent . . ."

"Well, I could predict that."

She ignores him, " . . . very violent, and I see . . . a something in de Bronx, an oil or gas leak . . . no, it's radiation, and everybody tinks it's an accident. But it isn't, it's no accident at all. Bad times" —she shakes her head—"bad times a comin' in de nineties . . . beginnin' of de end . . . wars and de axis of de earth it shifts and cities are swept away when all de icebergs and glaciers melts . . . beginnin' of de end."

Dancer is more fascinated by Tequila's accent than her prophecies. He is sure he could find the same predictions in any book by Jeanne Dixon or Ruth Montgomery, but her voice is like a kaleidoscope. It keeps changing. The syllables dip down and then sail up and turn around and round and are never stressed the same way twice.

"Now dis for you," she says. "I see cameras, many cameras. And I see a man, 50's or 60's wit a camera. A Cancer and Leo rising I tink. I tink between the 3rd and 6th of July he was born. Do you know dis man?"

Miles? Dancer thinks. But he says, "No, not at all."

"Maybe he isn't a big part of your life now, but he will be...he will be." Now she is silent a moment or two, and she is still shuffling the cards back and forth to some rhythm only she understands. "You know somebody who recently died?"

"No, not anybody at...no one I knew anyway."

"Two deaths this week, and you will benefit from both...a great lady, she be involved too...a great and bootiful lady. You have met her before."

He thinks of Anne. "Is she going to die?"

"Everybody dies. Is how you live dat matters."

"But this great and beautiful lady? What..."

"Shhh, let Tequila concentrate. I see struggle...struggle followed by amazing success...phenomenal. Everybody luvs you." Now she stares him straight in the eyes. "Why do ya fight me?"

"What?" he asks, on the edge of her every word.

"You're fighting me."

"No I'm not...I mean I don't mean to."

"No, but you do. Why?"

"I'm sorry, I don't know what you mean...really."

"Maybe, but..." She flashes him the surliest smile. "When did you first learn of your powers?"

"Powers?" He is completely baffled. Maybe she means his writing ability. "You mean my writing powers. I'm a writer."

"No, not writing. I mean your other powers."

"I don't have any."

"Oh yes you do—a very great power, or you couldn't fight me."

"I told you I'm not fighting you. Aren't you going to spread the cards down on the table?"

"What do I need cards for? Ya don't tink I actually read dem do ya? Day are only for show. Mah power goes through dem"—she flashes him her sickly grin again—"but ya know dat already, don't ya?"

He is frustrated. She isn't doing what she's supposed to do. "But you read the cards for the man before me."

Tequila shrugs. "He was a fool. He doesn't have de power, so I gave 'em a show. Oh, he'll be amazed." Now she taps the stack of cards softly against the table. "Such a handsome young man, ya are. Have ya evah been to Heaven?"

He assumes it's a joke. "Once or twice, just to sightsee."

"Is dat all?" She seems curious.

He thinks that Tequila may be an example of life imitating liquor. "Well," he adds, "all that I can remember."

"Uh huh. When were you born child?"

"1965."

"The date."

"February 8th."

"February *8th,* 1965?" She gasps. "So, you're the one!"

"Excuse me?"

"I can't believe it. I never thought I'd get to meet you. You know, something told me to stay late tonight. I've always trusted mah intuition, and now I know why...so you're de one." She looks at him as though he fell from the sky.

"I'm sorry, but you must have me mistaken for someone else."

"No, there is no mistake. You're the one all right—the great leader, but I nevah knew you would be so, so handsome. You with your angel's face... such an angel's face. Oh, but it's good, it's real good. Are you a good boy?"

"I'd like to think so."

"Yes you are, too good." Her face turns dark. "But there is another one too"—she lets out a cackle that would freeze the surface of Venus—"and he is even more handsome. He has to be to fool everybody. I have spoken with him as well, and he also says that he is a good boy. Oh yes, such a very good boy. Ha, ha ha!"

"Listen, I just came by for a plain card reading, just like you did for the guy before me."

"Cards? You still want cards? We do cards if ya want...but you're special. Ya don't need them."

"Really, I think I better be on my way, it's getting..."

"What ya want to know? I tell you anything." She raises her eyebrows and her eyes sparkle.

He thinks this is more like it. "Well, I want to find out about my career."

"Do you?"

"Yes I do."

"And what do ya want ta know? Go ahead, tell Tequila."

"I've got some manuscripts out, well really a few short stories and a novel. I was wondering what's happening with them."

"Oh, you'll nevah go hungry or be without money, not you."

Dancer thinks this is certainly a misfire.

"But you must be patient. You...you are too intense. Yes, be patient. Your kingdom will come in the 90's, the early 90's it begins."

Kingdom? "Listen you really do have me mistaken...really. Millions of people were born in '65."

"I don't make mistakes," Tequila says indignantly. "Ask anybody whose fate I've transposed. There will be two kingdoms. One is based on confusion. Not confusion, no...deception—a kingdom of deception. But yours, yours will be the other. All the walk-ins, the ones who are coming in now to relieve the souls who don't want to go through the 90's, to relieve the ones who can't make the journey through the acid fires, the fallout, the wars and blood and sickness and disasters, yours will be theirs." Tequila seems to be in some sort of trance. Her accent is completely gone, and she is pronouncing her words crisply and sharply. "But the other, the dark one who is blond and appears so wholesome, you will have to meet him and..."

"I don't understand what you're talking about. I just want to find out about my books."

"But I haven't written it yet," Tequila says.

"What?"

"It's still in mah head, up heah." Her accent is back and she is pointing all nine fingers at her head. "But you will get it. It will find its way to ya when de time comes. I won't be here then, but don't worry. You'll get it."

Crazy old bat. "No, I meant *my* books."

"Your books? What kind of books are dey?"

"Children's books."

"I see, so you get the little children first. Yes, oh yes, start with the children when they are young so you will have a legion when they are old." Tequila is gasping for her breath. "I've met you before."

"When?"

"Don't you remember?"

"I've never met you."

"Uh huh."

"I haven't . . . ever."

"That's a pretty chain you have around your neck."

His blood runs cold.

She says, "I think it belongs to me. Do you know what it means?"

"No . . . how could it, I thought, but you don't even look like . . ."

"You are really good. You will fool them all, everyone, but you can't fool me. Oh, you'd like to think you can, so I played along. In fact, you almost did when you first sat down . . . you and your angel's face, so charming you are. You lie low for now and everybody tinks you are so nice, such a good boy." She crosses her legs and twirls her parasol and smiles. She still shuffles the cards in one hand. "Nervous are you? Upset that I see through? Testing me, aren't ya? Dat's what you are doing, to see how good I am."

"I really . . ."

"Listen to Tequila."

"I really have to go now. I hope you understand if I don't pay you anything." He stands. "It's been a pleasure though."

She smiles. It's all warmth and forgiveness. "Good God boy, you look like you've seen a ghost. Sit back down here and be sweet. Listen heah"—she leans over to whisper in Dancer's ear—"honey, I didn't mean to skeer ya. Don't pay no attention to nothin' I say . . . I'm a fake." Now she leans back laughing and slaps her knee. "Chile, but I thought ya was goin' to jump out of your skin."

He feels like the world's biggest fool. "It's just when you pointed out this chain. I . . . I felt weird, that's all."

"What is it?" She clamps the hand with only four fingers around it. "I don't believe I've evah seen nothin' like it before."

"I don't know what it is. I sort of found it."

"Well, it must be good luck, whatever it is, 'cause honey you sure are a fool. God looks out after fools and children. You're a little of both. Now smile for Tequila." He does and so does she. "Ya won't tell nobody will ya?"

"Tell anyone what? That I'm a fool and a child?"

"No honey, that I'm, ya know, dat I don't have the gift—dat I'm just a lousy phony grubbin' a buck."

"Are you kidding. I'm going to tell everybody I know that you're nothing less than Nostradamus's twin sister."

She says thank you and gives him a big bear hug and pats him on the behind. "You're a gem, ya are. Now run on and don't evah do this foolishness again. They ain't been a prophet yet who wasn't a wulf wearin' fleece, and that's de truth."

As he stands he says, "I can't leave without paying you something."

She grabs him by the arm. "No, no I won't heah of it. Now shoo." He turns in the rain to wave goodbye and Tequila nods with her hands on her hips. She calls out, "Honey, I tink dat is nectar you're bleedin' after all, cause I nevah met nobody sweetah," and she grins her surliest smile.

The rain is beating down even harder now, but at this point buying an umbrella would be like buying a swimming pool— what would be the point? Dancer reflects on the things Tequila said to him and laughs. Even though she scared him to death, and even though she's a phony, she did it with flair—not a bad entertainer after all. He saunters along until Christopher Street runs into 7th Avenue, then figures he might as well be getting back to Brooklyn. First though, he's got to have a banana split with cherry vanilla ice cream and caramel sauce without the nuts but extra whipped cream. There's this place on Greenwich he knows of that even uses real bing cherries instead of those horrible maraschino kind that taste like latex pickled in cough syrup.

The Hispanic behind the counter—he guesses the man is Hispanic, he's not sure—is singing, "Don't fuck with me Argentina, the truth is I never liked you," as he makes Dancer's banana split. He tells Dancer that it'll be $4.50, and just like an old man, Dancer remembers when they used to be $2.25. But since he got paid yesterday, he's a rich man. So he takes out his wallet—his wallet!

"Tequila Mockinbyrd!" Dancer shrieks.

The Hispanic stares dumbly at him with the cash drawer open. "No, no," he says, "nana spleet. Nana spleet."

"Oh, my God!" Dancer dashes out the door and into the deluge.

The Hispanic calls out, "Dinero! Dinero!" but the words never catch up to Dancer who is running full-tilt through the raindrops. He hardly notices the eerie glow that rises off the street. (Like a J.M.W. Turner painting, the scene before him is all colored mist and harried vaporous light.) Instead, he is thinking the vilest thoughts about that witch, Tequila.

Of course, she's gone when he gets there. "Damn, damn, damn!" Just a rainy wet street corner and a tatty, candy-striped canopy flapping rain in his eyes. He wants to scream. He wants to knock his teeth against a brick wall. He wants to murder the first person that walks by him. How could he let this happen? He is always so careful, so fucking careful. And now, now to have his whole fortune swiped by an ugly, fat, swindling, flim-flamming fake charlatan... How could he be so stupid?

It won't do him any good to call the police. They'd probably sympathize with her anyway or laugh at him. Not even a dollar to ride The Train of Tears... again. Not to mention that he's soaking wet, cold, hungry and... it's amazing how completely one suffers when the opportunity presents itself. He leans against a brick wall and slides his back down until his chin is resting on his knees. An unbroken thread of water is dribbling on his left shoe, probably from a leak in the canopy above. He sees that in her haste, Tequila forgot to take her vinyl cushion with her, so he sits on top of it, and now at least his rear isn't sore from the concrete.

What should he do? He's too upset to even think about it. And people are stepping over him and turning their heads as though he isn't really here. One man throws a quarter at him and he throws it back at him. He instantly regrets it though, because he could have used the quarter to make a phone call. In any case, the man doesn't pick it back up, so Dancer gets up to find it. But he can't because no one ever finds money they drop, and he is no exception. But he does find something else... his wallet!

It's in the street, precariously balanced between the rungs of a drain grille, like a little leather island surrounded by a torrent of sewage. He snatches it up with his hands before the water can suck it down, opens it quickly and finds...nothing. Absolutely nothing! The witch took everything. How could she...from him, Dancer, who probably needs it more than anyone else in the whole city. She didn't even leave his dry cleaner's receipt or his driver's license, or even the halved ticket stubs from that movie he saw last week or...the hundred dollar bill. "Please, please, please," he prays, "please let her have overlooked it." He sticks his finger down into the slot, and luck of luck she has. He pulls it out, kisses it and thinks that it does pay to prepare for the unexpected after all. But there's something else folded up with it...a tarot card. One of Tequila's grimy old tarot cards. It's from the Major Arcana and it says, THE WORLD. He turns it over, and on the back is a quickly scribbled note—"I am not proud of myself, but you will one day have everting. Tequila will not."

He stares at the note for what seems like forever, until the rain has blurred the ink, and until the paper is so soggy it melts in his hand. For some reason the words make sense and suddenly, he realizes that he doesn't hate Tequila anymore, that maybe he even understands her. He recalls the words of the panhandler he met earlier, the one who held out a plate of nickels and asked him to make a wish and change the world. His wish had been that he might somehow make a difference. Maybe he has.

Dancer stuffs the hundred into a pocket and goes home.

THE BUSINESS OF
LEECHES

or

Chapter
6

IT'S THURSDAY NIGHT and the Palladium is hot, hot, hot!

Madonna is here! Cher left early and Michael J. Fox is dancing with Molly Ringwald. Professional debutante Priscilla Host is wearing streaked hair and looking fat, as she trundles after Boy George who's looking wired. And intermingled like glittery Christmas tree ornaments are—of course—Brooke, Bianca and some of the Brat Pack—although Bianca's glitter appears a bit tarnished, as though she may have spent one too many years cruising such melees. Tama Janowitz is in one corner scrawling notes on a pad, and celebutant Lisa E. is in another, chattering with a soap opera star whose name no one can ever remember.

Dancer is here too, compliments of Nova Grey Lovejoy who's been in California all day on business. Dancer didn't make it into work today. Tequila's shenanigans the night before left him unable to do anything but prop himself up in bed, popping Alka-Seltzers and worrying about things he has no control over:

Things like whether anyone at the Greasy Sleaze Bucket would even notice his absence, and if they did, would they get a temp to sit at his desk and disorganize everything on it, and would the temp find the *Playboy* and the gummie bears he'd stashed under his typewriter... things like how he's going to pay the rent this month, not to mention the piddlesome bills, and whether he should go home over the Fourth of July, and if so, will his Visa stand the strain (what Visa?)... things like remembering to put a halt on his Visa card that Tequila stole and to order another, and to get a new driver's license if and when he does go home so he'll not be able to drive his decomposing car, because he's never home... and he's got to call Macy's too, because God knows that Tequila has probably charged a new deck of Tarot cards and a Maserati and Jupiter's sixth moon on it by now.

In fact, going home probably isn't such a bad idea, because if he cries poverty long and hard enough his Dad might give him enough money to scrape by on until his next pittance check. It's a mighty big "might" though. He and his Dad are barely on "How's-the-weather-in-New-York" terms, and it's going to cost most of his remaining $99.00 (he spent $1 on a subway token back to Brooklyn last night) just to get there, but the Fourth is still several days away, which means his stash will be whittled down even more before he even steps on the plane, assuming he can get a new Visa beforehand. But at least he can eat well if he goes home, because God knows that eating is all anyone ever does in Alabama, that and drink bourbon and talk college football.

This morning, lying in Zinc's bed and staring at the paint-flaked ceiling, Dancer decided that thanks to Tequila there are four possible ways he could play his hand:

> (1). Risk spending most of his $99.00 to get home, on the off-chance that the man who loves to smile and say, "I told you so," will give him enough money to make ends meet.
> (2). Risk staying in New York on the miraculous chance that $99.00 will cover rent, food, the Visa bill, the Macy's bill, subway tokens, Dove Bars and fake-nun money for the next two weeks.
> (3). Use his $99.00 to open his own gypsy stand, which he can then use to flim flam naive types like himself.
> (4). Risk none of his $99.00 and luckily stumble across

an attaché case containing ten million dollars in unmarked bills.

Unfortunately, worrying doesn't help anyone but doctors of ulcer patients, so by the afternoon Dancer was feeling much better and managed to drag himself out to the Sheep Meadow to work on his tan. He even ate a hot dog with sauerkraut but no onions and a Larry's lemon ice that made his lips pucker. He also bought a ten-pack of Train of Tears tokens... so now he's down to $85.00 and dwindling.

You're young.
You're talented.
You're ambitious.
You're not even thinking about advertising.

Dancer's not sure, but he thinks he looks good tonight. His skin's got some color, and he's wearing a marbled silk grandpapa shirt with tails down to his knees, parachute pants with snaps at the ankles and sporty Capezios. The whole ensemble is black and white except for a tiny rose-colored leather bow tie fastened around his neck. He thinks that Tequila is going to have a pretty hard time buying that Maserati if she plans on putting it on *his* Visa.

Stars, stars everywhere and more than a drop to drink. He'll have to remember to swipe Nova's Palladium pass more often, because he's feeling very good right now. The music is blasting, the synthesizers are pounding and the video screens are whirling and twirling above the dance floor, flashing synchronized pictures of near-naked Australian lifeguards and women in lingerie. And twisting beneath them all are these sinuous, stunning people amidst green lasers and dry ice, slinging attitudes so hard it would injure anyone not armored in the trendiest fashions their careers can't afford.

He is tapping his feet and sort of gamboling near a pillar. Standing next to him is this eye-popping, kiss-my-ass gorgeous, 5′10″ brain-dead *Vogue* model. She's holding a syringe filled with a syrupy liquid, as she jabs a needle up her arm. She glazes at Dancer, grins and shouts above the noise, "B-12!"

He nods.

Now she fondles her hip-length hair and grooves down to the floor snapping her fingers, then grooves back up again real slowly like she's under water. "Like wooooow!" she says, her voice a shrill squeak. "This is some bitchin' beat!" She smacks her neon lips and says to Dancer, "Wanna shake it?"

Dancer suspects that this brain-dead *Vogue* model is not destined to be the future mother of his children, but alas, hormones have their own priorities, so he moves forward.

They dance for a while, with the model jerking about like a marionette caught in a blender. She licks her lips and shouts out outrageously-vile sexual fantasies, describing to him in exacting detail just what she likes to have done to her, while he stares back at her pretending he doesn't speak or understand English. And this goes on and on until he thinks that no matter how attractive a woman is, she still has to have a little sense; otherwise, being pretty is the same as ugly. He finally just tunes her out completely, closing his eyes and letting the beat of the music take him away.

The song changes and he opens his eyes to discover that Miss Vogue has removed her blouse and is now dancing in her bra on top of a speaker. This suits him just fine, and he is about to ask a brain-dead *Cosmo* model to dance with him, because one is smiling at him from the balcony above, when suddenly he sees an even greater beauty looking bored standing next to her, someone who isn't brain-dead, and who's blowing a plume of smoke into the air as she stamps out a fuchsia cigarette.

He cannot believe his luck. "Anne! Anne! Down here!"

"Oh my god!" Anne says, her face lighting up. "Dancer! Dancer from Alabama!"

They are sitting in the Mike Todd room talking across a table at each other through one of those vampirish black candelabras sprayed with aerosol cobwebs. Behind Anne's head billows a huge tapestry-like white sheet, which partly conceals three people be-

hind it groping toward a menage-a-trois. From somewhere Anne
has produced two champagne cocktails, and Dancer takes a sip of
one, feeling the beginning of an erection.

Anne says, "I tried calling you today to invite you to dinner, but
you weren't at work or at home."

"Yeah, I called in sick today and went to the park." He suddenly
remembers giving Suzanne Bernstein a hard time for doing the
same thing and feels a pang of guilt.

"A summer cold?"

"No... I'm kind of ashamed to admit it but this old gypsy fortune teller robbed me last night."

"Oh, I'm so sorry. I didn't have too great a night myself. Turk
never showed for a promo photo session, which made me late for
a wardrobe fitting, and then my idiot driver hit one of those bicycle messengers and..."

"Then that *was* you."

"What do you mean?"

"I was there when it happened. I was crossing the intersection,
and the bicycle swerved to miss me. It hit your car instead. I tried
to get your attention, but you didn't see me."

"Oh, I'm sorry, Dancer. I guess I was in such a hurry..."

"No, don't apologize. I should be the one doing that. It's because of me that he hit your car."

"Well, if it's any consolation, no real damage was done, just a
broken headlight." Now she laughs. "We're both so selfish,
Dancer. Neither one of us cares a whit about that messenger."

He laughs too. "Well, maybe if he had been more friendly..."

She sits her champagne down and rests her chin in her palm,
smirking at him. "I'll bet you thought I'd never call you again,
didn't you?"

"No, not at all. I know how busy you are."

"Busy hell. It works both ways though. You could have called
me too, you know."

"Well, I figured since you only gave me your number in L.A.,
you didn't want to be bothered before filming started."

"That's true," she says, slurring her words slightly. "I'm a big
star you know, but then bright young men are never a bother.
Besides, it's not only sexual. I'm not the sort of woman who

panders to, how shall I say it—opportunistic young men. No, I want you to know I've never done that. I'm only attracted to people of integrity, honor and manners; qualities that I recognized in you instantly. You're the type of person who only needs to be given a chance; a rare type, but with the right breaks you'll go far. Yes, it'll be interesting to watch what happens to you... you're going to do well."

"Well, I wish I had a dollar for every time I've heard that."

"One day you will, lots of them." He sort of bites the inside of his lip, not knowing how to answer this, and stares down into his glass. "So," purrs Anne, "I think we've already discussed if you've ever been in love but how about romance? What's the most romantic thing you've ever done? I mean"—she laughs—"*besides* letting little old gypsy women rob you blind."

He thinks that Anne, in the candlelight, is without a doubt the loveliest woman he's ever seen. He says, "Well, let's see," and in a playful mood begins inventing a story. "Once I made love under the stars on a catamaran... off the coast of Bora Bora. It was me and this Polynesian girl named Maia... and her boyfriend and his little sister, all four of us entwined like spaghetti on this boat as it rocked up and down, sensually, over the waves. We ate sea grapes and fed each other raw oysters that we brought up from the bottom. We were tanned and restless, and the wind blew all the time ... and this went on for three love-hungry days, this pure carnal freedom... and, and I'm not a good liar, am I?"

She smiles. "But you'd make a cracker-jack romance novelist."

He notices that the song has changed downstairs. "Would you like to dance, Anne?"

"You can't be serious. I look like death in a microwave."

"Well, then, do you want to get out of here and pretend we're on my catamaran?"

She mulls this over for only a second. "Everyone looks beautiful in the dark," she says, and they get up to leave. That simple.

He feels like he's hit the jackpot. After all, how many men in the world would absolutely kill to get a chance at making love with a movie star as beautiful as Anne Monet? A movie star! And not just once but twice he is getting this privilege. That's at least an indication he has something going for him other than just blond hair and bone structure... or is it? Maybe he's giving himself too much credit.

Taking her arm, he proudly leads Anne through the crowd, even though she seems a bit wobbly. He overhears a woman cluck her tongue and say to the person standing next to her, "That's what happens when you start to slide."

"Who's that with her?"

"God knows, her houseboy probably."

He ignores it. "Did you bring a coat or anything, Anne?"

"It's June."

"But I thought you movie stars wore minks year-round."

She guzzles the rest of her champagne and slurs, "Just in L.A., where we need them." Now she sort of trips down a few of the stairs, the ones made of glass cylinders with lights shining up through them.

He grabs her just in time and says, "Don't worry, I'm right behind you."

"Such a gentleman," she drawls, the words slurring badly now.

Dancer figures that what Anne needs at the moment is hot coffee, so they get in her limo and he tells the driver to head for the Empire Diner. The driver flashes his white teeth, and they drive uptown to Chelsea.

Dancer is sipping coffee on his barstool as Anne pushes her hands against the counter and spins round and round just as fast as she can. It's about 3:30 in the morning, and the place is packed. She stops, brushes her hair, takes out her mirror to apply lipstick, screams, puts her mirror back and begins pushing the counter again. Slowly she starts tilting sideways, and he grabs her just before she falls off completely. He has already given up hope of any sleep tonight, and he imagines there isn't much of a chance that a bed will be used for other things either. The actor/singer/model/waiter behind the counter wearing a leather cock ring on his wrist asks Dancer if the lady would like more coffee. He says that she would.

"No," Anne says. "I think I'd like a nice dry martini instead."

The actor/singer/model/waiter chews on his cheeks and says,

"Well woman, unless you brought your own bottle, you're out of your glorious luck."

To which Anne replies, "My young stud, what makes you think my luck is any gloriouser... any more glorious than anybody else's?"

And the actor/singer/model/waiter jiggles the earring in his right nipple and says, "Anybody's luck is glorious who's on your side of the counter."

"*Mine* isn't," Dancer says.

"It will be," the actor/singer/model/waiter says resignedly. He turns away to serve another customer as Anne opens her platinum case and takes out an orange "cigarette," taps the end of her cigarette over an ashtray and mumbles. "Fuckin' actors, anywhere's a stage," then turns to Dancer. "Never be an actor, because that's what happens to ninety-nine percent of them. Look at him," she says, pointing at the actor/singer/model/waiter, "thirty-two years old, ravaged, and still slinging shit in a hash house."

Dancer, playing the role of attentive student, nods reflectively.

"I used to work in a Howard Johnson's once," Anne says, "the one in midtown. I think it closed not too long ago... the same one where Lily Tomlin used to work." She begins to laugh now. "Lily used to get on the intercom and say in her Ernestine voice, 'Hello, this is Lily, your waitress of the week, here to faithfully serve you and your family the very finest cuisine on American soil.'" Anne shakes her head back and forth, "Lily didn't last too long at the Howard J's."

"I have a goldfish named Lily," Dancer says. "She used to have a friend named Ambrosia that swam along with her, but my stupid roommate fed Ambrosia to the baby pigeons on the fire escape, so now she's all alone."

"Just like me," Anne says, beginning to cry, "beautiful and all alone in my fishbowl... I do want love, Dancer... no, not love, I want someone I can talk to, I mean *talk* to. You know?"

The actor/singer/model/waiter saunters over and pours them both another cup of coffee. He winks at Anne with one eye and at Dancer with the other, and then like Dan Ackroyd impersonation of a wild and crazy guy, he gyrates into the kitchen, twirling his hands and swinging his hips while bent backwards like a calypso dancer. "Tha...tha...that's all folks," he says as the doors close on him. And they never see him again.

Anne rolls her eyes and suddenly shudders. She wraps her arms around her shoulders. "I think the air conditioning's too low."

"You mean a goose just walked over your grave."

She turns to him and crosses her eyes. "What?"

"That's what my grandmother used to say."

"One of those Southern expressions, I guess."

"Like shittin' in high cotton."

She laughs and draws on her orange cigarette. "And what does that one mean?"

"It means you've got it made."

"Do you think I'm shittin' in high cotton?"

"I did when I first met you the other night in front of the Plaza. You were like a goddess then, but now I see you're just like everybody else...somehow that didn't come out right. It wasn't meant to be a putdown or anything, I just meant..."

"Oh Dancer, you're just so cute." She grabs him and hugs him and knocks over his coffee. "Oops, oh damn."

"I'll get it," he says, dabbing the brown lake with Anne's napkin.

"Hurry, before Waiter Strangelove comes back and kicks us both out."

"There," Dancer says, and wrings out the napkin over the empty cup. "So what do you want to do now?"

"Go back in time."

"Back to where?"

"Oh, I don't know..." She takes out her mirror, sighs, and begins to work on her maquillage. "Listen, suppose you had a time machine"—Anne carefully outlines her lips with gloss while proposing this—"and you could use it to go either forward or backward to any point in history, so long as you stayed a year. Now of course, you'd be given the proper clothes and some money, let's say the equivalent of oh, two hundred thousand by today's standards. Now, where would you go?"

"I'd definitely go forward. Forward about a hundred years, and the first place I'd go to would be the library to see if I had any books in print. And I'd travel all over the world and..."

"But what if civilization is destroyed by then? What if the world is just a wasteland and the people are back in the Dark Ages? What would you do?"

"It won't be. It'll be a beautiful world. The people will be educated and intellectual, and they'll have solved the aging process. Everyone will be friendly too, because we'll all be wiser having been through the nuclear holocaust and its repercussions."

"So the world will be a lovely place full of young, gorgeous people?" Anne is scraping mascara across her eyelids.

"Yeah, in a hundred years. It's only the part in between that's going to be ugly."

"Beginning when?"

"I'd say in less than ten years."

"That soon?"

"That soon."

"Well, you know what?" Anne says, rubbing rouge in her cheeks, "I think you're dead right, and that's why given a choice, I choose to go back...back two thousand years to ancient Rome. I want to be Caesar's wife and be above reproach, Empress of the whole fuckin' Roman Empire, and throw fabulous orgies and bacchanals that last for days. Everything must have been so simple then, simple and decadent, just like I like it."

Dancer says, "My favorite cake is chocolate decadence cake. Have you ever had any?"

"Oh God, isn't it like the best thing on earth. I gain weight just thinking about it." Now she's pushing back her eyebrows. "They might have some here if you want to order a piece. Just keep it away from me though. I start shooting in two weeks and the last thing I need is a spare tire and pimples."

"I better not either. If I don't watch it, I'll have two spare tires."

"There," she says, clicking her mirror shut, "how do I look?"

"Like an eighteen year old on prom night."

"That's what I thought." She looks around at the crowd and says, "You know, Paulina comes by here *all* the time."

"The model?"

She examines her nails and says, "Beauty is such a strange thing. I mean, if you're beautiful it's *so* easy to be rich."

"That's not entirely true. I've known some pretty poor beautiful people."

"Then they're stupid and beautiful, because the smart ones know how to use it." She sips at her coffee. "I'll admit it's a rare hybrid though—beauty and brains... I mean *real* beauty and *real* brains. I don't have *real* brains. You see, I'm more shrewd than I am smart. And when the two are in a race, shrewdness will win *every* time."

"You've got lipstick on your teeth, Miss Shrewd."

"So does Elizabeth Taylor. Come on Dancer, it's only four-fifteen, let's get out of here and go to the Limelight."

Dancer and Anne are upstairs in the dimly lit stained-glass V.I.P. room of the Limelight nightclub, which in more pious times functioned as a cathedral. About a dozen others are here too—strange looking people with jaded stances and vaguely familiar faces from forgotten album covers of the 60's and 70's. Some are snorting and smoking drugs. Others are making out or just absorbing the eerie music in a catatonic trance. Dancer is sure he's committing some sort of blasphemy just by being here, even though he's been blessed on a regular basis all week.

He and Anne are sitting across from each other on a pair of Memphis style sofas, their cocktails and Anne's cigarette case resting on a glass table between them. He is unconsciously playing with the chain around his neck. "Did you ever find out who that woman in the subway was?" Anne asks.

"No, the papers didn't mention a word."

"Strange."

"Yeah."

"Oh, my God!" Anne says, looking over Dancer's head.

"What's wrong?"

"Turk just walked in." She grabs a cigarette and lights it quickly. "Shit! He's the last person I wanted to see tonight." Now she stands. "Just play along, Dancer, okay?"

"Sure."

"Turk! Turk, how are you?" Several of the has-been zombies look up from their stupor and enviously whisper among each other.

"Anne, luv!" Turk's eyes light up as he rushes over.

Introductions are exchanged and Turk takes a seat next to Anne.

"They're pluyin' me new single," Turk says. "Ear ut?"

"Catchy," Anne says.

"Yuh, et asn't been released yut ere in the Stites, but et's already number thrae in Britain."

"Well, God save the Queen," Dancer says half-aloud. He doesn't know why he feels such incredible antagonism toward this British rock star, but Turk has the most hideous teeth that Dancer has ever seen on anything other than a corpse in a horror movie. He's also cadaverously thin, with these dark veins in his neck that protrude like implanted licorice sticks. He has no chin at all, and his only claim to hair is a shock of orange stuff that hangs down his back like an orangutan's tail.

Anne pats Turk on the knee and says to Dancer, "Turk and I are starring in a new movie together. He's also doing the soundtrack." Dancer tries a smile, but Turk is fawning all over Anne, kissing her arms and nibbling her ear lobes. She is squirming around rather uncomfortably but giggling like she enjoys it, saying things like, "Stop that now, Turk. You're embarrassing Dancer."

"Ow cun Uh 'elp it luv if you're burnin' me insides out, yu know whu Uh mean?"

Anne giggles again, pries him off and says, "Let's make a toast." She picks up her glass, "To Turk, may we make beautiful music together."

Turk laughs and says, "Uh don't know 'ow beautiful it'll be luv, but it'll be as bluddy prufitable as the Queen's loo. Me agent tol' me last evenin' he already 'as three mill in advance sales for the soundtrack, and Uh ain't evun recorded it yet. Now ain't thut a bluddy riot!" He and Anne both laugh uproariously and clink their glasses together. Dancer thinks that with three million dollars in the bank, Turk ought to be able to at least afford some dentures.

"What's wrong, Dancer?" Anne asks. "You look upset."

"Nothing's wrong. I guess it's just the remnants of my Bible Belt upbringing. I still get nervous in churches that close after daylight."

Turk sort of grins and pours a stinking liquid from a blue vial onto a handkerchief. Now he stuffs the handkerchief into his mouth and inhales deeply. His face turns the most brilliant shade of tomato red. Anne doesn't seem to notice as she says, "Dancer is from Alabama. He's a writer, and some day he's going to be more famous than Faulkner."

Turk, who has already pulled three million from an album he hasn't yet recorded says, "Who's Faulkner?"

Now Dancer knows why he feels such incredible antagonism towards him.

Suddenly, just as Turk starts molesting Anne again, a camera flashes and a photographer says, "Thank you, Miss Monet. Could I have another with Turk on your left side?"

Anne pushes Turk off and screams, "Who let you in here?" She turns to the creature at the door. "Did you let him in here?" The creature just stammers inaudibly. She turns back to the photographer. "I had better not see that photograph. It's your career if I do."

"Can I quote you, Miss Monet?"

"Out! Out!" Several people rush over to escort the photographer to the door.

"We're sorry, Miss Monet. It won't happen again, Miss Monet."

"You're right about that," Anne snaps, "because we are leaving." She jumps up and Dancer stands.

"Please, Miss Monet," someone else says, this time in an authoritative way. He snaps his fingers at a waiter. "A bottle of champagne for Miss Monet and her party." He turns back to her. "We're terribly sorry, Miss Monet. It won't happen again I assure you, please, sit back down."

Anne takes a long draw on her cigarette and flips her hair. "I'm sorry too. I didn't mean to get so upset."

"There there, luv," Turk says.

"The responsibility is all ours, we assure you, Miss Monet. Enjoy yourselves." He disappears just as the champagne arrives.

Several bottles later they're all dancing downstairs and Dancer is sure it must be daylight by now, either that or they've turned on klieg lights behind the stained glass. He's running on inertia alone at this point, and every time Turk passes around the rag Dancer shakes his head no and waves it on to Anne, who shakes her head no too and waves it back to Turk. Shouting over the Beastie Boys' new single, Dancer asks, "What time is it anyway?"

"Time to get up," Anne says.

"Time to get down," Turk shouts, and he shoves his blue vial under his nose again, then wraps the handkerchief around his mouth like an outlaw. He flits about the floor, pointing his fingers like pistols at people until he crashes into the pulpit and starts bleeding profusely, and an ambulance has to come.

"Quick," Anne says, grabbing Dancer's hand. They run out of the Limelight and into the blinding light of day where he hails her limo, and they go off to breakfast. She slips a pair of sunglasses over her nose. "Oh God, if I didn't need him so much right now, I'd wish him dead...I don't mean that. Shit! Poor Turk, I hope he's all right, but the last thing I need is another scandal with my name attached to it."

"I don't really like him either," Dancer admits.

"He's a classic example of too much too fast—an English boy from a working class background, who overnight has more money than he ever dreamed existed."

"You two don't seem to have much in common," Dancer says, thinking about how Turk had his hands all over her. He wonders if he's jealous.

"We're friends because it's good business to be friends. It's business, Dancer...it's just the fuckin' business of leeches." She props her chin against the tinted glass window and says to the driver, "the Plaza."

The croissants and marmalade aren't as fresh this morning as they were on Tuesday, or maybe Dancer just isn't as fresh. He picks at his plate and sips at his juice. "What's wrong, Dancer?" Anne asks, but she isn't any hungrier than he is.

"I've got to be at work in fifteen minutes, and I don't even care. Nobody at work cares either and wouldn't care if I ever showed up again. I've written a good children's novel—at least, I think it's good—and nobody cares. I'm working on another and nobody cares. I can't get an agent because I haven't been published, and I can't get published because I don't have an agent. I have exactly $85.00 to my name and nobody cares whether I ever get a book published as long as I live, nobody except me. I just hope I'm in print by the time of my funeral." He pulls a petal from the black-eyed Susan in the middle of the table and rolls it between his fingers until it's a pulpy little ball. "Can I ask you a question, Anne?"

"Shoot."

"Was your success a fight against the world?"

"Not the world, Dancer... the whole damned universe. I mean, I've got more skeletons than Forest Lawn." She taps her butter knife against her saucer repeatedly to hear it ding. "You wouldn't believe the things I've had to do, things I'd be ashamed to tell the Devil himself. "She looks through Dancer rather than at him. "But I did them, by God I did them—and now my mother lives in a fabulous home in the Hamptons and doesn't want for anything, and my sister went to college... college!"

"Did you want to go to college, Anne?"

"For a while, it's all I thought about... but my parents couldn't afford it, my mother I mean. I haven't seen my father since I was a child." Her voice kind of drifts away, then she smiles, "You're going to think this is funny, but I always wanted to be a teacher."

"I thought you wanted to be a great actress?"

"Never great, Dancer, just famous. Besides, all little girls want to be actresses. There aren't too many who aspire to teach algebra."

"Math?"

"Honey, I was doing cube matrices when I was ten years old. I even handle all my own accounting and can tell you how much I'll owe in taxes without even filling out the form."

"I can barely add," he says.

"I think most creative people are like that. They're usually great in English and the Humanities, but horrible with numbers." Her expression suddenly goes blank again. "But anyway, not too many people know I'd really rather be in front of a blackboard than a camera."

"I feel honored," he says sincerely. "So why don't you go to school now?"

"I don't know," she says, giving a little shrug. "I guess it's just too late. I'm not sure it's such a passion anymore. I'm a little scared too. Maybe I wouldn't be as good a teacher as I am an actress. Or maybe I'm just too rich now."

He crosses his arms on the table and rests his head on the back of his hands. "Was it worth it, Anne? Your fight, I mean. Was it really worth it?"

She tilts her head back and smirks. "Dancer, it was worth every fuckin' dick I sucked." Now she smiles strangely as if remembering a time that wasn't too good, and she wraps her hands around her shoulders again and shivers. "I guess a goose just shit in my cotton."

"You mean walked over your grave."

"Yeah," she says vacantly, "a goose just shit on my grave."

MUSH MUSH IN THE BUSH BUSH

or

Chapter

7

NOBODY ELSE IS here yet, so he hardly needed to race. But Dancer has this thing about punctuality. He just hates to be late. Timeliness has always been an obsession with him, but now it's one bordering on paranoia—a condition not remedied by living in New York, but only exacerbated as he enters his mid-twenties and remains unpublished. It's a mixed blessing. On one hand, his race with time forces him to write when all natural instincts say, just put it off until tomorrow, but on the other hand, he sometimes gets so worked up over the passage of time that he only wastes more time worrying about it. The circle is so vicious.

Feeling the need for a cup of coffee, he scuttles down to the cafeteria, avoiding eye contact with anyone and refusing to acknowledge his reflection in the elevator's stainless steel doors on the ride back up. He feels like he's been trampled over by a herd of dinosaurs as he walks down the hall, the squishy carpet giving way under his feet. Every few feet there are soggy signs on the floor that say, WET CARPET. Does this mean he isn't supposed to walk on it? On top of his desk he finds this:

Dear Ann:

I have a problem. I have two brothers. One brother is in advertising. The other was put to death in the electric chair for murder. My mother died from insanity when I was three years old. My two sisters are prostitutes, and my father sells narcotics to high school students. Recently, I met a girl who was just released from a reformatory where she served time for smothering her illegitimate child to death, and I want to marry her.
My problem is—if I marry this girl, should I tell her about my brother who is in advertising?

S.S.

Dancer doesn't know what Ms. Landers might advise, but he personally believes that if S.S. goes ahead and tells his girlfriend *before* they're married, then she just might decide that she's better off single. After all, what would her friends at prison think?
"Like hi, Dancer."
"My God, it's Suzanne Bernstein." Dancer pushes the TIME button on his technologically advanced desk telephone. "And it's only 9:41!"
"Oh, Dancer, you make it sound like I'm *always* late."
"Aren't you?"
"No, I'm not, thank you. It's just that you are early *all* the time." She says this with as much disgust as she can muster.
Suzanne is wearing a suit today, and her kinky, artificially blonde hair is pulled back in a bun, like a dried out mop. "Interviews today, Suzanne?"
"Is it that obvious?" She twirls around with her arms outstretched. "Do you like my suit? You know, I've worn the skirt twice before, but the blouse is new and my white jacket complements it nicely, because it's like a linen blend, so it totally won't crumple or wrinkle. I was so hesitant to purchase it. I didn't even try it on." She sort of bats her eyes and giggles. "I was afraid that since I've been a little, you know, reckless lately on my diet, that it might not fit. "But"—she twirls around again—"as you can see, it fits like a glove."

"Like a glove."

"And what does that remark mean?"

"What do you mean, what does it mean? It doesn't *mean* anything."

"You never like anything I wear."

"Are you on the rag, Suzanne?"

"What, what did you say?" She stalks toward him like a wildcat. "I cannot believe what you just said."

"What did I say?"

"Don't you own an iron, Dancer? I mean, sweet Jesus." She looks him up and down with scorn. "Who dresses you every morning anyway—Ringling Brothers?"

"What's wrong with how I look?"

"You look like you've been sleeping in the park."

"I wish I'd gotten some sleep."

"My heart bleeds, Dancer. It really does."

"Morning, Earlybird," Miles says as he walks in. "Suzanne?" he says, reaching out to touch her arm. He looks at his wristwatch. "Is...is that really you?"

"Like who else would it be? I don't believe this; I come into work a little early and people act like I'm a ghost or something."

Miles ignores her and shuffles into his office. "Interviews today, Suzanne?"

"Boy," she says, "everybody's sure in a rotten mood today."

"Morning, Dancer"...crocodile spike boots and a dress by Fiorucci.

"Morning, Nova. How was L.A.?"

"A disaster. My plane was late leaving, and I didn't get there until about two in the morning, and by then they'd already canceled my room, so I had to change hotels. Then to top it off, the plane was late coming back again last night. They had an earthquake or something, and the whole trip was a mess. But we picked a really pretty girl for SILKEN. Anyway," she sits down at her desk, "how'd things go here at the office?"

"I was sick yesterday."

"Hmmm, you still look sick. You've been looking pretty bad all week. Have you been getting enough sleep? I think you need some more sleep."

"I'll work on it today, Nova."

She nods, apparently satisfied.

Miles pokes his head in. "Hey kids, what's pink, lives in a cave and only comes out for sex and ice cream?" He sticks out his tongue and scrunches up his face and then he's gone.

Back at his desk, Dancer drums his fingers on his note pad and worries again about his stolen wallet and all its repercussions. He calls his mother and tells her he'll be home this weekend for the 4th. "Of July?" she asks.

"No," Dancer says, "of June."

"But June ended yesterday."

"Yes, Mom, July. The 4th of July."

"Well, I don't know about New York City, but it's summertime down here. Make sure you bring some cool clothes."

"It's summertime here too, Mom."

"Do you need someone to pick you up at the airport?"

"Only if I can't talk the pilot into landing on the freeway near the house."

"Do you think he might do that?"

For as long as Dancer has known this woman, he has never been able to figure out if she is incredibly humorous or just incredibly dense. "I think I might need you to pick me up at the airport."

"Fine, just call me before your plane leaves and I'll be there."

"Thanks, Mom."

He calls Visa and delivers his sob story. Miraculously, they tell him that if he comes by their offices today, they'll issue him another card. He makes a mental note to visit the Visa office during his lunch hour, then calls People's Express and makes a reservation to Birmingham. They tell him that on Saturday every seat is booked, but they *always* tell him this, and he has learned that if he just shows up claiming he has a reservation they never check it out. He's told that a flight leaves Newark at 1:30, arriving in Birmingham at 3:30. That's the one he'll take. He punches his telephone again for the time, folds his fingers together, sighs and settles back to wait for five o'clock.

He can hear Ned Helix in the office behind him screaming at the people in the stock room. "Morons! I don't care! It's shit, S-H-I-T, shit! You've got thousands and thousands of dollars worth of merchandise down there and none of it's worth shit. This is a capitalistic society we live in, a society based upon competition, and unless there's a standard we can share, well, there's going to be a *lot* of aggravation. Hello? Hello! Bastards don't you hang up on me."

Ding-a-ling. Ding-a-ling. "Nova Lovejoy's line."

"Hi Dancer."

"Hi Sal." Sal doesn't sound too happy.

"Nova," Dancer calls, "it's Sal."

"Tell him I'll be right with him. There's a run in my fishnets."

"She'll be right with you, Sal."

"Thanks, Dancer."

He punches the hold button, presses the receiver down and glances toward Judith. She looks pale as she stares at a Snicker's candy bar that some prankster has put on her desk. The attached note reads, EAT ME, PLEASE!

A minute later the mail boy comes down the hall pushing the cart. As always, Dancer feels a rush of excitement. Maybe today, he thinks, maybe today he'll get an acceptance for one of his stories. "Anything for me?"

"Nope. See ya, Dancuh."

"Yeah, see you." Dancer notices Irving Koenig standing in his corner door watching the mailboy make his rounds. He looks expectant.

"Uh, Judith," Irving says. "Would you mind taking this supply list to the stock room and picking up these things for me?" Judith, still pale and speechless, grabs the list and leaves. The mail boy makes sort of a hand signal at Irving. Irving makes a signal back. The mail boy looks around to make sure no one is watching. Dancer pretends to be sorting everybody's mail. The mail boy ducks into Irving's office. Dancer hopes Irving doesn't donate blood to the Red Cross.

Now Dancer distributes the mail, noticing that Ned Helix has a little surprise. He slips the envelope marked "Confidential" under his door, the one with the pink slip inside. It looks like Dale Mandarino has a new head after all. Now he slides Nova's *Women's Wear Daily* under her door. He hears her slam down the phone. She's crying. "Nova?" he says, knocking on her door. "Are you all right?"

The door opens and Nova is dabbing a tissue at her eyes. "Hi, Dancer. Sure, everything's just fine. Come on in. Would you close the door behind you?" She lies down on her sofa.

"What's up?"

"I just had a talk with Sal."

"Big fight?"

"Oh no, nothing like that. Do you think I'd cry over a little exchange of insults? Dancer, could you pass me that box of Kleenex in the window. Thank you." She blows her nose. "Dancer, Sal's been let go from his agency. I mean, well, 'let go' isn't it exactly. He's been 'laid off' from his agency, that's how they phrased it. It's all political, of course. It always is. I mean, Sal has been an art director with them for ten years. Ten years! And now they just kick him out like a stray mutt.

"But why? He's so good."

"He's very good; he's excellent, but since when does quality mean anything in advertising? This business is so incestuous, Dancer. Incestuous and nepotistic. The senior C.D. there quit about six months ago, so naturally the new guy wants to bring in all his friends. Sal has never gotten along with the new guy anyway. He doesn't recognize good advertising from bad. He's one of those people who you wonder how he ever got to the position he's in. Sal calls him the Packaged Goods Whore...not to his face of course, at least not before today."

"He'll get another job, Nova. I'll bet he has another one in less than two weeks."

She places an arm across her forehead. "No he won't. It's the dog days of summer. Nobody's hiring this time of year, nobody. Besides, the market's flooded and he's fifty-one years old. Maybe if he were an accountant or a broker or in sales, something that requires no talent or young blood, but you know as well as I do that advertising is a children's game...and children only play with other children. Face it, I'm forty now and already playing for time. I was planning on a face lift when I take my vacation this fall. Now we can't afford it. Not with one salary we can't...and a woman's salary at that."

"Please Nova, it's not like you're out on the street."

"Not yet. Oh Dancer, you don't know the fears that haunt me. I see those poor old bag women pushing around everything they own in a grocery cart, and I think to myself Nova, that's you in twenty years. I worry every day for my job, especially with..." She points toward Irving Koenig's direction. "You can't even imagine the terror I live in."

Dancer feels caught in a real-life soap opera. He expects to hear organ music any second. "Listen Nova, everybody fears poverty, especially in New York where even the rich have to lower their standard of living. Just don't put so much pressure on yourself, okay? Relax a little. Hell, you're a V.P. now. Try to enjoy it."

"V.P. shit," she says, "it's just a way to keep me in middle management for the rest of my career. I'll never move one inch higher. There's no place to go but down. I don't know if you've noticed or not—this is strictly between you and me—but the morale around here is very low. I mean, it's practically apathetic. I don't think anybody's job is safe, and certainly not a woman's." She blows her nose again. "Hell, where's Norman Vincent Peale when you need him?"

Lunch hours are over and Dancer is now down to $78.00. At least he has a new Visa. "You've got DoveBar on your nose," says the seldom-seen black girl as he passes her desk.

"Oh thanks," he says and wipes it off. He believes this is the first time she has ever actually spoken to him. He wonders if it has anything to do with him being from the South. Maybe she has finally decided that all southerners aren't prejudiced. Of course, he has no inkling of what her name is.

He gets back to his desk just in time to see Suzanne Bernstein squirming around in her chair trying to remove her panties discreetly. Discretion isn't one of her hallmarks though. "Suzanne, what in the world are you doing?"

Suzanne turns a deep crimson. "Dancer, I can't believe you

noticed. I mean a bomb could go off and ordinarily you wouldn't even look up, but let a girl try to do one little thing in private..."

"In private? Suzanne, you're in the middle of the hallway."

"Well, I still have on something underneath. I mean, it's not like I'm wearing *nothing*. You know, I have on those panties and hose all in one sort of thing, but I wore my regular panties too, and they were feeling a little tight." She laughs. "I guess it does look a little strange, I mean a grown woman taking off her undies at her desk, but you know I just didn't want to go all the way to the bathroom, and this place is like a desert at lunch time anyway, so I didn't think anyone would notice and certainly not you."

"Why *not* me?"

"Well, ordinarily you live in your own little world. People have to knock to enter."

"That's not true. I notice everything. I may pretend that I don't but I do."

"Then pretend you didn't notice what you noticed." Suzanne throws her panties in a drawer and takes out a complex looking chart with a picture of the solar system on it. She fishes through her purse and finds a protractor, then begins plotting the stars.

"How'd the interview go?"

Suzanne doesn't look up, but says, "They're going to call me."

"It went that good, huh?"

"Fuck you." She lays her protractor down. "I'm sorry. I'm such a bitch today. It's just that I'm in a real pressure situation because my new boyfriend—well, he's really my old boyfriend because my sister dated him for a while—has come back to me again. Anyway, my boyfriend is taking me camping over this weekend for the 4th, and it's supposed to be like this real romantic thing, but I haven't had my period yet, and I'm worried."

"What does your horoscope advise?"

"It says, 'Be ready for new challenges.'"

"Pregnancy is certainly a challenge," he says.

"Too challenging for me right now. I just hope I don't have to go through another abortion." Dancer can't believe she's talking to him about this. "You know," she says, "guys are *so* lucky. They can just do it and then it's over, and they never have to think about it again. Sometimes I just wish I were a lesbyterian. I mean, things would be so much easier then. My sister's a lezzie, you've met my sister haven't you?" Nod. "She's such a thin one too, thin and pretty. Most of them aren't though. I mean, none of her girlfriends are."

"But I thought your sister was dating your old boyfriend?"

"You mean my new boyfriend."

"But isn't your new one the same as your old one?"

"Yeah, he's new again now because my sister dumped him, but that doesn't mean she likes guys. Come on, Dancer. I mean it doesn't mean she likes guys just because she dates them. She just likes to get"—Suzanne smiles—"you know, a little mush mush in the bush bush every now and then. It's just one of those natural feminine cravings. Sexuality has nothing to do with it. I mean, let's face it—a vagina wasn't made just to use the bathroom through."

Dancer certainly hopes not.

Judith floats by. A little more color has returned to her face. "Anybody need a Lotto card?"

"Oh I do," says the seldom-seen black girl. "I play every week but I've run out."

"A what?" Dancer asks.

Suzanne says, "Jesus Dancer, don't they have a lottery in North California . . . I mean Carolina."

"Alabama."

"Wherever. Don't they have the Lotto down there?" She shows Dancer her *Post* with a headline that screams, "JACKPOT JUMPS TO 50 MIL!"

Dancer suddenly realizes what all those lines at the newsstand were for when he was buying a strawberry Frozfruit before lunch. He says, "Lotteries are illegal in the South. They're considered gambling. But I did buy a ticket once when I first moved here. I forgot to watch the drawing though. God only knows where that ticket is now."

Suzanne says, "Dancer, you're such a space cadet. You could be a multimillionaire right now and not even know it."

"Water under the bridge."

"No it isn't. If you can find the ticket, it's good for up to a year. I buy five every week. Once I got three numbers and the bonus number and won only $85.00. That's because five thousand other people chose the same numbers, and we had to share the loot. It was a real bummer."

"I'll try and find it."

"Just remember, when you win don't forget who put you there."

"Dancer?" It's Nova again. Her tone indicates she's in better spirits.

"Yas'm Miz Scahlet?" Dancer goes into her office.

She is sitting at her desk, furiously drawing a beautiful girl on onion paper over her light box. Nova's face is cast in the ghastliest shadows from the under-lighting. He plops down on her pink gabardine sofa, and naturally the skeleton is shining right in his eyes. "Dancer, I don't know where Miles is and Miss Bernstein doesn't know her head from a mango. So"—she stabs her black marker twice to make eye pupils—"I'm giving you a chance to star."

"Star in what?"

"You're twenty-two, right?"

"Twenty-three."

"Whatever, my point is that college experience is still fresh in your mind."

"Sort of, but I didn't really learn anything new in college."

"No matter. The finalist that Nina Blanchard and I picked for the new SILKEN ad is just a living doll—from Phoenix. A real cactus flower. They're flying her in next week for the makeover and wardrobe fitting. Anyway, Otis doesn't want to use the standard boring headline that SILKEN normally uses. He wants something fun. Especially since this particular campaign is going to appear on billboards all over college campuses around the country."

"So he wants something with a collegiate sort of flavor?"

"Exactly, now I've got to meet with Otis in just a few minutes and I'm desperate. If you want to see what you can come up with then by all means give it a shot."

"Any sort of guidelines?"

"It has to be two lines, the head and a tagline, and the tagline has to say, 'SILKEN...Touch to Feel.' Here's the pose she'll be doing," Nova says, showing him what she's been drawing. It is a drop-dead gorgeous girl lying on her stomach as she gazes over one shoulder at the camera. She's wearing a backless gown, and she's chewing on a shoulder strap. "Now the headline can say just about anything as long as it's cute and has some spunk to it. Something like, 'How's that major in extra-curricular activities? SILKEN . . . Touch to Feel.' Of course, that's too long, too many words, but you get the picture?"

"I'll give it a shot."

"Brevity, that's the key. Just play around with it and see what you come up with."

He returns to his desk and writes down anything that comes into his head, none of which he thinks is particularly brilliant: "Finals make your skin crawl? SILKEN . . . Touch to Feel," "Sorority rush blues? SILKEN . . . Touch to Feel," and "Get an 'A' in Anatomy. SILKEN . . . Touch to Feel."

Just then Miles rushes in. "I'm sorry, Nova. I know we've got that meeting with Otis in five minutes, but I had to meet with my agent over lunch, and you know how it goes. It's that new book of poetry I have out. The fuckers aren't shipping it. Turns out that my publishing company owes them money, so they're holding all the new releases. If it's not one thing . . ."

"That's all right," Nova says. "I asked Dancer to see what he could come up with for the headline. I hope you don't mind."

Miles laughs. "No, not at all."

"Dancer," Nova calls, "have you got those lines ready?"

"Just a minute." He jerks the paper out of his typewriter. "Yeah, I don't know whether they're what you're after, but . . ."

"Dancer, these are good," she says, "really good. Look at these, Miles."

Miles does. "Yeah," he says rather unenthusiastically, "Dancer, these are good."

Nova says, "I love that one there—'Get an 'A' in Anatomy.' It goes directly for what the product is pushing—skin. Miles, what do you think?"

Miles swallows and says, "I like it. I like it, Dancer."

Uh oh, Dancer thinks.

Now Miles says, "But you know, I was kind of leaning toward something more traditional, kind of like, 'Earn a Gentleman's See.

SILKEN... Touch to Feel.'" He prints the lines in the air with his hand.

"What does it mean?" Dancer and Nova ask together.

"Haven't you ever heard that before?"

Dancer says, "This isn't the 50's, Miles," and he realizes immediately it's a mistake. Miles begins to mutter something under his breath.

Nova glances from one to the other. "Then it's settled," she says. "We'll use 'Earn a Gentleman's See,' and 'Get an 'A' in Anatomy.' We'll also try one of mine—'On Campus or Off.' This gives us three headlines to present to Otis, one from each of us. We'll let him decide which one seems most appropriate."

Miles and Nova head toward Otis's office, headlines and stat in hands, while Dancer remains behind, praying that Otis doesn't choose his.

In the meantime, he has to go to the bathroom. But in order to get there he has to get a key from the receptionist because somebody has stolen his. He debates whether he has to go badly enough to make pleasantries with the androgyn. He decides that he does.

"Hi," Dancer says, smiling. Luckily he/she has a new tan. "Could I borrow the key a minute? Nice tan. Where'd you get it?"

"Tar beach," he/she says with a grin.

Dancer imagines this is his cue to say, "Tar beach?" so he does.

"Yeah," he/she says. "You know, at St. Roof of the Manhattan Virgin Island."

Dancer manages an expression that says, "Gee, you sure are one funny guy/girl." And now he dashes away before it has time to wink at him.

Washing his hands, Dancer looks in the mirror at the two pairs of feet in the stall behind his back. He hears whoops of laughter followed by a succession of short sniffs which he tries to ignore. He can't decide if his hair is really blond or if it is really brown. But just when he's about to reach a verdict, the toilet in the stall flushes, and he hears one long sniff over the noise. He concludes that the color of his hair couldn't possibly have anything to do with the price of Coca-Cola, and he is about to leave when he notices a used condom on top of a wet paper towel. Could the mail boy just have left?

He hears the two pair of giggling feet behind him say to each other, "Okay now, pull it together and straighten up, it's time to be creative," and he decides he'd better return the key before the stall door opens, and it snows on his parade.

Damn, he's already used the tan line, so now he's got to come up with something else. Think, think, think. Good, it's reading a book.

"Thanks for the key . . . how's the book?"

"Okay, I guess, if you like Rita Mae Brown. I don't particularly."

You're young.
You're talented.
You're ambitious.
Advertising is crazy about you.

The meeting with Otis has adjourned. Nova Grey Lovejoy is grinning from ear to ear. She runs to Dancer and pats him on the butt. "You're in! Otis loved your line."

"Really?"

"Now let me just print it in, and then you can take it down to the Stat room. Tell them you want it twice up and mounted on foam board. I've got to take it to the client in just a few minutes and if they say yes, then we'll comp it and . . . My God Dancer, do you realize that there are copywriters who've been working here for years and haven't gotten a national ad. Do you know how lucky you are? And first time out too."

"Congratulations," Miles says, but he isn't smiling.

Dancer wonders if this means a promotion. He is scared to death it does, because if that's the case, he won't have any time to write. Not that he ever does anyway, but at least his present position allows him the opportunity should he choose to do so. People start appearing from nowhere; people he didn't think even knew he was alive, and they pat him on the back and tell him, "Good job."

Tweedle Dumb calls. "Dancer, who loves you baby?"

Suzanne Bernstein gushes, "Oh Dancer, now you're a *real* writer."

Judith says, "I knew you'd make it some day, Dancer."

Dancer is numb. He hasn't done anything, absolutely nothing except jot down a few random words, trite words at that. And everyone is acting like he's just won the Nobel for literature... everyone except Miles. "Eve Harrington!" he says suddenly. "Eve Harrington, that's who he is. Just like when Bette Davis was stranded in her mink on the highway and Anne Baxter went on stage as her replacement and became a star." Nobody can tell if Miles is joking or not. "I'm late by ten minutes and the buzzards swoop down for the kill."

Nova says, "For God's sake, Miles, calm down. I hardly think one little headline is going to cause Otis to replace you. Be good now, I mean you've had hundreds yourself."

"Not on billboards across the country I haven't, and he does it in ten minutes. Just see if I give him any more advice on where to send those tawdry stories he writes, just see if I do."

Dancer is practically in shock, and Nova is staring at him with her mouth hung open. He thinks, Is this the secret? Is this all advertising is?—ruthless competition and jealousy? If it is, he doesn't want any part of it. He's gotten more than his desired dosage from publishing.

Which brings an interesting fact to his attention. Once again, an entire week has slipped by, an entire forty-hour week, and what has he accomplished toward his career? Exactly half a page of one story. At the present rate, he figures he'll have about a 5,000-word story ready for submission in about a year. This means that by the time he's in his dotage he'll have just about enough stories for one good anthology. Maybe he really *should* consider a career in advertising. At least he could make some real money, and certainly if ever there was a time to ask for a promotion, it's now. These flukes don't happen just every day, especially to "creative assistants."

Suddenly out of somewhere, he's hit in the head with a "baseball." Otis Molansky and Keith "Box" Halley are playing an inning in the hallway. "Homerun!" Keith yells, and he sprints down the hall touching the seldom-seen black girl's desk, then Suzanne's desk and now Dancer's. "Didn't hurt you did I, Dancer?"

"Felt great," Dancer says as he hands the wadded-up story-board back to Keith.

Keith says, "Hey, congratulations man," and he throws the ball back to Otis who winds up his pitch again.

"Okay," Suzanne says, "let's hear some chatter out there."

So Otis, the seldom-seen black girl and Suzanne start heckling Keith, and soon the whole floor is caught up in a Thank-God-it's-a-holiday-weekend-mood. Everyone except Miles, who has gone into his office and slammed the door... and Ned Helix, who has just opened his confidential envelope. "I've been fired!"

This doesn't come as much of a surprise to anybody except Ned himself, so nobody seems too distraught. The game goes on. "All right," Keith announces, "the mighty Casey is up to bat." He swings his hips in circular motions and all eyes are glued to his crotch. "Come on Oatmeal, burn the ball, baby. Burn it in here." A cardboard poster cylinder is the bat. Otis throws. Keith swings. Everybody cheers as the ball soars over three desks, whizzes by Dancer's head and sails through Irving Koenig's open door, landing slap dab in the middle of the desk. You can hear a paper clip drop.

"Sweet Jesus," Suzanne says, gasping.

The silence is deadly. Will Irving ignore it or not? He does not. Irving emerges from his lair the color of ice. He holds the ball in one hand just above his head. "I believe somebody hit a foul," he says, but he is not smiling. Watching him, Dancer wonders just how cold his blood is? He saw a program last week on PBS about temperature. According to the program's narrator, scientists are able to produce a temperature that is 459 degrees *below freezing*. They call this, "absolute zero." He figures that Irving's blood is probably below "absolute zero."

The whole floor is staring at Irving Koenig—at his frozen face, his Arctic blue suit, his steel grey toupee, and his suspenders. Irving wears suspenders every day. No one knows why, but they suspect it's because his pants keep dropping. In any case, suspenders are his exclusive trademark. He is pulling on them at the moment and letting them snap back against his shoulder. "Keith, would you like to come into my office a minute." It is not a question.

"Gee Irving, thanks for the invitation, but after spending last night at my girlfriend's, I just don't think I could come again today."

The whole floor gasps now. Irving fights for self-control, but his body is trembling and everyone knows that any second now he'll point his finger, and poor Keith will be frozen solid throughout eternity. Irving says, "Then I'll just say what I have to tell you right here." No one is breathing. "You struck out. You're off the team."

Keith doesn't know whether he should try laughter or not. "Hey Irv, it was just a joke man... Irv, we were only having a little... it's a holiday."

"Otis?" Irving says calmly.

"Yes, sir."

"Find me another writer before the office opens again on Tuesday. Keith is leaving us. He's signing on with the Mets."

"Yes sir."

Keith says, "But... but..."

"No," Irving says, "it's bat, B-A-T, bat."

Ned Helix, having nothing to lose, applauds.

The rest of the afternoon is unusually somber. Dancer wishes Anne would call and say that she loves him or lusts him or something colorful like that. But she is probably still sleeping off the night. So, he guesses he should get back to work on either a story or his novel. But if he really cranes his neck he can see into Nova Grey Lovejoy's office, and she's not in there at the moment, and her window shade is up. Directly across the street is a hotel. He can see into five different rooms on three different floors. In one of them a maid is clearing off a coffee table. But in each of the rooms on opposite sides of her is a businessman, and the bald one is in bed with what looks like three twelve-year-old girls. The other is masturbating in front of the television wearing only his tie and socks. In another room, below the masturbator, are a man and woman arguing, and below them a man is attempting suicide.

You're young.
You're talented.
But are you ambitious?

Dancer wonders why this man is attempting suicide? Is it disillusionment? Is it because he thinks he's a failure? These are the reasons that Dancer would choose, and this makes him ponder the relationship between age and relative success. The man through the window doesn't look very old, maybe around forty. Dancer always tells himself that he'll commit suicide when he's twenty-five if he isn't published. But he doesn't really think that he will. Of course he isn't twenty-five yet either.

Now all sorts of irritating thoughts start percolating in his head. He's thinking of the friends he grew up with, like the one in Atlanta who just sent him a letter. He's a writer too. It seems that everyone Dancer knows is an artist of some sort, but one by one they're giving up their dreams, settling for nine-to-five. They're hitting their mid-twenties and realizing it's the point of no return. Somehow, the starving artist routine isn't as romantic as it once seemed. The odds against success aren't as easily dismissable as they were at eighteen. Money in the short run is like the bird in the hand. But this is where Dancer is different. He wants the two in the bush.

Anne Monet did it. Still though, she isn't happy, not really. And look at all that she's got: beauty, fame, money. Dancer wonders what would make *him* happy.

The answer is simple...money. And lots of it. But not just money from anything. Not money from writing advertising—"disposable fiction" as Miles puts it. The money has to come deservedly. The money has to be the by-product of the best writing he can possibly do. But this brings up another interesting question. Is wealth dependent upon greatness? If he uses Anne as his litmus test, then the facts seem to say no. She herself admits that she isn't a great actress. And this is a total contradiction to what he'd always been taught—that the best are the ones who make it. It simply is *not* true. It's never the best. It's the ones who are most driven...the ones who just won't give up. Miles once told him, "Initially, you don't need any talent at all. Initially, it's only whom you know. Ultimately, however, it's who knows of you. It's marketing, Dancer. It's *all* marketing."

Dancer thinks this through, and for the first time it really makes sense. Here he sits, at a tailor-made job for a writer, and what does he do? He procrastinates and mopes about all the time, thinking up excuses for not writing, blaming everything from climate to mental block, thinking that he isn't good enough and that no one cares anyway. It's all true, of course. He isn't good enough ... not yet. And no one does care ... not yet. So, he'll just have to make them care. He'll just have to overcome all the obstacles or die trying. (In his head the theme from "Rocky" is reaching a crescendo.)

Dancer watches as the man across the street dives out of his hotel window, and he has made his decision. He is not going to drop by the wayside. He's going to be a successful author if it's the last damned thing on this earth he does. And he's going to do it young too. He is *not* going to take the promotion. Underbrush will only slow him down. Instead, he picks up his pencil, and for the first time he really begins to write ... Dancer begins to write!

Part
II

LIFE'S DRAMA

A SHADE OF MALIGNANCY

or

Chapter
8

THE PLANE IS in the air. Dancer is on the plane. The plane is going home. He is sitting in a window seat overlooking the wing. He always gets stuck over the wing. A teenage Madonna wannabe is sitting next to him. She's wearing braces on her teeth and ten lbs. of beads and crucifixes around her neck. Her bleached, streaked, permed hair sticks straight up. Apparently, she doesn't realize that she's already three years behind the times. She keeps stealing glances at him, but turns her head when he looks back. On her fold-down tray is an assortment of nail polishes in colors that can only be found in hospital trash cans—varicose blue, pus yellow and hemorrhoid purple. She's painting each of her talons with a different one of these, sometimes mixing them to make a shade of malignancy not recognized by the A.M.A.

He ignores her and stares out his window into a cloudy green haze. He's nervous about seeing his parents, not just because he has to ask his Dad for money, but because once again he is returning home untriumphantly. He always hopes whenever he goes home he'll be able to say he's a published author. It's even more important since they really don't believe in him. They don't understand why he had to leave the South. They don't understand that in order to be successful he *had* to come to New York. They actually believe books are just written, mailed to a publisher and presto! You're rich and famous overnight.

Dancer used to assume this too, but he eventually learned that the days are gone when an unsolicited manuscript might be accepted on merit alone. It took him three years to realize this, three wasted years of sending off stories, of getting his hopes up, of worshipping the mailbox and receiving nothing in return but those dreaded form rejection slips—little 3 × 5 cards that all publishing houses mail out by the millions, it being their way of just letting you know you're no better than dirt:

> Dear <u>Mr. Dancer:</u>
>
> Thank you for sending your story <u>Just Call Me Dirt.</u> We regret to say that after careful consideration, we do not feel it would fit happily on our list. As always, we would like to be able to reject it personally, but due to the millions and millions of manuscripts we receive each day, we do not possibly have time. Therefore, we let our computer with its automatic xerox signature signer do it for us.
>
> Thank you for considering us. We wish you luck placing your manuscript elsewhere.
>
> John Doe, Editor

Of course New York hasn't exactly flung its door open for him either. But at least the potential is here, at least he's now in a position to learn how the business works from *where* it works. His parents don't realize this though. And the more time that slips by and he has nothing to show, the more their doubts are confirmed. His mother is more tolerant than his dad, but she is a woman who hasalways assumed that Dancer is innately talented, being her child after all—and where there is talent, acclaim naturally follows. She has no sense of cause and effect, no grasp of the time and effort it takes to become a success. She simply assumes he will be a success, and he must live up to assumptions as quickly as he can. His dad on the other hand, has already given up on him altogether. He never wanted him to be an artist anyway and certainly not a writer. He expected Dancer to take the paved road and major in business—get a real job. Dancer tried, he really did try; but after taking Introductory Accounting four times in a row and never grasping the difference between debits and credits, he returned relievedly to the humanities...and put himself through school.

So again he's homeward bound to face two opposing factions—his mother, who is proud of him for no reason, and his father, who always wanted a reason to be proud. His parents are divorced and live on opposite sides of the city.

The Madonna wannabe has finished her nails. They look like instruments of torture. She blows on them, looks at Dancer, looks back at her nails, blows on them, looks at him again, looks back, blows, looks, blows...until he wants to slap her. She scrounges through her purse, which is the size of a coffin, until she finds her *National Enquirer,* then casually flips through it looking and blowing on alternate pages. Finally she asks, "Do you have a girlfriend?"

"Don't you have any parents?" he asks back.

"Naturally."

"Do they know what you do to your fingers?"

She ignores the question. "Don't you have a girlfriend?"

"Naturally."

"Is your girlfriend ugly or is she reeeeeeal ugly?"

Dancer turns to the girl. He wonders if her parents would prosecute if he strangled her to death. They probably wouldn't. "She's very beautiful," he says, and to taunt her he adds, "she's a world-famous actress."

"Oh sure she is. And I guess she's on the cover of my magazine too." The girl shoves the tabloid under his nose.

He pulls his head back. "My God! That's her!"

The girl jerks her magazine away. "Oh, I see, you date Anne Monet. Yeah, I'm so sure. Yeah, that's the ticket."

"Let me see that a minute." He takes the magazine out of her hands.

"Hey," she says, "give that back." The people in front of them look over the back of their seats, and the people in back of them look over the front of their seats. He kindly gives the girl back her magazine. She is very covetous of it now. She leans toward the aisle holding her *Enquirer* close to her.

He taps his fingers on his arm rest. "Um, if you don't mind, could I borrow your magazine when you're finished?"

"No!"

He resists the urge to ram her head through his window. "Then may I please get a better look at the cover?"

She thinks about this one a little while. "Okay," she says, "but just for a second." True to her word she flashes the cover at him very quickly.

He taps his fingers again. "I'm sorry, but I really didn't get a good look at it. Could you do that one more time and just a little bit slower please?"

The girl thinks again, and this time she flashes it just long enough for him to make out the headline: MY LAST LOVE ROMP WITH TURK! The photo is one of a startled Anne backed against a sofa as Turk kisses her neck. Apparently, it was taken when the three of them were upstairs at Limelight.

"Would you mind if I just read the cover story?" he asks.

"Yes."

"Yes, you would mind, or yes, I can read it?"

"No, you can't."

He glares at her. "Why aren't you in school?"

"It happens to be summer break." She looks at the front of her *Enquirer* again. "How do you know Anne Monet?"

"I told you. She's my girlfriend."

"She is not. She's Turk's girlfriend."

"No, she isn't. She doesn't even like Turk."

"How do you know?" she asks. "Have you met Turk before?"

"I was dancing with him the other night?"

"Dancing? Are you gay?"

"We were dancing together... the three of us—me, Turk and Anne."

"I don't believe you. You're a liar. Anne only loves Turk."

"Anne hates Turk."

"Then how come my magazine says they were going to get married before he died? Answer that one."

"He died?"

"See, you don't know anything. He died yesterday. He fell down the stairs trying to save Anne from being kidnapped."

"He did not. He was dead drunk and strung out and crashed into the pulpit of a bar. He bled to death probably."

"My magazine says..."

Oh God, Dancer thinks as the girl prattles on, please let the plane land soon.

When it finally does, he races away from the Madonna wannabe as fast as he can.

"Hey," she calls out, "will you send me an autographed picture of Turk if I give you my address?"

"No," Dancer shouts over his shoulder.

"Slime Ball!" she shouts. "You're a liar and a slime ball."

Dancer's mom and her boyfriend are waiting for him. There are no hugs, no kisses, no display of affection of any kind. Dancer's family doesn't do those things. However, his mom does manage to ask, "How was the flight?"

"Fine."

Now they walk in silence toward the parking garage and get in the car. Dancer sits in the back. The boyfriend smiles at Dancer's mom. Dancer's mom smiles at Dancer, and everyone turns their attention to the windshield. Dancer finally breaks the ice by telling his mom that she looks like she has gained weight. She says she's lost weight. He says so has he. She asks why. He says he can't afford to eat. She says that's a shame, those sorts of things don't happen in the South. He says, "Obviously," and the boyfriend cranks up the car.

Dancer's mom and her boyfriend share a condominium in a suburb of Birmingham called Hoover—a very white-bread area located "over the mountain." The mountain is Red Mountain, so named for its huge deposits of iron ore. It is the maginot line that separates the white sections from the black sections. No blacks live "over the mountain."

Birmingham itself, a city of close to a million people, squats in a valley under "the mountain." It's really nothing more than an overgrown town—a town that ritually reminds itself that it could have been what Atlanta is. The rival cities are only 140 miles apart, and both were the same size back in the 50's. Back then however, Birmingham's steel union controlled everything, and the union was vehemently opposed to progress. Progress means only two things—sin and corruption. Consequently, Atlanta got the international airport; Atlanta got the glittering skyscrapers and the business conventions. Atlanta got everything, so now Birmingham's southern baptists are left with regrets for what could have been.

I-65 is the highway that circles the city. Dancer looks out the car window and is stunned at how much smaller everything seems. There are only three buildings that qualify as actual skyscrapers. Each is about thirty floors tall. One is occupied by Ma Bell and the other two by banks. Oddly, Birmingham has a sizeable Jewish population. Most all of them reside in the exclusive section of Mountain Brook, a neighborhood that prides itself on being one of the ten wealthiest in the United States and is naturally located "over the mountain."

Dancer rolls down his window and breathes in the air. It's so clear and fresh compared to what he's become accustomed to. Most of the steel mills are closed now and gone is the orange fermentation that once permeated everything. Strangely, it feels good to be home, even for a few days. He supposes it's true what they say about roots. They can never be completely severed, and as much as he so desperately had to leave this place, he's glad to be back. It's stabilizing.

The first thing Dancer does when he arrives at his mother's house is throw down his bags and call The Plaza. Anne isn't in though, so he leaves his number and a message for her to please call him. His mom says, "Home five minutes, and you're already on the phone to New York City."

"It was an emergency, Mom."

"I understand. All mothers should be so lucky as to have cosmopolitan sons. Are you hungry? There's some fried chicken in the refrigerator. Dick [the boyfriend] bought some peaches today at the farmer's market if you want one of those. I imagine you can't get too many fresh fruits and vegetables in New York City."

"Not too many," Dancer says, "only what the world can produce." He bites into a juicy peach. "Is there any rum? I'll make us all a daiquiri."

"That sounds good," his mother says. "I think it's in the pantry there. Dick, would you like a daiquiri?"

Dick says that he would. Dancer doesn't know why, but Dick will speak to his mom or at a wall or just into the air, but never directly to him. Dancer believes that Dick, who is a psychologist, doesn't particularly like him that much. Dick has also been through some hard times, so maybe he's just a little introspective. Dick has throat cancer, or *had* throat cancer as the doctors put it, but the cancer has been in remission for over five years now. When they removed Dick's vocal chords they said he would never talk again. And for a while he had to hold one of those little contraptions under his chin that made him sound like Darth Vader. He had to learn sign language and start counseling the deaf in order to stay in business. But slowly and miraculously his voice came back, and now he's supposed to be cured. Still though, Dancer's mom won't marry him. She's afraid if she does the cancer will reappear, and she'll be stuck with all the medical bills when he dies. Also, another marriage means her alimony immediately stops. And she's going to make Dancer's dad pay for the rest of his life.

Dancer chops up three peaches, drops the chunks into the blender along with ice and rum and turns it on. His mom opens the living room drapes to let the sunset in. Dick turns on a lamp and sits down with *The Birmingham News* in his lap. "So," Dancer's mom says with no enthusiasm, "tell us all the exciting things you've been doing up North."

"Not much of anything," Dancer says as he pours the daiquiris into a glass and passes them out. "To home," he says.

"Oh Dancer, these are so good," his mom says. "I guess if you don't make it as a writer you can always be a bartender." She laughs.

Dick laughs. Dancer does not laugh.

They have another round of daiquiris, get a little drunker, and his mom talks about the weather—how hot it has been and how it's the driest summer she can remember, that it's so dry the farmers are killing their livestock rather than letting them starve, and that some of the farmers are even killing themselves. Dancer says he saw a man kill himself the other day, that he dived out of a hotel window. His mother tells him it's nothing unusual in New York City where those things happen all the time. Next, she says how her father, (the old Indian) who lives in Arkansas, is starting to act his age. He's the same age as the year. His wife, Dancer's grandmother, died last August and Dancer didn't go to her funeral because no one bothered to tell him she died until a month later.

Dancer thinks that his mom looks a lot like his grandmother did, especially as she gets older. Even though she's fifty, she doesn't have a wrinkle on her face. Neither did his grandmother. Still, her cheeks sag slightly now, and the area around her eyes has gotten pudgy. She was once very thin and lovely. He thinks it's amazing how quickly people seem to age when you don't see them regularly. He also thinks he should start coming home more often.

"Shouldn't you call your father and let him know you're home?"

"I'll see him tomorrow," he says, and he goes into the kitchen to rummage through the refrigerator.

"Is your father going to the barbecue?" his mom asks from the other room.

"I think everybody's going to Grandmother's," Dancer mumbles through a chicken breast. (This is his dad's mother who is still alive.)

His mom says, "Well that'll be nice. I guess the whole family will be there. Your brother is coming up from Montgomery too."

"Montgomery? I thought he was still stationed at Fort Campbell."

"Dancer, he left that platoon back before Christmas, back when all his friends were killed in that plane crash with all those other soldiers."

"Well, how was I supposed to know? No one ever writes or calls."

"The street runs both ways, son."

"Well, what's he doing down in Montgomery?"

"I guess he's still working on helicopters. He called the other day, collect of course, from Louisiana of all places. They were on some test flight mission, and the blade just stopped... stopped twirling in mid air! Luckily, they weren't more than a few feet above ground. They landed the helicopter in some sugar farmer's field, and for about three hours they tried to fix it. Then, the farmer came out with his shotgun thinking they were drug smugglers. Drug smugglers! Can you even believe it? I tell you what, between the helicopter and the farmer it's lucky he's even alive." She looks at Dick then back at Dancer. "I guess your father's new wife will be there too."

"At grandmother's? I guess she will."

"I heard your father's new wife was in the hospital recently."

"Really," Dancer says, with absolutely no interest.

"Yes, I was talkin' to your grandmother the other day... come back in here son and sit down. You can eat on the sofa if you want. Move over, Dick. I was talkin' to your grandmother the other day, and she said Carla had been in the hospital for over a week."

"Really."

"She said she had a biopsy done on a patch in her lungs. Does your father's new wife smoke?"

"Does a chimney?" Dancer asks.

"Is your father's new wife pretty?"

"Mom, they've been married now for over seven years."

"You mean living together for over seven years. I don't think anyone actually *knows* whether they're married or not. Your grandmother says she hasn't seen a ring on her finger."

"You and Dick aren't married."

"That's right, we're not. I don't intend to get married either." She sips at her daiquiri and pulls one leg under her and rocks back and forth in her chair. "I don't believe in the Noah's Ark Syndrome. Of course, men are different. Men *hate* being single."

"I like it," Dancer ventures.

"You live in New York City too. Most men are remarried less than one year after they're divorced." She shakes a finger in the air. "Now personally, I think Dick would make a fine second marriage husband. He's sincere, easy going, dependable... why, he'll do just anything I ask him. Your father never would. Well, I take that back, your father is basically a good man... for a drunk.

Dancer"—she points a finger at the blender—"why don't you just pour me the last tad of that into my glass before it melts back to water. Dick," she asks, "would you like some more daiquiri? If you do, I'll let Dancer make us some more."

Dick looks up from his paper, smiles, shakes his head, smiles, and says to the lampshade, "No thank you, Dancer." He looks back at his paper. "No, I'm fine thank you."

"Dancer, do you and Carla get along?"

"We don't fight, if that's what you mean."

"Well, I hope your father is happy with her. I hope she doesn't divorce him."

"They seem to get along well enough. She likes to cook and talk. He likes to eat and listen."

"Carla enjoys cooking?"

"She's a great cook."

"Did you hear that, Dick?" says Dancer's mom. "Well, no wonder he married her. I guess she does housework too."

"They have a maid that comes by about twice a week."

"A maid! My goodness. I *knew* your father was well off. He never spent a nickel on me, but I knew he had it. Dancer, what do you think he does with his money?" She sits her daiquiri down. "He lives in a nice enough house I suppose, but it's nothing like what you'd expect a man of his means would have. What do you think he does with his money?"

"Invests it, I guess. I don't know."

His mom kind of squints her eyes and shakes her head back and forth. "Shrewd, he's a shrewd son of a bitch. There's no telling where he puts his money. That's one thing I have to give him credit for. He can keep a secret too, that man can keep a secret better than anyone I know. Why, he can be in a roomful of people, and they'll all be talking about something, and I guarantee you your father will know more about it than all of them put together, but he won't say *one* word. He'll just let them keep on talking, acting like he doesn't know a thing." Dancer doesn't comment. His mom thinks to herself for a moment and then she blurts out, "Don't you let him die and you not know what he's worth or where it all is. You and Silas are entitled to half of what he's got, and God only knows what that might be. When was the last time you spoke to your father?"

"Christmas."

"What? You mean you haven't spoken to your father since then?" She stares at Dancer long and hard then stares at Dick. Dick looks up from his paper and stares at the lamp shade.

"Mom, we just don't have anything to say to each other. There's no common ground. We're like strangers on a street. And even when I do call we both just listen mute while the phone crackles. Our conversations consist of "hello.""

"Well, I think it might be in your best interest to get on better terms with him."

"Mom, he doesn't even like me."

"That's not true. He may not show it, but your father loves you very much."

"You mean he loves Silas very much. The two of them get along great."

"You and your brother are different people, Dancer, completely different people. I've always asked myself how I could raise two sons so totally different. Silas isn't as independent as you are. You've never needed anyone but yourself. You're like your father in that way, and the truth is he's probably jealous. You're everything he wanted to be but couldn't. You're educated, you're handsome, you're smart. Things get handed to you. Your father came up the hard way. He just lucked out by getting into the tire business back in the 60's."

"Well, I don't know who tinted your glasses rose, but things don't get handed to me."

His mom says, "I remember once when both of you were still babies. You were about three I guess, so your brother must have been four. Both of you were playing in that sandbox your father built under the deck, and you had coerced Silas into stealing eggs out of the refrigerator so you could mix them with sand and make a huge castle. The castle had a moat and everything. You were so proud of it too, but just as you finished it, Silas kicked it over. Well, you came running into the house screaming, and your father turned to me and said the strangest thing. He said, 'Dancer will never have to work for a living. Silas always will.'"

"That's why dad resents me?"

"It's not resentment, Dancer. Your father just wants to be needed."

"Well that's good to hear, because I need him to loan me some money."

"Are you broke?"

"I was robbed the other day. My wallet was stolen."

"You were mugged?"

"Not mugged, Mom, robbed."

"Someone broke into your apartment?"

"The details aren't important."

"Not important. Of course they're important. Did you notify the police?"

"No."

"And why not?"

He sort of hangs his head sheepishly. "A fortune teller stole it."

"You wasted money on a soothsayer!" She turns to Dick. "Did you hear that Dick?" She turns to Dancer. "Your credit cards too?"

"Everything. But I had them stopped. Visa already gave me a new card. That's how I got down here."

"I don't believe this," his mom says. "Dick, do you believe this?"

Dick shakes his head indicating his disbelief.

"How much do you need? Or a better question is, how much have you got?"

"About $41.00."

"To your name!"

"Maybe a little less. I bought some LoveBites before I got on the plane. $39.00, I guess."

"What are LoveBites?"

"Ice cream."

"Only you, Dancer, would spend your last dollar on food."

"It's not my *last* dollar, Mom."

"You never could save a nickel. I got a letter from the bank the other day. Apparently your IRA was closed out just around the time you disappeared for New York City."

"What a strange coincidence."

"They had never closed one out before. You were the first...

and you owe twelve dollars in penalties. I paid it though."

"Thank you. It took them long enough. I mean, I withdrew it over a year ago."

"Please," his mom says, "you're hardly in a position to belittle the bank. How much do you need anyway?"

"About six or seven hundred dollars."

"Seven hundred dollars!"

"Mom, New York is expensive. I've got to make my car payment, rent, credit cards, utility bills...not to mention things like laundry money and subway tokens. And food."

"No one makes you live there."

"I know that, Mom. I know that only too well. Nobody made me go to college either, but I did it...and put myself through by waiting tables."

"Your father would have paid for it if you had asked him."

"That's right, he would have. And I would have had to major in business too, and be eternally indebted for the rest of my life."

"Regardless, your college was an education."

"You don't think New York is an education?"

"Only if you're studying to sell drugs and be rude. What happened to your IRA money?"

"What happened to it? I spent it of course. There wasn't but $500.00 in it to begin with."

"When do you get paid again?"

"About two weeks, but rent is due on the 5th."

"You haven't paid July's rent?"

"Mom, have you even been listening? I was robbed."

"Well, what kind of idiot carries around all his money at one time?"

"An idiot who has an even dumber idiot for a roommate, one who bounced last month's rent check, so this month we have to pay in cash."

"Can't you borrow the money from him?"

"Mom, this is a person who can't even remember to close the refrigerator door or set the phone back on the hook. Besides, I haven't seen him since Tuesday."

"Aren't you worried he might be dead by now?"

"No, I'm not worried."

"Do you worry about anything?"

"Yes, I worry about whether I'm a fool to believe I'm even good enough to call myself a writer. I worry about growing old and accomplishing nothing... I worry about all the rain forests being destroyed and everyone suffocating because there's no more oxygen being produced, I worry about the extinction of the black rhino and the ivory-billed woodpecker, the death of Broadway, acid rain, Chernobyl's long term effects on the environment, PCB's, the inevitable collapse of Social Security, the greying of the baby boomers and where have all our heroes gone? I worry about all those things. But most of all I worry about money... how does anyone ever get started when there are just so many fucking, petty little things keeping them down?"

Dancer's mom looks at Dick, and Dick looks at Dancer's mom. Their expressions seem to say, "He's finally cracked."

"Dancer," Dick says to the lampshade, "you're what we call a frustrated dreamer..."

"Shut up."

"Dancer," his mom says, "you know I'd love to loan you the money, but..."

"I didn't ask you to loan me any money."

"I know you didn't." She looks at Dick. "I know you didn't, but if I were in a position to do so I would. I'd love to. Unfortunately though"—she smiles at Dick lovingly—"unfortunately I've just invested everything I have into Dick's ranch."

"Ranch?" Dancer stares listlessly at the sunset.

"Yes," his mom says, "a snail ranch."

"A what?"

"A commercial snail ranch for processing and canning escargot."

"Heliculture," Dick says. "Its a relatively simple set-up. All you need is a greenhouse."

Dancer's mom says, "We just invested everything into a greenhouse, a big greenhouse with heating units and fans and air conditioning. It was once used to grow hydroponic tomatoes and lettuce."

"But now," Dick says, "it's filled with rows and rows of covered plastic buckets containing snails, about 500 to a bucket. They're fed on a protein-rich diet of soybeans and crushed oyster shells."

"Then," Dancer's mom says excitedly, "we starve them for two days, and after that they're parboiled, picked from their shells, canned in water and cooked again in the can. Oh, they're just delicious, nothing like those rubber bands in a can you get from Europe. Of course, at this stage we're still working out the kinks, but in the future we hope to be able to pack as many as 3,000 cases a month. Just think, 3,000 cases a month! One day, escargot will be as common as... as kiwi fruit. Isn't it exciting!"

"Yeah, exciting," Dancer says. "Excuse me." He goes into the bedroom to call Anne again, but she still isn't in. He walks back into the living room and sits down. His mom and Dick are watching the news on television.

"You really should call your father," Dancer's mom says softly.

"I told you mom, I'll see him tomorrow."

She nods silently. "How's your writing going?"

"Not too well."

"No word on your children's novel?"

"I've given up on it and started another one. It's not for children though. It's an apocalyptic mystery called AMBER WAVES."

"Interesting title," his mother says uninterestingly. "What's it about?"

"A race with time to avoid human extinction. For some unknown reason, all the women in the world of child-bearing age have suddenly become infertile. There are no longer any new people replacing the old. As population diminishes, we begin to suffer severe economic and social upheaval. Manufacturers of baby products are the first to collapse, followed by the school systems. A domino effect begins. Thirty years pass, and the women who were little children when it all started know that a solution must be found soon if mankind is to survive. Human cloning is seriously considered. But at the last minute, it's discovered that the culprit is wheat, the only food source the entire world shares. It seems that a small meteor which crashed into the Atlantic thirty years earlier had released something into the atmosphere that caused a reorganization of the wheat gene structure. In essence, any food product containing wheat had become a natural contraceptive."

"Uh huh," his mom says, "well I must admit it *is* imaginative."

"I like it!" Dick exclaims. "I like it a lot!"

His mom smiles proudly upon Dick's approval. "It's my side of the family where he gets his talent. Dancer will be world famous some day. World famous some day soon."

Dancer sighs and stares at Dan Rather. He's rambling on about something called the Dow Jones Industrial Average, another subject Dancer is completely ignorant of. "And now for some tragic news. British pop star Turk died late last night after suffering a cerebral hemorrhage earlier in the day. Turk, known for his flamboyance and eerie, surrealistic vocals, had collapsed at a well-known New York nightclub, accompanied by his fiancée, actress Anne Monet. The two were to begin filming a movie together later this month. An autopsy revealed high levels of barbiturates and alcohol in his blood. Funeral services will be held in London on Monday. Turk was twenty-nine years old."

Dancer leaps up and turns the set off. His mom looks at him strangely. "What a waste," she says. "Money, fame, a beautiful girlfriend like Anne Monet, and where does it get him?" She shakes her head. "What's that poor woman going to do now? You know, I've always loved her films." She gets up and asks if anyone is still hungry, and if they are, would they like to make dinner. No one is though, so she reluctantly bites into a piece of cold chicken. "Do you have a girlfriend, Dancer?"

Dancer says that he does, that he's been going out with Anne Monet. His mom laughs and says that his sense of humor is rather black and ill-timed. He says it's the truth. Dick tells the lampshade that Dancer is a dreamer. His mom tells Dick that a fantasy world isn't a healthy world, and doesn't he agree. Dick does indeed. His mom tells Dancer to consider some free counseling. Dancer calls Dick a quack. Dick proves it by quacking. Dancer leaves and drives his car to Atlanta where he stays out all night with his friend Tommy doing God knows what. They talk about old days, run his Visa to the hilt, and Dancer drives back the next morning in time for his grandmother's holiday barbecue.

A BIRD'S NEST IN A TREE

or

Chapter
9

DANCER SNEAKS HIS car into his grandmother's graveled drive, shuts off the engine, sighs, and doesn't get out immediately. He rolls down his window and looks around. Judging from the number of vehicles, everyone else is already here—probably out back. He sees smoke rising up reluctantly through the water oaks from the barbecue behind the house. A few of the cars he recognizes, others he doesn't. He recognizes his dad's of course, but this is its purpose—an ostentatious wine-colored Cadillac, bigger than any of the others because he is a bigger man, both figuratively and literally. At 6'7", 240 lbs plus, he is not the sort whom people question or say "no" to. He looks like a hybrid of Andy Griffith and Frankenstein's monster—stolid, craggy-faced and physically imposing. He's well aware of it too. He used it to raise his family and become a rich man—the sight of him alone is enough to make anyone obey. Briefly, Dancer debates whether he should just turn around and leave before anyone notices him. As broke as he is, begging from his dad suddenly seems worse than poverty. It's not that the man wouldn't give him any money, he probably would, but not without making him grovel for it first. His dad is a powermonger. Besides, having been out all night Dancer looks like warmed-over death, which would only confirm his family's opinion that New York is Hell on Earth.

He cranks his car back up, but then turns it off again as he thinks of his grandmother. She's the only true selfless person he's ever known, the glue that holds his family together, and she'd be heartbroken if he didn't see her while he's home. He even bought her flowers with practically the last of his money—coral roses, her favorite—leaving him with exactly $17.64 between him and starvation. For a moment he ponders what will become of his so-called "family" when his grandmother dies. As it stands now, she is the *sole* reason any of them even see each other for the few times a year that they do. Holidays in Dancer's family serve one function only—to force relatives into mandatory, albeit temporary kinship... and he's just as guilty as any of them.

"Damn," he says as he pounds his hands against the steering wheel. But he grabs the roses and forces himself out of his car and onto his grandmother's porch. Voices float up from behind the house and in through the open windows, creating a sort of funneled echo—voices talking about how Alabama is not only going to win the SEC this year but the National Championship as well, proving once and for all that the Tide still rolls even without the almighty "Bear"... voices about how wonderful the new Galleria is with its glass dome, about how progressive the South is becoming, about the evils of horse racing and how the boiled peanuts don't have nearly enough salt... voices about pollution on the Cahaba River and how purdy the crepe myrtles look this time of year... about how dry and brown everything is, so much so that "you can't see the niggahs for the trees,"... voices about the weather, about Wallace, about water moccasins and about... Dancer?

"A blind hog lookin' for an acorn" says the voice of his detestable Aunt Pinky—a shrew with narcolepsy, the sleeping sickness. She falls asleep in mid-sentences, only to wake up if somebody nudges her. "That's what he is. He's always been like that. Prancin' off to New York City just like that"—she snaps her fingers high in the air—"thinkin' them publishin' places are just gonna..."

"Pinky," her husband, Uncle Dove says, "Pinky, wake up honey, wake up now."

"Thinkin' them publishin' places are gonna just snap him up like a duck on a June bug, just like that." Aunt Pinky snaps her fingers again.

"Yeah, but he is the lucky one," Uncle Dove says. (Dancer has always liked Uncle Dove.)

"You're right," Pinky says who'll agree to anything and always wants the last word. "Why, he's luckier than a dead man on Easter Sunday"—she drops to sleep again but quickly jolts out of it—"and if he don't go to Hell first he'll sure go to Heaven." Dancer decides if he's ever going to make his entrance he should do it now, while his luck is still up. So he walks around the front of the house and down the cinder block steps toward the shady barbecue area.

"Dancer!" his grandmother exclaims. "You made it after all." She smiles and opens her arms. "I'm so glad you could make it, honey. Come over here and give me a big hug. Look everybody, Dancer is here."

"Dancer!" Aunt Pinky squeals with shrewish delight. "Come over here and give me a big hug, honey. We was just talkin' 'bout you." She flits over to him, her pinkish-red hair bouncing dizzily, beating everyone else to the first hug. "Why, what's this?" she says peering over his shoulder. "If it ain't the purdiest roses I ever saw in my whole life."

"They're for grandmother," Dancer says modestly, "I thought she might like them." He produces the bouquet from behind his back.

"My goodness," his grandmother says, "they're just beautiful Dancer, thank you. Thank you so much." She holds them under her nose and sniffs. "I'm going to put them in some water right now and set them in the middle of the table for folks to admire."

Aunt Pinky hugs him again, and Dancer suffers through the embarrassing affection as everyone stares at him with both awe and surprise. To most of his relatives, actually returning alive from New York is more amazing than if he had crossed the Sahara naked. Somebody asks, "So how's the big apple been treat-

in' you?" But somebody else waves his arms and tells him to
hush, the answer being obviously not too well. A cousin asks,
"Seen any famous movie stars up there?" like it's the moon.

His grandmother returns with the roses in a vase saying, "Now
don't you be asking Dancer such silly questions, he's probably
hungry." She sits the flowers down. "Are you hungry honey? Grab
yourself a plate over here." She gets one for him. "There's the
forks, Sugar," she says, handing him one. "I made a squash casse-
role just for you and German chocolate cake too."

He sits on the picnic table and pours himself some tea. Two of
his younger teenage cousins are arguing about which of them
loved Turk more. "But you didn't even see him in concert when
he came to the Omni in Atlanta," one of them says.

The other sticks out her tongue. "But your best friend didn't get
to go backstage and see him like mine did. Turk even signed his
autograph, and I saw it."

"Hush girls, please," one of Dancer's aunts says. "No one wants
to hear you arguing about dead people."

The prettier of the two turns to Dancer. "Dancer, did you ever
see Turk up in New York City?"

"Now honey," the girl's mother says, "New York City has millions of people, of course Dancer never saw him."

Dancer says to the little cousin, "I was with him Friday when
he died." The little cousin giggles.

He looks to the barbecue grill. His dad is standing next to it,
stabbing a skewer into smoking slabs of meat and ribs. "Hi
son," he says uneasily. Carla, seated a few feet away, doesn't
even bother acknowledging him. Instead, she finger-combs her
waist-length black hair and then pretends to adjust the diamond bracelet on her wrist. Even from where he sits, Dancer
feels the tension between the three of them—Carla outright
loathing him, his dad not particularly thrilled to see him and
Dancer not understanding either of them. He doesn't see his
brother anywhere.

Aunt Pinky snatches up a plate and says, "Now Dancer honey,
just look at all these goodies. I know you ain't seen food like this
in a month of Sundays. Whatever you like just tell me." Without

waiting for an answer she says, "A little fried okra with some green tumatahs"—she scoops up a blob of the stuff and slings it on his plate—"and a little creamed corn and some squash, Dancer you like squash don't you Sweetie…"

He sips at his tea and crunches on ice as he surveys the lounging crowd around him, scattered about the back yard like so much flotsam from a shipwreck. Like Pinky, all his aunts have red hair. None of his uncles do, however, and neither do any of his cousins, except for the youngest one. He's about six years old—a demon who's already been in reform school for burning down a house with the people still inside. Dancer watches him pull the hair of his Aunt Camille. Hers is brick colored. Camille is his favorite aunt, mainly because she is rather artsy herself and has an unfailing conviction in Dancer's talents. She's painfully Baptist though, and the whole family believes she's still a virgin even though she's been married to Uncle Snow for nearly fifteen years. They have one adopted son named Rambler. He's an overachiever and tends to be chunky. Aunt Camille starves him by combination-locking all the cabinets and the refrigerator. She's a maniacal perfectionist and housekeeper, like the automatons in *The Stepford Wives*. She waxes the trees in her front yard and cooks meals by precise recipes. The only time Rambler gets to eat is when he's at grandmother's.

"…and a little of these deviled eggs and some dumplins with giblet gravy and some pumpkin bread and…"

"Pinky," Aunt Camille says. "Somebody catch her."

"…and some pumpkin bread and a dab of this green pea salad that your Aunt Rena made…"

Dancer thinks that his Aunt Rena is just the opposite of Aunt Camille. She abhors housework even more than Dancer's mom. No one here really likes his mom except his grandmother, and everybody else is quite relieved she's no longer part of the family. He supposes she's just too unconventional and iconoclastic for their taste, especially Aunt Rena's. Aunt Rena can be a lot of fun though, and today she's dressed in red, white & blue. But she's always been the kind of person who spoils her children. He imagines this is why her younger child is a demon. Her older one turned out okay, cousin Maggie, even if she is a little fickle. She can spend an hour just deciding between a chicken leg or a chicken thigh.

Aunt Rena's husband, Uncle Syracuse, won't live much longer. He only has one kidney and can't find a donor to match his tissue type. One of Maggie's would probably work, but she flatly refuses because the scar would show when she wears her bikini. Uncle Syracuse retired as an Admiral or General or something impressive from the Air Force, and he has invented a parachute that opens at 100 feet, which he's trying to patent so that when he dies, Aunt Rena and Maggie and the demon child will be provided for.

"...and just a titch of my special pepper sauce over these turnip greens, everybody loves turnip greens." Dancer hates them. "And some sliced cucumbers and a pickled Vidalia and..."

His cousin Celra is lying on a blanket looking far away and beaten. She's worn out at twenty-six, having once been very beautiful and vivacious. Celra—she turned to drugs...Celra who could have married any man she wanted; Celra who took your breath away when she entered a room; Celra who depended too much on her looks to get by, but threw even that away. Dancer watches her pull one finger down the middle of her face, beginning at the top of her forehead and traveling down to her chin as though drawing a line where she plans to split her head into halves. He doesn't want to catch her eye. They were so close once, but he can't bear dissipation...Celra always wears long sleeves.

As for the rest of his relatives, Dancer doesn't know that much about them. Either they're dull, colorless people just drifting around in their lives, or whatever they've hidden has been hidden well. There's Uncle Bobo, who everyone considers a blithering idiot. He has become a millionaire by selling second-hand auto parts, getting started in the business after someone crashed his car through Bobo's kitchen wall and ran away from the accident. To this day the wall hasn't been repaired. There's his cousin Rhoda who sorts eggs in an egg factory. The brown ones are harder than the white ones to sort because she can't see the cracks as easily... Uncle Milford who draws a disability pension from the Korean War...Aunt Minnie who won second place for her plum jam at the Mississippi State Fair in 1969...Cousin Nancy, whose doctor just recently discovered that her blood flows backwards...the Tootle twins who suffer severe dyslexia, children of Aunt Ira and Great Uncle Pip, both first cousins once removed...Little Burr with his cowlick...cousin Kale, born with one green eye and one blue eye...Old Aunt Roo, the last of the Shakers...Uncle Dove who went bald at twenty-two, only to have a full head of hair come back to him in his middle-age...cousins Cindy-Jean and Lyla who both swallowed a thimble once, and the list goes on. Tiringly on.

Suddenly, Aunt Pinky falls asleep again, wavers a moment, then turns Dancer's mounded plate upside down all over her dress. No one bothers to wake her up this time. "She'll only scream if we do," Aunt Rena says.

"Dang if it ain't hot," somebody grumbles.

"Than a witch's titty," Uncle Bobo says.

"Colder you mean," drawls Uncle Syracuse who's administering self-dialysis with this portable plastic bag of clear fluid.

"Syracuse," Aunt Rena asks, "do you have to do that here where everybody's eating?"

"But it ain't cold," Uncle Bobo says, "it's hot."

"I know it's hot," Uncle Syracuse says as he pushes a tube into the hole in his side, "but the expression goes, 'It's colder than a witch's titty in a brass bra!' If you're gonna say hot, you've got to say, 'It's hotter than Hell.'" He turns to Rena. "And yes, I have to do this here. It's time."

"Well," she snaps, "you could have told me and I woulduv helped you upstairs to the house. Maggie, help your father into the house."

"Yes'm." But Dancer sees that Maggie makes no effort to get up.

"I guess he could have said it's hotter than a blister on a sunburned Apache," Great Uncle Pip says.

"That's purdy hot," cousin Rhoda, the egg sorter agrees.

"There aren't many Indians around any more," old Aunt Roo croaks. "I haven't seen any in the longest."

"Transmission gaskets neither," Uncle Bobo moans, "not in the longest since I can remember."

"Or football players," whines cousin Nancy, who just broke up with her boyfriend at Auburn. Dancer wonders if his blood flows backwards as well.

"Have you seen the purdy ball of yarn that Minnie was knittin' her afghan with?" Aunt Camille asks one of the Tootle twins.

Aunt Ira answers, "Wasn't it just the purdiest color of green anybody ever laid eyes on?"

"I don't like green," cousin Lyla says, none the worse for having once swallowed a thimble.

"I wish it would rain and make things green," Uncle Milford says as he pats his leg with the shell fragment in it. "And my leg says it just might."

Dancer is already feeling nauseous, and he hasn't eaten a thing. "Excuse me," he says, getting up from the picnic table, "I think I'm going to walk around a while." Dancer's dad opens his mouth as though to say something but changes his mind when Carla glares at him. He jabs the smoldering meats. As Dancer passes Carla's chair, she turns her head toward the garden, as though noticing some rare vegetable previously undiscovered by science.

"Silas is down in the woods lookin' for golf balls," Celra whispers from her blanket in the sun. Dancer nods. Celra whispers in a softer tone that she has a horse if Dancer would like to ride. He shakes his head and strolls reminiscently toward the woods. He remembers these woods with fondness. They cover only about two square miles at most, serving as a buffer between a golf course and his grandmother's property. He and his cousins used to love to come to grandmother's. They'd spend hours building forts from fallen trees, or searching for golf balls and playing in the creek. He walks to the edge, where the long-leaf pines surge 120 feet up from the yard, but he doesn't enter. He'd only be disillusioned now. The creek wouldn't be the Amazon; the trees wouldn't be sequoias. He'd rather just remember than be reminded. Some things shouldn't change, but they do.

He realizes it was a mistake to come home just to ask for money. He has never been able to ask his dad for anything, and he's a fool to believe that a year in New York has either toughened him any or made his dad more sympathetic. Maybe New York has awakened him to the grimness of reality, even given him a thicker skin—an insensitivity that he didn't have before he left. But he's not in New York now. He's home, and for the first time he thinks he may not be part of the South anymore. For as long as he can remember, he's wanted to escape. Call it wanderlust, but the South moves too slow for him, too stiflingly slow, and he's always had to move in a hurry.

Up ahead he sees his brother approaching, pockets bulging with golf balls. "What's up?" Silas asks expressionlessly. Dancer sees his brother hasn't changed a bit...no, "Hello Dancer, it's great to see you again," no, "How have you been little brother?" ...just, "What's up?" As though they still see each other every day of their lives.

"Not too much," Dancer says, and this is the extent of their conversation. He thinks to himself, "What else is there to say?" It's funny...he knows he lived with this person for over eighteen years. He rode the school bus with him, ate at the same table, watched television together, and sometimes even talked—but he can't recall one single moment they actually *shared*. His mom is right—how *did* she raise two people so utterly different? They don't even look like brothers. Silas has deep brown hair, brown eyes, freckles and is left-handed. He never displayed any sort of artistic acumen, hordes money like a skinflint and builds helicopters. Basically, Dancer guesses he's a simple person, the kind who'd live alone in a log cabin in the Klondike had he been born 100 years before...Dancer has never understood people who don't desire the moon and stars gift-wrapped on a silver platter.

Silas is wearing one of those military camouflage outfits splashed with patches of color. Dancer imagines they're so comfortable they make you tired, and that's why they're called, "fatigues." On Silas's head perches a baseball cap that says, DIFFERENT DAY, SAME SHIT. "How long are you home for?" Silas asks as Dancer steps in with him, and they walk back toward everyone else.

"I'll probably go back tomorrow. I have to be at work again on Tuesday."

Silas grunts and juggles two golf balls. "You see dad?"

"I saw him, yeah."

"He's buyin' me a truck, a fuel-injected four-wheel-drive with an electronic dashboard, and a camper on the back so I can take it fishin' and stay down on the river."

"Sounds nice," Dancer says, but he's thinking, *You're twenty-four-years old and Dad is still giving you toys. At least I've got a little independence. Yeah, sure Dancer, that's why you're home, because you're so damned independent.*

Back under the shade of the oaks, an uncle says to Silas, "I see you found some golf balls."

Silas says, "Yep."

"Lot of golfers out today?"

Silas says, "Not too many, a couple I guess."

Dancer sits beneath the eaves of the house and bends an ear to the chitchat. He nervously taps the aluminum arm on his lawn chair and watches his dad battle a fly. At the same time his dad listens to the demon child attempt to weasel a free bicycle tire out of him. (It seems the demon child experienced a blow-out yesterday while running over a puppy.) Dancer's dad doesn't actually own the tire company that employs him, but he's pretty close to the top, and anything that's round and made of rubber they've produced—car tires, tractor tires, tricycle tires, even tires for match box toys. It's always amazed Dancer that his dad climbed from grease monkey to top management in such a short time—his dad who has no more than a tenth grade education. Dancer thinks it's the kind of American success story people only dream about. Why is it then that his dad is so miserable?

Dancer can't tell if his dad has been drinking today or not. He usually waits until the evening. But he's become such a pro at it through the years, learning to hold it so well, that Dancer just isn't sure. His dad is always somber and troubled looking, like he has been places and seen things people aren't supposed to see. Carla may have influenced him to slow down a little too, although at the moment she's nursing her "tea" awfully slow. Looking at the two of them together, Dancer guesses they're compatible, but not in a sexual sort of way. Theirs seems to be more of a mutual remorse; a shared self-pity for what they either were or could have been but gave up...like two people committing suicide together, because they don't have the courage to do it alone.

The barbecue is winding down. People have pushed their plates aside. Old Aunt Roo has fallen asleep in her chair and a butterfly is resting on her nose. Dancer's grandmother is stacking plastic cups into a column, and Carla has lit up a cigarette. Dancer's dad throws water on the hickory logs and they seethe slowly. Aunt Rena and Aunt Camille are stacking the ribs and things onto some flat pans. What isn't finished off at supper, people will carry home with them. Aunt Pinky is still slumped over the table with food stains drying on her dress.

Dancer steals a glance at his grandmother as she pushes the column of cups aside and pours a bottle of pastel colored pills onto a saucer. One by one, she sorts through them, selecting the prettiest to swallow first. These are her after-a-meal pills. She has to take just as many before each meal. Still, her blood sugar is dangerously high, and usually she's feeling much worse than she ever lets on...diabetes has turned her into a time bomb and she knows it. She rubs her eyes, squeezes her brows together, grimaces and downs a pale blue tablet. "Grandmother," Dancer asks, "are you feeling OK?"

"Oh honey, don't worry about me, I'm fine...if those aren't the prettiest flowers."

"Can I get you anything mom?" Aunt Camille asks as she wraps aluminum foil over a platter.

"I told you I'm fine, just fine." She blankly gazes at the youngest children as they play hide and seek between the corn stalks in the garden. Lazy clouds drift by overhead, blocking the sun with patches of shadow that creep through the greenery like blight.

Celra now looks up from her blanket again and says dreamily to no one in particular, "I'll be so happy on August 8th, 1988. It's the only time this decade that the month, date and year share identical numerals. Just think, it won't happen again until September 9th, 1999, like the eruption of Mt. Vesuvius or something." Nobody looks at her strangely except Dancer.

"Honey," Dancer's grandmother says to him, "you haven't eaten a thing. Are you sure you don't want nothin' before we cover it all up?"

"I'll eat something later, grandmother." He is too concerned about approaching his dad for money to worry about food. Come on, he thinks, go ahead and just ask him. God knows it's not going to break the man just to lend you a few hundred dollars. Hell, he just bought Silas a carnival on wheels. Dancer looks at Silas. He's folding up one of his ears and trying to stuff it inside his head. Besides, Dancer tells himself, how else are you going to get back to New York? But he can't ask him here, not with everyone else around. Carla mistakenly catches his eye and attempts a guilty half-smile before striking up a pointless conversation with the demon child about perfume.

Dancer's father isn't the first in the family to get divorced. But he's the only one who divorced his wife to marry another woman. What surprises Dancer is how quickly everyone accepted her. Of course, his dad's position in the family hierarchy had a lot to do with it. His dad is the oldest child. Naturally, Dancer's grandmother feels a special empathy toward him. Being rich doesn't hurt either. Dancer's grandmother's only source of income is her Social Security check, so his dad helps her financially, and has helped others in the family too. Apparently, money forgives anything.

Dancer doesn't though. It's not easy to forgive what his dad put his mom through. Dancer was ten years old when it started, and he remembers it as happening almost overnight. His dad came home very late and very intoxicated one evening, and simply never came home early or sober again. There followed six years of madness, of torture and pain, before the man finally divorced his family to marry Carla. By this point, Dancer's bond with his father, always a fragile one, was shattered forever.

He can look at it abstractly now, as though recalling a movie on television, but he wouldn't go back to being a teenager, not for all the money in the world plus a dollar. It has taken too long for the scars to heal. Piece by piece Dancer has buried all memories of his adolescence—the good with the bad, shoveled into the same grave. Sometimes though, the horrible things still rear their heads, proving that they're only buried, never dead—the screaming arguments laced with obscenities, happening almost nightly year after year, like some kind of satanic ritual... the insults and drunken accusations... and the hideous, incomprehensible words he heard repeated over and over again in the angriest tones, words that even today make him flinch when he hears them—"divorce," "custody," "not again," and "you promised"... the most painful of all being, "I didn't mean to hit you." This he heard only one time though, and the worst thing he ever had to do was turn his back on the person he once respected most.

Somehow, Silas grew up oblivious to it all. But Dancer guesses Silas was blinded from the start. He and his dad have always been buddy/buddy. Their relationship was never strained. It wasn't an effort for his dad to speak to Silas like it was to Dancer. Thinking about it, Dancer decides he's not so much jealous of the relationship his dad has with Silas as he is upset with the reasoning behind it. He's always suspected his dad doesn't necessarily like Silas more. He just likes Dancer less... his favoritism being some sort of revenge. Also, as with the rest of the family, Silas's love is easily bought. Dancer thinks it's ironic he came home for money.

His dad, seeing that Dancer seems intent on sticking around, now fakes a yawn, stretches, and finally asks, "So how's your car running, son?" He always starts a conversation with Dancer about automobiles. This is because he knows Dancer is completely ignorant of them. In that way his dad gives himself an immediate edge, increasing their distance from each other and thereby assuring an extremely shallow and brief conversation. His dad loves rigged contests.

"Oh, it cranked right up," Dancer says warily.

His dad wipes his hands on a napkin. He hands it to Carla who folds it up and places it on her knee, using it as her "tea" coaster. She stares back out to that undiscovered vegetable. "When was the last time you changed the oil, son?"

"I don't remember, how often is it supposed to be changed?" Immediately Dancer realizes he has played into a trap.

His dad sighs, and does so with the greatest aplomb, proving to himself and everyone else that Dancer hasn't gained an ounce of sense from his year up north. "It's supposed to be changed about every seven thousand miles. I change mine every three though."

"But it hasn't even been driven."

"It still gets dirty, son."

Dancer figures that as long as he's being taken for the court jester, he might as well give an entertaining performance. "Well, I don't guess it has ever been changed."

"How about your antifreeze, have you checked it lately?"

"Dad, I just got in yesterday afternoon. Antifreeze wasn't exactly the first thing on my mind."

"Fine, but when you come home for Christmas, don't complain to me that your engine block is cracked. He looks at the others as though to say, Can you believe such a fool exists? Dancer asks what an engine block is. His dad groans, "Come on, I'll check everything out for you. I've got a few extra quarts of oil in my trunk. I might have a little antifreeze too." Dancer reluctantly follows his dad around the house while Silas trots along behind them like a faithful dog.

Without an audience, his dad doesn't seem nearly so threatening. The unshaded sun also makes him appear older and not in the best of health. His hair is dull and colorless. The pock marks in his face turn to craters, and he's suddenly paunchier and stoop-shouldered—a giant melting monster. Dancer also notices that his dad's walk isn't without a stagger...hitting him up is going to be a delicate maneuver.

He opts for the literary approach. "I got an acknowledgment from a journal called the East Shore Review about two weeks ago. They're considering a story I sent them. I should know for certain by the end of the month."

His dad seems not to have heard him. He's standing in front of his Cadillac examining the grille as though it could possibly be a centimeter out of plumb. "You gotten anything published yet?"

"Not...not yet, it takes time you know." His dad nods his meaty head doubtfully. Silas throws a rock at a squirrel and misses. His dad goes over to Dancer's car and opens the hood. Silas walks slowly around it, kicking at the tires one by one.

"How much can you make off a story?" his dad asks, these mirage-like fumes floating around his face like a seared halo.

Dancer shoves his hands in his pockets and shifts his weight from one leg to the other. "Umm, well maybe a couple hundred, it depends."

"On what?" Silas asks. "What does it depend on?" He picks up another rock and fires it at the squirrel again. This time he doesn't miss. The squirrel chatters crazily for a second and drops from its limb with a thud.

Dancer would like to throw a rock at Silas. "It depends on whether you've ever been published before or whether you've got any name recognition, that sort of thing."

"But you don't have any of that," says the man with the burned halo. Silas snickers and tries for a red bird this time.

"But I'm working on it," Dancer says. "I've been writing very seriously lately. It's really competitive though, even cliquish. Nobody wants new blood to get in, and everybody's out for himself."

"Son, that's how the world works."

"I realize that only too well, dad. But still, when every writer wants into *The New Yorker* and only one is allowed, who do you think gets in—the unknown or John Updike?"

"He a writer?" Dancer's dad asks.

"What's *The New Yorker*?" Silas asks.

Dancer sighs and leans against the fender.

"How long does it usually take to write one of these stories, son?"

"A week or two usually."

"You waste two weeks just to get a couple hundred dollars? Seems to me like an awful lot of work for an awfully small return."

"Me too," Silas agrees.

Dancer thinks that maybe he shouldn't have taken the literary approach. "Writing is accumulative, dad. The more I write, the more I'll have to submit, which means I increase my chances of getting published and eventually making more money."

"More money? But you haven't gotten *any* money from your writing yet, isn't that what you said?"

"Yes, but..."

"Well then it's only simple arithmetic that you'll make more than nothing, but making more than nothing is still not making a living." Silas misses the red bird.

Why does Dancer feel like he fell down the rabbit hole? His dad pulls this metal stick out from something and holds it up to the sun. "Damn son, you don't have a drop of oil in here. Silas, see if you can get me that oil out of the back of my car." He turns back to Dancer. "You've been in New York City for what, over a year now, right?"

"Just a little over."

Silas gets his dad a can of oil. His dad takes a pocket-knife out of his pants and stabs two holes in the top of the can. He turns it over and the blue oil streams down into some hidden crevice somewhere. "Well, it seems to me that a year ought to be long enough to do just about anything."

"Dad, sometimes it takes up to three months to even get a rejection."

Silas snickers again.

"Uh huh," his dad says. "And have you been keeping up your car insurance?"

"Car insurance? It's rather pointless, if I never drive the thing."

"Oh I see, but it's not pointless for me to waste my oil?" He unscrews a cap. "But at least your antifreeze is okay. It'll last you through the winter."

"Should I shout hallelujah? You know dad, I didn't ask you to put your oil in my car."

"Well, I've done you a lot of favors you haven't asked for."

"Jesus," Dancer says, and he realizes he no more knows who these two people are than he knows the unknown soldier. "I'm not going to get into an argument with you about cars if that's what you want."

His dad closes the hood and brushes his hands together. "Son, what *I* want has never been much of a concern of yours anyway, has it? You've always done exactly what *you* want."

"What I've done is what I've had to do, not necessarily what I *wanted*." His dad crosses his arms and shakes his head back and forth, and Silas is gaping at Dancer like one would at a snuff film. "Listen dad, I can't afford the damned insurance anyway."

"Why don't you sell the car then?"

"Because it's the only thing I own, the only thing in the whole world, and even if I never drive it again at least I have something to call *mine*."

"Just don't wreck it, that's all I'm going to say. And when you do, don't expect me to bail you out."

"I never expect anything from you, certainly not a bail-out."

"Oh really," his dad says, and Dancer knows he's been trapped again. "How are you doing financially by the way?"

Why does this man always keep Dancer on the defensive? His mom was right—Dancer's dad is shrewd. He knew from the moment Dancer arrived that he had come for money. "Okay, I'm doing okay." Silas grins and his dad doesn't say a word. Dancer rubs his eyeballs, like he did when he was a kid to see the colors. "All right," he blurts shamelessly, "so I'm broke."

His dad lets out a deep breath—the cue that his sermon is about to begin. "I don't understand it; I don't understand it at all. You had everything going for you son, everything, but..."

"I was only treading water here, dad. I was going crazy."

"Please." His dad holds out his hand. "Please Dancer, just let me finish what I'm saying." Dancer bites his lips and nods. Silas picks up another rock and throws it at a bird's nest in a tree. A mama robin flies away and this yellowish egg juice dribbles through her fractured home. "Even with a degree in, in literature or whatever you call it, you still could have gotten a decent job in something like public relations or real estate...even being a teacher would have been more respectable than just nothing."

"I'm doing a little more than 'just nothing,' thank you."

Dancer's dad doesn't seem to hear him. "But what did you do? You flew off to that city of yours expecting to find something, God knows what, and call yourself a writer...a writer? Dancer, you'll starve to death." Silas throws another rock and knocks the nest out of the tree. It lands upside down like a twig igloo, sticky powder blue egg shells stuck to it. "I don't understand what you're expecting to find, son." A moment of silence follows, the most awkward silence Dancer has ever had to endure, broken only by the crunch of sticks as Silas stomps on the igloo. Finally, and with great deliberation, his dad slowly says, "But you chose your life, against all advice you chose it, and I'll be damned if I'm going to support a lost cause." On this note, the two strangers turn and walk away.

Dancer nods his head in their wake and says, "Oh, before you go, here." He pulls out his wallet. "I'm . . . I'm sorry I wasted your time. I've got a little money left, let me pay you for the oil." He takes out a five and brings it to his dad.

"Son, the last thing I want from you is your money." He passes the bill to Silas, who stuffs it into his pocket. They turn to walk away again, and his dad very loudly asks the air in front of him, "I'm just confused about one thing, Dancer—why are you so determined to throw your life away?"

Dancer looks at the ground and then to the sky. He scratches the back of his neck and kicks at the lawn. "I'll tell you why," he shouts suddenly. "I'll tell you why." His dad and brother stop and turn to look at him. They're about fifteen feet away. "Because I swore to myself a long time ago that when I grew up I would be everything you're not."

His dad manages something similar to a smile. "Well, you've certainly succeeded, son. You're more successful at failure than anyone I know."

"You won't even give me a chance," Dancer says. "You *want* me to fail."

Other relatives come from around the house to see what all the commotion is about—Aunt Camille, Carla, a few uncles, his grandmother. They hover wide-eyed behind his dad. "What's the problem here," Uncle Bobo says, "car trouble?"

Dancer's dad looks as though he could bend plated armor; he starts breathing heavily, torn between what he wants to say and what he won't say. "I've only wanted the best for you, son. And I've done things you could never understand just so you and your brother would have what I didn't. Maybe I didn't go about it the right way, but look at yourself. You could be anything, anything at all . . . but here you are wasting your life away . . ."

"Wasting *my* life away? *My* life. No, you're the expert in that department, dad."

"Please," his grandmother pleads, "let's not have this."

Carla, a drink in one hand and cigarette in the other, says to Dancer's dad, "Come on, honey." She starts leading him away. "You're getting all riled up over nothing."

"Why have you always been at war with me, Dad? Didn't you ever have a dream? Didn't you ever want something so badly that you didn't even have a choice but to pursue it? Writing is what I *have* to do. It's what I'm supposed to do, and that's the best explanation I can give."

"Dancer, everyone ever born has had dreams, but most eventually face up to reality, and more than anything I don't want you to be disappointed."

"Is that what *you* did, dad—face up to reality? Well, I'm certainly not disappointed in you. Everyone should be so lucky as to have an alcoholic father."

"Please," his grandmother says, nearly in tears.

"And dad, was it reality you were facing when you walked out on mom and left her with two children—a woman pushing middle-age who hadn't worked a day in her life? Is that what you call 'facing reality'?"

Carla gulps at her glass and leans upward on her toes, whispering something in his dad's ear. She pulls at his arm, but he jerks it away and shakes it at Dancer. "Don't you dare talk to me about your mother, don't you *ever* preach at me about your mother. She may talk poor mouth, but I know what she's up to, shacked up with that man...I've seen him, I've seen him. I've had them followed. And you better damn well tell her that I'm cutting off every cent of her alimony, every penny. So she just better damn well marry the bastard fast."

"I hate hypocrisy, dad. It's what I hate the most about the South; it's what I hate the most about you. You walked out on her for another woman. Don't you forget that either, you destroyed our family and you walked out on her."

Carla, smoking and sipping, turns on her heels and storms back to the barbecue. Dancer's dad is using every ounce of restraint to keep from lunging at Dancer like an animal. "Get out of here," he says between gritted teeth. "You've insulted my wife... Get out of here."

"Just go have another drink, dad. Drink yourself to death."

"That's enough!" Dancer's grandmother screams. "That is enough! I won't have this here, this is my house and I won't have it, I tell you!" She wipes her eyes with one hand. "No one is going anywhere, not unless *I* ask them. Now what's done is done; there's no going back—not to yesterday, not to last year, not to a second ago. Let's just make the best of it... please."

No one says a word for a few seconds after this. Uncle Bobo pretends to get something out of his car. Aunt Camille is in a state of shock. Silas runs off chasing a chipmunk with a stick, and Dancer's grandmother stares first at her son and then her grandson before softly saying, "Someday we'll all have to answer for what we've done in our lives—the mistakes we've made and the people we've hurt—but all I've ever wanted is for things to run smoothly. They don't always do, and probably most of the time they don't, but that's not to say we can't try." She wrings her hands together. "It's all I ask of you."

Slowly, very slowly Dancer looks at his dad. He has never seen a pair of eyes so glazed. Uncle Bobo, having not found what he pretended to look for, takes Aunt Camille's hand and leads her back around the house, leaving Dancer alone with the stranger and his grandmother. Dancer wonders if the stranger is going to apologize or if he should be the one to do that. His grandmother looks very distraught. Is this all my fault? he thinks. Am I responsible? The last thing he ever wanted to do was hurt his grandmother. And to think that he created this mess for the most piddling of all reasons. Money. He wonders if he is experiencing vertigo. The whole yard, his whole life, seems to be spinning around him—himself not actually a part of it, just the reciprocator of its madness. *When was the last time I ate anything?* Unwanted images and realizations, caught in the centrifugal force, are suddenly pressed against the edge of his mind: the fact that he has only $12.64 left to his name now, that Silas (blood of his blood) stole five of his precious dollars after Dancer so magnanimously offered to buy his dad's oil, that he has no way to get back to New York, that he'll just have to live off his family, that Fate is sometimes so cruel.

"Grandmother," he says humbly, "I'm... I'm sorry about the

scene I made." Miraculously, the pinwheel around him starts slowing down a little, his grandmother and his dad are focusing again in front of him, and the weighty things pressed against his mind are rolling back to their cracks and crannies. Balance is a wonderful thing.

A hazy reality follows. His dad says something to his grandmother, then he says something to Dancer, something about how it would be a good idea if Dancer leaves. Dancer says maybe he should. He goes to his car and gets in. His grandmother says something to his dad. His dad goes back to the smoke under the oaks behind the house, leaving the two of them alone. She takes something out of her apron, it looks like money, like a hundred dollar bill, but Dancer won't take it. He says that he can't, that she needs it more. She tells him that when he has lived as long as she has, he'll learn the true value of money, that it really is *just* money, that she doesn't need it anymore anyhow, that she'll be leaving soon just like he must, that they're both going on to great places. He says he can't come home again and she says, "I know honey, I know."

The mama robin has returned to her tree, but senses something wrong. She pecks the bark and hops listlessly from one limb to another, finding neither her home nor her children. Eventually, she perches on a limb while bobbing her head and offers one sweet chord of music to an audience that isn't listening... With great reluctance, she flies away.

THE GRIEVING DIVORCÉE

or

Chapter

10

"WHERE HAVE YOU been?" Dancer's mom asks as Dancer walks through the door. She is putting something in the oven. Dick is tinkering with a camera at the kitchen table. The entire condo reeks of garlic and withered snail-meat sizzled in butter. "Um mmm," says his mom to the bubbling dead mollusks.

"The barbecue," Dancer mumbles as he flops down in a chair.

"What about last night? It's none of my business, of course, but Dick and I were worried." She sets the plate of snails next to Dick's camera. "Here Dick," she says, "test this batch. I used a little less garlic this time and just a smidge of cinnamon." Dick tastes them, burning his tongue, and says they're still not right. Dancer's mom says she wishes she'd learned how to cook back when she was younger, the implication apparently being that cooking, like ballet, is a skill which diminishes with age. "Dancer, would you like a snail?"

"I'm not hungry . . . I went to Atlanta last night."

"What's wrong honey?" She pours herself a glass of ice water and wipes her brow. "You know, we apologize for that little incident yesterday. Dick didn't mean to call you a dreamer, did you, Dick?"

Dick says, "No, not at all," to a roll of film.

"Just as I'm sure you didn't mean to call Dick a quack." Dancer says she's right, he didn't. "Good," his mom says. "Dick and I are about to go to Vulcan and take pictures of the skyline for the tin can labels. Would you like to come?"

"Why not."

"Dancer, how do you like the name we've chosen—'Dixie Valley Escargot?'"

Dancer doesn't think she could have chosen a stupider name. "It's nice, I like it."

"See," she says to Dick. "Dancer likes it." Dick nods at his camera. "Is the camera loaded and ready to roll, Dick?" Dick says that it is. "Good, and luckily it's a beautiful day. We ought to get some nice clear pictures. I'd like something really panoramic you know, something so wide it wraps all the way around the can. Let me just get my purse." She runs into the bedroom, leaving Dancer alone with Dick. Fortunately, Dick is so engrossed in his tinkering that he doesn't expect any pleasantries.

That's good, thinks Dancer, because he doesn't plan on making any. "Mom," he calls, "did I get any phone calls?"

"You mean like from any Hollywood movie stars?" she chides, returning from the bedroom.

"Exactly."

She gives him a stern look, as though he'd better not start up this foolishness again. "In fact, you did get a call from somebody. I think it was a prankster though. He was in a state of hysteria and said his name was Calcium or Iodine or something like that. He claimed to be your roommate. I said I didn't know where you were or when you'd be back."

"Zinc?"

"Yes, that's it...Zinc. Now what kind of name is that? Is his father Frank Zappa?"

"Did he leave a message?"

"He said to call him as soon as you could, that it was important. I think he was crying."

"Zinc was crying?"

"Well, I couldn't really tell. There was a lot of traffic noise in the background. It must have been a pay phone. He called twice."

Dancer grabs the phone and dials his apartment.

"Honey, can't that wait," his mom says. "We're just about to go out the door and besides, you've already put two long distance calls on there. You're going back tomorrow anyway, aren't you?" He ignores her. The phone rings about ten times but Zinc doesn't answer. "Dancer, you'll see him tomorrow anyway."

He hangs up. "Did he say anything else?"

"Who?"

"Zinc!"

"Not that I remember." She grabs her keys. "Come on now. We've got to get there while the light's still good."

Less than thirty minutes later the three of them are riding the elevator up to the observation platform inside the 125-foot tall marble pedestal on top of Red Mountain. A fifty-five-foot cast-iron statue of Vulcan stands on top of the pedestal. The reason Dancer knows these dimensions exactly is that the computer is talking to them as they ascend. He remembers from his scanty studies in Greek mythology that Vulcan is supposed to be the God of fire or blacksmiths or something like that. And from somewhere he also recalls that Vulcan is the second largest statue in the U.S., the first being Miss Liberty. (He thinks it's boggling how the human mind can store so much useless trivia.) Vulcan holds aloft a glass torch, illuminated either red or green, depending on whether someone has died in an Alabama highway accident within the last twenty-four hours. Today it is red, so somebody must have.

The view from the donut-shaped observatory is breathtaking. The entire city glitters. He sees his college, U.A.B., sees Southside where he used to live (the Bohemian section of town), and he sees the bridge over the expressway where he once had to talk his old friend Raine Freeman out of jumping because he was tripping on acid and thought he could fly. Dancer leans against one of the viewfinders and wonders what ever happened to Raine, to all his old friends for that matter. Then he thinks about Zinc. God knows, anything could have happened to him, and as for Anne, well, he'll have to remind himself to call the Plaza once more when they get back.

"Great, nobody else is up here," Dancer's mom says, "now Dick won't have to deal with people getting in the way of our pictures."

Dancer points the viewfinder toward his old apartment, the one he simply walked out of one day never to come back. It's amazing how long a year can seem. "Mom, do you have a quarter?"

"A quarter? Didn't your father give you any money?"

"No."

"What? He didn't give you anything?"

"That's what I said, didn't I?"

"That bastard. Why not?"

"He told me I was wasting my life."

"And what else did he say? Dick, can you believe this?" Dick can't. "There honey," she points, "get that shot over there, that's a good one." Dick gets it.

"I really don't want to talk about it."

"But you have to, honey. Was your father's new wife there too?"

"Yes."

"I might have known. What else did he say?"

"He said you had better marry Dick because he's cutting off your alimony. He hired somebody to follow you."

"What!" Dancer's mom nearly falls through the glass. "Follow me!" And suddenly she looks like a double-crossed witch. "I put up with seventeen miserable years of marriage to that redneck, and he had just better think twice before he messes with me. I'm not the ignorant little country girl from a cotton patch anymore, and I'll have his tail slammed in a courtroom quicker than he can say 'Johnny Walker Red' if that's what it takes." Dancer has never seen his mom so livid.

Dick looks down at his shoes and ventures, "Maybe marriage isn't such a bad idea."

"Shut up," Dancer's mom says. "Oooooh, I didn't say one word when he cut off Silas's child support eight months early just because he joined the army." She turns to Dancer. "And I didn't say one word when he cut off your child support a year early just because you went off to college, but I'll be damned if I'm going to stand by while he cuts off *my* alimony. I earned every penny of that money and more. He's going to pay me my back child support too. I am *through* playing the grieving divorcée." The elevator opens and two greasy teenagers step out to face a screaming harridan. They leap back in and jab the DOOR SHUT button. "Why,

I'll squeeze his bank account 'til it bleeds. He'll end up hocking Carla's six carat diamond bracelet surrounded by rubies just to keep his house. I'll do it too, just see if I won't."

Dick actually catches Dancer's eye and makes a worried face. Dancer's mom leans against the railing and glowers toward the city as though casting a silent spell. She fidgets restlessly and whips around to face Dancer. "Did you ever wonder why your father makes so much money? Did you?"

"What?"

"Did you?"

"Yes, yes of course I did."

"I guess you just assumed he worked hard and got lucky, didn't you?" Dancer has a feeling he's about to hear a revelation. His mom turns back to the window and fondles the bow on her blouse. "We had so many bills after Silas was born. He was in the hospital nearly a year. Twice they told me he wouldn't live. Twice I picked out the clothes I'd bury him in. But by the time you came along he was more or less fine. Your father and I never told you about his problems because you weren't old enough to understand anyhow, and when you finally were old enough, well, it just seemed like something from the past that nobody wanted to talk about. You never even knew he was sick, did you?"

"No, I had no idea," Dancer says, shocked. "What was wrong with him?"

"Your father used to pace that hospital waiting room like a caged tiger, worrying himself into a fit over where the money was coming from. Live or die, we just didn't have enough money. You see, your father never went to college, why he practically came in on a load of watermelons."

Dancer goes to the window and stands next to her. For a long time he's been meaning to ask her a question that he never had the nerve or opportunity to ask before. Now, however, the time seemed right. "Why did you marry him, mom?"

She doesn't speak for a few seconds but finally says, "Well, when your daddy's a dirt farmer then you marry the first man who promises to get you out. I wasn't going to end up like all my girlfriends, another sharecropper's wife, not me...I suppose it's just as much my fault as your father's. I'm the one who kept pressuring him, kept hounding him to make more money ... to do *something.*" She breathes in deeply and says, "Your brother wasn't born ... normal. Oh, he looked okay. He had two legs, two arms and two eyes, but things inside him weren't; they weren't right. I'm sure it's because of what happened at the plant. Your father should have known he was playing with fire when all those fish turned belly-up."

"What?" Dancer is thoroughly confused. "Mom, you're not making any sense."

"Maybe I should have told you sooner, before you were grown. It might have made you understand your father better."

"I don't have any proof of course, and it's taken me a while to figure it all out, but your father's drinking started just about the time they quarantined the plant. That night they ordered everyone out and locked the doors was the first night he didn't come home. He offered no explanation for where he went. I was worried sick."

"Quarantined? You mean the place was contaminated? I don't remember anything about this."

"How could you? We never told you, but those environmental safety people just marched right in and bolted the doors shut. Presto, everybody was out of a job until they could establish a new site. According to the papers, the lake out back had gotten polluted with some kind of deadly chemical, something so bad they don't even make it anymore. Fish were dying, birds were dying, meanwhile the lake water was being piped into the building to cool the machinery. The environmental people were afraid some of it might be getting into the rubber tires. Who knows? Anyway, they built a new plant at a site twenty miles away, using all the money they made from suing some chemical manufacturer. It was millions, I mean millions! Yes sir, they tripled the plant's size, quadrupled its employees, and your father just got one promotion after another. I guess he hasn't drawn a sober breath since."

"Wait a minute, Mom. Are you saying they paid Dad to contaminate the lake?"

"Either that, or he was the one who came up with the idea. All I know is that during the time that the plant was closed we didn't suffer one bit. Suddenly, there was plenty of money, more than enough to pay off all our bills and even enough to buy a new car. I was flabbergasted."

"Hush money?"

"Well, your father was always handling chemicals. That's all artificial rubber is you know, and back then, before the energy crisis, the car industry was booming. The company needed to expand, and they wanted to do it the most profitable way possible—at another company's expense."

"Dad told you this?"

"Your father never *told* me anything. I figured it all out myself —a piece here, a piece there. Your father never wanted to hurt anybody." She turns to Dancer with tears in her eyes. "He only wanted to be a good provider. They offered him a chance at more money. He *had* to do it...the bills, so many damned bills. Unfortunately though, it backfired, and now he's become a victim. He's trapped, Dancer, trapped just like he was thrown in prison...you see, I think Carla saw him do it."

Dancer is absolutely dumbfounded. "But how did she..."

"She was a secretary there at the time. Maybe she saw a way out too."

"Blackmail?"

"Makes sense, doesn't it? I don't know what the circumstances were, whether she stayed late one night and actually caught him rolling drums down to the lake, or whether they were having an affair and she decided to manipulate his guilty conscience, I don't know."

Dancer's head was reeling. All his years of confusion are beginning to clear—the overnight descent into alcoholism, the favoritism toward Silas, Carla's iron influence—suddenly clear as glass. "Mom," he says, "weren't you worried about having another child after Silas was born?"

"Not at all. Like I said, this whole horrid thing is just something I pieced together through the years. But looking back, I remember how upset your father was when I told him I was pregnant again. He nearly hit the roof, which only sent me into immediate depression. I was so puzzled, because he'd always said he wanted at least two children, maybe even three. But there he was, insisting I have an abortion, and that was before abortions were even legal. God, I was miserable, but there was no way I was going to have an abortion, especially since his only argument was that we couldn't afford another child, when it was obvious that by this point we could."

"So it's just lucky I wasn't born maimed, huh?" Dancer feels dizzy.

"We don't know that for sure. Your father got promoted shortly after Silas was born—an executive position. So he hadn't been handling any chemicals for nearly a year before you were even conceived."

"It was still a crap shoot though, and he knew it too. What shame he must live with... what guilt." It's not a lack of respect Dancer feels toward his father now, it's only pity. Dancer looks at Dick, but apparently Dick has heard this story before.

Dancer's mom says, "If it weren't for Dick's therapy, I don't think I could have told you. I don't think I could have admitted it to myself even. Damn that bastard. He doesn't know I've figured out any of this. He thinks he covered his tracks so well. Hmph! Well, let him just try to cut off my alimony. Let him just try."

The elevator opens again and some more people get out. Dick takes the arm of Dancer's mom and they drive back to the condo. Dancer pours them all a glass of wine, and they sit around morosely, staring at each other until Dancer's mom says, "The irony of it all is that the family he loved and risked his dignity for is exactly what he sacrificed."

Dancer sips his wine and thinks about this. He wonders if he'll come down with some strange kind of liver cancer or something in about twenty years. Finally he says, "Do you think Carla had the insight to know dad would get rich from this deal, or could she actually have fallen in love with him?"

"Oh, I'm sure she convinced herself she loved him. No woman wants to think of herself as a shameless golddigger. Besides, your father isn't without his good qualities. I just hope they're happy together. I'd hate to know he'd entered another unhappy marriage."

"I wonder if he can sleep at night."

"Not without his cocktails." His mom stares distantly into her wine as she swirls it around, repeating what she said yesterday,

"But your father's basically a good man...for a drunk."

"I don't hate him anymore," Dancer says. "He knows he made a mistake, and I'm sure he's paying for it. It doesn't erase the past; I can never be close to him, but at least I understand him now."

"Well," his mom says, standing up suddenly as the phone rings, "so much for happy homecomings." She picks up the receiver. "Hello...just a minute please, may I ask who's calling?" Dancer watches his mom's eyes grow wide and her mouth hang open. "Who?...Oh my God! You don't mean it..."

"What is it?" Dancer asks, leaping up. "What's wrong?"

"I can't believe...I just...Oh, I've seen all your old movies, Miss Monet, every single one of them. Oh my God!"

Dancer quickly jumps out of his chair and tries to take the phone, embarrassment written all over his face. "Mom, I think it's for me."

His mom snatches the phone away from her son. "Stop that! How often do I get to talk with a real live movie star?" She speaks back into the receiver, her voice suddenly as fluid and coddling as fine brandy. "Oh Miss Monet, you know I've always admired you so much, and now to have you calling my Dancer, well it's a genuine thrill."

"Mom! Mom, you're embarrassing me."

"Oh, and we're all so sorry to hear about your fiancé. We heard it on the news last night...I know what it is to lose a loved one..."

"Mom, give—me—the—telephone!" He grabs it from her. "I'm sorry, Anne." Dancer's mom backs slowly away as though in the presence of the Pope, and sits softly down on the sofa next to Dick. She clutches his hand and smiles ethereally. "Hold on a minute, Anne," Dancer says, "let me get it in the bedroom."

"No, no Dancer you don't have to do that," his mom says, "we won't listen, will we Dick?" Dick nods that they won't. Dancer ignores her and takes it in the bedroom. "Anne?"

"Dancer, who was that woman?"

"My mother. I apologize for her behavior. It's just that she didn't believe me yesterday when I told her about you. She's never met an actress before."

"Don't worry about it. I'm used to it."

Dancer notes that her voice doesn't sound very cheery. She sounds like she's been crying, and he hears all sorts of clanking, clattering noises in the background. "I read about Turk on the plane and tried calling you yesterday. I left several messages but..."

"I checked out. The reporters wouldn't leave me alone so I just checked out."

He hears some more clanking and clattering, alarms going off and people shouting. "Where are you, Anne?"

"Oh Dancer, I'm so depressed I could lay down and scream. You're the only one who listens to me, the only one."

"Anne, have you been drinking?"

"Drinking, doping, destroying my health. I'm having a very alliterative and sinful Sunday afternoon." She begins to cry. "I've been fired, Dancer. They fired me from the picture."

"Oh, no. Anne, I...I know how much it meant to you. It hasn't been a good weekend for either of us." He hears a siren and some bells and clickity clackity sounds. "Anne, where for God's sake are you?"

"Dancer, they didn't even wait until his body was cold. I didn't even know he had died. They called me late Friday night and said, 'Turk is dead and you're fired,' just like that, all in the same breath just like that." Her voice begins to trail away.

"Anne? Anne are you there? Speak into the phone."

"And you know what my first thought was, Dancer. Do you know?"

"No, what was it?"

"I thought, 'Oh dear God, where am I going to find another picture?' No sympathy for Turk, no remorse, no feeling toward him whatsoever. Only for my own selfish self. Dancer, what's wrong with me?"

"Nothing's wrong with you. It's not your fault he died. Anne, please tell me where you are."

"Atlantic City," she says. "I'm in Atlantic City at Caesars and I've lost $17,000."

"What? You what! Anne, that's more than I make in a year!"

"Ain't it the truth. And it didn't take me twenty minutes to blow it."

"Anne, listen to me. Leave right now. Go back to New York. I'll, I'll meet you at the airport."

"No, no Dancer, you come here. I'll get you a plane ticket. I need you to go with me to Turk's funeral tomorrow. We're leaving tonight. Please, say you'll come with me. I can't do it alone."

"Anne, I can't come there. I . . . I can't go to Turk's funeral. Hell, isn't he being buried in London?"

"Tomorrow afternoon at Westminster Abbey."

"They don't bury rock stars at Westminster Abbey."

"Well shit, it's somewhere around there. Dancer, I can't go alone. I can't stand to be alone. Please, say you'll come. We'll have a good time. I'll show you all the sights."

"I've seen all the sights. I was in London just before I came to New York. It's where I met my roommate."

"He's British?"

"No, he was just there. He got lost or something on his way to California."

"Well, all the more reason to go back. It'll be nostalgic."

"But I don't have any money. Besides, I have to be at work again on Tuesday anyway. I can't just . . ."

"My God Dancer, you said yourself they don't care whether you show up or not. They won't even notice you're gone. Listen, I know we haven't known each other long, but for some reason I feel . . . well, that you're one of the few people I can trust. You're just that sort of person."

Dancer thinks about this. It's true, he's never really gone out of his way to be a shoulder to cry on, but for some reason people have always trusted him as their personal confidant. Nova, who tells him everything; Miles, who treats Dancer like a bar crony; even Suzanne Bernstein—with all her inane patter about Scrabble and diets and abortions.

"I guess I missed my calling," he tells Anne. "I should have been a psychologist like my mom's boyfriend."

"So you'll come?" she asks, knowing he's weakening.

"I didn't even bring a suit."

"We'll buy you one. The plane leaves at 11:30 tonight from New York. It's 3:30 now . . ."

"It's 2:30 here."

"All right, it's 2:30 there, but here's what you do. Catch the next plane to Newark. I'll have a ticket waiting for you at the counter. My driver will meet you at the airport. He'll be holding one of those signs with your name on it. Just look for him at the gate. He'll drive you here and we'll take a helicopter to Kennedy."

"Can't I just meet you at Kennedy?" *Why is he even considering this?*

"No, I want you here. I need someone here, a crutch to lean on. I'm feeling so sad, Dancer, so lonely and sad."

He sighs. This is all getting too melodramatic. For the next few minutes he works out the logistical details with Anne, then tells her he'll see her soon. The instant he puts the phone down, his mom comes bubbling into the bedroom. "Are you going to be in a movie, Dancer?" She turns to Dick. "Oh I just knew he'd do it, Dick, I just knew it!"

Dancer suddenly starts hurling clothes into his suitcase. "I need you to drive me to the airport."

"To Hollywood!" Dancer's mom says. "He's going to Hollywood!"

"I'm going to Atlantic City."

"Atlantic City . . . New Jersey? Is it a movie about gambling?"

"There is no movie, mom. I'm going to a funeral."

"A funeral? But who died?"

"I'll explain it on the way to the airport. Just get your keys."

SEA FOAM FUDGE

or

Chapter

11

THE FLIGHT TO Newark pitches Dancer into a welter of anxiety. First off, he barely makes the plane and unluckily, the Madonna wannabe, like a social disease, is back again. He pulls his bag up to his face to avoid her and slinks to a seat in the rear, whereupon he begins brooding about his lack of money and the gnawing emptiness in his stomach. The last quasi-nutritious thing he consumed was that peach daiquiri he made yesterday, and Lord knows its nutritional value wasn't exactly a pitch for longevity. He asks for some of those tasty honey-roasted almonds but the prissy flight attendant never does bring him any, vexing him no end. While he waits in vain for the flight attendant to meander back to his area, he stews about rent, about bills, about Zinc; reminding himself to call the apartment again when the plane lands. What's he going to do? They'll both be kicked out! Not only did his gamble backfire but now his dad despises him, his mom worships the ground he walks on and his grandmother is out $100.

True to her slurred word, Anne's driver is standing at the gate, holding up a sign that says, DANCER. He takes Dancer's bag and grumbles something about "the shitty weather"—a rather enigmatic complaint since the weather is perfect. Dancer supposes it's his standard line, feeling he's required to say *something*. Dancer also notices that one headlight is still busted, but foregoes mentioning that it is his fault. The driver slams Dancer's door and they're off.

Dancer pours himself a cocktail, stretches out across the leather upholstery and revels in the luxury. He watches a little television, the all new version of Hollywood Squares, or maybe it's just the old version because Paul Lynde is in the middle and Dancer recalls that Paul Lynde is dead now. In any case, it's just as silly and dumb as it can be, and Dancer finds it disturbing to realize that someone is making millions of dollars off this, someone other than himself. He turns it off and passes some whiskey (upon request) to the driver. The driver says his name is Constantinople and asks Dancer if he knows how to play Botticelli. Dancer admits he has played it in the past.

"Good," Constantinople says, "you can explain me the rules."

Dancer tries to wriggle out of it, claiming you can't really play with only two people. But Constantinople is adamant, so Dancer says, "All right, let's say I give you two initials, T.T. let's say. Well, you have to figure out who T.T. is by asking me clue questions— something like, 'Is T.T. a singer?'"

"But whut if she ain't though?" Constantinople asks.

Dancer scoots to the middle of his seat and leans forward, crossing his arms over the back of Constantinople's seat. He watches the yellow lines in the highway slither under the car. "Well, that's what I'm getting to. I have to say, 'No, T.T. is not Tina Turner, or no, T.T. is not Toni Tenille, the point being that I have to name *somebody*, otherwise you get to ask me a 'yes' or 'no' question. However, just because T.T. isn't Tina Turner or Toni Tenille doesn't necessarily mean that T.T. isn't a singer. T.T. could very well be Tiny Tim."

"But what if the singer is Michael Jackson or Melba Moore?"

Dancer pauses a moment, trying to locate the thread. "But neither of those begin with T.T.."

"Does it always have to be T.T.?"

"No, no of course not. You can pick any set of initials you want. But when your opponent asks a question he has to be thinking of somebody with those initials, and if you think he's bluffing, you can challenge him."

"To a fight?"

Dancer shakes his head and looks behind him, watching the yellow lines race out from the other end. "Maybe we should try something else. Let's just go through the alphabet and name foods. You go first."

"Buttermilk biscuits," Constantinople says, through a swig of whiskey, "hot from the oven and swimmin' in sorghum."

Dancer pleads a sudden disinterest in such child's play and turns the Hollywood Squares back on. Rose Marie is being asked a trick question, something about French Impressionism and who created a greater impact—Henri Matisse or Hieronymus Bosch. She says Bosch, and the man in the X chair disagrees. "Good for you," says the host, and proceeds to inform Rose that Bosch was neither French nor an impressionist. Rose says, "That's funny, I always had a good impression of him."

By the time they get to Atlantic City both Dancer and Constantinople are feeling pretty mellow. The whiskey bottle is nearly empty and Dancer isn't the least bit worried that (A) he has absolutely no idea what he's doing in a limousine with a drunk driver, or (B) they're driving across a giant Monopoly board. He doesn't see the Miss America contestants anywhere. Maybe it's the wrong month. God, is Atlantic City seedy and dilapidated! He didn't exactly anticipate Victorian architecture and ladies strolling with parasols, but he certainly never expected a ghost town with boarded over store fronts and flaking paint on crumbling brick facades. For some reason he is reminded of a Jacques Cousteau special he watched last month on the indigence of Port-au-Prince, Haiti. Where is the revitalization that was supposed to come with all the gambling loot?

As they pull up to the hotel, Constantinople warns him that he better get rid of the empty bottle. Dancer shoves it under the seat. He gets out and is overwhelmed by the unexpected gaudiness, which seems an affront to the ghetto across the street. He thinks the contrast would make a perfect thesis for an economics major; but being an English major himself, it's just killing him that "Caesars" has no apostrophe between the "r" and the "s."

He has never been inside a casino before and is overwhelmed by its size. It must cover two acres. Wall-to-wall slot machines and crap tables, baccarat dens and blackjack tables, cocktail waitresses in togas and waiters like chariot racers. And the people! Tacky, tacky people—coarse women in purple polyester with yellow hair piled on top their heads, tattooed men with beer guts wearing too much jewelry, bucolic housewives chewing cigars through hangovers while toting plastic tumblers full of $1 slot tokens. All of them lit by a murky bloodish glow.

"You lost?" a pasty-faced guard grunts at Dancer.

Startled, Dancer says, "I'm looking for the elevators."

"Over there," the guard says, pointing.

Dancer thanks him and moves forward. He feels like the lost lamb who's fallen into a wolf pit—the eyes. Eyes are watching his every move. It's a horrible feeling: cameras in smoky glass bubbles clinging to the ceiling, security guards whispering into walkie-talkies and bulbous thugs standing by staircases sucking in every moment. It's not just him alone though. They're watching everyone...suspicion...avarice...doubt... Dancer wonders, If the Mafia were contracted to build Heaven, would this be it?

He finds the elevator, ducks in, and soars breathlessly to the eleventh floor as though riding a magic carpet up from Hell, not entirely convinced that what he left below was real. He wonders if whiskey is a hallucinogen. The doors make a pleasant ding before they open, and he steps out into a plushly carpeted corridor. Anne's door is at the end. He knocks.

"Dancer?"

He decides to be cute. "'Tis I, oh worldly one."

"Wait just a minute." Some muffled sounds within, then, "Okay, c'mon in." Dancer opens the door and there's Anne wearing pleated slacks the color of flesh but naked from the waist up. She's standing by the window sultrily squeezing half a lemon over her breasts and arms. The juice is rolling down her stomach and gathering in her navel. "Who am I?" she murmurs.

"Susan Sarandon in *Atlantic City*."

She throws the lemon at Dancer. "How'd you know that?"

"I saw the movie." He closes the door behind him.

"I was born for that role," Anne says, flouncing onto her bed. "She got an Oscar nomination, but I would have won the damned thing." He picks the lemon up off the floor, blows off the lint, and asks her to turn over on her stomach. He massages the citrus in slow, caressing circles along her spine. "Ummm," she says, "miss me?"

"I was worried about you."

"Everyone worries about me." Now she turns onto her side and props herself on her elbows. "Dancer," she says, smirking. "You've been drinking, haven't you. I can smell it from here."

"I had to put something in my system, otherwise I'd have fainted from hunger."

She pulls her hair away from her neck. "It wasn't an accusation." She lays down and closes her eyes. He applies pressure to the lemon. She asks, "Don't they feed you in Alabama?"

"I was too nervous to eat. My dad gave me the whole works —the guilt trip, paternal supremacy and family banishment. I knew it was coming, but I didn't think it would be this time."

"A little higher, Dancer. That's it. Oh God, that feels wonderful." She stretches out her arms and moves them in a slow flapping motion, as though making snow angels on the bed spread. "I would be a perfect mother, but I know other women who are perfect mothers too. They have horrible children. Perfectly horrible. I don't ever want children. You?"

"Someday maybe, if I'm rich and if the world is a safer place. I only want one though. I believe overpopulation is the root of all our problems. There's no space anymore."

She laughs and tells him he sounds like a Californian, and then for a reason that he doesn't understand, she says that only two hundred years ago a squirrel could travel from the east coast all the way west of the Mississippi without ever touching the ground. Next, she speculates that if people were more like lions then "the family" wouldn't be a myth. "Children shouldn't feel obligated to keep in touch all their lives. They should be weaned away at a certain age and told they must survive on their own, like you, Dancer." Somehow, this isn't heartening to him. The lemon has run dry and Anne flips over, asking if he wouldn't mind massaging her temples, and has he even noticed that she is now "sober as a fence post thank you?"

He says, "If I'd just lost a year's salary I'd be sober too." He massages her temples with his index fingers in slow circles.

"Oh God Dancer, what is my problem? I just don't seem to have any direction anymore." She points to a gargantuan fruit basket wrapped in translucent gold cellophane near the window. "Why don't you take out that bottle of Moet for us and pop the cork? In fact, just bring the whole basket over here. We don't have time to order dinner. You'll just have to wait 'til we get on the plane. What time is it anyway?"

He glanced at the clock on a dresser. "7:33." He gets up and hands the basket to Anne. She peels off the crackly cellophane and gives him the champagne. "It's warm," he says.

"There's no time to chill it. The helicopter leaves at 8:15."

He smiles and nods at Anne's exposed breasts. "No time to finish undressing either?"

"If there was, do you think I'd still be in my slacks?" She pulls on an ivory blouse, and he passes her a flute of bubbles. "Cheers," she says, and they tip their glasses together. She points toward his bag. "Is that all you brought?"

"I was only planning on a weekend at home, not a world tour." He stuffs some mint chocolates into his mouth and bites into a banana.

Anne admires herself in the mirror, grabs the Moet, a clump of white grapes and says, "Just leave it here. I'll have my driver pick it up when he checks me out. We'll get you some new stuff in London."

Dancer stops chewing and says, "Uh oh."

"What is it?"

"I don't have my passport."

Anne shrugs as she puts on an earring. "Don't worry about it. They'll let you in . . . you're with me."

"Anne, I hardly think foreign countries grant the same courtesies as the Palladium." He drops into a chair. "What am I going to do?"

"It's a funeral, Dancer, they'll make an exception." She adjusts the stud in her ear. "Just one of the many inalienable rights of passage provided to celebrities. It's not legal, but we're above law. Ask De Lorean."

"You're not kidding, are you?"

"When you're famous you'll understand. Are my earrings straight?"

He nods. She looks around the room. "I guess we're ready then. Have you ever seen the boardwalk?"

He shakes his head through a mouthful of imported chocolate.

"Come on then. The helicopter leaves from Resorts, a few hotels over."

So they get in this thing that looks like a backwards rickshaw. A person stands behind them and pushes it, and the noise it makes on the boards is like a stick being dragged along a wooden fence. Anne is eating grapes by holding them above her and biting them from below. The beach is on their right, trashed with litter, and people are copulating under piers.

On their left is a garish strip of shops selling cholesterol poisoning under the guises of "sea foam fudge" and "original salt water taffy." A dingy mattress is plopped in front of one of these shops, called Miss Tena Annette's palm reading pit. On it wallows a deformed fat girl with her tongue hanging out. It's an exceptionally long tongue. Standing next to her is an emaciated crone singing "Amazing Grace" while holding out her apron for money to be pitched into it. Even the President needs money, Dancer thinks, wondering where that line comes from. Then he remembers—the soundtrack to *A Star Is Born*. The song is titled, "Hellacious Acres."

Admission's free, you pay to get out.

The heli-pad is at the end of the pier behind the Resorts hotel. Anne and Dancer step out of the backwards rickshaw. Dancer gives the person who pushed them a tip—$5.00. He now has $100.64 but tries not to think about it. Money does make him think of Zinc though. He remembers he ought to call him, especially since he's leaving the country... *I'm leaving the country!* "Anne, do we have time for me to call my roommate?"

"We've got about seven minutes. Is that enough time?"

"If I can find a phone it is."

"Through here," she says, and they push on this frosted glass revolving door and find themselves magically inside another casino. "You see one anywhere?"

"There," he says, "by the roulette tables." He races toward them, fumbling through his pockets for change, but pulls out only his 64¢ and the hundred his grandmother gave him. "Damn! Anne, do you have enough change for a long distance call?"

She hurriedly goes through her purse then stares at the doors. "Dancer, they've started the blades. People are getting on."

"Anne, it'll only take a minute. I've got to call him."

She pulls out a lipstick tube, an old autographed press release, two tampons, a bottle of turpentine—"keeps my hair shiny," she says quickly. "I don't have any, Dancer, not even a nickel." Dancer's hundred catches her eye. A strange look crosses her face. She halts her search for a second. "You ever gamble before, Dancer?" He shakes his head quickly, alternately glancing between the doors and her bottomless bag. "You mean you're a virgin?"

"What? What are you talki..."

"Ohmigod Dancer, do you know how lucky you'll be!" She snatches the bill out of his hand.

"Anne, no!"

"Just this one, Dancer. Please."

"But that's all the money I have."

"You'll make more."

"I'll lose it all."

"You'll make a mint."

"Anne, please give me back the hundred dollars."

"Just one bet, Dancer. Trust me." She leans across the felt table, her eyes gleaming. "A color and a number, Dancer. You name it."

"Oh God no, Anne. We have to be at the helicopter in less than two minutes, we don't have time to..."

"Lucky number two," Anne shouts. "A hundred's worth of chips on number two." She turns from the dealer to Dancer. "Red or black?"

Dancer is not sweating bricks. He's sweating whole quarries. This can't be happening to him. "Anne please..."

"Too late, Dancer. Just pick a color, hurry."

"Red," he says softly. "Red!" he practically screams.

"Red it is," Anne says, as though being the first on Mars.

The dealer releases the silver ball into the rotating abyss and everyone around the table, all the tacky people, hold their breath hypnotically. Some plead. Some beg. Dancer merely looks. His hands drop to his sides. His sixty-four cents rolls silently across the plaid carpeting and vanishes in the noise. He watches the tiny little sphere, his whole world, roll around and round and round and lower and lower and lower... He has read about people who leave their bodies and experience something beautiful, something which must be like death, yet they are able to return from it and speak of warm lights and tunnels and lovely places of flowers and gold... but this doesn't happen to him.

Horror is what happens to him. Panic is what happens to him. True, $100 wasn't enough to pay his debts, to keep them in their apartment, but it was *something*. He could have made it stretch to payday at least. Oh, why can't he be more like Zinc? Why does he worry about these things out of his control? Zinc never worries. Zinc never worries about a thing, and somehow he gets by. Anne never worries. She complains a lot, but she never worries. *Am I the only one on this Earth who actually worries? Am I?*

Slowly, like he's under water, a numb apathy washes over him. What's the point? Why care? What can he do?... Nothing. Nothing matters. His whole life, his future, has always been molded by others' foolishness. Why does he fight it? As Zinc would say, "Just go with the flow, man. Chill out." So with no feeling at all, not caring whether he wins or loses, he stares at the silver sphere clank across the perforations, scuttle to a halt and gleam dizzily under the smoke and fuzzy lights.

"Number two red," says the dealer, "a winner."

> *Someone saved,*
> *Someone saved,*
> *Someone saved,*
> *My life tonight.*
>
> —ELTON JOHN

III

THE CIRCLE
OF LIFE

THEY DON'T HAVE ICE IN ENGLAND

or

Chapter

12

"THERE'S A FINE line between rationalization and impulse."

"You're wrong," Anne says. "There's no line at all. One justs wastes more time than the other. I told you I knew you'd win. If we had rationalized it, not only would we have missed our flight but you wouldn't be sitting on $2,000 right now."

Dancer instinctively feels his bulging wallet again and has to admit she's right. "Anne, it's just too good to be true, I mean this day has been so strange. I've felt the lowest and highest that I've ever felt in my life."

"Literally," Anne says, referring to their present position 38,000 feet somewhere above the North Atlantic.

Sure enough, customs waved Dancer right on through at the gate before take off. Anne had to play the Hollywood bitch, which didn't work. So she resorted to Turk's pathetic widow, which did. And now the attendant is asking "Widow Monet" if she and Dancer would like another drink. They would. The attendant gives them not one but two, offering her condolences to Anne. She has read about the tragedy in the papers. Anne feigns sadness. Next, someone dressed like a Samurai chef serves them a delicious platter of jade scallops and chunks of pink lobster meat on skewers to dip into three kinds of sauces plus fortune cookies on the side. Most of the other passengers are asleep. Dancer needs to be, but the food is so good, Anne is so beautiful and Zinc is so stupid. Dancer has called him twice from the phone on the plane. Until today he never realized there were phones on planes. If he had, he wouldn't have tried to call Zinc from the casino, and he'd be $2,000 poorer. Nobody answered the first time. The second time, a recorder told him the service has been disconnected. So he just says to hell with Zinc and enjoys his sybaritic surroundings. God, it's great traveling first class with a star.

He pushes his plate aside, picks up his cookie and says, "I've always believed in fortune cookies."

"Oh, so have I," Anne says. "You go first."

Dancer snaps his in two and pulls the slip of paper out. "Reality is for those who lack imagination." He looks at Anne. "I can't tell, is it a good fortune or a bad fortune?"

"Good, I think. It means you're above the commonplace, being an artist like you are."

"Well, what are you waiting on? Open yours."

"Oh God," she says, and she sets the cookie on her plate and brings her fist down on it like a mallet. "Damn, I don't believe it, I always get the bum cookies."

"What does it say?"

"Here." She hands it to him.

" 'Hell is paved with good intentions?' What kind of fortune is that?"

"Ill fortune. I knew I shouldn't be going to Turk's funeral. It's all his fault." She opens her platinum cigarette case and removes a chartreuse cigarette.

"How'd you get through customs with those?"

"I tell them they're dope, and they never believe me. What color would you like?"

"I'll pass for now." Somehow, it doesn't seem too bright to smoke dope on a plane, even if you're with a movie star. Then too, he has a fleeting image of Nancy Reagan shaking her finger at him.

They sit in silence a few minutes. The attendant removes their plates and sniffs the air. Anne smiles wickedly and proffers her cigarette. The attendant accepts, and soon both she and the Samurai chef are laughing up a riot behind the curtains. So much for airplane etiquette, Dancer thinks. He stares out the window and notices that the sky is just beginning to turn an orangey color. He asks Anne the time—two A.M.—and says they must be crossing the International Date Line. "You only live for the future, don't you?" she asks suddenly.

He crunches on his cookie and thinks about that one. He's wondering if Anne is referring back to their conversation about time machines from the other night. He says, "But everybody lives for the future. You have to, it's the only thing coming."

"No, you don't have to. Some people live for the past, some for the present."

"I can't think about the past. All that's back there is childhood, and it hurts too much. As for the present, nothing is really happening. My career is at a standstill. The future is all I've got."

She pulls down the shade on her window. "I wish I had a future, but everything wonderful is behind me now. Turk was my only hope for a comeback, and now he's dead. I'm over the hill, Dancer, a has-been at thirty-six."

"And I'm a never-was at twenty-three. Which is worse?"

"Don't feel sorry for yourself, Dancer. It's unbecoming."

"Take a look in your mirror, Anne."

"I have a right to feel sorry for myself. You don't. Your career is just beginning..."

"And it's been 'just beginning' for about three years now."

"Give it time. My God, you're so intense sometimes." She heaves a great sigh. "I wish I were half as serious as you."

"Anne, your only problem is that you've got too much time on your hands. What you need is work."

"And prisoners need dynamite, but I doubt they'll be getting any." She smushes her chartreuse cigarette and lights up a mauve one. "The rainbow is running low. I should contact my friend in Jamaica."

Dancer says, "I don't understand why people aren't just knocking down your doors to offer you work. I mean you're gorgeous; you're talented; you've done lots of other films... what's the problem?"

Anne twist-shuts the circular air vent above her head and pulls a blanket up around her chin. "The problem is that I'm, and this is a quote, 'A boozed-up, drugged-out leftover flower child incapable of bringing emotion or passion to any role other than that of playing myself.' The worst thing about it is that it's perfectly true."

"You believe that?"

"I don't know what to believe. I believe I'm afraid, that's what I believe. Someone once said, I think it was my psychiatrist, that boredom and self-righteousness are the two greatest forms of fear. If that's true, I must be absolutely terrified."

"But what are you afraid of? You've got everything."

"It all means nothing, less than nothing. Maybe I just don't have any innocence anymore. I've seen too much. I've done too much. Hell, I feel like I'm 250 years old." She pulls the blanket up higher around her face. "I want it back again, Dancer. I want the attention, the accolades..." Her voice goes thin. "I think the sad truth is that my initial success was just a fluke." She bites her lip. "You know, I've never done any stage work. Know why?" He doesn't. "It's because I can't *really* act. I can be pretty. I can be glamorous. I can even be demure, but style is a far cry from substance. With film you get to do it over and over again until it's right. Plus you've got distractions like camera angles and props and lighting—they can hide just about anything. But you can't fake a live audience."

"I don't agree," he says. "Did you ever hear the joke about the boy who stopped a man on the street and asked how to get to Carnegie Hall?"

She smiles and says, "Practice, my son, practice."

He shrugs. "There you go."

"You're so optimistic, Dancer. I mean it's good. Hell, it's great."

"My mom's boyfriend says, now mind you he doesn't say much, but when he does it's usually worthwhile. He says that people can be divided into two groups—those who are driven by the fear of failure and those who are driven by the desire to succeed. Both work, but only one of them makes the odds irrelevant. You can do it again, Anne. All you need is the right material."

She turns to him and looks him over. "So you're a writer, Dancer. Write me a screenplay." Immediately, their eyes lock.

Something clicks. Things spring to mind, things like "fate," things like "destiny." She says, "I just had a déjà vu. You ever get those?"

"I had one too," he says.

"What do you think it means?"

"My mom says it means your life is going according to plan."

"We can help each other, Dancer."

"I know."

"There must be a word for this."

"Symbiosis," he says.

"I thought that only applied to one-celled organisms."

"One-tracked organisms."

"Go to sleep, Dancer. We've got a lot of work ahead of us."

"You're on." He clicks off his overhead light.

Aside from the dollar having dropped, London isn't much different from the city Dancer remembers being in a year ago. It's still wet; it's still cold; it's still old. Only the circumstances that brought him here have changed. Back then, he was just out of school—his glorious future shining not one kilowatt brighter because of it. What could he do with an English degree anyway... teach? Not a chance. This was still the anxious eighties, after all. There was no way he was going to tolerate a teacher's salary for the rest of his life.

So the question was one of direction. Where does one go, when like a chrysalis, one emerges from the safely constructed college cocoon? He couldn't dry his wings on a limb forever. But his only employable skills were, "Would anyone care for a cocktail before dinner?" He had been waiting tables every night of his life since he was eighteen. By day he schlepped to school. In his nonexistant spare time he studied, and God knows how he ever managed to write a novel in between. Burnout was not the word.

But as is always the case, just when he reached the point when he could take no more, the point where something had to give... it was over. He graduated, and a way of life Dancer had lived for as long as he could remember didn't exist anymore. Within that same month—as though everything around him had been timed to shut off simultaneously—he finished his novel; his apartment lease ran out, and the restaurant where he worked closed down.

At first he was a little dazed. He had at least hoped to continue waiting tables long enough to save some money. But mismanagement dictated otherwise. He showed up one night, and the doors were chained. They hadn't even given him his last check. What should he do now—temporarily move back in with one of his parents? Impossible. His dad wouldn't let him move in with him. His mom couldn't. She was in between apartments at the time, debating whether to move in with Dick while staying with one of her girlfriends. So once again, desperation was the order of Dancer's day. He supposed he could get a job in another restaurant, but why stall? Someone was obviously telling him the gig was up. Move on, big dreamer, move on. So Dancer did.

It was St. Patrick's Day. That was the day he left. He figured it was a good omen since St. Patrick's Day is an Irish holiday; and since Ireland is part of the same general land mass as England, well at least, just an island over, sort of like Hawaii and Oahu; and since Dancer has a little Irish blood in him from somewhere way back anyway... but anyway if he had rationalized it, he would never have done it. After all, what kind of lunatic walks out his door with a suitcase, a manuscript, $600 and a one-way ticket to a foreign country that he has never visited in his life and where he knows not a soul? A lunatic who has nothing to lose. That's what kind.

The choice of London was more the result of elimination than anything else. He harbored no mad, desperate need to see the mother country, and he didn't believe he had lived there in a past life or anything like that. He had considered warm, fun places like L.A. or Nassau, and exotic places like Paris and Amsterdam, even Sydney (kangaroos are his favorite animal). None of these cities, however, were very big on publishing. So the only logical choices were either New York or London. But the thought of living in New York, where people are slaughtered in broad daylight as others watch, scared him to death. (Dancer was still molded by the southern mentality at this point.) Also, he had mailed sections of his novel to countless New York houses, but no one seemed to realize its true brilliance. One editor, perhaps just to stop Dancer from submitting it yet again, suggested he try the European market. "They are more likely to publish an allegorical children's fantasy than America," the editor said, citing George Orwell's *Animal Farm* as an example, which of course was all Dancer needed to hear. (He later found out that Orwell was not quite "unknown" at the time he published *Animal Farm*. He already had *1984* under his belt.)

He told no one about his exodus; not even his friends who were plotting their own escapes, and especially not his family. They would only try to dissuade him. Since he didn't even have a girl-friend at the time, there was no one to wish him farewell or throw him a going-away party. He simply drove his car to the Iron & Steel Credit Union, closed out his I.R.A., collected his $500, drove to the bank, closed out his savings account, collected his $100, drove back to his apartment and called a cab to drive him to the airport. While waiting, he placed the door key under the mat and dropped the letters in the mailbox. Each letter was addressed to a different friend, notifying them of his departure and of what they might take from his apartment. Not being a slave to capitalism, it never occurred to him that he should sell his possessions. Nor did it occur to him that his parents might wonder what had become of their second son. He figured he'd notify them of his where-abouts once he got settled. When the cab arrived, Dancer slid in and never looked back.

The weather was absolutely gorgeous when he landed at Gat-wick Airport, spurring Dancer to wonder if the legendary London fog and drizzle were only rumors concocted by the British to keep out crass Americans. He decided they were, that the clear skies were a symbol—luck would smile on him in England. An hour later, however, it started raining murderously; but at that point it didn't matter, since it's only your initial impression that deter-mines your degree of luck. (This is a theory Dancer invented himself, and is therefore subject to change depending on how much he must rely on self-deception in order to keep a state of panic at bay.)

Not knowing where to go from the airport, he merely followed the crowd, and what a morose crowd it was. (Contrary to myth, the English aren't a very jovial people, not anymore.) Anyway, he ended up on a train that whisked him to Victoria Station where he bought an unbelievably delicious Cadbury's candy bar embedded like sedimentary rock with raisins and nuts. After licking off his fingers he figured he might as well get a hotel room, and a girl in a booth who reserves that sort of thing asked him how much he'd like to spend and in what section of town he'd care to stay. He said, "Precious little but someplace nice."

"*Americans,*" she said. "Would you care to try a youth hostel?"

"Youth hostel?" He had never heard the term before. He imagined a place like a fraternity house yet inhabited by angry people. "How much is it?"

"Six pounds per night."

"I'll take it."

"It's in Earl's Court," she said.

"Is that a good area?"

"You'll like it," she assured him.

Dancer did. Apparently, Earl's Court is a sort of borderline area —not quite respectable but not quite the black hole of Calcutta either. A lot of artists live there, and homosexuals and Aussies. Even Princess Diana once lived there back when she was just a pudgy kindergarten teacher. So if nothing else, the place has color. Dancer was pleased.

During his first week, Dancer just wandered about and did the things visitors were supposed to do. He sipped tea in Wedgwood at four and felt refined; he ate kidney pies in pubs and felt repulsed; and he sampled those extraordinarily tasteless excuses for biscuits with jam called scones. He was unimpressed by both the Tower of London and Buckingham Palace. If you've seen them once, he thought, then you've *seen* them. However, he was quite impressed by the zoo, especially the live panda. He had never seen one before. (Well, that's not entirely true. When he was in the sixth grade he was on the safety patrol. You can't be on the safety patrol unless you make straight A's, so he was very proud to be on it. Anyway, the safety patrol took a field trip to Washington, D.C.; the year before, President Nixon had been given these two baby pandas by the government of China. One was named Ling Ling and the other was Ping Pong or something like that. He got to see both of them, but he really doesn't remember them very well. So for all intents and purposes, he saw his first live panda in London.)

During his second week, Dancer tried unsuccessfully to get an agent to represent his classic children's novel. He was in the National Portrait Gallery's gift shop, debating between a postcard of either the Brontë sisters or Rupert Brooke, when he stumbled as if by fate across "The Writers' & Artists' Yearbook," which alphabetically lists every agent and publisher in Britain. Most of them thought he was rude though, since he would just show up with his manuscript at their door unannounced. But he only resorted to this after they refused to speak to him over the tellie.

English telephones were another thing that didn't impress him. They just don't work. The English apparently don't go to the bathroom either, because he found no public restrooms anywhere. Nor do they take showers. He had to take baths the whole time, something he hadn't done since he was four. Nor do the English have ice. All drinks are served at room temperature which Dancer guesses evens out, since most rooms are ice cold . . . they don't have heat in England, either.

By Dancer's third week, he had tromped through every tourist attraction and hounded every literary agent to the point that he was ashamed to be an American—a fact which everybody in London always pointed out to him usually in the most derogatory manner. He was running low on money too (England has the most beautiful money), feeling depressed and glum, when who should stop him one night at Piccadilly Circus asking directions to a nightclub called the Hippodrome but his future roommate and nemesis, Zinc.

"Hey man," he asked, looking a little dazed as though unsure of where he was, "do you speak English?"

Considering what country they were in, Dancer thought this a strange question to ask. Even back then it seems, the things that came out of Zinc's mouth didn't quite hit the mark. But at least he looked friendly and apparently he was just as relieved as Dancer to meet a fellow American. They exchanged names, chatted a few minutes, and upon Zinc's invitation, Dancer accompanied his new friend to the ultra-glitzy Hippodrome. Zinc said he was into "absorbin' a few sounds and generally just chillin' out man." So it was during the course of doing exactly these things that Dancer learned Zinc was in England only as a result of the most bizarre accident (or so it seemed bizarre at the time, but as Dancer would later discover, Zinc and bizarre accidents are one and the same).

Listening to Zinc's story drunkenly unfold there at a table on the top tier of the Hippodrome's futuristic amphitheater, Dancer began to draw the conclusion that either Zinc was a shameless liar with a flair for adventurous storytelling, or else he was just so indifferent toward life that he didn't give a damn what happened to him, thereby involving himself in any number of dire predicaments. Whatever the case, Dancer had a hard time taking seriously the story Zinc told, not because it *couldn't* have happened, but because the better Dancer began to know Zinc, the more he realized it probably did happen, which only made it even more unbelievable. Anyway, according to Zinc, his reason for being in London (in a nutshell) went something like this:

It was spring break at Pratt, so Zinc decided he needed to get the hell out of Brooklyn and go somewhere to catch a tan. California seemed to be the natural choice, and luckily he had an old girlfriend in San Diego—a specialist in sea otters. She had moved there against a palm reader's better judgment, but Zinc figured he'd visit her for a week anyway. After all, a week wasn't really enough time for her bad karma to rub off on him, but it was plenty of time to get a good solid tan.

Well, in Kennedy airport he asked one of the airline employees where to board his flight. But the employee (in retrospect, obviously suffering from a hearing impairment), thought Zinc had said "Santiago," as in the capital of Chile, and Zinc didn't think the large number of Spanish-speaking people on the plane was anything unusual since San Diego was so close to Mexico anyway. Plus, he fell asleep before the aircraft even left the ground because he'd spent six hours that morning in the gym pumping iron so he'd look good on the beach. (Dancer didn't bother interrupting Zinc to ask if he ever noticed he'd been directed to the international terminal. Why muddle a good tale?)

It seems Zinc didn't think it was one bit strange that he had to show his passport either. He assumed it was newly instituted airport policy designed to curb the dispersion of illegal aliens. (Fortunately, he'd brought along his passport, just in case he and the sea otter specialist decided they wanted to cruise down to the Baja Peninsula.) Additionally, no one even bothered checking his boarding pass before boarding. Zinc speculated that this was due to the fact he was eating a limburger sandwich as he flashed the pass (the sandwich being a gift from a woman whose bags Zinc had helped carry). So it was only after the plane landed, and Zinc stumbled sleepy-eyed out of the airport and into the South American morning sun that he realized he wasn't in California at all.

Dancer believes that a normal person would have explained this mix-up to an airport official and gotten on the next available flight to San Diego. Zinc, however, decided that as long as he was in Chile, he might as well see what Chileans have to offer.

Anyway, to make a ridiculous story short, Zinc spent about a week checking the place out, eating foods he didn't recognize and sleeping on the beach, until one day he ran into a beautiful French woman—a marine biologist who was in Chile researching the unexplainable coastal appearance of a particular species of manatee, previously thought to live only in the Red Sea. A romantic relationship quickly ensued, since the marine biologist had a thing for blond Caucasians, who were scarce thereabouts. Also, Zinc flim-flammed her into assuming he was an expert on rare sea mammals, a misinterpretation based entirely on what he had retained from his conversations with the sea otter specialist. The fact that Zinc had purchased a healthy stash of hashish from one of the local Santiagans also helped.

It happened that the marine biologist was finishing up her taggings of the manatee and asked Zinc if he would care to accompany her, the crew and one pregnant manatee back to France. She told him she would be more than happy to put him on the payroll, Zinc being "expertly trained in veterinary pediatrics" like he was. Fortunately for Zinc, when the pregnant manatee went into labor somewhere east of Bermuda, the entire crew was high on Zinc's hash, so the last thing on their minds was the welfare of a pregnant animal. She handled things well enough on her own though, producing two adorable manatee calves, one of which Zinc named after himself.

By this point in the story Dancer was certain the entire thing was just being made up as Zinc went along, but he listened intently nonetheless, especially fascinated with the part about what happened after Zinc's arrival in France. There, the marine biologist bade him adieu and went back to her husband, and Zinc set out on a bicycle toward Paris. Along the way, he passed by a nuclear reactor and a group of students chained to a fence asked him in French if he would like to participate in their nonviolent no-nukes demonstration. Not understanding French, Zinc didn't know what they were talking about, but the girl who threw him a pair of handcuffs was pretty, so he chained himself next to her, and it turned out that she was British and liked hash just about as much as Zinc, coke even more. French was really only a second language for her.

This was how Zinc first met his current girlfriend, Cheryl. It was something like love at first sight, but there at the fence it began raining, and they both contacted such bad cases of flu that they ended up in a hospital. Two days later, Cheryl's parents took her home to London without even letting Zinc say goodbye or find out where she lived. All he knew about her possible whereabouts was that every Friday night she went dancing at the Hippodrome.

Thus, came out the reason why Zinc happened to be standing that night inside the club telling this amazing story to Dancer. Sure enough, Cheryl eventually showed. There were tears and kisses. Everybody cried, even Dancer, and it was agreed that either Zinc or Cheryl would have to leave their country if they planned to spend their lives together. God, it was romantic.

Swept up in the giddiness of the moment, Dancer suggested an immediate marriage—his argument being that marriage would make each of them a citizen of both countries thus solving a passel of immigration problems. Both Zinc and Cheryl agreed it was an excellent idea, and so they all stumbled out of the Hippodrome in search of a minister. They were barely out the door when Zinc suddenly remembered that he might already be married. It seems some poor waif in Chile had begged Zinc to marry her so that she

could go to America and start a new life. Zinc may or may not
have complied. He didn't remember. He was high at the time and
forgot all about her once he met the marine biologist. In any case,
he didn't think it was a legal marriage. But polygamy, whether
real or imagined, didn't set too well with Cheryl.

So Zinc and Cheryl decided they'd just have to live together in sin
until they could confirm or deny Zinc's vague memory. It was
determined that the three of them should pool their money and go
back to the States the next day; but that Cheryl should try to find an
American to marry her as soon as possible, in order to keep from
being deported. Dancer briefly entertained the idea of volunteering
for the job himself, and Zinc even had the gall to ask him if he
wouldn't mind—Zinc, whom Dancer had known approximately
two entire hours at that point. "After all," he argued, "what is
marriage but a scrap of paper anyway?" Dancer agreed he'd think
about it, but he pointed out that he might want to get married for
real some day, and what would his prospective bride think? Zinc
agreed that women were touchy about this sort of thing.

Finally, having no other choice, they agreed to trust in Fate,
and all three departed for New York—there to seek out a suitable
marriage partner for Cheryl. Of course, Dancer had his own reasons for going to New York. Having made no headway in London
as far as his career was concerned, the next logical port-of-call
was the Big Apple. He just hoped he'd be able to keep the mug-
gers and psychotics at bay long enough to find a publisher.

Luckily, he landed a job within a week (no doubt because of
Nova taking an instant liking to him), so New York wasn't as hard
on him as it could have been. As that first spring turned into
summer though, he found that living in the very epicenter of the
world's publishing empire didn't necessarily mean his chances of
becoming an integral part of it were any less difficult than when
he'd lived in Birmingham. In fact, instead of proximity being a
plus, he realized only too clearly just how much competition was
actually out there. Literally, he was one of millions—all dreaming
the same dream, all praying for that one break, that one chance to
prove themselves worthy of seeing something they'd written in
print.

While Dancer bemoaned the odds that confronted him, he wrestled with life's mundane tasks, becoming increasingly aware that living in a one-room apartment in Brooklyn with *both* Zinc and Cheryl was not all it was cracked up to be, if indeed it was ever cracked up to be anything.

Had Cheryl not eventually found a husband, Dancer might have been driven to some unspeakably desperate act. As it was, Cheryl's betrothal changed things dramatically. Her new husband was wealthy, he was under forty, and he wanted a wife for appearance's sake only. No offense, but women just didn't do a thing for him, and he had a spacious deco loft in Soho where he almost never stayed, so Cheryl moved out. Why live all cramped up in Brooklyn when she could live in Manhattan in this unbelievable space for absolutely free? Why indeed! In New York, after all, this is equivalent of a miracle, and all she had to do was change her last name. Zinc was delighted. He could sleep over any night he pleased. Besides, did it really matter that Cheryl's husband-to-be seemed to be operating a nocturnal courier service from his apartment?

Dancer wanted nothing to do with the man, refusing even to go to Cheryl's wedding or her housewarming party. He'd been placing that ad for a husband in the *Village Voice*, anyway. Ads attract weirdos, and there was definitely something fishy about Cheryl's new husband; something more than just the fact that he always wore dark sunglasses in public, or that he changed his phone number once every two months, or that he refused to answer the phone himself, or that he constantly bragged that he paid no taxes. After meeting him once, instinct told Dancer to stay away. He warned Cheryl to be wary of him; but when Cheryl asked why, Dancer couldn't come up with a solid answer. It's hard to argue distrust based on "fatuous" observations, especially when the other party doesn't want to listen.

Dancer soon noticed that Zinc was spending an inordinant amount of time around Cheryl and her new husband. Zinc started looking a little underweight and glassy-eyed, sometimes disappearing for days on end. Eventually, it got to the point that he was spending no more than one night a week in Brooklyn if that.

Dancer sensed that something was wrong, wanted to help him, but Zinc didn't seem to want his help.

And now, with these mysterious phone calls to Dancer's mom and Zinc in tears, things had apparently taken a turn for the worse. It's enough to make Dancer wonder what Cheryl meant the last time he talked to her, when he asked how things were going and she countered, "Mind your own friggin' business or somebody else will." Dancer didn't chat too long.

SWIMMING FOR THE LIGHT ABOVE ME

or

Chapter

13

THEY ARE IN the Knightsbridge section of London, Dancer and Anne, buying Dancer a dark, raw silk suit, European cut, for him to wear to Turk's funeral that afternoon. Modeling in front of the mirror, Dancer can't get over how suave he looks—that is, if he does say so himself. "A perfect fit," the salesman says, down on his knees and pinning the hem. "They were made for you." Now he bends up and pulls the tape measure along Dancer's inseam. "Do you dress to the left or to the right, sir?"

"The left or right to what?"

The salesman looks embarrassed. "I need to know which side to add the extra cloth to."

"Extra cloth where?"

"Oh for Christ's sake, Dancer," Anne says, "he wants to know which side you wear your cock on."

"What? But neither... I mean it's, it's in the middle."

"You don't wear boxer shorts, sir?"

"I wear briefs, one-hundred percent cotton, white briefs."

"Loose briefs or tight briefs, sir?"

"What business is it of yours!" Dancer can't believe this.

"I'm only interested in your comfort, sir."

"We're in a hurry," Anne tells him. "Comfort isn't important. Fashion is. Now what about shoes?"

"One moment, Miss Monet." The salesman zips away but returns in a jiffy with a pair of loafers. He looks at Dancer. "A size 11, I presume?"

"Good guess," Dancer says.

"Sizing is my specialty, sir." He tosses his head.

Dancer slips them on. "They feel fine, but what kind of leather are they? Some sort of reptile?"

"Alligator, sir."

"No, I won't wear an endangered species."

The salesman takes a step back. "Oh but sir, we would never dream of slaughtering an endangered species just for its skin. No, no I assure you this alligator was raised on a farm. One of millions."

Dancer looks at Anne. "You belong on a wedding cake," she says.

"Sir, the alligator himself didn't wear them so well."

"Well, all right," Dancer agrees reluctantly. "They do look nice. I'll wear them out."

"Very well, sir."

"The suit too," Dancer says.

"Oh but sir, it will be at least three days before we can possibly have your trousers ready."

"Don't you have any already hemmed?"

"Sir," the salesman says, gasping. "You are in Harrod's!"

"Then I'll just have to wear them pinned."

The salesman swallows hard. "Very well, sir."

Two body guards, courtesy of Scotland Yard, escort Dancer and Anne out of the store. Ever since they stepped off the plane it has been the VIP treatment all the way. A black Rolls Royce picked them up at Heathrow and whisked them to a suite done in peach at the Dorchester. A phalanx of police had to hold back the crowds as Anne stepped out of the car. Paparazzi shoved microphones at her asking how much she stood to inherit; what was Turk like in bed and who was her young escort? The British love a scandal more than anyone. Dancer and Anne have already made the cover of *The Sun*—an assemblage of half-truths and speculations so sensational it makes the *New York Post* look like the Bible. Today's headline screeches, ANNE TRADES COLD TURK FOR HOT CHICKEN! Dancer recalls a quote from the biography of Joe Orton, a now deceased British playwright whose jealous lover beat his head in with a hammer. Joe said, "The English are the most tasteless of civilizations, that is why they place such great store by it." Dancer couldn't agree more.

He has only been to one funeral in his life—his grandfather's on his dad's side. In fact, as he thinks about it in the back of the Rolls, he realizes he is amazingly inexperienced when it comes to milestones. Most people, by the time they're twenty-three, know of at least someone other than a relative who has died, someone who has gotten married, someone who has had a child. But Dancer doesn't. He has never been to a wedding, never held a baby in his arms, and aside from his previously mentioned grandfather's, Turk's is his first real funeral. By "real" he means a black-veiled affair—limousines with their lights on, robed priests, obsequious speeches and a floral representation rivaling even the Garden of Eden's—all the morbid spectacle. Turk, disappointingly however, plays the renegade even in death.

The burial is taking place not in a cemetery but in Turk's own back yard . . . in his olympic-sized heated swimming pool. As they pull into the drive, Anne tells Dancer that Turk wanted a burial at sea, but some glitch in maritime laws strictly prohibits it. (Apparently it's illegal unless you're in the Navy and die during time of war.) Dancer, being the pragmatist that he is, asks what will become of his body once it is dumped in the pool. "At least out at sea the fish would have eaten it." Anne says she doesn't know, but the Rolls Royce driver says he read in *The Sun* that they're going to fill in the pool with cement once everyone is through swimming and after the casket sinks.

The Rolls stops in front of Turk's castle and is stampeded by reporters. Anne does her Jackie imitation, pushing her sunglasses against her nose and feathering the tulle veil on her new, black, crimped Oleg Cassini pillbox hat. Everything old is new again. The veil stops just below her eyes. "I'm nervous," Dancer says. Anne whispers, "Just let me do all the talking," and she pastes one of her famous smiles on her face, one that says, "Yes, I'm a star even in these sad times I live in," and she puts her arm through Dancer's and they step out into a barrage of flash bulbs and questions.

"Miss Monet, over here Miss Monet, who is the young man you're with? Is he your new lover?" Dancer doesn't know whether he's supposed to smile or look annoyed or act too bereaved to care.

Anne pretends the reporter is a fool for even asking. "Why, this is Dancer of course. He's writing my next screenplay."

"Dancer who, Miss Monet?"

"Dancer," stresses Anne, "the author."

"Miss Monet, is your relationship with Dancer, the author, a personal one or a professional one?"

"Extremely," Anne says.

"Miss Monet, do you advocate May/December relationships?"

"Only during the summer months, when it's the hottest."

Another reporter edges in. "Miss Monet, is it true Turk willed all his song rights to you?"

"I've seen no will."

"Miss Monet, can you confirm that Turk has a leather-padded pleasure room in his dungeon?"

"No comment."

"Miss Monet..."

"No more questions please," a guard says as he lifts a red velvet rope to let Dancer and Anne onto the drawbridge. It clanks upwards after they cross over it, leaving the reporters and their cameras, like a herd of wildebeests, stranded on the opposite bank of the moat.

Anne and Dancer sign the guest register. Dancer's hand is shaking for some reason and his "D" ends up looking like a number "eight." He recognizes a few of the signatures—an MTV VJ, a famous social climber, a marchioness, a movie producer and someone who is famous for no other reason than that he is. A girl in the foyer with a whiny cockney accent wipes her hands on an Elizabethan tapestry and asks Anne if she prefers a one-piece or a two, and whether Dancer would like a speedo or trunks. She suggests the speedo, but Dancer lies and says he can't swim. Anne does too. The whiny cockney girl shrugs and points them toward the party out back, saying the funeral will begin in about half an hour.

Dancer figures Turk's castle must date back to the Middle Ages, back before even the War of Roses maybe. He never could remember who fought that war or why. All he knows is that one side uses a red rose as the emblem on their flag, the other a white rose. Personally, he likes white roses better, red being such a cliché, but he doesn't know if the white side won or not; and as he stands around trying to look sophisticated in his pinned trousers he wonders how both sides would have distinguished themselves if they had chosen a marigold instead. *What a stupid thing to think of.* He can only blame it on the liveried butlers milling about with their shiny trays offering goodies which he assumed were mints...obviously they weren't.

He has no idea what you'd call the thing constructed above the pool, but it's this huge contraption made of wood girders and a spiraling fiberglass water flume, much like one of those rides at Six Flags where you're supposed to be in a runaway log on some untamed river in Saskatchewan. To Dancer it looks more like a giant spindly-legged spider taking a leak. Way up on top of it is a coffin, behind that, something that looks like a guillotine. A long rope is attached to the top of the guillotine and its other end is tied around the end of the diving board. No one here seems to think it's anything unusual though. Anne explains that Turk had it built a year ago, as a contingency plan in case he couldn't be buried at sea. "Death was his favorite subject, and when he wasn't trying to molest me, he usually talked about his funeral. He always intended to die young, saying that if he could have one wish in the world, he'd wish to go pointlessly at the peak of his career. I don't know how many times I heard him say, 'I don't care that much about eternity, just immortality.'" Anne pulls off her pillbox hat and hurls it into the pool. "Yu know whu Uh mean, Luv?"

"It's so sad," Dancer says, not feeling sad at all but believing he should follow funeral protocol. He hopes he didn't take anything too damaging off one of those trays.

"Sad, Hell. That son of a bitch knew all along what he was doing. Just like Jim Morrison. Just like Janis. Not a talented bone

in his body. Dead before he's thirty. And he's going to live forever!"
She drops into a wrought iron patio chair. "We've got to come up
with a screenplay soon."

"We need a theme," he says.

"Something brilliant. Something Oscar-caliber."

Dancer's mind wanders. There must be a thousand people
here. Some are dressed; some are undressed; some are swimming, some are eating. A buffet like Dancer has never imagined
is set up under a black circus tent amidst this topiary of ivy
dinosaurs and dragons carved from shrubbery. To get to the
buffet though, you have to go through a boxwood maze about
ten feet high, which must cover two acres if an inch. He hears
some people, apparently lost, screaming for help. Others are
screaming only because it seems to be the thing to do. He
swears an ivy brontosaurus just moved. He wonders if he
should scream.

"Are you feeling okay?" Anne asks. She crosses her legs and
arches her head back, letting her dark hair cascade luxuriously
into the air. "I feel perfectly wonderful myself."

"What was on those trays?" he asks.

"God knows... snips and snails and puppy dogs' tails."

Another of the liveried butlers comes by again. He's dressed
like a Chippendale model, wearing just a bow tie and briefs and
hands them a glass of something. "You know," Anne says, sipping
at her something, "we've got to make a decision about our future
relationship."

"What do you mean?"

She pauses a moment, as though trying to think of the best way
to explain a delicate matter to a child. "You don't love me, do you,
Dancer?"

He wasn't quite expecting this. "Well, even though I've only
known you a week..."

"Because I don't want you to fall in love with me. We mean too
much to each other to ruin it. It wouldn't work anyway. I'm a
bitch—a selfish bitch who's got a decade on you."

He nods. "You don't have to say any more. I understand. I have
to be at work again tomorrow anyway." He stands.

"What?" She laughs. "No, sit back down. You don't understand.

I'm not giving you the heave ho. Hell, if I was going to do that, I would have done it the other night at the Palladium. All I'm saying is that we're going to be spending a lot of time together on this project, and ... as fond as I am of passion and all that implies, well I just think it's in our best interest if we keep things as uncomplicated as possible. Believe it or not, I am very disciplined when it comes to my career."

He sees that it has started raining. Funny, the water doesn't even feel wet. A few people open their umbrellas but for the most part, no one seems to notice. His new raw silk suit is getting ruined, not to mention his loafers, his farm-grown alligator loafers. The hem on his trousers starts coming undone, and some of the pins poke out, threatening to stab him in the ankles. He just goes ahead and pulls them all out, all the while wondering if Nova Grey Lovejoy has an alligator purse.

"My point," Anne says, "is that if we want to make this thing work, our relationship should be a purely professional one from here on out. Don't you agree?"

"Well, I suppose that would be best." He sits down in the saturated grass next to Anne and throws his shoes into the pool. He doesn't know why, but everyone else is throwing something of theirs in too. It seems to be the thing to do. Accidentally, one of his shoes hits a bald girl. She climbs out of the pool and throws it back at him, giving him a piece of her mind in the bargain. He asks Anne why the bald girl is painted green. Anne hypothesizes that she is symbolic of one of the seven deadly sins, envy perhaps, and he thinks Anne might have a point because two of the other bald girls are arguing, and they're both fat, so one must be Miss Gluttony and the other Miss Sloth.

Sitting in his socks in the grass in the rain, he suddenly feels very vulnerable. "I don't have any stability in my life, Anne. Not financial. Not emotional. After this weekend I can't go home again, and there may not be a job waiting for me when I get back to New York." She reaches out and strokes his wet hair. Someone puts in a tape of Turk's soon-to-be released posthumous album. A haunting melody floats through the loudspeakers, and the music-insiders who already have the copies start singing along with the lyrics:

I think I can make it
If I don't look back.
I hear a crunching sound in the snow.
Something is behind me.
But I can stand that,
For the room is very beautiful
And I may not see the wolf...

Anne says, "I know how you feel, Dancer. I really do. It's the emptiest feeling in the world..."

"I feel like I'm underwater, down at the very bottom of the ocean, and there's all this pressure on me that I can't overcome. I'm swimming for the light up above me. The water there is like soft crystal, not dense and black. The air is sweet. It must be, or I wouldn't keep trying. I've got to hurry though, before I drown. But if I rush too quickly, I'll get the bends. Time is always against me."

Anne kicks off her pumps and pulls her knees up under her chin, wrapping her arms around her legs. "You're only twenty-three? Sometimes you seem so much older. No one worries about stability at twenty-three. No one I ever knew, but then the eighties are so desperate. I don't understand it. Where are we all heading?"

It begins raining harder. Lightning flashes, illuminating the guillotine at the top of the spindly spider. A girl wearing a necklace made of ice cubes jiggles over to Anne and tells her how much she admires her work. Anne returns the favor by telling her how much she admires her necklace. The girl seems pleased, says that she finds the melting cubes comforting. As she talks, Dancer watches rivulets of water race down her cleavage.

I am almost inside the warm room.
Only my foot remains without,
Held by the door.
There is a wolf chewing on my foot.
But I can stand that,
For the room is very beautiful
And I cannot see the wolf...

A dancing transvestite now sashays over and asks Dancer if he'd like to take a bite of his edible lace leotards before the rain melts them off. Dancer declines. The transvestite asks him if he's sure—they're mulberry flavored after all. Dancer says he's quite sure, but if he gets hungry later he'll definitely call him over. The transvestite boogies away and is replaced by another of the liveried butlers who admits he's really a member of Turk's band, but that they're all dressed incognito. This one claims he's the bass player. Anne says she thought she recognized him but wasn't sure. Her makeup is running in the rain. She holds her head high in defiance. The liveried butler offers Dancer another goodie. Dancer shakes his head this time and says that artists and amphetamines should never mix.

An alleged ring leader of a child prostitution ring comes up and joins them. He says he'd like to change careers and is thinking about getting into acting. A woman into necrophilia asks Anne if it might be possible for her to "view" the corpse. Anne tells her she can bury herself alive with it for all she cares. The alleged ring leader of the child prostitution ring now breaks down in tears and admits that he doesn't have a penis. All eyes involuntarily dart to his pants. He says you can't really tell unless he's naked because otherwise he's always wearing a jock strap stuffed with socks. The liveried butler dressed incognito laughs and drops his tray of "mints." Everyone but Dancer and Anne scramble to pick them up before they get too muddy.

Now a man with scar tissue covering the entire right side of his face walks up to Anne and introduces himself, saying he's Turk's attorney and that he's heard a lot about her—only good things. He says he's sorry, but that Turk bequeathed all the money left over from the funeral to the Royal Institute of Paranormal Sciences. The bequest will be used to study Spontaneous Human Combustion—an inexplicable phenomenon in which people explode into flames and burn to a cinder. "You know," he says, "S.H.C." He smiles and accepts a slightly soiled mint from the liveried butler, then turns back to Anne. "Turk did, however, leave this lovely castle to you."

Anne turns to Dancer and says, "Tell me this is a bad dream."

Soon all my flesh will be eaten away.
I can then pull my leg inside,
To wait until I bleed to death.
But I can stand that too,
For the room is very beautiful
And I never saw the wolf.

Someone turns down the stereo and asks if he can please have everyone's attention. Once he gets it he announces that the man with no penis, the girl with the ice cube necklace and the dancing transvestite will deliver the eulogy. (Actually he calls them by name, but Dancer can't remember what he calls them.) The three stand up by the diving board and each says a few empty words. The dancing transvestite, whose leotards have completely melted by now, tries repeatedly to light a candle but the rain keeps putting it out. The girl in the ice cube necklace is still jiggling but her exposed breasts are turning blue. She's making eyes at the man with no penis... and through all this Dancer is saying to himself: At least I've got two thousand brand new dollars. At least I can pay my bills another month. He remembers he owes his grandmother $100 and vows to pay her back. Can it be that he was in Alabama only thirty-six hours ago? It's hard to believe he's on the same planet.

What follows is more Grand Guignol. The dancing transvestite finally succeeds in lighting a candle, but only by holding his palm above the flame. He stifles a grimace and moves the candle beneath the rope, the one attached to the diving board at one end and the guillotine at the other. People start chanting and fluttering their fingers from the ground up to the sky. The girl with the ice cube necklace sucks on her cubes one by one and does something like an Egyptian version of the hula around the pool. The rope above the candle begins turning black and frazzling. Turk's attorney whispers to Anne that he realizes it's an inappropriate time to discuss business, but that he has some papers for her to sign. Perhaps they could have lunch tomorrow? A jagged sliver of lightning flashes again, the rope snaps and the guillotine blade lurches suddenly upwards instead of down. Turk's coffin, painted enamel red, pops out from between the guillotine and drops into the water flume, where like a nightmare galleon, it gushes downward and scrapes around the spiral with all eyes helplessly glued to its descent. Dancer turns to Anne with a baffled look on his face. "I'm ready to leave anytime you are."

Anne grabs his arm. "I'm right behind you."

They push their way through the chanting worshipers, into the castle (Anne's castle) and past the whiny Cockney girl. Dancer opens the front door for Anne and quickly looks back through the rain-spattered windows. He hears applause as the red casket shoots like a bloody bullet from the flume, barely avoiding a collision with one of the bald-headed seven deadly sins—Miss Lust, it looks like. He slams the door shut. He and Anne dash across the lowering drawbridge and he gets splinters in his feet because he's only wearing socks, wet socks at that. They leap through the congealed mob of reporters and into the back of the Rolls. "Hit it," Anne shouts, and the car skids away.

Anne finger-combs her rain-matted hair. "God, I hate groupies," she says.

"Where to, Mum?" the driver asks.

"The Dorchester." She takes a drenched handkerchief out of her bag and wipes the smeared mascara from around her eyes. "Can you believe Turk? willing all his money to some hokey Spontaneous Rejuvenation crap—frogs from rain and turtles from mud—leaving me nothing but that heap of bricks?"

"Human combustion," Dancer corrects. "Spontaneous Human Combustion."

Anne rolls down her window and lets the rain blow against her face. "Rejuvenation...combustion...water and fire...birth and death...all the same thing, I guess."

Dancer thinks he has never seen Anne look so beautiful as now with the wind and the rain flying around inside the car. He moves toward her, loosens her dress straps and lets them drape at her elbows. He massages her soft wet shoulders. She asks, "What is the meaning of life, Dancer? I mean, seriously." He nuzzles his head against her neck and wraps his arms around her waist, then lifts her hands to his mouth and nibbles her fingers one at a time.

"If you think about it," he says, "nothing *really* matters." He takes off his jacket and tie, unbuttons his shirt and pushes his chest against her back. Her wet crepe dress is clammy yet warm against his skin.

The driver looks over his shoulder and the Rolls swerves, tossing Dancer and Anne onto their backs.

"It seems like life should have a purpose," Anne says. "Like we should be moving *toward* something. But we all keep running in circles..."

Dancer lifts himself over Anne and pulls up her dress. She unsnaps the buttons on his trousers (they're so continental, they don't even have a zipper). He pulls down her silk Peek-A-Boo panties. The driver takes off his cap and wipes his forehead. "Well," Anne says, raising her mouth to meet Dancer's, "so much for professional relationships."

IT WAS THE MUSHROOMS THAT DID IT

or

Chapter

14

SHACKLED TO THE walls of the dungeon are three emaciated wax victims, their frozen features sadly gazing up Marie Antoinette's severed head in a basket. A strobe light sizzles across a man strapped in a steel chair—Gary Gilmore is being electrocuted. Dancer hears screams followed by slicing sounds and then hooves on cobblestones. Jack the Ripper has dismembered another prostitute. In the garrotte, one man is being slowly strangled as another tightens the screw in an iron collar around his neck... It's late in the afternoon and Dancer and Anne are at Madame Tussaud's House of Wax.

Dancer now feels pretty normal. After the funeral he and Anne took a hot bath and a short nap. Anne then suggested they do a little sightseeing, but first they did the proper thing and had tea. It wasn't good tea though, or at least he didn't enjoy it because it had these little stems in it that tasted like licorice. Sex in a Rolls followed by licorice tea followed by the Chamber of Horrors. Things sure do go downhill in a hurry.

"Where do we go from here?" Dancer asks.

"Well, we could go to the planetarium next door, or shopping down Sloane Street, or..."

"No, I mean where do we go with the screenplay? Are you staying in London? Going back to L.A.? New York? Is this going to be a collaboration or am I just supposed to mail it to you when I'm finished? We don't even have an idea of what it should be about."

She says, "But I'm sure we'll come up with something in a few days."

"A few *days!* I can't stay in London that long."

"Sure you can. We'll discuss it over dinner tonight."

"But Anne, I've got to go back to New York tonight."

"Why tonight?"

"Well, first, I have a job—a job I can't afford to lose. Second, my roommate and I will be kicked out of our apartment if we don't pay our rent by the fifth, which is tomorrow. Third, I'm actually worried about what might have happened to the moron."

She sighs. She and Dancer are watching Jean Paul Marat bleed to death in his bathtub. "All right," she says, "but at least wait until tomorrow morning. If you left tonight you'd just have to go directly from the airport to work. They won't fire you for missing one day. Besides, I really do need to discuss some things over dinner with you... I've been thinking about what you said about stability."

"That I don't have any?"

"Exactly." She smiles and kind of cocks her head. "I have a proposition for you."

"Oh..."

"Not that kind of proposition," she says.

"What kind?"

"We'll discuss it tonight, over dinner and wine."

He casts his eyes downwards, so he doesn't have to look at her. "Are you staying in London?"

"Just until the end of the week. I've got to sign those papers for the castle. I don't want it, but if it's going to be handed to me, the least I can do is accept it."

"And where to at the end of the week?"

"Why," she teases, "will you miss me?"

"I will."

She clucks her tongue and stares at a smiling woman serving her husband poisoned soup. "You really are so different, Dancer."

"I'm not different. I'll just miss you, that's all."

"Well, if it's any consolation, I'll miss you too. I feel so relaxed around you, like I've known you for years. You like me not because of who I am but because I'm me. That means a lot." She runs her fingers slowly over the glass eyes of a man hanging from a meat hook. "Just think, these people will be tortured forever, never getting any older, never dying, but always in pain."

Dancer looks long and hard at the wax victim. *What is it about...? Something she just said...* Slowly an idea begins to form. "Wait a minute," he says. "That's it. Anne, that's it!"

She jerks her hand away. "What?"

"Your screenplay."

"A man on a meat hook?"

"Someone who doesn't age."

"I'm not doing a vampire movie. I refuse. I may be hard-up, but I'm not a fool. No legitimate actress does horror."

"I'm not talking about horror. I'm talking about tragedy. I'm talking about a beautiful, sad woman, a woman who for some reason she doesn't understand, has stopped aging...just stopped." Anne's eyes begin to brighten. "But rather than a blessing, it's a curse. She has to keep moving all the time, never staying in one place for more than a few years, never being able to fall in love, no roots, no stability, no past or future, only the eternal present."

"Oh, my God," Anne says softly. "Dancer, you know, I think it could work." For a few moments she seems lost in thought, then the corners of her lips turn up in a wide smile. "It's the script I've been waiting for. The script I've been dreaming of. It's perfect. Why, it's an Oscar!"

It is now 10:00 p.m. and Dancer and Anne are having dinner and fine wine in a posh club on the roof of a tall building. The club, appropriately named The Gardens, has glass walls that look out onto a beautifully landscaped Babylon, resplendent with live flamingos, palm trees, a gurgling brook and fountained arbors where people smoke illegal substances and indulge in self-promotion. Below them twinkles the city—a million diamonds on dark velvet.

He pours her another glass of Pouilly Fumé and lights himself a cigarette (lemon yellow) upon request. He inhales and blows the smoke slowly into her eyes. She asks him to do it again. "How about now?"

"Not yet," he says.

"Again then." He blows again.

"Now?"

"Okay," he says, "they're red."

"I look like I've been crying all day?"

"In mortal agony."

"Perfect," she says. "There's no telling who we'll run into in here. Appearances are everything." She swigs her wine and rubs her temples. "Whoa, but talk about a passive high."

The waiter clears away their plates. "Would you like to walk around on the roof, Anne, get some fresh air?"

"Why not?" she says.

They carry their wine through glass doors, and Anne chases four water birds, egrets or ducks or something, into a pond. Dancer sits on a stone and explains how he saw a television program last month about food in China, that in some of the rural provinces the peasants use ducks instead of fishing poles to catch fish. "It's a method they've used for centuries. They tie a rope around a duck's neck and drop it into the water. The duck is able to bob for fish but it can't swallow them because of the rope. All the peasant has to do is yank the duck back into the boat, squeeze its neck, and the fish pops right out." Dancer pulls at a clump of flowers and sprinkles them into the water. "And these stupid ducks will do this all night, never getting anything at all to eat."

"But the bright side," Anne says, "is that neither party has to mess with worms." She smiles. "There must be a moral here somewhere." They wander up to an elevated plateau of the roof, sit down cross-legged and gaze out over London drinking their wine.

"Isn't it beautiful," he says.

"A second-rate country living on the dole," she says. "And to think they ruled the world only a few years back. See what happens if you don't adapt to change—you slowly disappear. Like me."

"Hey, lighten up a little. We have a gorgeous view in front of us. Besides, you're too much a survivor to disappear."

"Tell that to the dodos, Mr. Darwin." She moves closer to Dancer and places her hands inside his. Her violet chiffon dress and train-length matching scarf ripple in the breeze. She tosses the scarf around her neck. "Just call me Isadora." The moonlight turns her skin to alabaster. (Dancer has only the vaguest idea what alabaster is, but he imagines the comparison is an accurate one, albeit a trifle overused.) Staring out at the city lights, Anne says, "Should she have just discovered she's stopped aging, or has this been a problem of hers for quite some time, a few hundred years maybe?"

"*Who?*" Dancer asks, still caught in the spell cast by Anne's beauty.

"The tragi-heroine in our screenplay."

"Oh," he says. "Um, why don't we say two hundred years, no wait, let's go back even further, give her some real history."

"Not too far though. I don't look good in animal skins."

"Well... how about the early eighteenth century?"

"Yeah... yeah, that's it. She was a Puritan. Of clean spirit and humble faith, a good woman." She turns to him. "Actresses cast against type *always* win Oscars. Think of a name, Dancer. She needs an exotic name. Something turbulent. Something ageless. Something beautiful."

"Ramara," he says without hesitating. "Her name is Ramara."

"How pretty. What does it mean?"

"Nothing, I just made it up. But this woman, Ramara, got deathly ill on her thirty-sixth birthday—"

"Thirty-fourth birthday," Anne says. "I can easily pass for thirty-four."

He pours more wine. "Okay, she got deathly ill on her thirty-fourth birthday, but—"

"It was the mushrooms that did it," Anne says. "She loved wild mushrooms."

"Fine then. Ramara got deathly ill on her thirty-fourth birthday from wild mushrooms, but somehow she pulled through. Then, let's see... we fast-forward. Ten years have passed. She should be an old woman by the standards of her day—"

Anne interrupts. "All her friends' hair have turned gray, their facial muscles are sagging, eyelids drooping, but Ramara, to everyone's amazement is unchanged...you know, I like that name, it kind of rhymes with tomorrow."

"People," Dancer says sinisterly, "begin to talk."

"They accuse her of being a witch."

"And drive her out of town."

Anne takes a big gulp of wine. "She has to survive on her own now, a female Daniel Boone alone in the savage wilderness for the next hundred years. No women's lib. No automatic cash machines. No facials at Elizabeth Arden. Just Ramara, hiding alone behind false names and dreams of super malls."

"What do you think she should look like?" he asks. "I don't see her as a thin woman..."

"I'll wear padding," Anne says with delight. "Oh, this is too good. And through the years, as she picks up more and more polish, she begins to diet, she loses her accent, has a nose job—a transformation! Another sure bet for the Oscar!"

He says, "She realizes she needs a steady income, but something that allows her to keep a low profile at the same time. So she starts investing in gold and copper mines as the West opens up, oil fields in Texas and coastal property in Southern California..."

"Selling it at an astronomical profit a hundred years later. And every fifty years she hocks all her furniture at antique prices. By the twentieth century she's this elegant, sophisticated creature, wealthy beyond all dreams. But still she isn't happy. She wants love. She wants a man."

"Time painfully passes," Dancer says. "Ramara grows more and more paranoid that her secret may be discovered. She slowly turns into a recluse, alone in her mansion, rotating a new staff of servants every five years. She doesn't allow any photographs to be taken. She has no birth records, no social security number, she can't own a driver's license or an American Express card...it's getting harder and harder for her to live in a modern world."

"But she has the most beautiful period portraits hanging on her walls," Anne says wistfully. "Ramara by Whistler, Ramara as a Gilded Age socialite by John Singer Sargent, Ramara as a flapper by Augustus John—and every morning she wakes up and looks to her portraits and then to her mirror, hoping against hope that she'll see a wrinkle or that first gray hair; something to prove that she's mortal after all. Until finally, just when she's abandoned all hope, it happens... her first crow's feet! She's euphoric. At last she can start a normal life—get married, go to parties, have a listed phone number—because after nearly three centuries of heartache and loneliness, Ramara knows she is going to die!"

"Music up," Dancer says, "credits roll."

"Oh God, Dancer, it's perfect. "Time-defying movies are really in right now. And the twist on aging, that someone would actually want to grow older, to die, why it's brilliant. We can really milk it down to the nitty-gritty too: how she lives in constant fear of getting ill, a cold or the flu, that she'll have to see a doctor, and he'll find out she's somehow different and want to exploit her, or better yet, use her as his human guinea pig. The possibilities are endless." She tosses her just-call-me-Isadora scarf again, pulls it like a boa from around her neck and flings it over the side of the building. It drifts and flitters up and away, tumbling into the darkness until it vanishes. "It'll be the comeback of the decade. Hollywood loves a comeback. Comebacks give hope to all the fallen stars, a reason for them to say, 'Well, Anne Monet did it, washed-up Anne Monet, so maybe I can too.' That's what they'll all say." She paces around a big tree strung with shimmering lights. "Why I'll be box office all over again—the best tables at Spago and Lutece, invitations to the White House, the cover of *People* magazine, an interview with Barbara Walters... Cybill Shepherd eat your heart out."

"You're assuming it's going to be a blockbuster?"

She stares him dead in the eyes. "You're damned right I am. Always strive for the impossible, Dancer. Because it's true what they say—you can have anything in the world, you can be anything you want... anything. Most people don't actually believe this. They'll repeat it. They'll think it can happen to others, but never to them. And the reason they won't think it can happen is that they won't *make* it happen. We, my friend, are two people who will."

"And God bless America."

She smiles to herself for a moment, reveling in her certain glory. "You know, I'd like to be able to show a producer a final draft by the end of the summer."

He leaps up. "The end of the summer? Jesus Anne, come down to Earth. It's already July. I'll be lucky if I can send the first draft to you by Christmas."

"But Dancer, we've already figured out the plot. How difficult could the rest of it be?"

He shakes his head. "You don't understand. Brainstorming is the easy part. The execution is something totally different. I mean, this story takes place for the most part in the past, right? Do you realize how much research is going to be involved? I've got to find out how people lived back then, how they talked, what they talked about…I've got to verify dates, pore over medical journals to learn about the aging process…this can't be just some made-for-television hatchet job, you know. I don't want any anachronisms. Every detail has to be authentic. Perfect. The very best, Anne. If for no other reason than personal satisfaction."

She says, "Screw personal satisfaction. It has to be the best for one reason only—the sake of our careers." She adjusts the bracelets on her wrists and throws her wine glass over the side of the building. He hears it shatter against something way down below. He throws his over, too, but for some reason it doesn't shatter. God knows what he hit. "Tell me how you write, Dancer. How long it takes you, how you revise and edit, that sort of thing. I don't know about you, but I can't give a good performance if my life isn't in order. How do you even concentrate without any stability?"

He picks at an imaginary thread on his new suit (the one he bought on Sloane Street, right next to the pet shoppe where he found a replacement for Ambrosia). "That's just it, Anne, I can't. Ideally, I need to be all by myself when I write, but somehow that's a luxury I can't afford. So usually I write at work, but even at my job there's always some piddling distraction."

"What about at night?"

"I can't write at night. Don't ask me why. I just can't. When I was in college, I always had to wait tables at night. Maybe I trained myself only to be creative during the day."

"Maybe. I heard Hemingway could only write standing up. I'd like to hear the story behind that one." She looks out into the wafting clouds. "I guess all artists have their little quirks though. It's what makes them special." She touches his arm and points to a tiny star peeping through a gap in the sky. "Make a wish, Dancer. Hurry, before the clouds cover it back up."

He closes his eyes for a moment. "Okay," he says, "I made one."

"What did you wish for?"

"If I tell it won't come true."

"Silly boy, that only applies to birthdays, when you can't blow out all your candles. If you wish on a star you're supposed to tell. It doubles your chances of coming true."

"Does it now?"

"Uh huh."

"If you really want to know, I wished that we stay friends forever."

"Déjà vu," Anne says, smiling. "I wished the same thing."

"Well, you know what that means, don't you?"

"That our lives are going according to plan?"

"Uh huh." He suddenly feels guilty. "Anne, I'm sorry about this afternoon in the back of the car. I . . . I should have respected you. It wouldn't have happened if I hadn't taken that—"

"You didn't hear me screaming rape, did you?"

"Just the same. You're right about our relationship. It'll be strictly professional from now on."

"A professional friendship," she says, extending her hand.

"A professional friendship." He gives her hand a shake, then pulls her up on her feet. "Should we go back in?"

"Just one more thing." A smirk crosses her face. "It's time for that proposition I mentioned earlier." She takes his hand and leads him to a sort of Byzantine alcove. "Sit down."

"Oh no," he says, "sounds intense." He sits on a bench, leaning against a trellis of exotic flowering vines. Across from him a marble lion's head on a wall drools water into a big oval pool of lily pads. Shining up from the bottom of the pool are hundreds of gold and silver coins.

Anne sort of twirls serenely around the pool in her violet chiffon dress. The wind catches between the layers of chiffon and for some reason Dancer thinks of faerie nymphs and vestal virgins and ancient Greece. "Dancer," she says, holding the outer layer of chiffon above her head like a religious shroud, "did you know—" Just at this moment she's interrupted by an arguing couple walking over.

It's a wrinkly old prune and his twenty-year-old girlfriend. The twenty-year-old girlfriend is wearing a silver lamé dress and a diamond choker, but she rips the diamond choker off in a wild fit after the wrinkly old prune tries putting his arm around her. Dancer figures he must be seventy if he's a day. Next the girlfriend slaps the diamond choker across his face and says, "Your wife just better die bloody damned soon, that's all I have to say."

The wrinkly old prune looks apologetically at Dancer and Anne, but his wrinkles change position as he recognizes Anne. "I don't believe it," he says. "Anne Monet! After all these years."

Dancer notices the color drain from Anne's face.

"I directed one of your first movies, don't you remember, Anne? Why, it must be twenty years since we've seen each other." He smiles rapaciously. "You were just a teenager then . . ."

Anne doesn't say anything. She merely pulls her holy shroud down from around her head and fixes her hair.

"Yes, well," the wrinkly old prune says, "how time stagnates." Dancer can't tell if he's being cute or not. He does notice, however, that the wrinkly old prune's eyes are like flat-black balls, sucking in all the light but reflecting none back. They roll slowly back and forth, sizing up Dancer and Anne's relationship. "Anne," he says, "I can see you've hardly changed a bit."

Anne looks quickly at the girlfriend and says, "Likewise," in a barely audible breath.

The girlfriend sulks at a distance, plucking diamonds out of her choker and throwing them into the sky. She looks a little sloshed. Both of them do. The wrinkly old prune sort of nods toward her and smiles at Dancer and Anne, his dentures a dazzling and lecherous white.

Anne manages to ask the wrinkly old prune, "What brings you to London?" in a voice that indicates she not only couldn't care less what he's doing in London, but that she wishes he were anywhere else in the world.

"I'm casting a revival of Tennessee Williams's *Sweet Bird of Youth,* but we're having the worst time finding a lead for the role of Princess Kosmonopolis, the drug-addled and ravaged old actress." He looks into Anne's smoke-red eyes. "You know, Anne, you'd be *ideal* for the part."

Now it's Anne's turn to slap the wrinkly old prune (W. O. P.) which she does with a vengeance, as if this is something she's been waiting all her life to do.

The W. O. P. backs away, saying, "You're hardly in a position to jeopardize what's left of your miserable career, my dear, especially after the untimely but highly farcical death of your fiancé, 'Turk the Turd.'"

Anne slaps the W. O. P. again. "You and... and your little girlfriend there can just go straight to Hell and fuck yourselves."

The girlfriend plucks another diamond and snaps, "We already went there earlier tonight, thank you, and we quite enjoyed ourselves."

The W. O. P. rubs his cheeks and gives the girlfriend a menacing look, one that says a beautiful child is put on this earth for two reasons only—to be looked at and played with, not listened to. He turns back to Anne and says, "You'll pay for that remark. By this time tomorrow you won't even be able to get a job with the circus."

"Hah!" Anne says. "You flatter yourself if you think you have that much power."

The W. O. P. shakes a pruny finger at Anne. "At least I'm still respected in this business." He scowls at Dancer. "At least I haven't resorted to hiring for sex."

"How dare you insult my friend with your senile presumptions."

Dancer thinks, now there's a good one—presumptuous old prune—P. O. P. He'd punch P. O. P. in the stomach if P. O. P. weren't so incredibly old and so incredibly drunk. As he is though, a punch might just kill him. So Dancer decides to take a more reasoned approach: "I think it would be a good idea if you and your lady friend went back inside."

Anne says, "Dancer, there's no call for politeness." She whips about to face P. O. P. "Just what do you call Little Miss Glitter Rocks there, your nurse?"

P. O. P. grins. "Little Mi... Kit just happens to be a very fine, up-and-coming actress." Dancer thinks P. O. P. is only saying this, as opposed to actually believing it.

Anne says, "Well, there's no denying that last adjective I'm sure."

"Listen to the jealous bitch," P. O. P. says. Dancer can't believe he's hearing such ungentlemanly accusations. "You never got over the fact that you can't play the ingénue forever, did you?" He motions Little Miss Glitter Rocks to his side and puts his arm around her. Little Miss Glitter Rocks sort of grinds her diamond choker between her hands impatiently, twists her head and tilts up her nose.

Anne circles around the two of them, glaring at P. O. P. with a hatred Dancer hopes he never sees again. "God damn you!" Dancer is glad Anne doesn't have access to any sort of lethal weaponry right now. "At best you were never better than second-rate, just daddy's little boy trying his hand at the family business. The only reason I even worked with you at all was that I was just starting out and you were the only thing I could get. You had no idea what you were doing; as inexperienced as I was, I could see that, and what's more, you were too drunk to care."

Suddenly, Dancer is back in Alabama... at the barbecue yesterday. It's not Anne screaming these accusations at some dirty old man he's never met, it's Dancer screaming at his dad. Was it only yesterday? Wasn't it more like a century ago?

"It was only blind luck that the film was a hit," Anne says. "Blind damn luck!"

True, Dancer thinks, it was blind luck that I even met Anne at all. What if the adult of Islam had never tried to steal money from me? What if the woman in the white dress had not gotten shoved in front of the Train of Tears? What if I hadn't made a mistake in Grand Central... what if I had given the fake nun a one dollar bill instead of a ten dollar bill after all?... I would never have met Anne, that's what. And we would never have come to London. We wouldn't be writing a screenplay. I wouldn't have won $2,000. Why, I'd be sweating bricks in Brooklyn, worrying about how I was going to pay the bills, how I was going to survive. My career would have been over before it had begun.

P. O. P. laughs at Anne and squeezes Little Miss Glitter Rocks's ass. Little Miss Glitter Rocks takes the remnants of her diamond choker and slaps him across the face again. This time she draws a tiny rivulet of blood. P. O. P. savagely rips a sleeve off Little Miss Glitter Rocks's lamé gown and dabs it at his face.

Little Miss Glitter Rocks stands back and stares at P. O. P. in unbelieving horror. "My dress, you bloody ripped my dress!"

"Be glad I didn't bloody rip your arm off with it."

Dancer reminds himself again not to forget to return his grandmother's one hundred dollars. He doesn't know why this should come to mind now. It just does.

P. O. P. turns back to Anne. "Well, as long as we're writing on the walls here, why don't we just finish the story. Do you think you were the only one forced to work with second-rate talent? I begged my brother to replace you...beeeeged." P. O. P. looks at Dancer and says, "He was the producer, my brother." Then he looks back at Anne. "But he wouldn't touch you—a talentless little upstart, and he wouldn't touch you. Just make the picture as quickly as you can, he said. Naturally, I kept asking him, why the rush? Why not spend some money? Why not get some real talent? Why use a bimbo who keeps screwing up her lines. Finally, one day he told me. Because she fucked my son, he said."

"Liar!"

"That's right. Fucked him and then threatened to scream rape."

"You goddamned liar!" Anne turns to Dancer. "Not a word of it's true. Not a word."

"Just another teenage runaway peddling her ass on Sunset Boulevard. That's all she was. A thousand came before her, and a thousand came after her."

"That's *enough,*" Dancer says. "It doesn't matter." Dancer is now glad he's the one who doesn't have access to any kind of lethal weaponry.

For some reason Little Miss Glitter Rocks is laughing so hard she can barely breathe, and in between gasps for air she sings to the tune of a nursery rhyme, "Bah bah, blackmail, have you any pull?"

"But Miss Monet here was different," P. O. P. says. "She was much smarter than the others, even remembered my nephew's license plate. I'll bet you remember it to this very day, don't you, Anne? Come on and tell us. You *never* forgot a number."

Anne clutches her ears and sinks slowly to her knees in the grass. She doesn't even seem aware anyone is speaking to her. Dancer puts his arms around her and shouts at P. O. P., "Stop it! None of it makes a difference now! For God's sake, stop it."

Little Miss Glitter Rocks is holding her stomach to keep from doubling over. "Yes sir, yes sir, one cunt full."

"One of her regulars worked in the police department, a greasy toothless bum. They had a deal set up. Once a week our innocent Anne here gave him a free piece of ass. In exchange, he'd run all the numbers she'd collected through criminal records and call her back if anything looked promising. With my nephew she hit pay dirt. You see, another little actress had already tried Anne's scam, so he'd been indicted for a possible rape once before. We got him off because he was a minor himself at the time. But Anne knew he wouldn't have a chance in Hell the second go around, no matter whether a jury knew she was a whore or not."

Suddenly, like a wild tiger Anne springs at P. O. P., raking her nails into his already bleeding face. She knocks him against the drooling marble lion and pummels him with her fists.

P. O. P. laughs, too drunk to feel the punches. "Too bad about your movie deal. What's it been now? Going on five years, isn't it? That's professional suicide in this business."

Anne bites into P. O. P.'s neck. P. O. P. raises back his pruny hand and strikes it against Anne's shoulder.

"Get her! Kill her!" Little Miss Glitter Rocks shouts.

Dancer pleads, "Anne, no! Don't play his game. That's what he wants you to do." He tries pulling her away.

"Leave me alone, Dancer. I've been waiting to kill this bastard for the last twenty years!" She shouts at P. O. P. "Why don't you tell the whole story? Why don't you mention how your precious nephew beat me up and dumped me on the side of the road? Why don't you mention that I was in the hospital for nearly two months, that I almost died."

"Liar!" P. O. P. shouts.

"Kill her," Little Miss Glitter Rocks yells.

Reflexively Dancer slaps Little Miss Glitter Rocks, but instantly regrets it, realizing he has set her off. She kicks him in the knees, kicks him in the groin, punches him in the stomach. He tries grabbing her arms, but Anne rams the toe of her pumps square into Little Miss Glitter Rocks's butt, knocking her face first into the lily pool. Uh oh, Dancer thinks, we've had it now.

Little Miss Glitter Rocks stands up screaming and dripping clumps of slime. "Pervert! Pervert!" Now P. O. P. kicks at Anne. Dancer punches P. O. P. It doesn't kill him, thank God, but he stumbles into the pool too. Little Miss Glitter Rocks hurls a fistful of gold coins at Dancer, grabs his sore knees and drags him wincing toward the edge. Anne tries to hold Dancer back from the water, but P. O. P. pulls Anne's chiffon dress, ripping it in the process. And before any of them realize it, they're all four in the lily pool—dripping slime, clawing at faces, ripping at clothing, and smacking each other with lily pads.

It's nearly dawn.

The police department is in a dilapidated old building and the walls are the same color as rotten apricots. No one has filed any charges except The Gardens. The four of them—Dancer, Anne, P. O. P. and Little Miss Glitter Rocks—will have to split the cost of replacing the lily pads they destroyed, and naturally they were some of the rarest in the world and have to be imported from a swamp valley in the Congo somewhere. If that weren't enough, Dancer is sitting in yet another wet and ruined suit, and his underwear is climbing up his crotch. Sitting next to him, Anne looks like the grand prize winner at a Halloween fright ball. Both of them are caked in green sludge.

"I wonder if we'll make the cover of *The Sun* again?" Dancer asks. He rather liked that photograph of himself on yesterday's cover.

"Naturally," Anne says, lighting up a cigarette.

Someone gives them a form to sign. Anne smiles and accepts the pen. Dancer guesses that P. O. P. and Little Miss Glitter Rocks are in another room signing the same form. All four of them have been warned that neither party is allowed to see the other as long as they're still on English soil. This suits Dancer just fine. He accepts the pen from Anne and scribbles his name. The policeman in front of them snort of sniffs the air and Anne flashes him one of her I'm-a-celebrity-so-go-fuck-yourself-smiles. He looks the other way and asks if she wouldn't mind autographing his coffee napkin before she leaves.

"Not at all."

Now the policeman (he really is a nice policeman) asks if Dancer the Author wouldn't mind signing his name as well.

"Me?"

"My Missus is a big reader. She'll get a bloody kick out of a famous author's signature."

So Dancer happily obliges, and Anne, in a swirl of tattered muddy chiffon and muck-plastered hair, leads the way out. "You look like something that escaped from the sewers," Dancer says once they're out of the building.

"And you the Prince of Decomposition."

So the Sewer Escapee and the Prince of Decomposition walk along in the pre-dawn darkness. It's raining of course, and they kick at the sidewalk and maneuver around garbage cans heading back toward their hotel. "Well, there goes another night of needed sleep," Dancer says.

"You can always sleep on the plane," Anne says wearily. She picks up a discarded umbrella and tries opening it. Two of the little metal sticks poke out the top, but otherwise it seems to work well enough. "I'm *so* tired," she says. He takes the umbrella and holds it over both of them. She places her head against his shoulder as they walk. "Do you hate me, Dancer?"

"Of course I don't hate you. Why do you ask that?"

"Because I would hate me if I were you."

"No, you wouldn't. You would love you if you were me."

"Damn, you're good with pronouns. It's a gift. It really is." She pauses a moment. "I wish I had a gift. But all I ever had was my looks, and I knew I'd have to use them if I ever planned on making anything of myself." He puts an arm around her muddy waist, and they listen to the sound of their shoes on the sidewalk and the rain pattering on top the umbrella. "So one day I just got on a train and left Brooklyn forever. I had sixty-three dollars to my name. All I ever wanted was a better life, that's all, just a better life. Like the people in the movies."

"You don't have to apologize to me, Anne."

"I know. It's just that... well, sometimes I wish I had been a little more scrupulous."

"From what I heard tonight, it doesn't sound to me like scruples are exactly the ticket to success in Hollywood."

"Dancer, it's a vicious place. At least in New York people don't bother with facades. If they're going to slit your throat, they at least look the part and tell you so. In L. A., everyone is friendly. Everyone is beautiful. And they're all wearing masks." She squeezes his hand and says, "I just want you to know that I took my mask off a long time ago. I'm not the same person I had to be back then. I've changed."

"I believe you, Anne. I really do. And I like the person you've become."

She wipes at her eyes. "Oh God, Dancer. What did I ever do without you?" She plants a big kiss on his cheeks.

They cross over a small bridge, and Anne throws their umbrella over the side. It drifts down and rests on top of the water. They watch it float under the bridge and come out on the other side. She says, "You know that proposition of mine?"

"You never got around to it."

"Good, because it's no longer a proposition. It's a command." The umbrella floats into a swifter current and whirls around in wobbly circles until it drifts away to where the stream and sky merge together. "Did you know I have a beach house in Laguna? It's my retreat from the world, a place I go to get away from every-thing—plenty of privacy, an inspirational place... a perfect place for a writer to work."

"You mean like the writer of an Oscar-winning screenplay?"

"Yes, that kind of writer." They lean over the railing of the bridge and watch their faces in the mirror below. "Do you know what Friday is, Dancer?"

"Other than the 8th you mean?"

"Friday is your last day of work at that ad agency."

"The Greasy Sleaze Bucket," he says.

"Friday is your last night in New York."

"The Big Rotten Apple."

"So guess what that makes Saturday?"

"The beginning of my life?"

"Do you have any furniture you'll need to take? I've got plenty you know, a typewriter and word processor too—state of the art stuff. The place is fully furnished."

"You must have been expecting me."

"For quite some time now."

"Where should I meet you? When?"

The corners of her mouth go up. "The fountain in front of the Plaza. Noon Saturday."

Now the mirror below them reflects a soft cobalt color as the first ray of daylight breaks through the clouds. Anne gets a determined look on her face. "We're going to have this screenplay finished by the end of the summer. At that time I'm going to sell it to a producer. By this same time next year I'm going to be the number one box office attraction, and you, Dancer dear, are going to be the hottest script writer in the business. Now what do you say to that?"

"There's no business like show business."

A CLOUDY FILM OF FLOUR

or

Chapter

15

GETTING BACK THROUGH customs at Kennedy is *such* a bitch. They won't believe Dancer when he explains his reason for not having a passport. "Oh sure you were at Turk's funeral with Anne Monet," they say, "and I suppose you played croquet with the Queen too." Dancer shows them his *Sun* cover, but they say that his picture in a newspaper does not constitute international immunity.

"Well, why don't you call the Dorchester and talk with Anne Monet personally?"

"Oh, somebody's going to talk all right, but it's sure not going to be Anne Monet." As they lead him into a private room one of them asks him, "Have you ever seen *Midnight Express?*"

He hasn't, and he doesn't think he wants to either, because once in the private room they frisk him and ask him to please remove his clothes. He tells them he'd rather not. They ask him again, but this time it doesn't sound too much like a question. He reluctantly complies and one of them opens a drawer, removing a rather small but streamlined flashlight. "Would you turn around and spread your legs please?"

"For what?"

"Because I'm in love with you," he says flatly.

Dancer gives them all a once-over. He debates whether to just run as fast as he can, but decides a naked man running through an airport might look suspicious, so he closes his eyes and turns around, hoping this indignity will be over quickly. What they do with the flashlight he thought only happened in triple-X movies.

"Nothing," the one with the flashlight says.

"You can put your clothes back on," another says. "Why are they so wrinkled and wet?"

Dancer says, "Because London is old and rainy."

"Why are they wrinkled and wet?"

"I was fighting in a lily pond."

"Why are they wrinkled and wet?"

"I'm an anti-American Soviet communist drug smuggler, but try as I might, I can't tell the difference between Russian dressing and Thousand Island."

None of them smile. "What's in the plastic bag, son?"

"My goldfish, Ambrosia. What does it look like?"

"Oh, it looks like a goldfish all right, but don't you realize that the transportation of tropical fish is illegal?" Dancer says he doesn't think goldfish are a tropical species, that he even saw some swimming around under a layer of ice when he went to the botanical gardens in Brooklyn this past March.

"What's inside your goldfish, son?"

"Organs and things," he says.

"We believe you," they say as they dump poor Ambrosia on a table and hack her in two. Both pieces flop around on the steel table for a few seconds and then the organs and things stream out into a gelatinous blob. He guesses it's just his destiny that any goldfish of his will die of mutilation.

Finally, after what seems like hours, he has the sense to ask if the same customs inspector who passed him and Anne through two days before is working today.

"I think he might be," the one in love with him says.

And luckily he is. They bring him in. He recognizes Dancer, warns him to never let this happen again, that he could have been "a terrorist with a bomb up his ass, and then all our tails would have been fried," and they let him go. As Dancer makes his way to the train he finds himself wondering what happened to the character in *Midnight Express*. Did they let him go? He thinks that when he gets back to work, he'll have to ask Miles. Miles knows everything.

Why is going to Brooklyn always such an ordeal? So far Dancer has spent two monotonous hours riding the JFK Express (whoever thought up that name certainly had a sense of humor), and now he's standing on the platform at the Broadway-Nassau station, leaning against a pole and waiting for the A train (the Alcatraz). He's thinking about all the things he has to do in the next three days. He's got to close out his bank account at Chase, all eight dollars of it. He's got to inform Visa and Macy's of his new address in Laguna... his new address in Laguna! Anne wrote it down on a piece of paper somewhere. He hopes he hasn't lost it. He's got to fill out a change of address at the post office so that all his rejection slips won't get lost. He ought to call his mom. *What about dad, though? Ah, let him find out on his own, the bastard.* He's got to clean out his desk at work. God knows how many pounds of unfinished manuscripts he has in there. He's got to hand in his resignation. What a joke—his resignation. And they'll probably have the nerve to point out he's not giving two weeks' notice. "Screw 'em."

The Train of Tears thunders into the station, and Dancer looks behind him to make sure no one is getting any bright ideas about shoving him in front of it. He sees that some of the cars have an "A" in their windows, so he guesses it must be the Alcatraz. You never can tell though, because each car usually has several different letters on it, forcing riders to assume that the greatest number of matching letters correlates to the correct letter of the train. Why can't the Transit Authority get its act together? Why can't they just color code everything like they do with the Tubes? What in the heck is their problem? Thank God he only has three more days of this.

Something has happened while he's been away. Something terrible. Dancer senses it even before he turns his key. He pushes at the door. "Zinc?" He leaps back into the hall as a stenching wave of rotted food overwhelms him. The open refrigerator washes an eerie light across the plundered cupboard. Glass jars and dishes lie smashed on the floor, a cloudy film of flour and sugar and coffee settled over them. (Dancer hadn't even realized he and Zinc owned such sundry goods.) He pokes his head in. Footprints are everywhere. Two little mice scamper away to wherever little mice scamper. "Zinc?" Again there is no answer. He cautiously enters, puts down his bag, and quickly switches on all the lights in the foyer. "Oh my God!"

In front of him, the living room looks worse than how Dancer imagines Rome looked after the carnage: Their dining table has been overturned, its legs broken off; their television and stereo have been bashed in, with stray knobs lying here and there like toadstools sprouted after a storm. All their garbage bags of clothes look as if they've been run through a shredder, and the sofa (the sofa Dancer sleeps on) looks as if it's been attacked by a pack of marauding bears. Zinc's mattress is even worse—its insides have been gutted and spread like mutant snowflakes over everything.

He is afraid to even look in the bathroom. He eventually does, but not without first picking a knife up off the floor and standing back as he kicks the door open. The first thing he sees is that the shower curtain has been torn from its hook and wadded up into the tub. His eyes travel to the curvy pipe which should be under the sink, but has been ripped from its joints and used as a hammer to break the tiles on the walls. Above the sink, the medicine cabinet has been looted, with every tube and bottle either squeezed or poured onto the floor and then smeared over all the porcelain fixtures like finger paints. On the wall next to the shattered mirror is written in toothpaste, YOU CAN SHIT IN ONE HAND AND WISH IN THE OTHER, AND SEE WHICH ONE GETS FULL FIRST.

He vaguely wonders if this is a coded message or just an exercise in bathroom humor. He closes the door and goes back into the living room where he throws open a window. Between the emptied chemicals and the rotted food, he's beginning to feel nauseous. The stuffing snow drifts up from the floor and wafts around the wreckage, creating a sort of Dr. Zhivago effect. He squats down on the floor and tries to think of what he should do now. Call Cheryl? But naturally he doesn't know her wealthy tax evader husband's number, and the phone is disconnected anyway. He feels like he's inside one of those nativity toys, those little plastic bubbles filled with water that you shake to make it snow. He wonders if anyone is looking at him. In front of him floats Lily, upside down in her half evaporated bowl. One of the stuffing snowflakes settles on top of her, and she sways a little. Dancer guesses she starved to death.

Oddly, he doesn't feel in the least bit of danger, though he can only imagine where Zinc might be right now. "Damn him," he says out loud. "Just what am I supposed to do?" But he has half a notion not to even let it bother him. After all, he's leaving for California in three days, what should he care about Zinc for? *He never worries about me. I could disappear and never be heard from again, and it wouldn't even cross his mind that I was missing.* But of course, he is too much the humanitarian not to worry. He thinks, maybe the Creature next door knows something. So he goes next door and knocks, but no one is home. He is actually glad. The Creature is some sort of Satan worshiper anyway, weird as they come, and every time Dancer finds another headless doll in the garbage dumpster, he's pretty sure it originated from the Creature's apartment.

Dancer now tries the other side, but no one is home there either. He tries the apartment across from them. "Who is it?" a decrepit old voice asks.

"Dancer, ma'am. I live across the hall."

She doesn't answer.

"It's Dancer."

"I don't support the arts. Go away."

"No, no I'm not *a* dancer. My name is Dancer. I found your cat last month on the roof . . . I live across the hall from you."

"What hall?"

"This hall. This hall I'm standing in."

"I thought Vitamin C lived over there."

"Zinc, ma'am. His name is Zinc. But I live there too. I've been gone a few days, and someone has broken into our apartment."

"He's a dancer too?"

"No, no ma'am he isn't. Could you open the door please? I think we're having trouble communicating."

"I don't open the door to strangers. That's how I've lived as long as I have, but if you get Vitamin C then I'll open the door for him. He was nice enough to find Persia for me."

"I'm the one who found Persia, not Zinc. His name is Zinc. That's what I'm trying to ask you. Do you know where he is?"

"My sink is fine. I had a little trouble with my toilet the other day, but I bought a new plunger, and it's fine now too. It took me a little while. You know I've got three cats, and they're all just as curious as they can be."

Dancer sighs and leans against the door. "Thank you anyway, ma'am." He goes downstairs to the pay phone at the corner of DeKalb. The good thing about collect telephone calls, he thinks, is that you don't even need a quarter to make them. All he has to do is pick up the receiver and tell the operator his name and the number he wants to call. Isn't living in America great?

"I have a collect call from a Mr. Dancer, will you accept the charges?"

"Well . . ."

"Mom, say yes."

"Dancer, son is that you?"

"That's who the operator said, didn't she?"

"A collect call from a Mr. Dancer, will you accept the charges?"

"Well, how much is it going to be?"

"Mom, just tell the woman yes!"

"All right, yes. I'll accept the charges . . . Dancer, how is Atlantic City? Are they giving you lots of scenes?"

"I told you, Mom, I didn't go there to be in a movie."

"Well, why are you calling me then? Anne Monet dump you?"

"No, it's not that kind of relationship. I called to ask if Zinc called back again while I was away."

His mom doesn't answer immediately. He hears a heavy sigh. "Dancer, I'm afraid I've got some bad news."

"I knew it. Oh God, what is it?"

"Brace yourself, son . . . we lost the ranch."

"Ranch? What ranch? What are you talking about?"

"The *snail* ranch!"

"Mom, did you even hear what I asked?"

"Dancer, did you even hear what I said. We *lost* the ranch."

"Mom, did Zinc call?"

"Someone poured salt in every one of the breeding buckets. I have a suspicion of who it was too."

"Did Zinc call?"

"I think it was your father. I called him Sunday afternoon, right after we dropped you off at the airport. And did I ever lay down the law too. Your father's new wife answered the phone, naturally, and it was all I could do to even be civil to the slut." His mom snickers. "My alimony check is being doubled...doubled!" She snickers again. "I'm getting every penny of my back child support too! Of course, this morning is when Dick discovered all the dead snails. Have you ever seen 15,000 withered snails before? It's not a sight for sore eyes, believe me. I'm suing your father, naturally. I have no proof, but I'm certain he'll settle out of court, guilty or not. He'd hate for me to yell DDT, if you know what I mean."

"Mom, did Zinc call?"

"Zinc? What do you keep pestering me about this Zinc person for? Who in the hell is he anyway?"

"He is my roommate! Z-I-N-C!" Dancer pounds the sides of the phone booth.

"No, no the only time anyone with that name called was last Saturday night. Anyway, Dick and I are starting a new project with my extra money." She pauses a second for effect. "Don't you want to hear what it is?"

"No."

"Son, why are you so rude? And what is all that noise in the background?"

"I'm on the street."

"Don't they have phones on the set? I thought they always took caravans of Winnebagos on these location shoots."

"I—am—not—starring—in—a—movie! How many times do I have to tell you? Will you please just listen to me? I'm back in New York."

"Well, then what's wrong with your own telephone?"

He tries to remain calm. "It has been disconnected. Our apartment has been destroyed, and I think something has happened to my roommate. I don't know what to do."

"Well, my God, why don't you just call the police? I've never understood how the most logical things escape you. You ought to have expected this sort of thing living up there in New York City anyhow. Now do you want to hear about mine and Dick's new project or not?"

"The suspense is killing me."

"Get ready now. Are you ready?"

"I'm on the edge of my seat."

"Aren't those telephone booth seats uncomfortable?"

"*Mom.*"

"All right, all right. Are you sure you're ready?"

"I'm sure."

"Flavored condoms!"

Dancer nearly drops the phone. He's too shocked for words.

"Condoms in assorted flavors. Think about it. The timing is perfect. And you know why? I'll tell you why, because even though the condom market is booming right now, people are growing bored. They know they can't practice standard sex anymore but they don't enjoy using rubbers either, so what are they going to do? Where do they turn? I'll tell you where, Yum Cums, that's where."

"Oh my God!"

"It's so perfect. Dick and I are planning to introduce Yum Cums in a twelve-pack assortment to begin with. One size fits all. Each condom will be color-keyed and individually wrapped in its own sealed, tamper-resistant flavor packet. The red ones will be strawberry shortcake, the black ones hot fudge sundae. They'll also come in champagne, garden mint, peaches and cream, cherries jubilee and my personal favorite, lemon zinger."

Dancer has recovered sufficiently to get off his own zinger. "Sort of like the way you felt as a kid when you opened your first box of Crayolas."

"Exactly," Dancer's mom says. "We're putting the fun back into fellatio."

"I can't believe I'm hearing this from you," he says. "Mothers are not even supposed to talk about this kind of stuff, much less make a career out of it, especially in front of their own children."

"Oh son, don't be such a prude. Look at you. You're the one living up there in sin city, exposing yourself to God knows what. One of the reasons I'm pioneering this crusade is to protect the multitudes of people living in that horrible place."

"By selling some nonsense called Yum Cums? Mom, these quick-buck schemes of yours get more hare-brained every time. Please, just don't do me any favors, okay? I only wanted to know if you'd heard from Zinc. That's all I wanted to know."

"And I told you already, I haven't. I don't understand why you have to be so belligerent. You *asked* me to tell you about Yum Cums."

"Asked you? You *made* me listen."

"Fine!" says Dancer's mom.

"Fine!" says Dancer.

"Fine!" they both say together; and now a silence follows, a silence that neither one of them wants to be the first to break. Seconds pass, making the situation more awkward. Eventually Dancer says, "I'm moving to California on Saturday."

"That's nice," his mom says. "Maybe you'll learn to like avocados. God knows I could never get you to eat anything green. Will you be living in Beverly Hills?"

"Laguna Beach."

"Is that near the ocean?"

"What do you think, mom?"

"Well, I don't know, you never can tell about Californians. They aren't even real people . . . have you told your father?"

"No."

"Good. How about your grandmother?"

"Not yet."

"She went back to the doctor again, you know."

"No, I didn't know. How would I know?"

"It's just her blood sugar again. I hope she's all right. I never could figure out how such a good woman could bear a child like your father. But I guess your father is basically good too, for a—"

"Yes, I know mom. Well, I should be going now. I've got to find Zinc. I'll send Grandmother a letter when I return her money, and I'll call you once I get to Laguna."

"Take care, son. Don't get too tan. You know how you always used to get those little white spots on your skin from spending too much time out in the sun, and I just don't—"

"Bye, mom."

"Bye, son."

Click. Click.

Dancer goes over to the stoop and sits down. *Now what?* He doesn't know who else to call, and he's certainly not going to call the police. What would the police do anyway? They would file some meaningless report and ask him a lot of pointless questions, and he would end up having to spill all the beans about Cheryl and her wealthy tax-evader husband. They would probably want the husband's name, and how could Dancer legitimately claim he doesn't *know* his name without looking like a fool and a liar both? Also, how would Dancer explain what Zinc does when they inevitably ask, "And what line of employment is your roommate in?"

So Dancer decides to do nothing. He's just too weary to worry —too weary from traveling all day and too weary from not having really slept since he can remember. God knows that sleep on a plane is hardly quality sleep. Trudging back upstairs, he just hopes he'll be able to wake up come tomorrow morning, seeing as how the alarm clock is in the same condition as the stereo and the television. Usually, he's very good about coming alive just a minute or two before the alarm goes off; but usually he doesn't have jet lag. *Why should I even care if I'm late or not?* he thinks. *I'm quitting at the end of the week anyway.* He wonders if he's a type A personality. Will he have a heart attack before he's fifty, brought on by too much stress and an improper diet? He guesses he will ... if he lives that long.

No one should worry as much as he does. It's just that his life has changed so much this last week, and he's got so much to do in the short time he has left in New York. For instance, as tired as he is, right now he's worried about whether there is enough left in the way of clothes to assemble a whole outfit for work tomorrow. He's worried about whether there's enough shampoo left in the shampoo bottle to wash his hair in the morning. He's worried about giving Lily a proper burial, as opposed to just flushing her down the toilet. He imagines no one else would worry about these things, but then no one else is him. He's unique in that regard.

And being unique like he is, he picks a spoon up off the floor, scoops Lily out of her half evaporated bowl and carries her to the flower box in the window. God, how the magenta petunias have grown! "Shoo pigeon, shoo." He waves the bird away and sees that two more doomed eggs have been laid. He places Lily on the sill—she's kind of stiff because rigor mortis has set in—and he plows her out a grave as far from the eggs as he can. He's heard that if you touch a bird's eggs before they hatch, the mother can smell the human scent and won't come back to the nest. Of course it's a moot point with pigeons, since their chicks always die anyway.

Unexpectedly, quite unexpectedly and with only one scoop of dirt left to go, the spoon strikes something that makes a definite crinkly-crackly sound, something that sounds more like cellophane than dirt. *Uh oh.* Why couldn't he have just dug Lily a shallow grave, why did he dig a full inch deeper than was required? Quickly he pulls down the window shade and roots up the package. He brushes off the dirt. It's rectangular shaped, about the thickness of a good-sized trashy novel, *Valley of the Dolls* maybe. All right, it doesn't have to be a trashy novel, it can be any novel, *Moby Dick,* say. (Luckily, he never did have to read that.) And it's filled with white powder, which he seriously doubts is baking soda. He wonders if this is what people in the drug business call a kilo. But he has no more idea of what a kilo is than he does a milligram.

He wonders if this kilo is what the people who destroyed his apartment were looking for. You dummy, he thinks, don't be naive, what else would it be? But will they be back tonight and kill him, that's the pressing question? Maybe he should rinse all the coke down the drain and pretend ignorance. Then again, maybe he shouldn't. Maybe he should use it as a tool to bargain for his life. Or for Zinc's life, if Zinc is still alive. *Questions. Questions. Questions.* Ever since he's come back to American soil he has been plagued with nothing but questions.

He reburies the coke and fixes himself a pallet from the shredded mattress and sheets on the floor. The way he figures it, he's too tired to make any rational decisions about anything right now. And as horrible as the questions are, their answers can only be worse. So he pulls up the sheets and closes his eyes.

Maybe I can sell it!

Go to sleep Dancer.

AN OBNOXIOUS,
HAUTEUR BITCH

or

Chapter
16

YES, ALL HIS worries proved justified: his automatic mental alarm clock didn't go off when it was supposed to, and it was only sheer luck that the Creature next door started his live animal sacrifices at 8:30, because if his monkeys hadn't screamed Dancer might still be asleep. And of course, there wasn't so much as a drop of shampoo left in the bottle, forcing him to wash his hair with a glob of something that he scraped off the cracked bathroom mirror. It *looked* like shampoo, and his hair *is* clean, but now his scalp feels like it's on fire. Luckily, he did manage to assemble a complete and unshredded outfit. True, the pants are sea green cotton with vertical aqua stripes and a draw string around the waist (Zinc's beach wear). And true, the shirt is salmon pink with a yellow collar. So he looks like an ad for color photography, but at least no one murdered him during the course of the night.

Dancer steps off the elevator shaking his burning wet hair and panting, because he ran all the way from Grand Central without even stopping to give the fake nun his spare change. He doesn't know why this makes him feel guilty, especially since she has not once God-blessed him like the regular street people have the decency to do, but he knows he'll probably worry about it all day just the same. Worry number one though is how to best approach Irving Koenig with the news that he's quitting on Friday. Of course, he could just procrastinate until it's too late, which is what he'd like to do, but flouting etiquette would cause him too much anxiety.

He goes to his desk to further think this out. As late as he is, he's still earlier than everyone else—everyone but the anorexic Judith, who suddenly appears. "Morning Dancer," she says distractedly, "Everyone missed you yesterday, did you have a nice Fourth?" He sees that she is clutching this stack of cardboard against her chest and has a frantic look on her face. "Oh God," she says to the column, next to his desk, "they're everywhere!"

Dancer looks at the column, then back to Judith. "But they support the building," he says, convinced that lack of nutrition has finally robbed Judith of all pretenses of sanity.

"No," she says, "these signs." She rips one off the column and holds it up for him to see. On it is painted an arrow pointing toward Irving's door with a caption that reads, "this way to the AIDS quarantine." She says, "I've been finding them all over the place."

Dancer looks over at the next column. "Only five more yards to the AIDS quarantine." He looks at Irving's door. "At last! Catch AIDS here!"

Judith rips the signs down and stuffs them into a garbage can. "Did I miss any?"

Dancer asks, "Who do you think did it?"

"My guess is either Keith Halley or Ned Helix. I'm sure they both kept their I.D. cards. One of them must have snuck in last night—probably Keith." Judith leans over and whispers into Dancer's ear, "Do you really think he has AIDS? I mean he does look like he's lost some weight."

At this moment the ice man himself rounds a corner. "Morning Judith," he says frostily.

Judith stifles a squeak and backs against Dancer's desk. "M... Morning, Irving."

Now Irving's door slams closed, entombing Irving in his quarantine. Judith looks at Dancer, shrugs, and Dancer shrugs back. He doesn't think he'll tell Irving he's quitting after all.

*   *   *

The next worry on Dancer's mind is that perennial favorite—money. He's not even going to think about Zinc. After all, Zinc knows Dancer's work number. If he's still alive he'll call. In the meantime, Dancer picks up his technologically advanced desk telephone and calls to notify Visa and Macy's of his change of address. With this out of the way, the moment he's been dreading arrives. Exactly how much of his $2,000 does he have left?

Well, let's see here. His fourth of the Congo-imported lily pads came to about 300 pounds (or about $450 if he really wants to wince), and the money he spent on ruined clothes was at least that much. Add to that all those little nit-picky things: tips, taxis, admission into Madame Tussaud's and one mutilated goldfish. He takes out his wallet and dares to count what's remaining. *Five hundred? Is that all! But I couldn't have spent fifteen hundred, not in two days. No, no, I couldn't have!* He counts it again, but the amount remains the same.

Suddenly, his thoughts turn to that kilo of cocaine buried in the flower box. *No...absolutely not. People have gone to prison for that kind of thing, caught people anyway. And you know what happens to young men in prison...besides, you don't know the first thing about selling coke. Aside from that, it isn't even your coke to sell. But what if Zinc is dead? It would be mine then. What if he isn't dead, though? What if he's still alive and he comes back to find that you've sold all his coke and sold it at undermarket value too?* Dancer finds himself wondering just how much a gram of coke costs, and what a "gram" actually is.

He looks up from his desk, his fantasies of illegal profit temporarily put on hold, and sees Miles Caesar shuffle in. Miles waves at him from down the hall, motioning him to join him in his office. A second later he's at Miles's door being told to sit himself down. "What do sex and snow have in common?" Miles asks.

Dancer thinks it is a rather apropos riddle. "I don't know, an Eskimo in heat I guess."

Miles says, "You never know how many inches you're going to get or how long it's going to last."

"Not one of your better ones, Miles."

"None of them ever are."

Miles has a blue gabardine sofa. Dancer guesses that the company which manufactures these office sofas got a good deal on gabardine. Miles sits in his chair, pulls a beer from a brown paper bag and pours it over a bowl of raisin bran. "I'm allergic to milk," he says.

"What does it taste like?" Dancer asks.

"Piss and prunes," Miles says through a mouthful. "You missed the hot news yesterday."

"What's that?"

"About Tenesia? You didn't hear?"

"Who's Tenesia?"

"The black girl, you know, Otis Molansky's assistant."

"Oh yeah," Dancer says, "the one who's never here. What about her? Did her mother finally die?"

"I'm the one who nearly died," Miles says. "The little wench won the lottery. Fifty million dollars!"

"You're kidding," Dancer says, his excitement quickly ripening into jealousy. How dare the seldom-seen black girl win fifty million dollars when he's distraught over only having five hundred.

Miles says, "Can you believe it? After taxes she'll be getting about two million tax free once a year for the next twenty years. I'm telling you it gives hard work a bad name."

"It just isn't fair," Dancer says.

"Yeah," Miles says, "but that's okay, we'll get our reward in heaven." He gives an ironic chuckle.

"How long did it take her to quit?"

"About a millisecond. She's spending the rest of the week being fitted for a wardrobe before she leaves on her cruise around the world." Miles crunches slowly on his piss and prunes. A little of the piss dribbles down his chin. "Maybe it'll make her miserable though. We can at least hope for that."

Dancer says, "Not a chance. She'll spend every nickel with elation."

"True," Miles says, "Misery is the luxury of the proud." He puts down his spoon and picks up his pencil. "That's pretty good in fact. I'll have to use it in a poem." Now he tucks the line into his pocket and takes a newspaper from his briefcase, "Look at this," he says.

Dancer assumes it's going to be an article about the seldom-seen black girl, but he sees that it's a picture of a refrigerator instead. It's a very nice refrigerator, stocked with just about every kind of produce that America could be proud of. "This is what I bought yesterday," Miles says, his voice filled with capitalistic pride. "How much do you think it cost?"

Dancer wonders if this is Miles's way of rubbing in just how much larger his income actually is. "$600?"

"Higher."

"$1,600."

"Lower."

"$1,000."

"Higher."

"Why don't you just tell me, Miles?"

Drumroll. "It cost me $1,400. $1,400," he reiterates, just in case Dancer was suffering a temporary hearing loss the first time. "I never dreamed I would, in my lifetime, pay so much money just to keep my cabbages cold."

"Yeah, that's sure a nice-looking refrigerator," Dancer says.

Miles now takes back the paper and pushes his bowl of piss and prunes to one side. "But that's not why I called you in. You know, the client is having problems with your line, 'Get an A in Anatomy.' They don't think 'anatomy' really draws the consumer into the fact that we're selling skin with SILKEN."

"Whatever," Dancer says. He has never felt particularly proprietary about the line. Now, he feels even less so.

"Well, they just want something that says more about how soft SILKEN makes you feel, but still geared toward the college set. Of course, I think your line works perfectly well, so does Nova, and you know we were so proud of you and everything for thinking it up...I hope you didn't take me seriously when I went around calling you Eve Harrington on Friday."

"But—"

"But nothing. Since it was your line originally, I think it's only fair we give you a chance to come up with another."

"But Miles, I don't even care."

"Which is precisely why you'll go so far. It's always the apathetic ones who get what others would kill to have. Just give it your best, Dancer."

"You don't understand, Miles. I *really* don't care. I'm quitting advertising. I'm moving to California at the end of the week."

Now Otis Molansky sticks his head into Miles's door and says, "Well lookie here, if it isn't the Nobel Laureate Circle."

"Or what will Vanna wear next?" says Miles, arms flourished and wearing an artificial smile.

Enigmatically, Otis says, "I meant what I said, and I said what I meant, an elephant's faithful one hundred percent." He withdraws his head and moves down to the next office, repeating the same thing into their door, but changing the elephant to an Indian cobra. The meter goes slightly off though.

Miles looks straight at Dancer. "What are you running from?"

"Nothing, Miles, I'm leaving to write a screenplay for the movies."

"Why, of course, and when did this inspiration strike?"

"Yesterday morning, at dawn in London. Actually Anne Monet, the actress, and I came up with the idea together. It's the chance I've been dreaming of. I know I'm not making any sense at all."

"Not any. What are you doing for lunch today?"

"I hadn't made plans."

"You can join me then. I'm going to dissuade you from leaving. Twelve-thirty okay with you?"

"It won't work, Miles."

"Twelve-thirty?"

"Fine." Dancer gets up and pours himself a glass of water from the cooler before going back to his desk. He wishes he hadn't said anything. He wishes he had bought a lottery ticket. That's what he wishes.

Nova Grey Lovejoy slinks by in a diaphanous lucite dress, polished brass shoes, fingerless lace mitts up to her elbows and a purse made from the scrotum of a blue whale. "Oh God Dancer, I'm so upset. I am so upset. Come into my office."

"What's wrong?" he asks following her in.

"Well, I can't tell you," she says, slinging her whale scrotum purse against her Crayola crayon. The crayon tips over and breaks a femur bone on one of the skeleton's legs.

"Then if you can't tell me why did you ask me into your office?"

"All right, I can tell you, but you can't tell anybody."

"What?"

"Irving, that fucker, wants to take SILKEN away from me. He wants to give it to that new girl, Boom Boom, the fucker!"

"Boom Boom? Who is she?"

"Ned Helix's replacement. She started yesterday. Knockers out to here. I mean she makes me look positively masculine."

"But Nova, you made that account what it is today. (Dancer knows just how to play Nova.) Why would Irving even think of taking it from you?"

"I don't know, he personally told me that the exploratory Miles and I did had some very good stuff in it, so I can only assume he's practicing his usual favoritism toward the beautiful and overly endowed. I'm not going to stand for it this time though. I'm going over his head, straight to Chester." Now Nova stands sideways and examines her shape in the glass frame of the girl at the urinal. "I may not have as *much* as Boom Boom, but what I do have doesn't droop even a centimeter. Not a centimeter."

It's about 11:30. For the last hour Dancer has been trying to sketch out a basic outline for his screenplay. During the snags, he plays with a toy he stole from Suzanne's desk called the Mop Tops. It's a piece of cardboard with the bald-headed faces of a man and a woman on it, and over their faces is a plastic window in which is trapped metal shavings. The toy comes with a magnetic wand, and the trick is to see how many different hairstyles he can make for the couple. He has given the woman a sort of sixties bouffant, and he has made a beard for the man, turning him into a hippie. The thing is though, Dancer keeps jiggling the board, making hair grow even out of their eyes. It's like a hairstylist's nightmare.

Chomp chomp chomp. (Guess who's arriving?)

"Oh God, Miles, I am *so* late. Can I tell you something, I swear I was going to be *so* early. But listen to this, everything on Third Avenue just stopped. I sat for an hour on that bus with no air conditioning and it moved a total of two blocks. Miles, I promise I was really going to be *so* early, but a truck overturned or something and I just gave up. I even got up an extra ten minutes early. I know you don't believe me, but it's so true."

From where Dancer is sitting he can't hear if Miles accepts Suzanne's apology or not. Dancer watches as she approaches her desk, throws down her bag and replaces her tennis shoes with a pair of satin espadrilles. She then unwraps a dietetic chocolate candy bar and swivels around in her chair to begin her double super acrostic crossword. Suddenly, she turns to look behind her. "Oh hi, Dancer. You do anything special over the weekend? We missed you yesterday."

"I went to London."

"You're so full of shit." She turns back around.

He decides to give the woman Mop Top a hair-do like Suzanne's. "I knew you wouldn't believe me," he says and takes a copy of *The Sun* over to her (he'd brought it to work anticipating disbelief).

Suzanne says, "Oh Dancer, this is nice. You know I had one of these made for a Hanukkah present to my boyfriend last year. It was me on the cover of *Playboy*. Did you get this done at that little magazine shop in the East Village?"

"It's real, Suzanne."

"Yeah, they did a great job. You can barely even tell they superimposed Anne Monet next to you."

"But they didn't."

"Face it Dancer, you couldn't tell a lie to save your life. Did you see Sunday's *Post*? Tenesia was on the cover for real. The *Daily News* too. Fifty million dollars, can you like even imagine that much money?" She sighs and bites a hunk out of her dietetic chocolate candy bar. "One day, Dancer. One day I'm going to be so rich I'll even buy designer underwear."

"That's rich all right."

"You know, it's like only one more month 'til my birthday next month. Now Dancer, don't get me anything please. I mean there's just no need to. I won't be offended. And especially don't get me anything in a size 12 or 14, because you know it won't inspire me to keep my weight at its optimum level, not that I wouldn't appreciate it, but it's just that my sister is so naturally slim, the-bitch-I-hate-her-for-it, that it forces me to keep dieting just so I'll have all those extra pretty things to wear. And Dancer, you've seen her clothes; I mean my sister has some pretty things."

"Is she going to get pregnant, too, so you'll be able to wear her maternity clothes?"

"It was a false alarm, thank God. You know I finally had my period Saturday. I don't understand it; it's like ever since I've been dating my new boyfriend I've been late." She pauses for a moment. "Actually, I do have this one theory"—she giggles—"but I can't tell you..."

"Try me, Suzanne."

"Well,"—another giggle—"my boyfriend is large, you know. I mean I have to make him stop about two-thirds of the way in."

"At least it gives you something to work towards, Suzanne."

"Yeah, yeah I guess it's sort of like the *New York Times*. You don't need it all, but it's nice to know it's all there."

"I guess," he says.

Now Suzanne says, "You know, Dancer, why is it that on the most gorgeous weekend when everyone else goes to the beach, I go camping where there's like *total* shade? I mean where my blanket was there was like one spot of sun, you know, so I kept having to move the blanket all the time and still I didn't get much of a tan. But guess what, I mean you'll never believe this... I used the bathroom in the woods. I mean not just used the bathroom, because I've been like peeing in the woods ever since I can remember, but you know this time I had to like dig a hole... I bet you thought I was too jappy to do something like that. But you know, I really like wearing the same clothes three days in a row. No, no it doesn't bother me, and not wearing any make-up. I don't mind. I love it. Just a little mascara, that's all. You know, my sister had one of those mascara tattoos done. Everybody's doing it now, and it lasts like your entire life..."

As Suzanne continues her monologue, Dancer reflects that three days can be a very long time indeed.

You're young.
You're talented.
You're ambitious.
You're filthy rich no thanks to advertising.

It's ninety-one degrees outside, high noon, and here she comes, folks! Swooping down the corridor in a floor-length, so-black-it's-blue Blackglama mink, with white hot diamonds bigger than eyeballs dangling from her ears. Rigid spine. Gliding gait. Smiling with condescending radiance through newly bonded teeth and running ten manicured talons through her coiffure. Yes, you can look but don't touch the Empress Tenesia, a.k.a. the seldom-seen black girl. Dancer wonders where the dancing boys are, the ones who wear black coats and tails and kneel on the floor tipping their top hats in succession as they break into the theme song from *Mame*.

"Oh, Tenesia," Suzanne gushes, wrapping her arms around her. "You're so beautiful. You're so lucky. You're so...so..."

"Rich," says the seldom-seen black girl.

Dancer starts thinking about how money changes people. The seldom-seen black girl will obviously gain nothing from her new wealth. Within a year she'll be an obnoxious, hauteur bitch. He thinks about Anne. She can be a bitch too, he decides, although he has not personally been a witness to her bitchy side. He wonders if he'll turn into a bastard too when he has lots of money (may that day come soon!). He thinks he won't, but it's probably only human nature to think he'll be different. In all honesty, he knows change is inevitable. People expect it. And he has always, if nothing else, tried to live up to expectations. So the question remains—which is better from a personality standpoint, to be rich or to be poor?

"Oh poor is always better," Miles says, as he stuffs half a slice of New York cheesecake topped with blueberries and graham cracker crumbs into his mouth. "Some of our greatest historical figures starved to death."

Dancer doesn't bother asking who. He's too worried that the blueberries Miles is eating aren't real, that they're just bluish-clear paste with glumpy things in it, like the stuff found in the middle of "blueberry" pop tarts. (God, how he detests those.) Of course the restaurant is kind of seedy, so what does he expect? It's on Lexington Avenue down in the basement of a bar, and the marquee in the window proudly claims to staff "the world's rudest waitress." Dancer guesses that's who they got. Her name is Flo, if you can believe the cliché, and she wears badly frosted hair in a style popular two decades ago; just like what Dancer made for the Mop Tops.

In the middle of the blue-checkered cheesecloth table is a big bowl of pickles. Miles has warned Dancer not to touch them, that they're never rotated, so the same pickles stay in the same bowl for months on end, and he had the most uncomfortable gas pains for nearly a week the last time he ate a bowl. Flo comes by and snatches away Miles's plate before he's finished. "Hurry up and get out. You two have been in here nearly half an hour. I've got customers waiting." Dancer says he'd like some coffee when Flo gets a chance. Flo tells him, "You see the pot don't you, get it yourself!"

So Dancer gets his self up and pours his own coffee. The pot is just beneath the blackboard on which is written the daily initials. If the daily initials match your own then you get a free meal. Today's daily initials are M and C. Miles says he has been patronizing this establishment every single day for over two years hoping for just such a treat. So even though Flo is less than ecstatic, Miles is in a sort of soothsaying and superior-to-life mood. He says, "I've been thinking about what you told me about this Anne Monet. I admire her acting, but she doesn't sound to me like a very contented woman. You know, the problem with people today is that being "comfortable" just isn't good enough. I remember back in the fifties, if we had a house and a car and a decent job, well we were happy. But now everyone wants to live like Joan Collins on "Dynasty," and they want it all before their first crow's foot. I'm telling you, people have gotten too damned greedy."

"Do you think I'm greedy, Miles?"

"Hell, yes. You. Me. The whole world. More, more, more! What

I want to know is what's going to happen when the dinosaur stumbles?"

"What?"

Miles takes a sip from Dancer's coffee. "For the first time in our history the United States is importing more than it's exporting. Did you know we make up roughly only four percent of the world's population, yet we consume more than forty percent of the world's goods? Your grandchildren are going to be shocked that you lived in such an age of excess. Take a long look around you, Dancer. And take my advice, don't be in such a rush with your life."

"What are you saying, that I shouldn't want money?"

"What I'm saying is that Anne Monet is only going to set you up for disappointment." This isn't what Dancer wanted to hear. "And in any case, money is not the end to a means."

Dancer says, "It is when you don't have any. It is when it's the only proof of success your family will recognize." He takes back his coffee. "And don't pretend you're above the material world either. Otherwise, you wouldn't have just bought a brand new $1,200 refrigerator."

"$1,400," Miles says.

Dancer laughs. He stirs some more sugar into his coffee. "I'm going to miss you Miles, you more than anyone else in New York. You're the only one who took the time to help me with my writing. I realize I've still got a long way to go, but without you I might have just given up altogether."

"Did you ever hear anything on that children's novel you wrote?"

"Nothing positive. I'm going to rewrite it in a few years though, when I'm better."

"Is that your ambition, to be great? Or do you only want fame?"

"I don't know. My only real ambition is to be published and invisible. I'm not good enough to be great, and I'm too insecure to be gawked at. In fact, sometimes I think the whole trick to my life is just to get through it without actually touching anything."

"But Dancer, you can't have your cake and eat it too."

God how Dancer wishes Miles wouldn't answer everything with a platitude! He gets up again and pours himself another cup of coffee. Flo shoots him a bird. He sits back down, and now Miles spouts off some statistic about the link between caffeine and colon cancer. Dancer resists the urge to tell Miles what he can do to his rectum, and instead says, "Well, it's the only thing keeping my eyes open. I don't think I've had a decent night's sleep in two weeks, and this last week you can't even imagine. It's been like the Theater of the Absurd, starting with me nearly getting murdered on the subway only because I gave a fake nun all my money by mistake—I'm convinced it was divine intervention. From there I lusted after a famous neurotic actress who chain smokes marijuana cigarettes in assorted colors. The next day a gypsy charlatan with nine fingers robbed me penniless. I've been excommunicated by an alcoholic father who hasn't even heard of *The New Yorker,* and ignored by a mother who just lost her snail ranch. On no money I've traveled from New York to Birmingham to Atlanta to Atlantic City, where I won $2,000 and jetted blithely to London without a passport, only to be accosted by these funeral groupies of a dead rock star and taken to jail after fighting off a ninety-year-old man and his pubescent girlfriend in a lily pond on the roof of a building. I've been frisked with a flashlight where the sun doesn't shine and survived the deaths of three goldfish—two of which were brutally butchered and one that starved. My drug-dealing roommate has vanished from the face of the Earth; our apartment has been ransacked; I've found a kilo of coke under a nest of dying pigeons, and everyone I know is making the cover of newspapers!"

Miles belches and says, "Well, you want to know the secret to an organized life?"

"Please," Dancer says.

"Filing."

You're young.
You're talented.
You're ambitious.
And what has it gotten you?

It's fast approaching five o'clock. Dancer is convinced Zinc is dead by now. He hasn't called all day. Dancer wonders if this means he gets to keep the Brooklyn hovel and sublet it at an outrageous price in order to support himself while he's in California. Actually it's a good idea, solving as it would all of Dancer's financial woes and enabling him to keep a place here in New York. When asked where he's from, Dancer could smugly say, "I'm bicoastal,"...Yes, maybe it's not such a bad thing Zinc is dead after all.

Suzanne is already replacing her espadrilles with her sneakers when Judith comes over to Dancer's desk and says, "Irving would like to see you before you go." Suzanne looks at Dancer. Dancer looks at Judith. Judith says, "I guess that means now."

Why is Dancer about to panic? Even if Irving accuses him of writing those AIDS signs and fires him on the spot, why should he care? Just the same, he hesitates before knocking. He looks behind him. The entire floor is peeking timidly out their office doors to see if they're about to witness another immolation equivalent to Friday's baseball game. Dancer knocks. "Enter!" bellows the voice. "Close the door behind you."

"Judith says you wanted to see me?" Dancer ventures.

"Have a seat, son." Irving stands and pulls at his suspenders. He's actually exposing his fangs into something that resembles a smile. He begins pacing in a circle around his desk. "As you're well aware, GS & B recently merged with two of our competitive agencies, organizing ourselves into what is now the world's largest creative superpower."

This is new to Dancer.

"Even with problems yet to be resolved, the opportunities that lie ahead are tremendous and exciting."

Irving doesn't sound too excited.

"We can do what no other agency group has yet accomplished —set new standards of creativity on every level of client service from local to global. We can all be part of an enterprise that once and for all proves there is no conflict between bigger and better. We can reach undreamed of heights on the wings of creative excellence."

Dancer thinks Irving has been fed one too many advertising slogans over the years. It's obviously affected his ability to speak English.

"My point, son, is that you can be an integral part of the well-oiled machine. I saw that SILKEN line you contributed on Friday, and it's good. It's fresh. It's dynamic. It's exactly the type of input and creative edge needed to keep GS & B where it is today. As you know, Keith Halley left us on Friday to join the Mets. I'd like you to be the one to take his place. Of course, there is a substantial salary increase, and you'll be given an office with a window, even one overlooking Madison if you like." Irving walks over to where Dancer is seated and ever so slightly brushes his crotch against Dancer's shoulder. It could be a completely unconscious act. It could be.

"So talk to me, son. Tell me where you'd like it... your new office."

Dancer sort of leans as far from Irving as he can and stammers, "Well... you... thanks for the offer, Irving." He stands up and backs against Irving's mahogany desk. Irving turns to face him, his back to the door. "I mean I really appreciate it..."

Irving says softly, "Just how much do you appreciate it," and pulls his left suspender strap down from his shoulder.

"Uh, Irving..." Dancer wonders if he should lunge for the door.

Irving pulls down his right suspender strap. Both loops dangle around the outside of his legs. He says, "It's not every day of the week that an assistant gets the opportunity to become a copywriting superstar of the highest esteem at the world's largest creative global superpower." He places both hands on the fly of his pants and pulls from the middle. The zipper slowly unzips. "Uh oh," Irving says, "pop goes the weasel."

Dancer sees that indeed it does, rearing its weasely head higher and higher. "Wait a minute, Irving." Dancer holds his hands in front of him. "Stop right now. You don't know what you're doing. Uh, I'll just go right now and forget this ever happened. I'm leaving on Friday anyway. Friday's my last day."

"So let's have a going away party," Irving says. He takes a step toward Dancer, petting the weasel with long caressing strokes. The weasel seems to like it. Dancer takes a step sideways. Irving steps with him. Dancer steps the other way. Irving steps with him. "I've wanted you, Dancer. I've wanted you from the first day I interviewed you."

"Irving, you're saying things you'll only regret."

"I never regret, Dancer. I could be good for you. Just relax a little." He takes his free hand (the hand that isn't petting the weasel), and dips it into his shirt pocket. "Quaalude?"

"I'm leaving."

"You go and you're fired." Irving seems very calm. He must do these promotions a lot.

"I quit," Dancer says.

"Don't be so hasty," Irving says. "Rash decisions are always regretted. Things have to be well-planned in order to work. You must be willing to open up to new dimensions." With his foot he kicks a button on a baseboard near the door. His twin, green gabardine office sofas begin unfolding into a double bed. "Some nights I have to work late," he says, "*hard* problems must be solved." He removes his coat, loosens his tie, clamps both hands at his shirt collar and yanks outward. A machine gun of buttons shoots everywhere. His belly flops out. He smiles, removes his shoes and steps out of his slacks, buck naked except for his silk tie and his argyle support socks. He massages the weasel. "You ready to feel the power, son?"

Dancer takes a step backward. "You've gone too far this time. I'm not the mail boy. I'll have you fired."

Irving just laughs. He jumps onto the double bed, motioning Dancer to join him. Dancer takes the opportunity to bound for the door. Irving, refusing to be foiled, springs to his feet and leaps into the air for a tackle, but within this fraction of a second, as Irving is descending spread-eagle from mid-air, the door suddenly swings open and who should enter but Chester A. Lark, president of the entire creative global superpower that is GS & B. By his side is none other than an angry-faced woman with hair the same color red as the middle Gucci stripe, furious at having lost the plum SILKEN body bar account to an over-developed bimbo named Boom Boom.

"Watch out!" Dancer yells as he steps aside. But before the words are even out of his mouth, Irving has landed on top of Nova

Grey Lovejoy, knocking her to the floor. In such a position, the combined forces of gravity and sexual arousal, and body friction against diaphanous lucite, cause the rock-hard weasel to suddenly explode in a shuddering ecstasy of fluid fireworks. Pulsating eruptions, like milky snow drops, rain down on Nova's exposed abdominal region, her dress being hiked up around her shoulders.

"Get the fuck off me," Nova shrieks, practically hyperventilating with horror as Irving's juices roll down her stomach and fill her navel, the overflow trickling down the curves of her thighs. "Aaaaaaaah!" Dancer imagines that the subsequent screams emanating from this pile of flesh can probably be heard from the northern tip of Manhattan all the way down to the Bowery.

> *"Good night, good night,*
> *parting is such sweet sorrow."*

> —WILLIAM SHAKESPEARE

Irving's been fired!
Irving's been fired!
Irving's been fired!
The glorious news ricochets through every floor, down every hallway, into every corner and crevice of the building. Employees embrace each other, joyous tears streaming down their faces. The cafeteria sends out for magnums of champagne. Hopes, wishes and prayers have finally been answered. Ding dong, the witch is dead!

"It's mine now," Otis Molansky shouts as he does a jig down the hall, "all mine. Ten wretched years of subordinance." He sticks his head in Irving's office. "Roses are red. Violets are blue. At last I can say it—GO FUCK YOU!" He cackles, raises his arms and shakes his whole body with glee. "Oh sweet comeuppance!"

"It's the New York *Times* again," a pale Judith says, her state-of-the-art technologically advanced telephone ringing off the hook. "What do I tell them?"

"Tell them no comment," the two men from security reply, both sent up to guard Irving's door as he gets dressed and packs his things.

Judith brings her hands up to her face. "I can't handle these things. I can't! Where will I go now? They always throw out the baby with the wash. I'll starve."

"You're only a meal away right now," Suzanne says. "Anyway, they're not going to throw you out. Otis needs someone to take Tenesia's place. Just ask him, for Christ's sake."

Dancer says, "Or you could take my place. I'm leaving too."

"*Leaving?*" Judith wears a pained look on her face.

Suzanne says, "You mean Chester fired you too?"

"I quit."

"But why?" Judith asks. Dancer wonders if she's really as distraught about it as she sounds. He also wonders if her boyfriend has died.

"I'm moving to California."

Both Judith and Suzanne sort of raise their eyebrows.

"Don't even ask why. It's too long a story."

Suzanne says, "Well Dancer, this is so surprising. We'll have to throw you a going-away party. Like when's your last day?"

"Friday, but don't throw me a party, please. I hate cheap sentiment."

Suzanne says, "You're so snooty sometimes, Dancer. Just for that, we're going to throw you a huge party."

"Besides," Judith says with stars in her eyes, "everyone thinks you're a hero."

"Because I was nearly sodomized?"

"Because no one has to worry about losing their jobs anymore."

"Yeah," Suzanne says, looking around to make sure no one can hear her, "Otis is so thin-skinned he couldn't fire a match. Why do you think Tenesia lasted as long as she did?"

"I don't care," Dancer says, "I am not coming to any party."

"Yes you will."

"No I won't."

"Will."

"Won't."

"Will."

"Won't."

WHERE DO YOU EXPECT A MURDERER TO BE?

or

Chapter

17

BALLOONS AND CONFETTI and colored streamers are everywhere. Nova Grey Lovejoy, wearing a 1966 Betsy Johnson original made from nothing but old fashioned soda-can pop tops, is doing the Twist with Miles, and looking slightly wrinkled from a series of cleansings she has undergone to purge any remaining traces of Irving. The whole creative department is crowded into Otis Molansky's new corner office, popping corks and prophesying glorious days ahead. Actually Tweedle Dumb and Tweedle Dumber aren't creatives but have sworn on their mothers' lives to keep their mouths shut if only they can stay... Dancer is sharing in the general euphoria, but the reasons for his happiness are more complex. Ironically, it all relates back to the night before last when he seriously considered jumping off the Brooklyn Bridge into the East River with cinder blocks tied to his ankles.

What happened was this:

It was right after all the post-sodomy pandemonium. Dancer was walking home from the Train of Tears station and almost feeling sorry for poor Irving. Well, *poor* wasn't quite the right adjective—as usual Dancer was frantic over his own cash-flow problems and thinking that Irving at least had plenty of money to fall back on, thanks to years and years of accumulated profit-sharing. What added to his depression was his realization that two days probably wouldn't be enough time to sublet the apartment even if Zinc were dead, but the seeds of suicide weren't actually planted until Dancer's nightmarish encounter in the lobby of his tenement.

He knew something was wrong when he let himself in, and three cats, Persia and her sisters maybe, clawed at each other trying to be the first out the door. All instincts told him to run with them, but then he saw the wall of brass mailboxes gleaming dully at the far end of the lobby. He hadn't checked the mail since before going to London so, he reasoned, his chances of finding a publisher's acceptance in the mailbox had to be higher than normal. He decided to have a look. It was then that the apparition leaped at him from out of nowhere, sticking its cratered old nose into Dancer's eyeballs and shoving him against the mailboxes.

"Ah hah!" it shrieked. "Don't you run from me, boy. Oh, I've a been waitin' on you all day long." He pressed his craggy nose even closer. Dancer could practically feel the pits in it. "Don't you know what this is? The sixth. It's the sixth!"

Dancer shrunk as far away from the old hairy, pitted nose as he could. "But Mr. Queece, let me explain. I just got back in town last night and my roommate—"

"Hand it over."

"Hand what over?"

"Damages and rent." He held out his spotted hands. "Right now."

"But... but I don't have it on me right now."

"Open your wallet." He grabbed at Dancer's aqua striped beach pants.

"What are you doing? Are you crazy? Get away."

"Give me my money."

"What is this, your second childhood? Get away, I'm not paying you anything. I'm leaving at the end of the week."

"Like Hell, you're leavin' tonight." He grabbed at Dancer's pants again.

"Mr. Queece. Be reasonable."

But Mr. Queece wasn't. Like an old octopus his arms flailed and thrashed and sucked at Dancer's pockets... In a lightning stroke he picked Dancer's wallet, plucking out all five hundred dollars and flung the wallet into Dancer's face. As Dancer threw up his arms, Queece crammed the money down a slot on top of a locked iron wall box marked LANDLORD.

Just like that. Tequila Mockingbyrd all over again.

Dancer remembers punching at the iron box, clawing at the lid, screaming obscenities at Mr. Queece; and Mr. Queece only laughing as he slipped inside his apartment and removed Dancer's money by opening a latch from the inside. There followed a shouting match through the door about who had the more legitimate reason to call the police—Dancer accusing Mr. Queece of thievery and Mr. Queece accusing Dancer of withholding rent and destroying leased property. Dancer said he had nothing to do with it, that he found it that way. Mr. Queece said he'd had enough of both of them, especially that "shiftless piece of shit" Dancer lived with. What kind of place did they think he was running anyway?

Dancer kicked his feet against the door. He tried breaking the door knob off. He backed up and rammed the door with his shoulders. Nothing worked. He wondered if Mr. Queece was looking at him through the peephole. Looking and laughing. Dancer thought of a cartoon he once saw, *The Far Side,* he thinks it was, which showed a man knocking on a row of apartment doors, stabbing an ice pick through the peepholes as people asked, "Who's there?" All the peepholes had blood dribbling from them. Dancer wished he had an ice pick.

"Do you think I'm some kind of fool?" Mr. Queece said. "I saw what kind of things went on up there. It was comin' if you want my opinion." Dancer didn't. "Damn foreigners, bringin' their trashy ways over here. This country ain't no dumpin' ground you know. That girl deserved everything she got... the same for that tanned crap you lived with."

"Zinc? What happened to Zinc?"

"What's it worth to you?"

Dancer pressed his forehead against the door and pounded on it with both fists. "You bastard! You've got all my money. I don't have any left. Tell me what happened to Zinc?"

"Jail," Mr. Queece said. "Where do you expect a murderer to be?"

"Murder?"

"Surprised? She was dead before the cops even got here."

"Zinc murdered Cheryl?"

"Just thank your lucky stars you weren't here when he done it. Otherwise you'd be with him."

Dancer leaned against the mailboxes, head in his hands, legs feeling suddenly wobbly. It was just too much to absorb at once—robbed again, kicked out of his apartment, a murdering room-mate—he couldn't believe it. How had things gone so bad so fast? Things like this just weren't supposed to happen to him. Not thievery and murder! He was Dancer, Dancer of Alabama, whose life had always been circumscribed by fantasy. Reality was never supposed to slip in.

Mr. Queece said, "That's all I know. If you want more, you've got to call the police. Now get out. I ain't runnin' no shelter for the homeless or no front for drug smugglers. Get!"

Somehow Dancer pulled himself up the stairs to gather his things (those that weren't slashed, that is), and then sat down to wallow in his misery. He had been kicked out of his apartment for something that wasn't even his fault; Zinc was in jail; Cheryl was dead; and he was without even enough money to make a phone call. Everything had been going so well up 'til now. Just two more days and he would have been home free. Strange how Cheryl's death neither surprised nor saddened him. He started thinking about how much of an uphill battle his whole life had been, how everytime things began to look bright somebody always shattered the bulb. Like a zombie he got up from the floor and stuffed shirts and pants into his only suitcase. He thought of Anne—she seemed like a dream, some fantasy of his, created to justify his existence. Things began to blur and waver. He wished he knew someone to call. He wished the phone worked. He wished he had a quarter. He wished he wasn't crying. He wished he was dead.

But once again fate stepped in to save him. Someone knocked on the door. Dancer shouted out that no one was home. The person knocked again, not so politely as before. Dancer said, "Go away. Everyone living here has died, goldfish and present company included." This time the person knocked the door down.

"I'm Yeti," the man said. Dancer looked up and took a staggering step backwards. Yeti must have been seven feet tall, over five hundred pounds and as abominable looking as the snowman he was named after. In one beefy hand he daintily held a Pee Wee Herman lunch box, in the other a carving knife.

Dancer said, "If you came here to rob me, you're ten minutes too late."

Yeti sliced the air with his carving knife. "You Zinc?" He took a step forward. "If you ain't you're in trouble." He sliced the air again. "So are you Zinc?"

"Uh yeah, yeah, I'm Zinc." Dancer let his suitcase drop to the floor. The clothes spilled out in a heap. He thought this had to be some kind of crazy joke. It was all just too surreal. Maybe he was on one of those hidden camera television shows, the kind that takes immense pleasure from emotional embarrassment and pain.

Yeti held his knife out in front of him, blade upwards. "Well?" he said with a grin.

Dancer felt it was time to do some quick thinking. Undoubtedly, Yeti was some connection of Zinc's, and undoubtedly he had come for what lay buried in the flower box. Dancer sure picked a good night to stay in.

"I don't have forever," Yeti said.

"Uh right, right." Dancer went to the flower box and dug up the kilo. Yeti grabbed it from his hands, rolled the bag around to examine all sides, licked the tip of his knife and stabbed it into the bag just far enough to turn the tip white. He tasted it and smiled. "Vino said you'd be virgin pure."

Vino? Dancer thought. The name rang a dim bell. Suddenly he remembered. Vino was Cheryl's wealthy tax-evader husband.

Yeti stuffed the kilo into his shirt and the knife into his boots and turned to leave. He threw the Pee Wee Herman lunch box over his shoulder as he went through the door. "Hire yourself a maid," he said. And that was how Dancer came into fifty thousand dollars . . . tax free!

* * *

Dancer smiles to himself as he stands apart from the revelers. In front of him, Tweedle Dumber is sitting on the gabardine sofa bed, holding the androgynous receptionist's hand, explaining exactly how long it took him to die when he was crushed beneath a grand piano on board the *Titanic* in his previous life... according to his hypnotist. The androgynous receptionist is reading a book and nodding occasionally. Tweedle Dumber asks him/her if it's a good book. "Fairly," he/she says, "if you like Gore Vidal. I don't particularly."

Judith offers Dancer a piece of cake. She's been holding it in a napkin for the last half hour, occasionally pinching at it and pushing around the crumbs because Suzanne told her that she didn't think Judith was, like, capable of swallowing anything inhabited by calories. "Will you ever come back to New York again?" she asks.

"Off and on I suppose."

She pinches at her cake again and looks around the room. "Will you call me if I give you my number?"

"I thought you had a boyfriend?"

She casts her eyes down. "He left me."

"What?"

She nods.

"Oh Judith, I'm sorry to hear that." Dancer really is.

She shrugs, and ripping off a corner of her napkin, bravely dabs it against her cheeks. "I guess it happens to everybody at one time or another."

"Well yes," he says, not really knowing what to say. Consolation has never been one of his strong points. "That's as healthy an attitude as any."

"I think I really loved him though."

"Did you tell him that?"

"Uh huh," she says, her head hanging down, "and he said he loved me too, but that... but that..." She doesn't finish, choosing instead to pick some more at her cake.

"Go on, Judith, but what?"

"But that he couldn't bear to watch me commit suicide on the installment plan, and unless I start eating again, he isn't going to see me anymore."

"Oh, is that all," Dancer says, expecting something heinous.

"Is that *all?*"

"Well, come on, Judith, is eating such a hard thing to ask?"

"Then you agree with him?"

"Of course I agree with him."

"But I'm so fat, Dancer. I look in the mirror and..."

"Fat? If you're fat, then I must be the Hindenburg. Give me that piece of cake?"

"It's mine," she says, holding it away from him.

"I'm going to feed it to you."

"But I'll gain weight."

"Judith, I think you have a problem understanding the relationship between food consumption and life sustainment. If you don't eat, you die. It's that simple. So either take a bite of cake right now, or I'm personally escorting you to a hospital. What's it going to be?"

"But Dancer..."

"*Eat.*"

Judith stares forlornly at the confection in her hands, a look on her face no less wretched than if she were being forced to eat raw the heart ripped from her boyfriend's body. She sniffs at it and sticks the tip of her fingernail into the frosting, as though testing it for arsenic or potassium cyanide.

"Dammit, Judith," snaps Suzanne, who's been eavesdropping on the whole conversation, "it won't kill you."

"You can do it," Tweedle Dumb says from across the room, "the first bite's the hardest."

"We're pullin' for you," Dumber says, his hand now resting on the androgynous receptionist's knee. He starts chanting, "JUDITH...JU-DITH...JU-DITH." Suzanne joins in, soon followed by the rest of the party, until Judith can't stand it anymore.

She clutches her free hand over an ear and yells, "All right, I'll do it, if it'll make you all shut up, I'll do it." Shutting her eyes, she slowly brings the cake up to her face, her hand shaking, and holds it in front of her mouth. She takes the tiniest little nibble—a nibble a gnat couldn't taste—and without chewing it, swallows it like it's a ball of lead. A cheer goes up, and to Dancer's relief Judith smiles. "I did it," she says, astonished. "I really did it. And you know what? It tasted good. I liked it."

"She *liked* it," Dumb and Dumber say in unison, "she *liked* it."

"Oh Dancer," Judith says through another nibble, "now my boyfriend will take me back, and I have you to thank."

"It's only the beginning, Judith," Suzanne says. "Today an ounce of cake, tomorrow a leaf of spinach, the next day a whole peanut."

"Don't make fun of her, dear," Nova shouts to Suzanne from across the dance floor, smoothing down her dress over her twenty-four-inch waistline. She grabs Miles's arm and with a jerk of her bangled wrists spins all 250 lbs. of him into a pirouette. Dancer hopes Nova will ask him to dance when the song changes, although she and Miles seem to be having a pretty good time together. Dancer would ask Judith to dance, but she's actually eating a real bite from her cake. He doesn't want to retard her progress. The cake looks tasty though, so he sets off to get his own piece, when some junior copywriter whose name Dancer doesn't remember sticks his head into Otis's office and says that Dancer has a phone call.

Dancer is sure it's Anne. He's been trying to get in touch with her ever since Yeti's visit. He runs out to his desk but stops short just before picking it up. Something tells him not to answer it. He watches the red light blink off and on, wondering how long the person will hold. It could be Zinc. Dancer has already called Rikers Island, and they told him that Zinc is indeed there, but that Dancer will not be able to say goodbye to him until Saturday morning during visiting hours. The thought occurs to him that maybe Yeti discovered he was only an imposter and will threaten to kill him when he picks up the phone. Still, curiosity gets the best of him and he answers it. "Hello?" he says, "Dancer speaking."

"Son?"

For a second Dancer considers slamming the phone down. The impulse passes. "Dad?"

"It's me, son, I tried calling you at home early this morning, but your phone's been disconnected."

"Yeah, I know." He is too stunned to explain the reason or to point out that even if it hadn't been disconnected, he wouldn't have been home to answer it. (He's been staying at the Plaza these last two nights, his fifty thousand dollars safely tucked in the hotel safe.)

Neither of them says anything. Dancer stands and paces beside his desk as far as the cord will let him. He stares at the flap of black construction paper on Nova's door, the one that says 25¢ 50¢ A PEEK. He wonders if he should actually look at what there is to peek at now that this is his last day.

"How are you?" his dad asks finally.

"Okay . . . okay." He wishes that something other than monosyllables would come out of his mouth.

"I'm . . . I . . . Do you still need money, son?"

"No, no, I'm fine. Thanks though."

"Oh . . . Say, I washed your car for you. It was really dirty, all this dust and everything. We haven't had a good rain in the longest."

"Thanks."

"Son, you're not making things easy."

"Dad," Dancer says exasperated, "I don't know what to say. I wasn't expecting you to call. It's really a bad time anyway. Maybe I'll talk with you later."

"Wait, wait son. I called for a reason." He begins to hear sniffles, as though his dad is trying to keep from crying. "Dancer, I lost you a while back. I don't even know how it happened, but I . . ."

"Don't dad. Please don't. You don't have to apologize. I shouldn't have asked you for money."

"But son, I've never been there when you needed me. Hell, I feel like I don't even know who you are. You never would talk to me about your problems."

"This isn't the place dad, please. We're different, that's all. We've never seen things the same way." He leans against Nova's door. "We're just different."

"Maybe." His dad blows his nose and sucks in a long breath. "I want you to know that anytime you need a place to stay, well, you're more than welcome to stay here with Carla and me. Anytime you want."

Dancer nods into the phone and nervously fondles the top flap of the construction paper. He's dying to know what's back there. "Thanks dad, I appreciate it."

His dad sighs heavily. "I hear you're leaving New York."

"Tomorrow," Dancer says. "I'm moving to California." He takes his hand away from Nova's door deciding against a peek after all.

"Yeah, that's what I heard. That's why I called you. I think you'll have to make a detour. It's...it's about your grand-mother..."

FAIT ACCOMPLI

or

Chapter 18

I**T'S LIKE SOME** kind of miracle.

They've turned on the fountain in front of the Plaza hotel. Beautiful, sunlit water pours out of a naked bronze sylph holding an urn. The water cascades gently over tiered pools stacked like a wedding cake, gushing across giant concrete sea shells and spilling from one level down to the next. Dancer has read in numerous biographies of F. Scott Fitzgerald that he and his schizophrenic wife, Zelda, used to dance in this fountain during their bacchanales in the twenties. (Zelda hailed from Montgomery, Alabama.) But Dancer can't even enjoy it.

He can only stare down at the fountain from his window lamenting. Why, oh why didn't he return his grandmother's hundred dollars when he had the chance? It's a question that's been plaguing him all night, especially since he'd even remembered to put the money in an envelope and had taken the trouble to stamp and address it. He was going to hand it to the mail boy when he saw him pushing his cart towards him from the end of the hall. But then naturally Nova had called Dancer into her office for some piddling little reason (she needed her shoulders massaged), and by the time he got away he had forgotten all

272

about the envelope, which he had left lying upside down on his
resplendent white laminated desk. In fact, he didn't even think
about it again until three days later when he got the phone call;
not that his grandmother would have had time to use the money,
but of course she didn't know that. Besides, it's the principle of
the thing. Dancer didn't want her to die thinking he was an artistic failure dependent upon his family for support. And now it's too
late.

He takes a mint off his pillow, unwraps it, chews it and flops
across the bed on his stomach. His eyes wander from the fountain
to the New Orleans style jazz band playing in the surrounding
plaza (for which the hotel is named, Dancer supposes), to the line
of horse-drawn carriages parked along Central Park South, to the
windows of F.A.O. Schwarz across Fifth Avenue where herds of
stuffed toy animals gape back at him, to Bergdorf's waxy rigid
mannequins draped in ten thousand dollar pieces of fabric, to the
long black and silver cars, the vendors and the congealed masses
of people. But he sees none of these things. He sees only his
grandmother. She's frying peach pies in an iron skillet and telling
him to stand back so the grease won't pop on him. He sees her
rocking slowly in the old lawn swing. She's humming. He sees
her shelling peas under the water oak in the back yard. He sees
her teaching him how to play dominoes the proper Chinese way,
how to transplant saplings in the fall so the roots won't die...
these things that contribute absolutely nothing to the march of
civilization, he sees.

He props his elbows on the bed and his chin onto his palms and
squints up at the *Newsweek* clock. The time says 9:05 A.M. *Why
hasn't Anne called yet?* He's left at least a half dozen messages for
her at the Dorchester since yesterday afternoon. Of course, she's
probably somewhere over the tip of Iceland right about now. *But
she could use the phone on the plane couldn't she.* He gets up and
walks in circles around the room. Even though their agreed upon
rendezvous isn't until noon, he's sure it would be just like Anne
not to show up until exactly twelve o'clock, or even be fashionably
late; and today of all days, when he has neither the time nor the
inclination to play her prima donna games. As it is, he's got to
leave right this minute if he plans on getting out to the prison and

back again before twelve. His flight to Birmingham leaves at 1:30, meaning that all he'll have time to do is explain to Anne what has happened and that he'll just have to catch up with her in Laguna later in the week. Why do people have to die at the most inappropriate times?

He gives the phone one more chance to ring. It doesn't, naturally. So he closes the door behind him and runs downstairs to hail a cab. Getting inside he tells the driver, "Rikers Island," and sits back to stare pensively out the window trying to absorb the beauty of his last day in New York, preserving it in his memory to reflect back upon in some distant future. Suddenly though, an uncomfortable thought crosses his mind. *What if this whole California thing is just a joke at my expense? What if Anne has no intention of showing up today?* He nibbles his nails. *Why didn't she call me all week? I have no job, no place to live and no place to go.* But he tells himself, *Don't get so uptight. You worry too damned much. She'll show.* He keeps repeating this to himself and rolls his head around on his shoulders until his neck pops. Nervously, he taps his feet. He looks down at them. A smile appears.

In any case, Dancer old chap, I think you're forgetting you have fifty thousand crispola dollars stuffed down your boots... (His boots are made out of iguana skin. Iguanas are *not* on the Department of the Interior's list of endangered species)... Which brings up some interesting questions. Should Dancer tell Zinc about the money? Does the money even belong to Zinc? Does Dancer care whether it does or not? As he sees it, illicit profit can be lumped under the same axiom as love and war... all's fair.

> You won't always be young.
> Your talent is arguable.
> You're at least ambitious.
> Thank God you're not in jail.

Dancer sits down at this thing that looks like a row of connecting school desks, divided by a high bullet-proof and soundproof glass wall rising up from the middle of it. Each desk has a telephone, with which to speak to the poor imprisoned soul unfortunate enough to be stuck on the opposite side of the bullet-proof and soundproof glass wall. Some overdressed and overweight woman wearing a rock on her finger the size of a quarter is sitting next to him. She's crying fake tears into her telephone and petting some weird breed of dog sleeping in her lap. The dog has absolutely no hair at all. The fat woman doesn't have much. "Well, how would I know what happened to the money," she cries innocently. "I'm telling you I couldn't find it. It's not where you said it was, it's just not." Dancer thinks the lady doth protest too loudly. Now she glances his way, snarls at him, and the hairless dog wakes up and does the same thing. Dancer looks away but keeps his ears pricked. "Of course I wouldn't lie to you," she snipes into the phone. He can't see who she's sniping at. A pole is in the way. "What? Well, my mother left me this ring. What do you mean? Of course, you've seen me wear it before. Lower your voice. Don't you dare use that tone with me. You're scaring Twinkles." Dancer guesses that Twinkles is her hairless freak of a dog.

Now a guard opens a door on the other side of the glass and points Zinc to where Dancer is. Zinc waves as he picks up his phone. "Hey dude!"

"Hi," Dancer says cheerily, trying to sound as if they're meeting for lunch at 21. He sees that Zinc could use a hearty lunch in fact. He's lost a lot of weight and his face is covered with scratches.

"Good connection," Zinc says flatly, "almost like we're in the same world."

"They treating you okay, Zinc?"

Zinc sort of shrugs and rubs a hand through his hair. His hair hasn't been washed in a while. "Free food. Free bed. Free sex. None of it my favorite brand, but what the hell, ya know."

Dancer can only imagine. "How far away is your trial?"

"Six months...a year maybe, I dunno." Zinc examines the flesh on his arms. "I'll probably never have a tan again." Somehow this sounds like the greatest worry on Zinc's mind. He presses his nose against the glass and makes a face at Dancer. "You know, you're lookin' a little green at the gills yourself."

"My grandmother just died. I've got to fly home this afternoon."

"What a bummer. Everybody's dying all of a sudden."

Dancer plays with his hands on his desk. He intersects his

fingers and presses his palms together to make the church. Now he raises his index fingers and joins them at the tips to make the steeple. Now he turns his hands under and folds back his palms and wiggles his fingers. His fingers are all the people inside the church. "I'm sorry I wasn't home the other night, Zinc. I tried calling you but by then the phone had been disconnected. If I'd known you were in any real trouble, I'd have—"

Zinc shakes his head. "Hey man, it's not your fault." He doesn't elaborate further but instead turns his head to look at the man on the other side of the pole that Dancer can't see. Twinkles snarls at Dancer again. Zinc turns back around. "How's the apartment, man?"

"A wreck. We were kicked out, you know. I've been staying in a hotel."

"Yeah? I'm sorry about that." He hangs his head. "I guess Queece told you what happened?"

Dancer nods and bites his lips together. "He said you murdered Cheryl."

"Yeah, well Queece can go piss on a forest fire. There's nobody I loved more than Cheryl. Hell, you know that. No, I turned myself in for murder, but I didn't kill her . . . she OD'd."

"Why'd you turn yourself in for murder then?"

"So that husband of hers, Vino, can't get at me. I'd be dead too if I weren't in here."

"I don't understand . . ."

Zinc looks away again. "Maybe that's best. There's no sense in dragging you into all this."

"How do you know I'm not already involved?" Dancer asks, planting the line just to see Zinc's reaction and to determine if he should reveal any more.

"*You,*" he says, snorting. "Dancer, you've never been involved in anything more dangerous than a paper cut your whole life."

Dancer doesn't know why he takes this as an insult. He taps his boots against the floor and looks at the fat woman. Twinkles stands up in her lap and barks at him.

Zinc says, "Hey dude, don't look so hurt. It was a compliment." He sighs heavily. "You really want to know what happened?"

"Yes Zinc, I really do. For once I'd really like to know what you've been up to. I mean *I've* been through Hell, and I was only a bystander."

Zinc's eyes begin to water up in the corners. "Everything was fine until last Saturday," he says. "I mean I was even thinking about asking Cheryl if she wanted a kid."

"You mean a *baby*?"

"Yeah man, we woulduv made a great baby. But then like I got to wondering if Cheryl could even stay straight for nine months runnin'. I mean you were never around her that much. You don't know how bad she got. That husband of hers, Vino the bastard, he sells the shit for a livin'. Cheryl got to where she was doin' two, sometimes three G's a day. Anyway man, Saturday morning she came over, and I could tell she'd already had a few shoots and toots. She like staggered through the door and said we were goin' to have a celebration, and Jesus if she didn't open her purse and pull out this bag of junk that must have weighed three pounds if it weighed an ounce. I mean I nearly lost my tan."

Dancer has a feeling he's going to regret asking to hear this story. Already, he's beginning to sweat.

Zinc says, "I asked her where she got the shit, but you know like all she'd say was that she found it in Vino's closet. Vino's *closet*. Well, then we got into this big fight. I told her she had to take it back that minute, before Vino woke up and found it missing. But she said he was out of the country, that he wouldn't be back until the end of the week, and that her plan was to sell the shit so we could run off to Barbados together and start a new life in the sun. I told her it wouldn't work, that Vino would kill us. Dancer, you don't know what a bastard he is. He tricked me into being a middleman for him, always threatening to call the Immigration Bureau and have Cheryl deported if I didn't play along. Cheryl said she had it all figured out. She had found Vino's address book and called his buyer to come pick the stuff up at our place on Wednesday. She'd made up some lie about her being Vino's personal secretary. This guy's name was "The Snowman," that's what Cheryl called him. And according to her he was supposed to like just waltz into our apartment and hand over eighty thousand dollars in exchange for the bag. Then Cheryl and I would just get on a plane and fly away into the sunset. Like we lived in a fuckin' fairytale."

Eighty thousand, Dancer thinks, more than a little upset. *Why, that swindling crook.* He's tempted to pull his boots off right now just to recount his loot. He says, "So what did you end up doing with the bag of coke?" As though he didn't know the answer.

"You're not going to believe this dude, but Cheryl started eating it, I mean just scooping it into her hands and swallowing it like it was sugar or somethin'. She'd get real crazy when she was high. I tried grabbing the bag away from her, but she only grabbed it back and started clawing my face. That's why I look like this." He picks at a long narrow scab. "Then she took the bag and locked herself into the bathroom. I could hear her snorting the stuff and breaking things and throwing things all over the place. Hell, I didn't know what to do. I was afraid she'd get hurt. I tried calming her down, saying nice things to her, but she was like an animal. After a few minutes though, it got like totally silent. I could hear her breathin' heavy and I called out to her, but she wouldn't say anything back. I mean I was so scared she'd hurt herself that I just ran downstairs and called an ambulance."

"Our phone had already been disconnected?"

"I guess man, it hadn't been workin' for a day or two." Zinc begins to sob.

"Hey," Dancer says, "it's all right." He knows it isn't, but he can't think of anything logical to say.

Zinc wipes his eyes. "When I got back upstairs, she was . . . she was in a coma on my bed. I don't know what she did with the coke, whether she ate it all or flushed it or hid it. I mean, I ripped that place apart trying to find it before the ambulance arrived. I guess old Queece heard the noise and called the police. She, she was dead before they got there. That's when I turned myself in. I knew Vino would only kill me when he got back, but he can't touch me here. Christ, why do I feel like I'm in fuckin' confession?"

"Zinc, I wish there was something I could do." He really does.

"It's no good, man. There's nothin' anyone can do. At least you came to visit me. What with your grandmother dying and everything, I know you're not exactly in the mood for somebody else's troubles. I appreciate it. You're the only friend I've had besides Cheryl. My parents haven't even spoken to me in four years."

Dancer feels so incredibly guilty all of a sudden. Here he is with all this cash in his boots, the sweet irony being that Zinc and Cheryl won't even miss it, don't even know there's any *to* miss for that matter. After all, as far as Zinc is concerned the coke was flushed down the toilet, so of course how could it have been sold? And as for Cheryl, well, a dead woman can't very well tell anyone she buried a kilo beneath the petunias. In fact, the only person besides Dancer who knows what he does is Yeti, "the Snowman," and Yeti assumes Dancer is Zinc. It's all so perfect for Dancer, and here Zinc is telling him he's the only friend he has left.

Zinc says, "Maybe Queece kicking us out of the apartment was a blessing in disguise. I mean there's no telling how many pieces you'd be in right now if you'd been home Wednesday when the Snowman showed up."

Dancer rubs his forehead. He knows he's got to tell the truth. He couldn't live with himself otherwise. "Zinc, I *was* home Wednesday."

"You were? And the Snowman showed up?"

Dancer nods. "I didn't know who he was, he just barged through the door with a knife and a lunchbox telling me my name had better be Zinc. What was I supposed to say? I had a pretty good idea what he'd come for. The night before when I was burying Lily, I found the coke under the flowers. I traded it with him for the lunchbox."

"Well, I'll be damned."

"I wasn't going to tell you this, I mean I needed the money so badly, especially after Queece robbed me in the lobby for rent and damages. It was like a gift from God or something."

"The money was in the lunchbox?"

"Yeah."

"And where's it now?"

Dancer holds up his legs and points to his feet. "It was only fifty thousand though. He must have kept thirty for his commission."

"Thievin' bastard."

Dancer says, "I guess the money belongs to you . . . if you need it to help post bail . . ."

"I don't want bail. They'd get me. No, you keep it dude. That must have been a pretty scary experience you went through, you deserve it. Anyway, I've got plenty more in a safe-deposit box for when I get out . . . Vino's been a good employer."

"You know, you could probably bargain for clemency. I'm sure the feds would love to know Vino's occupation."

"I'll probably do that in a few months. But hey, do me a favor in the meantime will ya?"

"You name it."

"If Vino starts askin' you any questions, just say you don't know where I am, okay."

"Deal," Dancer says only too happily. "I'm leaving for a while anyway. That's why I came to see you, to say good-bye. I'm moving to California."

"Hey, all right. You'll love it out there. It's everything New York is but without the hassles." He leans forward and cracks a smile for the first time. "Not with this Anne Monet chick?"

"She's the one."

Zinc clucks his tongue and laughs. "Of all the fuckin' luck. You beat all I've ever seen man, things just always work out for you don't they?"

"Not without a price, Zinc. No one's that lucky."

"Yeah," Zinc says, "prices keep risin' all the time." The guard comes back in and taps Zinc on the shoulder. "Well dude," he says, "I guess recess is over."

"Take care, Zinc."

Twinkles barks.

Zinc pushes back his chair and gets up. He winks and waves over one shoulder as the guard escorts him out of the room.

They both know they'll never see each other again.

The New Orleans style jazz band is still playing by the fountain in front of the Plaza. They've just struck up "When the Saints Come Marching In." A crowd has gathered, clapping their hands and tossing quarters and dollar bills into an already overflowing trombone case. The weather and temperature are too perfect. Dancer can't remember a nicer day than this. The sky is a deep glossy blue, the trees in the park heavy with leaves. People are everywhere—enjoying the music, strolling hand in hand, basking in the sun—using their Saturday to relax with a vengeance.

Dancer squints up at the *Newsweek* clock again. 12:07. He just checked out of the hotel (no message from Anne). He tries mentally to calculate exactly how long he can afford to wait for her before running the risk of missing his flight. To calm his nerves he buys a watermelon ice with real seeds in it. He sits down on his suitcase and begins eating the ice slowly, spitting the seeds out one by one into a bed of nasturtiums. He wonders if the seeds have a prayer of sprouting, or if being frozen for so long in all this sugary slush has destroyed their strands of DNA and RNA, or their zygotes and gametes or whatever it is that might prevent seeds from germinating.

He's trying not to think about anything at all, trying just to steep himself in the pleasures of the day, but it's not working. If Anne doesn't show within the next few minutes, he thinks he'll probably have an aneurysm. What will he do? He looks up at the clock again. 12:22. *How could fifteen minutes have gone by? Stay calm,* Dancer. Stay calm. *Give her 'til twelve-thirty.* The seconds tick by. All right, he thinks, all right, let's just assume, just *assume* mind you, that she doesn't show...what then, huh? What next for the hotshot screenwriter without so much as a credit to his name?

He pushes his hands down into his pockets. He pulls them out again. He makes another church and steeple and all the people. He pushes them in again. His nails have been bitten down to the nubs. Unconsciously, he pulls out the never-mailed envelope containing the unreturned hundred dollar bill. He starts chewing at the corners of it. He supposes he could purchase a funeral arrangement with the money—some coral roses—but the one eccentricity of his mom's that ever made sense is not wasting money on the dead. "They can't appreciate it," she'd say, "so you might as well just give it to charity or to someone who can appreciate it. When I die, I want you just to drop me down a hole and forget about me." With this in mind, it suddenly occurs to Dancer what he should do with the money. Something that makes such perfect sense. Something that will not only ease his conscience, but probably make his grandmother proud if she could see him now.

He's got to hurry though. The *Newsweek* clock says twelve-thirty. He's resigned himself to another no-show from Anne. It's just one of those things. He's only thankful he was able to share the time with her that he did. She might have become a good friend and an influence on his career, but he refuses to feel sorry for himself by dwelling on what might have been. He picks up his suitcase and walks toward the corner. "Taxi!" he calls.

A cab from the opposite side of Fifth veers over, but is cut off by a long black limousine. Constantinople's big shiny face smiles at Dancer from the front seat. He pulls to a stop and a tinted window slides down in the back. A face shrouded in a white linen hood and sunglasses turns to him. Nobody says anything for a moment. Finally, Anne breaks the silence. "Do you think I'm beautiful?"

Dancer doesn't know whether he should feel perturbed or delighted. She smiles at him, trying to sway him toward the latter. He, however, opts for perturbation. "Anne," he says, choosing his words with care, "you know, ordinarily I can just shrug off your power games, but you can't treat people like inanimate objects. I deserve at least a little respect." Now he just stares at her, sun in his eyes and straddling his suitcase.

"Is that any way to treat your business partner?" She steps out of the car, all tanned and breezy, garbed in an ivory-white peasant dress and glass bracelets on her arms. She pulls back her linen hood and shakes her hair. It bends into the wind, long and lush.

"Isn't that Anne Monet?" someone asks behind Dancer.

"Who's the guy?" someone else asks.

"Must be her new boyfriend."

Dancer crosses his arms. "Didn't you get any of my messages?"

"I'm sorry, Dancer. Don't be mad. I did get them, but not until it was too late to call. I thought you'd be asleep. You wouldn't believe the hassles I've gone through with that castle. Some distant cousin of Turk's is contesting the will, claiming she has "blood-rights" to everything. I mean I've been tied up with lawyers sixteen hours a day just so I could have it all straightened out by today." She pinches him on the cheek. "Besides, I guess I did want to make you sweat a bit. We've been watching you from the corner for the last forty minutes."

"You *what?*"

"I wanted to see how long you'd wait." Now she kind of tilts her head and looks quickly from left to right. "I don't know, I suppose I just wanted to test your sincerity."

"Great," he says, "just great. And how did I score?"

"Well, actually I thought you might have waited longer."

"Well, I would have waited until midnight except that an emergency came up. I had a reason for needing to get in touch with you ... my grandmother died yesterday afternoon. I was very close to her."

"Oh *no,*" Anne says. "Oh God, Dancer, I had no idea. I ... feel like such a schmuck. I'm sorry." She wraps her arms around him.

"It's okay, but I've got to make a flight to Birmingham ... I didn't think you'd show."

"Well here," she says, "What are we stalling for. Get in." Constantinople runs around the side of the car, picks up Dancer's suitcase and throws it in the trunk. He closes Anne's door. Her window glides up shutting out the gawkers. She takes Dancer's hand and holds it in her own. "I'm going with you ... if you'd like me to that is."

"I would," Dancer says, his tone rather detached.

"Well, it's the least I can do, especially after you stuck with me through Turk's funeral. We can go on out to California next week sometime. I've never been to Alabama before. Which airport, Dancer?"

"LaGuardia."

Constantinople opens his own door and slides into the front seat.

"Const, did you get that?"

"Yes ma'am."

"Then step on it."

"Wait," Dancer says, "first we have to make a quick stop at Grand Central Station. I've got to give an envelope to someone."

Anne gives Dancer a look. "Are you sure there's time?"

"It'll only take a minute... it's something I have to do."
"Well Const, you heard him. *Hurry.*"

The limousine pulls up to Grand Central on the 42nd Street side, a canyon wider than most. The sun is able to infiltrate down to street level here. Anne closes the curtains in her window and pours herself a little something from a decanter. "I'll be right back," Dancer says. "Keep the car running." He gets out and pushes through the sun-washed entrance. A long, wide ramp leads down to the sub-levels of the station—a confusing maze of low, vaulted corridors lined with eateries, large empty marbled caverns known as "waiting rooms," archways and even more ramps and narrow halls descending at odd angles, some emptying down into smooty caves of train tracks and others to world famous restaurants, like the Oyster Bar—the core of all this being a room big enough to store an ocean liner, but designed to look more like the world's largest crypt; all cold stone and echoing footsteps and even an artificial night sky, complete with twinkling stars.

He runs down the ramp, boots clomping and eyes alert for a wimpled woman in black. At the bottom of the ramp he stops. To his right is a tunnel going down into the Antechamber of Hell. Above the tunnel it says, TO TRAINS ON LOWER LEVEL. Directly in front of him is another tunnel that says, TO TRAINS ON UPPER LEVEL. In addition, several other narrower tunnels are appendaged onto these, all interconnected by vestibular shops. It's through one of these that he dashes to get to the main chamber (the crypt with the twinkling stars). Here, like a spelunker trying to find his rope, he searches out his usual route to the Greasy Sleaze Bucket, figuring he's bound to cross paths with the fake nun at some point.

And there she is! He catches glimpses of her through the rushing people. She's sitting peacefully in her usual chair, her arms crossed and buried beneath the drapes of her habit, her dish of money resting unheld in her lap, as though being a member of a holy sect is tantamount to immunity against quick-handed thieves. Her face is the only exposed flesh on her body. Her eyes are cast down to the stone floor. She's totally unsmiling and seemingly oblivious to the fury of the world around her.

"Hi," Dancer says, running up. "I've been looking all over for you." He opens the envelope and places the hundred dollar bill on top of the change in her dish. She says nothing. "Hello," he says again, breathlessly adding, "remember me? I give you money almost every day. Last week I gave you ten dollars by mistake, a far-reaching mistake if you want to know the truth. I mean, if I hadn't done it, then I would've had plenty left over by the end of the day to buy a token, and I wouldn't have nearly been killed by the Islamic, and I wouldn't have met this beautiful woman who's waiting for me in her limousine up on the street this very second." The fake nun continues to say nothing. "Anyway, you kind of saved my life in a way, and this hundred dollars here, well, it has a lot of sentimental value attached to it. And...and I guess I'd just like you to have it. That's all."

And lo and behold if it isn't a day of multi-miracles, for the fake nun actually says, "God bless ya, mah angel," and she tips her wimple and smiles. She really does. She smiles. The fake nun smiles. It starts in the middle of her lips and slowly seeps around in both directions until having nowhere else to go, the corners lift upwards, pushing the area around her eyes into sparkly crinkles. Dancer is reminded of a special he once saw on PBS about the Namaqualand, a place located along the southwest coast of Africa. He made Zinc tape it. The Namaqualand is a desert, a wasteland of scorched boulders interspersed by an occasional grove of a most bizarre cacti known as elephant trunks. (Elephant trunks are the slowest growing plants on the face of the Earth—literally. Most predate Christ. They grow only in the Namaqualand and look exactly like withered green elephant trunks sticking up out of the sand.) But in the Namaqualand, once every twenty years or so, an amazing thing occurs. The Namaqualand blooms, and not just a few scattered blossoms here. No, it blooms as far as the eye can see, in every direction, in every color, in every shape and size and variation. Every inch of the Namaqualand is transformed into an ephemeral paradise. It vanishes, however, just as quickly and as mysteriously as it appears...just like the fake nun's smile.

She takes her hands out from under her habit and folds up Dancer's bill until it's square shaped, then she pushes it down into her dish burying it under all the change. He takes a step backwards. Something about her hands is ominously familiar. He had never paid much attention to them before. He was always in too much of a hurry to get to work, but now he's seeing her as though for the first time. He studies the fingers, counting them one by one . . . all the way up to nine. He studies her face. She holds out her arms. "Come over here and give me a big hug," she says. He withdraws. "Well, if ya don't want to give me a hug, then take a picture and ya can luk at me longer." He takes another step back.

Now she pushes her hands down into her habit again and pulls out a wad of gold jewelry. They're all identical, all chains with cartouches attached to them on which hieroglyphics are engraved, exactly like the one hanging around Dancer's neck. "Ah make these mahself. Everbody has to have two careers in New York," she says. "Everbody has to live. Everbody has to die. Everbody leaves somethin' behind." She inserts the four-fingered hand into the sleeve of her other arm, as though about to pull out a white rabbit, but instead produces a newspaper clipping. She holds it out in front of him. "Come on," she says, "read it."

Dancer's angels begin fighting over whether he should turn on his heels and run, or whether he can succumb to the overwhelming curiosity that's consuming him. The more masochistic of the two wins. Cautiously, he reaches out and grabs the clipping. He recognizes the photograph instantly. It's the murdered woman in the white dress. The headline reads, "Who Is She?" and the article goes on to say that the Islamic who killed her has been apprehended and is being held in custody, but that the "Ghost of Grand Central," as the woman is referred to, had no identification in her purse, and unless somebody identifies her soon, she'll have to be buried at city expense in a numbered box at Harts Island (formerly Potter's Field).

"Wuzn't you lookin' to find who she wuz?" the fake nun casually asks. "I found that write-up in the paper yesterday. The poor woman. Nobody even knows who she is . . . nobody but me." And with a great sigh—one that says "Why is everyone so much dumber than I?"—she reaches into the sleeve of her habit again, this time producing a ladies' wallet. "After she buys a necklace from me the other day, Ah gives her a great big hug. Affection and love is the most important things in the world, mo' important than all the money they is. Are ya sure ya wouldn't like another chain?"

Slowly Dancer backs away, one step behind the other. People pass in front of him, swirling and milling in all directions. Soon, he only sees vague glimpses of her face in between the empty patches of the crowd. Yet still he hears her speaking to him, even as he turns to start running through the tangled catacombs. "I knew ya wuz a good boy!" she shouts. "And ah told ya the wurld would be yours some day. Old Tequila didn't invent the rules and she sure don't want to play by them, but remember angel, they're the only rules there are."

With each step Dancer moves a little quicker, overcoming this shadowy underworld of despair, of hope, of shameless survival, until he finds the sun-dappled ramp leading up to the entrance. Beyond waits a new life. "You're the lucky one," are the last echoing words he hears her cry. And he dances out into the brilliant light, where things that are real don't seem so, but nothing lasts forever.